Saturday's Child

Ruth Hamilton is the bestselling author of twenty-five novels, including *Mulligan's Yard*, *Dorothy's War*, *The Judge's Daughter*, *The Reading Room*, *Mersey View* and *That Liverpool Girl*. She has become one of the north-west of England's most popular writers. She was born in Bolton, which is the setting for many of her novels. She now lives in Liverpool.

Ruth Hamilton

Saturday's Child

PAN BOOKS

First published in Great Britain 2002 by Bantam Press,
a division of Transworld Publishers

This edition published 2012 by Pan Books
an imprint of Pan Macmillan, a division of Macmillan Publishers Limited
Pan Macmillan, 20 New Wharf Road, London N1 9RR
Basingstoke and Oxford
Associated companies throughout the world
www.panmacmillan.com

ISBN 978-0-230-75712-7

1 3 5 7 9 8 6 4 2

A CIP catalogue record for this book is available from
the British Library.

Typeset by SetSystems Ltd, Saffron Walden, Essex
Printed and bound by CPI Group (UK) Ltd, Croydon, CR0 4YY

Visit **www.panmacmillan.com** to read more about all our books
and to buy them. You will also find features, author interviews and
news of any author events, and you can sign up for e-newsletters
so that you're always first to hear about our new releases.

My heartfelt thanks to Diane Pearson,
my editor since 1987.

Diane, you will be missed.
You were my friend and my backbone,
my teacher, my sister-in-words.
Go forth disgracefully – remember – purple
slippers in the snow.

Were I to live for ever, I could never repay you.

Love from Ruthie.

I dedicate this work to the memory of my little sister
Susan Mary Nixon

Susan died 25 August 2000 in Hamilton, New Zealand,
aged 52 years.

Acknowledgements

My thanks to

Dr Rory McCrimmon, for saving my life.

Diane Pearson, my editor, for her patience and help.

Dorothy Ramsden, my secretary, for unfailing support and faith in me.

Avril Cain, my 'bezzy' mate, for the laughs and the poetry.

David, Michael, Sue, Lizzy and Alice, my long-suffering family.

Gill and John, housekeeper and gardener, for minding the home front.

Sweetens Books, Bolton, the best shop in the hemisphere.

Chris Watson for tech support.

Macmillan, for republishing.

Liverpool, for being here; Bolton for being there.

My readership – God bless them, every one.

A very special thank you to Bill Strain of Johnson City, Texas, USA for his support and for the forensic research he did on my behalf.

Saturday's child works hard for a living.

One

Few people spoke to Nellie Hulme.

For one thing, she hadn't cleaned and stoned her step since the turn of the century, while the inside of her house was reputed to be worse than Charlie Entwistle's rag-and-bone yard. Lily Hardcastle, who suffered the questionable fortune of sharing party walls with Miss Hulme, was inundated with mice, silverfish, cockroaches and some little brown things for which no-one could discover a name.

Lily was worn out with it all. She felt like bringing in the sanitary people, but she couldn't quite persuade herself to do it. There was something sad and pitiable about the lonely woman next door, that shambling figure that made its way from home to shop, from shop to library, out of the library and back home to squalid isolation.

Another reason for avoiding Nellie Hulme was that she stank like old books, aged sweat and, for some strange reason, over-boiled cabbage. According to theory, she never cooked, living instead on chip shop meals, pasties, pies and the odd sandwich on a Sunday when shops were closed. As cabbage was not a part of this odd equation, the folk in Prudence Street guessed that some ancient vegetable matter had found its resting place beneath piles of newspapers and rat droppings.

Whatever, the old lady was a disgrace, while her house

should have been condemned years ago – even the bombed-out properties in the street were in better condition than number 1. Yes, the first house in Prudence Street was a festering boil, and something should have been done about it years ago.

Lily Hardcastle, who was scrubbing her step and her 'first flag' – decent people always scoured the slab just outside their front entrance – stopped the movement of brush and sandstone when Nellie Hulme's door opened. Even now, out in the so-called fresh air, Smelly Nellie's aroma tickled Lily's nose. The woman was a disgrace. Soap and donkey-stone cost nowt. Nellie had enough old clothes in that house to swap for a hundred scrubbing stones off a passing rag cart. Should Lily have another go at getting through to Nellie? Did she have the energy for such a confrontation?

Lily sat back on her heels. It was no use; there was no point in going through all that mee-mawing again. Nellie Hulme was deaf and dumb. To communicate with her, a person had to enunciate each syllable and match the words to invisible drawings produced by hands waving about in the air. Lily was fed up with carrying on like a windmill. It was all right for everybody else in the street, because Nellie's house was an end one, so poor Lily was the only one who suffered the constant smell and the frequent invasions by wildlife of many denominations. 'Mucky owld bugger,' she said under her breath. 'House wants burning down, everything in it and all. Aye, the lot needs shifting.'

Lily's youngest, an urchin named Roy, joined his mother in the doorway. 'Her ashpit's got maggots in it,' he declared, 'loads of them. I reckon I could sell them to people what go fishing. I wonder how much I could get for 'em?'

Lily clouted him across a leg with her floorcloth. 'Get

out of me wet,' she ordered, 'mind me donkey-stoning. Any road, you're supposed to be in bed, lad. Have you been scratching them spots? What have I told you about that, eh? If you keep digging away like that, your gob'll be smaller than the pox.'

Roy was not a thing of beauty; his freckle-spattered face was topped by a bright red thatch, and his skin was not improved by several bloody pits from which he had dug the pustules of chicken pox. 'You'll be marked for life,' chided Lily. 'Get back inside before I clout you again. And I hope you've not been poking and piking about over yon.' She waved a chapped hand in the direction of next door. 'It's trespassing, is that. One of these days Nellie Hulme'll get the police on you, me lad.'

Roy went back inside. He had 'gone over' once more, even though Mam had told him to stop. She had told him so often that his backside had stung from many a slapping, yet he could not resist climbing the yard wall to have a dekko through Nellie Hulme's scullery window. It wasn't easy, either, all that muck inside and outside the panes, but he had scraped a bit off and now wanted to tell somebody about the tree. It wasn't every day a lad found a tree growing in a scullery.

Mam came in, her body bent sideways by the weight of a bucketful of water. 'You've been and gone and done it again, haven't you?' she asked. 'After all I've said, you've been hanging about in that filthy midden next door.'

He nodded mutely.

'You'll catch summat. You'll catch the back of my hand and some terrible disease and all if you keep going over that back wall.' She clattered the bucket onto the flagged kitchen floor. Curiosity overcame her. 'Well?' she asked. 'What did you find this time? More maggots? Rats as big as cats?'

'There's a tree growing in the sloppy,' he said.

3

'Dirty owld bugger,' muttered Lily. 'In the slop-stone? It'll be an onion. She likes raw onions on her cheese butties, or so I've heard. What else?'

The thin lad raised a shoulder. 'I saw a mouse eating some bread. Well, I think it were bread and I think it were a mouse – could have been a small rat. Tins everywhere, milk gone green, newspapers on the floor. And the kitchen fire's been raked out all over the place, ashes everywhere.'

Lily leaned against the table. She was getting wearied to the back teeth with Miss Nellie Hulme. Here she was, doing her best against all odds, three lads, a husband who liked his ale, a tuppence-halfpenny job at the Prince William, not a decent rag to her back. And at least half her day was taken up by fighting this losing battle against Smelly Nellie. 'I'll have to fetch the town,' she declared. 'Because it's not right – we shouldn't be living next to all that. She should be cleaned up and moved out. We'll all be coming down with some sort of a plague – you mark my words.'

Roy picked at another itchy spot on his forehead. Mam was always going on about how everybody should mark her words.

'I said mark my words, not your face. Now, give over doing that – I've told you,' yelled Lily. 'Scarlet fever'll get into your system through them holes what you keep digging. Mithering about round ashpits while you've got open wounds – have you got no sense at all?'

Roy sighed. He didn't know what to do with himself, because he didn't feel ill, yet no-one was allowed to come near him until he had stopped being infectious. Although he disagreed with the theory that education was a necessity, he had to admit that school was a damned sight better than being stuck here with Mam, washing, ironing, cooking and scrubbing. He couldn't even go next door.

4

Nellie Hulme didn't seem to mind; she had seen him, had made no effort to chase him off. 'I've nowt to do,' he moaned, wishing immediately that he could bite back the words. 'I can find summat,' he added hastily, 'I could read in me bedroom or ... or I can make sums up, practise, like, for when I can go back to school.'

Lily skewered him with a hard look, handed him the Zebo and some rags. 'Get that grate shining,' she ordered. 'Use plenty of leading and elbow grease. No finger marks, no dull bits and wash your hands when you've finished.'

'But Mam—'

'You heard me, so shape.'

'The heat makes me spots itch,' he moaned, 'and I'm still not well. See, I've got a fever, all sweaty and ... and...' His voice died. The expression on his mother's face declared that all negotiation was fruitless, that there would be no treaty, no quarter given. 'All right,' he mumbled. He smeared Zebo on the oven door and wished with all his heart that he had kept his mouth shut, because Mam often found work for idle hands, declaring that she would use them before the devil did. That was yet another of Mam's sayings – the one about the devil and idle hands.

Lily stood in front of the dresser mirror and looked at the reflected stranger. She was only thirty-eight. Her eldest was seventeen, her middle one fourteen, her youngest, now making a feeble effort to shine the oven door, was nine. 'I suppose I'm a lucky one,' she mouthed. After all, Sam wasn't at her all the time, wasn't forcing her to have a baby every year. And there were ways and means, methods unavailable to the hordes of Catholics across the street. Aye, things could have been a damned sight worse, she reminded herself yet again.

But she looked so tired, so faded. It was a toss-up, she supposed, between poverty caused by too many children, or the same produced by a man who drank half his wages, thereby rendering himself incapable of procreation most nights of the week. Well, she would try hard to be grateful, she really would. The inner voice wore a sarcastic edge.

Lily wanted more than this, more than a life that had become a fight against many kinds of filth. Even thinking about the men's lavs at the Prince William made her gorge rise, all those deposits left everywhere, vomit, faeces, phlegm. And some of it was likely Sam's, as he was one of the ne'er-do-wells who frequented that particular hostelry. Yes, she hated cleaning that pub. She was meant for better things, for a decent home, a pleasant life . . . wasn't she? Was any member of her generation going to step outside these mean streets with their soot-coated walls and ill-tasting air? Where was there a decent life? Where should she go to seek it out? God, she had no idea what she was thinking about.

She'd been a bonny girl in her time, apple-cheeked, auburn-haired, straight of spine, strong in wind and limb. But now . . . She stepped closer to the speckled mirror. She could have been any age over forty, just a white face whose definition had become blurred by the fatty deposits from a poor diet, faded hair that was almost mousy, tired eyes, a forehead lined by care.

'Mam?'

'What?'

'Do I have to finish it?'

Lily swallowed. Marriage finished it every bloody time. She thought about the friends she'd had at school and in the mill, every last one of them worn down by motherhood, poverty, some by abusive husbands. That was the other good thing about Sam – he had never lifted a hand to her or the kids . . .

'Mam, I'm tired.'

Aye, they were all bloody tired, all pale-skinned through living in narrow alleys supervised by mill walls, mill chimneys, mill smoke. There had to be more than this, she told herself. The best she could expect was a chara ride to Blackpool once a year, some visits to and from relatives, a cigarette when she could afford one. There was no point in expecting new frocks and decent shoes, no sense in dreaming about a hairdo or a lipstick. And the idea of a better, cleaner life had to be the product of a disturbed mind. She had to accept it, live with it, just like everybody else . . .

'Mam?'

'Oh, leave it, Roy – you're getting on me bloody nerves – and that's swearing.' Not one of her sons could be described as either use or ornament. Like their father, they were selfish, thoughtless, feckless. No, that wasn't true, because Danny sometimes looked at her sideways before handing her an extra shilling.

'Mam?'

She rounded on him. 'Go,' she said, her tone dangerously quiet. 'Go and look at her next door's tree, her maggots, her green milk. I'm past caring, Roy. I'm past all of it. Only don't come running to me when you catch the scarlet.' She was tempted to add, 'Because I might not be here', but motherhood held back those words.

Roy studied his mother for a few moments. She had a temper as red-raw as any Irish Catholic's, but there was something a lot worse than temper in Lily Hardcastle. She had a cold place, a part of her that sat way below ordinary anger. Perhaps that was because she wasn't a Catholic. Catholics lived on the other side of the street. They were noisy, ill-kempt and full of fun. When he grew up, Roy Hardcastle was going to become a Catholic. They had singsongs, tunes played on a melodeon, fights, dramas.

He went outside and thought about climbing over the

wall, but the excitement had gone now that he had Mam's permission; things weren't half as exciting when adults approved. He scuffed clog irons on yard flags, kicked a stone about, admitted that chicken pox was not a good idea. He missed having people to talk to – even teachers were better than nothing at a pinch.

Lily sank into a fireside chair. She was in a funny sort of mood, one she couldn't quite get to grips with. Her thoughts were all over the place, darting about like a butterfly on a hot summer's day. And how many butterflies had she seen this year? How many chances had there been to look for a butterfly? Week after week, she went from posser to clothes line, oven to table, cleaning to ironing, the only change in routine a three-hour shift as dogsbody at the Prince Billy. Had she cleaned the ash-trays, did she know they were nine beer glasses short, when was she going to scrub the floors? And it would likely go on like this for ever.

'Thirty-eight,' she said aloud. 'Thirty-eight and bloody finished. Well, it's either me or them, and it's not going to be me. I've got to get out of here before I turn daft.' An inner voice told her that she couldn't go, but she shushed it, her tongue clicking impatiently against her front teeth. A door opened to let folk in and to allow others out. Surely stepping away would be easy?

She looked at the Home Sweet Home sampler above the fire, glanced at a few blue-and-white plates on the old dresser. Whatever was she thinking of? She had three sons, one down a Westhoughton pit, one ready for leaving school, Roy still a little lad. Then there was Sam, who was not the worst husband in the world. She noticed how she kept processing the same thoughts, the same excuses and reasons. She was staying put because things could have been worse, was trying to prevent herself from looking for better. This might be 1950, but women were still not allowed to wander. They could vote, could run a country while men ran about with guns, but they remained morally tethered to their duties.

She saw Roy through the window, knew from the noise that he was sparking his clogs against the flags. Normally, she would have berated him for wearing out his irons, but she couldn't be bothered any more. Something had ended today. What, though? What was different about today? What was suddenly so wrong? Perhaps she was having the change of life early.

There was usually enough food on the table; even when Sam drank his way through five bob, they managed to have sufficient to eat. But bellies were topped up by Lily's Prince Billy money. By rights, Prince Billy money should be saved for Christmas, for days out, clothes, kids' birthdays. He wasn't pulling his weight, wasn't Sam. He had never pulled his weight, come to think.

She tapped her fingers on the edge of the fireguard. Agitated on the surface, she was experiencing an inner calm that was almost frightening. It was ten minutes to one. Danny, her eldest, would be back from the pit at about six o'clock. She had a soft spot for Danny, who helped out as best he could when it came to money. Aaron, the fourteen-year-old, would be leaving school in a couple of months. That left Roy, nine years old and as much trouble as a barrel of monkeys. He was too young to be abandoned. Had she stopped loving her children, then? Was she one of those women who lacked true maternal feelings? Questions, questions, no bloody answers, no way of escaping the eternal circle.

And where the bloody hell did she think she was going, anyway? Buckingham Palace? 'Excuse me, King George, but I could do with a job – oh – and can my Roy go to school with the little princesses?' No, the princesses weren't young any more – the older was married with a baby son of her own. Lily was losing her mind ... or was she? A note to Danny – please look after Aaron. Aaron. Daft name, that. But Sam had insisted on it, as Aaron had been his grandfather's name.

Perhaps that was the answer – she had never been allowed much of a say in anything. Sam went to work, brought in the wage – after it had been depleted by his drinking – so he ruled the roost. Men ruled. They were in charge, which was why the world was for ever at war. 'I've got to do it,' she explained to herself. 'I have to get myself off out of here before it kills me.' But there was no certainty in the words, no conviction. It was a dream.

'I'm going,' she announced firmly. She would not run to her family. She was determined not to become a burden to anyone. So first, she had to find herself a job, somewhere to live, a new school for Roy ... Raising her head, she looked at him once more. He was hanging over the wall that separated the Hardcastle family from the disgraceful house next door. Roy adored his father. Lily could not discuss her half-formed plan with a nine-year-old. Born after his father's enlistment for war, Roy had made a hero of the man who had returned with a scarred face and one finger missing.

'I can't say a word to you until the last minute,' she whispered at a disappearing pair of legs. 'And if you don't want to come, I won't force you.' This was like a fairy tale, something out of a book with big coloured pictures inside. She wove the story, wished with all her heart that she dared to live the fable.

She took a deep breath. The twentieth century was half done and the war was long over. Some items were still rationed, many things were hard to get, and there was a restlessness in people, a feeling that things should be better after a five-year ceasefire. They had suffered deprivation beyond measure, had endured hardship because the country had needed to 'pull together' in the face of the enemy. Where was the reward? Where was the compensation? War widows existed on pensions too paltry to feed a cat, a few wounded heroes sat on doorsteps waiting for life to begin again. As for herself – Lily Hardcastle had lost two stone since the birth of Roy, had directed all rations at her children, had become old.

'I'm not ready for old,' she informed the grate. 'I don't love him any more. Sometimes, I wonder if I ever did really love him. Did I really think we'd be different, me and him?'

She thought about various men in the vicinity who had abandoned wives and children, could not bring to mind any women guilty of the same crime. When a man left home, people looked to the wife, pitied her, wondered whether she had treated her husband properly. How would they react when a woman took off? she wondered. Females stayed. They endured all kinds of ill-treatment, yet they remained simply because they were housewives, skivvies, creatures owned by their men.

Lily gulped. Even the thought of such a venture brought fear to her heart. No, she wasn't frightened, not really. Still calm, she was beginning now to worry about the children of a woman who had chosen to absent herself. Danny and Aaron would be talked about, but they would survive. As for Sam – well – he could drown his sorrows in another pint of Magee's.

Roy wandered in. 'Mam?'

'What?'

'Why does Smelly live like that?'

Lily stared at her son, through him, into a future that she needed to change. 'She's lost all heart, Roy. She just can't be bothered with anything.'

'Why?' His face screwed itself into a mask of questions.

11

Lily shook her head slowly. 'Well, she's deaf and dumb for a start. She's lonely and miserable, she's got nothing to do, nothing to hope for in the future.'

'She can read, Mam.'

'I know.'

'She goes to the library and reads all sorts. They've even made her her own corner because she stinks so bad. Nobody'll sit near her. And why is she always going to the picture house if she can't hear what's being said?'

Lily sighed and swung the kettle over the fire. 'Somewhere to go,' she muttered.

'Did she have a mam and dad?' Roy asked.

'Course she did,' answered Lily impatiently. 'Everybody has a mam and dad. But they'll be dead now. Nellie Hulme's not far off seventy.'

Roy looked at his own mam. She seemed different, a bit sad, down in the mouth. 'You'll never get the town to her, will you, Mam?'

Lily gasped. This was a rare moment of empathy, a few beats of time during which she realized that this boy, her youngest, understood her completely. 'No,' she said, 'I suppose I won't.'

'Because that'd be cruel, wouldn't it?' asked the voice of innocence.

'Yes, lad, it would.'

She heard him trudging upstairs, the metal-studded clogs crashing into each step. He had set her thinking about Nellie Hulme now. The mystery of Nellie Hulme – it sounded like a crime book, one of those her own mother had used to read.

According to folklore, Nellie had simply appeared one day, the adopted daughter of Sid and Edna Hulme, a childless couple in their late forties. They had lived here, in Prudence Street; the little girl had been kept at home and taught by them. She had learned to read, to write, to count, to do a bit of lip-reading, had grown up under the protective gaze of two solid, trustworthy citizens.

After their deaths, Nellie had remained in the same house, had allowed it to fall into its present state. Her original beginnings were unknown, though she never seemed completely bereft of money. So she had probably come from a comfortable family, people who could not cope with a deaf child, preferring instead to pass her on to folk who would take a wage for rearing her.

'Poor owld soul,' murmured Lily as she made a brew in a pint pot. 'Still, they must have left her a few bob.' Nellie had never worked, had kept her body and soul together on conscience money, no doubt, payments from her real family, a cache from which the now elderly spinster could take her weekly pittance.

Lily sipped at hot, sweet tea. Aye, this was a strange street, all right, Catholic on one side, Protestant on the other, never should the twain mix, though those rules had relaxed somewhat since the end of the war. The other end of Prudence Street had been bombed, leaving several houses uninhabitable, others flattened, two mills intact. 'Trust them to survive,' said Lily now. 'Bloody mills and pits, they'll never stop killing us.'

She thought her way along the houses, lingering on each dwelling as if saying her goodbyes. There was Nellie Hulme at number 1, sad, overweight, deaf, lonely. Then, at number 3, the Hardcastles struggled along – Lily herself, Sam, the three lads. Five Prudence Street housed Dot and Ernest Barnes whose family had long grown and left. Ernest and, for a while, his boys had been the Orange Lodgers, the taunters of the Catholics, though time and a bolting brewery horse had eroded their zeal for that cause. The sons had grown out of it and into sensible men, while Dot had never been involved at all. It had been him, Ernest, bad bugger he was.

13

Charlie Entwistle occupied the last house on Lily's side. He owned a rag-and-bone yard, was a miser and a target for many a woman's attention. Since his wife had passed away, Charlie had spent a great deal of time polishing his running shoes, as he had no intention of sharing his wealth with the women who chased him. 'What's he saving it for?' Lily asked out loud. 'No kids, no-one to leave it to. What's he doing living here? He could afford a grander place, I'm sure.'

Her mind's eye sallied across the street to the papist side. A lovely woman lived at number 2. She was named Margaret O'Gara, though most called her Magsy, a nickname she had acquired as a child. She had a daughter called Beth and a late husband who was buried in Italy. Then there were the tearaways at number 4, a brood reared by John and Sarah Higgins. Lily had lost track, though she knew that all the children were girls and that their names included Eileen, Theresa, Vera, Rachel, Annie – and others too numerous to mention. A running joke in the neighbourhood supported the legend that Sal Higgins called a register every morning just to make sure that all members were present and correct.

Which left only Thomas Grogan, the orphan. The sole survivor of an air raid, Tommy Grogan had been taken in by the Higgins family. He was their son, the boy they had never managed to produce. With her eyes closed, Lily saw the lad's face, eyes haunted by the sudden absence of his family. His dad, whose sight had been terrible, had never been called on to fight for his country. He had died in his home and in the arms of his loving wife.

There had been no division then, when the bombs had been deposited on Prudence Street. Catholic and Protestant had struggled side by side to release little Tommy from beneath a solid kitchen table. Oh yes, everyone had come together against the Germans.

He was ten now, little Tommy Grogan. He owned the face of an angel, cherub-cheeked, red-lipped, the beautiful countenance topped by a mass of blond curls which he flattened with water. After a few minutes, the curls would spring up again and all around him would smile. He was the perfect child. Although indulged by the Higgins family, Tommy Grogan managed not to be spoilt. Lily wondered where they all slept; rumour had it that several had beds in the parlour, while the lovely cuckoo in the nest occupied the kitchen at night. Well, Sal Higgins had best keep herself to herself – any more babies and they'd be using the scullery and the coal hole as sleeping quarters.

Time was passing, as it inevitably must. Lily rose and began cobbling together a stew that enjoyed a passing acquaintance with meat. Sam had drunk the black market meat money, of course. Oh, God, she couldn't go. She was the one who made sure that Danny and Aaron got a hot meal after work and school. As for Roy, he would never leave his father.

Lily dropped into a ladder-backed chair, peeler in one hand, carrot in the other. So this grim, grey life would go on and she, like so many others, would fade into her grave like a mere shadow, forgotten as soon as earth and sods were replaced.

She blamed much of her disquiet on Charles Dickens, a writer she had discovered in the big town library. A little boy in a graveyard, a woman sitting at a decayed wedding breakfast, a girl who would break Pip's heart. 'Great Expec-bloody-tations,' cursed Lily. 'Just a book, a pile of lies. Nobody meets a rich criminal in a cemetery, not in real life.'

Dickens had known all about real life, yet the man had dared to project a ray of hope onto the backcloth of merciless reality. 'They have to do that, writers,' she mumbled as she attacked vegetables, 'have to make sure it all comes right at the finish – otherwise, who'd bother flaming reading?'

There would be no Magwitch for Danny, Aaron or Roy. They would work down pits until their skin became blue with absorbed dust, until their eyes were reddened by that same gritty substance, until their lungs were scalded and too ravaged to do their job.

Lily closed her eyes, saw her father coughing into a blackened cloth, watched the black as it turned brown, then scarlet, heard the laboured breaths shortening as his body closed down. Oh, for a Magwitch! Oh, for just enough to buy a little business, sweets, tobacco, newspapers, bits and pieces. How could she sit and watch while Danny and Aaron donated their youth to coal?

'You're selfish, you are, Lily Hardcastle,' she informed herself in a whisper. 'You want to go off just because life doesn't suit, because you can't care about nobody except yourself. Well, get fettling and make life suit.' She got fettling, mustered her stew into order, piled ingredients into a soot-blackened pot, treated herself to a Woodbine.

As she inhaled rich Virginia, she thought about Charlie-at-the-end, that famous rag man who bestrode his useless fortune like an old hen squatting on a precious egg. He had money, yet his life was no better than hers, not really. Poor old Nellie in the next house had little but death and the Tivoli cinema to anticipate, while the Higgins clan across the street lived from hand to mouth, hardly a pair of clogs between two girls, barefoot on the cobbles, voices raised in prayer every night as they did the rosary.

What good had their prayers done? Lily squeezed the end of her Woodbine and placed the remaining half behind her ear. In the Vatican, Pius the twelfth lived among riches beyond counting, while those who supported him and his pastors had to take turns going to school, sharing clothes and shoes, headlice, fleas and diseases. It was a rum world, all right.

Lily stood up, smoothed her hair, retied her pinny. She stirred the stew, seasoned it, went to the front door for a breath of air. Across the street, Magsy O'Gara stood on a wobbly stool, a ragged leather in her hand.

This was daft, Lily thought. Why shouldn't she cross the street? In shops, everyone spoke to everyone without asking, 'You a Catholic or a Protestant?' And the war had pulled people together, while the religious maniac who lived next door to Lily was quieter in his old age. Surely those days of religious discrimination were over?

Pinning a smile to her face, she crossed over and steadied Magsy's stool. 'There you are, love,' she said, 'we can't have you falling, can we?' Bugger the Orange Lodge, thought Lily. Bugger the lot of them. It was time the women stuck together, whatever their denomination.

'Er . . . thank you,' said Magsy.

'You're welcome,' answered Lily. And she meant it.

Two

Nellie Hulme had a habit of smiling to herself as she waddled along, often completely oblivious of those who avoided her or gossiped about her. Although stone deaf, Nellie had a strong sense of atmosphere, while her sight was as sharp as any gimlet. But usually, she managed to absent herself, wallowing in a secret pride, a knowledge that in one particular area of life she was special, almost unique, certainly a one-off in the township of Bolton. What would they say if they ever found out? Would they want to become friends, to rub shoulders with her hitherto unacceptable persona?

None of them knew. Even the Hulmes, Nellie's adoptive parents, had not survived long enough to discover her talent. Nellie's vocation had been discovered on a wet day some forty years ago, a dismal Tuesday with low-hanging clouds, persistent drizzle and a chill that cut through to the bone. Every time she remembered that day, Nellie shivered, partly with the remembered weather, mostly because of its glorious outcome. She had side-stepped into a wonderland called Bolton Central Library, had wandered, cold and dripping, through the arts and crafts section.

Of course, the house had started to deteriorate soon afterwards, but the house had not mattered then, scarcely mattered now, though she thought about it sometimes, wondering how long it would take to clear up. What mattered most was the astonishing fact that Miss Helen Hulme of 1, Prudence Street, Bolton, Lancashire, was so sought after that people of note wrote begging letters, while her order book was fuller than a newly opened sardine tin, crammed with names, specifications, measurements. Miss Helen Hulme was a self-made star.

On her grimy parlour fireplace, crested cards were stacked three and four deep, messages from the staff of earls and dukes, two or three in the copperplate hands of princesses, one from the queen herself. Nellie lived in a world of bobbins and damask, of threads and linens and fine, sharp needles; Nellie was lacemaker to a king, to lords and ladies, to the newly rich and to the established upper crust. She was wanted, needed, valued.

She opened her door, kicked a few boxes out of the way. Nellie knew every creak of her floor, though she did not hear anything; she felt movement in boards, was aware of vibrations when a door slammed, when an unsteady sash dropped its window too quickly. She could see for yards ahead, was able to sense any change in weather long before it arrived, had the ability to sit for hours on end with pattern books, bobbins and threads. She was thoroughly focused on her calling and, apart from her visits to the library or the Tivoli Picture House, she devoted most of her time to the design and manufacture of household linens.

Straight away, she had known how to make lace. Her first set of bobbins had been extensions of her own fingers, implements she had recognized right away. Had she been here before, had she lived already in another time, in a place where women had sat in the Mediterranean sun, digits flying over cottons, silks and linen?

Not interested in newer, quicker methods, disenchanted by cheap materials, Nellie stuck to the old rules, her work cemented in centuries long dead, patterns culled from Brussels, France, Nottingham, Honiton. She was a true perfectionist, an artist with imagination, flair and the determination to succeed. So, while the residents of Prudence Street imagined her to be lazy, she was, in truth, dedicated to work that was absorbing and intensive.

She threw a pile of old clothes to the floor and settled her bulk on an ancient armchair. In a minute, she would get up and take off her coat, but she was so tired, so ... Her eyes closed and she was asleep in seconds. For the thousandth time, she was picking up the letter, *the* letter, the one that had changed her life. Beneath the crest of York, a few words, fourteen words, 'Thank you for the beautiful tablecloth; the duke and I shall treasure it always' ... And she had signed it herself, Elizabeth, Duchess of York. What a boost that had been to the ego of Helen Hulme. That same Elizabeth was now queen, while her gentle, frail husband occupied a throne vacated by a cowardly man who had chosen an easier way of life.

Nellie snored and snorted her way through the dream, recalling invitations to visit the palace, writing again in her sleep the polite refusals. She was too deaf to travel, too frightened, too ill. She was far too dirty for Buckingham Palace, though she never told them that. How could she inform a lady-in-waiting that, in truth, she was too weary to wash, too keen to sit up each night with her threads and bobbins? No-one would ever understand fully, so she made no attempts to explain herself.

Thus a scruffy, deaf woman from a northern town had become a maker of table linens for the gentry. One day, after her coffin had been carried from the house, the street would learn that she, Helen Hulme, had made and decorated cloths to cover tables bigger than her own parlour, had woven love into sets of sixty or eighty napkins, had served her king, her queen, her country. Royal heads rested on Hulme antimacassars, while silver coffee pots and delicate cups stood on Hulme tray cloths.

She shifted, and the dream changed. The world was big and green; a man dangled her from his shoulder, pretended to let her fall. Nearby, a pretty lady smiled. Birds sang. She heard them, listened to cadences so precious, so sweet ... Oh, what joy there was in the throats of those feathered creatures. The wind in the trees was audible, whispering and rustling among leaves before emerging at the other side to skip away towards other mischief. The pretty lady laughed, a tinkling noise that sounded almost like little bells rocked by a breeze. When the man laughed, Nellie shivered. His laughter was deep, low, almost threatening.

Nellie woke with a jolt. Sound. Only in sleep did she remember sound. Hearing had been taken from her, had been removed by the hand of ... Whose hand? Had God done this to her, had He visited this upon an innocent child? Perhaps she had been ill, laid low by a fever that had invaded her brain and her ears.

She needed to remember, had to remember, could not remember. And therein lay her bitterness, her unwillingness to comply with rules, to live as others lived. Because, once upon a time and in a faraway place, she had been a hearing, speaking child. But her fairy tale promised a different ending; there was no prince, no slayer of dragons. The words happily ever after were not on the page.

Roy ran into the kitchen, his face almost purple, a look of triumph decorating the homely face. 'Mam?' Breathlessly, he gulped. 'I've seen it. You won't believe it when I tell you, Mam, 'cos you'd never guess in a month of Sundays.'

Lily was doing shortcrust to make a lid for the stew. In

her experience, a layer of pastry on top of a dish made the food go that bit further. She moved a rolling pin to and fro, not needing to glance down at her handiwork. 'Well,' she said, 'you look suited. What have you done now?' He had at least six holes on his face and would probably grow up looking like an uncooked crumpet.

'I've seen it, I've seen it and she's come back, Mam.'

'Has she? I'm right pleased to hear that, Roy. And who's she? The cat's mother?'

Roy hopped from foot to foot. He was bursting with words, yet he couldn't organize them into a sensible sequence. 'Drainpipe,' he achieved eventually. 'I went up it while she were out, Mam. Smelly's drainpipe. It weren't easy to climb, but I managed at the finish – and – well, I saw it.'

Lily slammed the rolling pin onto the table's surface. 'You what? You daft little bugger. Everything in that house is rotted, lad, including the drainpipes. It's a wonder you're not lying in her yard with your back broke.' She noticed that his expression was one of shock and bewilderment. 'Well? Has the cat's mother took the tongue from your head?'

He sat down. 'Back bedroom,' he stammered, 'her back bedroom. Mam, it's clean. It's ... it's cleaner than our house, cleaner than owt I've ever seen.'

'You what?'

'It's clean,' he repeated.

'Clean? What do you mean, "clean"? Her's never batted a mat since we moved in here. As for a sweeping brush, I bet she hasn't got one to her name.'

'There isn't no mats. It's lino or oilcloth, I think, and the room's full of stuff. There's a big, long table, Mam, all shelves up the walls, boxes on them, a massive chair what she must sit on with a little table next to it and loads of oil lamps and books and cotton – big reels, not like what you have in the sewing box, Mam – and cloth, white cloth stood up in a roll and it's clean. It were like looking into a hospital room, all spotless, like.'

Seconds staggered past. 'Clean? Clean? She never has a bath. Yon tin bath in her back yard fell off the wall years since, when the handle rotted away.'

'One clean room, Mam. Window's clean and all. She must have sat out.' Sitting out was an activity that always frightened Roy. The women of the street often chatted to each other as they cleaned the upstairs windows, bodies outside, legs inside and usually pinned down by children whose responsibility was to stop their female parents from dropping to certain death.

'She's never sat out, Roy. I'd have noticed.' Very little in Prudence Street escaped the notice of Lily Hardcastle.

'She might do it at night, Mam.'

Pastry forgotten, Lily cupped her chin with her hands, thereby depositing self-raising flour all over her neck. 'Well,' she breathed, 'I'll go to the foot of our stairs and sing "Land of Hope and Glory". Whatever next?'

'There's a thing hanging on the door,' he offered now.

'A thing? What thing?'

Roy struggled once more for words. 'It's on a coat-hanger, but it's like … like a big frock, only it's not a frock.'

Lily waited, watched as gears fought to mesh within her son's nine-year-old brain. When was a frock not a frock? And was this youngest of hers all right in his head?

'It's like … like two sheets sewn up with a hole for her head and holes for her hands. Like a tent, it is.'

Well. Lily Hardcastle didn't know what to think or say, so she took the docker from its place of residence behind her right ear, lit it, inhaled deeply. A clean room? In Nellie Hulme's house? 'I thought she never went upstairs, Roy. I thought she slept in her front parlour.'

'It's not a sleeping room,' the boy answered, 'it's a making room. She makes things.'

'What things?'

He shrugged. 'Cloth things.'

Lily, seldom at a loss, could not lay her tongue across a single syllable. Cloth things? Anything coming out of Nellie Hulme's dump must have stunk to high heaven and low hell. And if the old woman was making clothes, why didn't she fettle a few bits for herself? There was neither rhyme nor reason to this. 'Are you sure, Roy Hardcastle?'

'Yes, Mam.'

'You're not making it up?'

'No, Mam.'

The mystery of Nellie Hulme was deepening fast. 'Put that kettle on, son, I need to get me brain working.'

He put the kettle on. 'And a paraffin stove.'

'You what?'

'There's a paraffin heater, Mam. That's clean and all, like shiny. It were that much of a shock, I near slipped off the drainpipe.'

'Then don't go up it again, else I'll tell your dad.'

'Right.' He inhaled deeply, hopefully. 'Can I have a dog?'

'No, you can't.' Roy often did this, distracting her then slipping in that same request, though sometimes he asked for a cat. He was desperate for an animal of some kind.

'Well, a cat would kill the mice,' he said, 'and a dog would chase the rats away.'

Lily threw her cigarette end into the fire. She draped pastry across her rolling pin, flicked it effortlessly onto the top of her brown baking dish. He wanted a dog, a cat, a rabbit and a good hiding. 'Did you see any of the things Nellie had made, Roy?' Lily scalded the pot and made tea.

He folded his arms. 'I could look after a dog.'

She sniffed. 'You looked after them goldfish, didn't you? Dead in a week, they were. You fed them enough to keep a whale going for a year.'

'Cloths,' he replied.

'What kind of cloths?'

'I'd take it for walks. I could take it to the park every day after school. It would guard the house and all.'

Lily fixed him with a hard stare. 'What kind of cloths?' she repeated.

'I could teach it tricks. They sit up and beg.'

'I've enough beggars round my table, so think on and tell me about them cloths. No use leaving me with half a tale – you know it'll mither me for the rest of today.'

He studied his mother, assessed that her mood was fair-to-middling. 'Holes in the corners,' he replied finally. 'At the pictures, in posh houses, they wipe their gobs on them while they're having their dinners.'

Lily popped the dish into the fireside oven. She had learned more today about her next door neighbour than she had found out in ten years. But she still couldn't work out how Nellie kept the stuff clean. Then she remembered. She'd seen Nellie once coming out of the Chinese laundry on Derby Street, a large brown paper parcel under an arm. Nellie in a laundry? It was like trying to imagine an iceberg in the desert.

'Cats don't eat much,' persisted Roy.

'Neither do I,' retorted Lily, 'and we're not having a cat, they howl in the night.'

'A dog, then,' he wheedled.

'I'll think on it.' She threw a handful of cutlery onto the table. 'Get shaping and set the places,' she snapped.

He set the places. Mam had said she would think on it. Next time the subject came up, he would remind her of that. Now, all he had to do was choose a name for the dog.

At the other side of Lily Hardcastle, number 5 Prudence Street, lived Dot and Ernest Barnes. Like Nellie Hulme, they had survived two world wars and had spent many years in the same house, doing the same things week in and week out, no hiccups in the regime, no excitement, few surprises.

Ernest, whose contempt for Catholics had become a legend in his own lifetime, no longer attended lodge meetings. The owner of a troublesome leg, he walked infrequently, with a limp and with the aid of two walking sticks. He slept in the parlour, read a great deal and listened to the wireless every evening.

But Ernest's main hobby, wife-beating, had been all but removed from him by a bolting brewery horse. Bitterness about this accident had twisted his face and his mind, rendering him coldly furious, implacable and verbally abusive to the point of slander.

Dot hated him. She hated him quietly but thoroughly, wishing him dead every moment of every day while she cooked, cleaned, washed and shopped her way through each waking second of time. Shopping was the best; she stayed out as long as possible, gossiping in queues, meeting old friends on corners, pretending that life was normal and liveable.

But when she returned to Prudence Street after these expeditions, her feet slowed, her expression changed and her limbs stiffened in anticipation of the greeting she would inevitably receive. She had married a bad man and had paid the price for forty-five years.

Still nimble at the age of sixty-five, Dot knew exactly where to stand to be beyond the reach of Ernest's heavy sticks. But sometimes he caught her unawares, sneaking up behind her when his leg was not too painful, cracking her across the back with a length of thick, polished wood. When this happened, Dot would absent herself by leaping through the scullery, out into the yard, and locking herself in the lavatory. It wasn't fear that drove her out of her home, not any more. When her sons had been in residence, she had experienced terror; now, she ran off into solitude to pray. She prayed fervently and endlessly for strength; she prayed that however powerful the temptation might become, she would not kill him.

Dot was bringing in her washing when Lily Hardcastle's face peeped over the wall. 'Hello, Lily,' said Dot, syllables contorted as they fought past two pegs gripped between her teeth. 'Bitter for September.'

Lily had never mentioned to Dot the noises she had heard over the past decade. It would have been impolite, intrusive, because, in spite of her situation, Dot Barnes was blessed with a quiet dignity that did not invite expressions of sympathy. 'Our Roy's been up Nellie's drainpipe,' Lily explained, 'and he says she's got a factory up in that back bedroom. Do you know owt?'

Dot shook her head and dropped clothes and pegs into a wicker basket. 'Nothing surprises me any more, Lily. I've gone well past shock, I have.'

Lily understood. Here stood the creature in whose soft-padded footsteps Lily might well follow. The woman from 5, Prudence Street was enough to put anyone off marriage. Dot had shrivelled into her current state, had allowed herself to be dried out by a man who should have been hanged, drawn, quartered, minced and thrown to the lions at Belle Vue. Lily jerked her head sideways in the direction of Dot's house. 'How's Ernest?'

'All right.' Dot folded a towel. 'Well, he's as all right as he gets, if you take my meaning.'

This was a different day, Lily told herself. Today, she had walked on the Other Side, the Catholic side where few Protestants trod now that war was finished. Of course, they were all polite to one another when they met by chance in shops or in other streets, but the quiet division remained here, on Prudence Street. 'Nowt prudent about it,' Lily said now.

'You what, Lily?'

'Name of our street – it means wisdom. What's been wise about it, eh? I mean, I know it's different now, but I had to think before crossing over to stop Magsy O'Gara falling off her chair.'

Dot managed a slight blush. 'Well, we know whose family were at the back of all that.'

A very different day, Lily realized. Nellie Hulme was running a one-woman industry, Lily had enjoyed a brief conversation with a papist widow, Ernest Barnes's wife had not only expressed an opinion but also had finally admitted that her man had caused more trouble than enough in these parts.

'He's not up to much these days,' commented Lily.

A corner of Dot's mouth twitched disobediently. 'No,' she answered after a pause, 'no, he's not.'

Lily waited for more, was not surprised when Dot offered nothing. 'I'll see you later, then,' said Lily.

'Wait.'

Lily froze.

'Have you got ten minutes?' asked Dot. 'Can I come in for a cup of tea?'

'Ooh, course you can. There's a good half hour before they come back from the pit,' said Lily, her 'they' encompassing her husband and her eldest son. 'And our Aaron's gone straight to the baths after school.' Roy was in, but he was upstairs with the *Beano* and the *Dandy*. Trying to keep the shock away from face and voice, Lily went back into her house.

Dot left her washing where it was, walked through her gate and into the entry, then through Lily's back gate. At the rear door of number 3, she hesitated for a few seconds.

'Come in,' yelled Lily from the scullery.

Dot hovered in the doorway. 'Eeh, Lily, I've not been in here since . . . I can't remember.'

'Since better and worse days, Dot.'

'Aye, since better and worse.'

Not much had changed about Dorothy Barnes, thought Lily as they sat at the kitchen table, each with a pint brew of Horniman's and a thin slice of walnut cake from Warburton's. 'Not same as home-made,' declared Lily, 'but it'll do at a push.'

'Aye, at a push,' said Dot.

Dot agreed with everybody, usually about three times. When she made a rare statement of her own, it dropped slowly from her lips and was underlined immediately by repetition. The visitor stared into her tea for a few moments.

'You all right, Dot?'

After a further pause, Dot raised her face. 'I'm not, Lily,' she replied. 'No, no, I'm not.'

Lily teetered, both physically and mentally, on the edge of her seat. People in these parts didn't go in for tea parties, weren't forever in and out of each other's domains. During the war, doors had always been left unlocked so that neighbours could have a borrow. Many was the time Lily had come in to find a note: 'I owe you two spoons sugar, Dot next door.' But things were a bit different now that rationing was less stringent. The camaraderie of war had ended with the signing of treaties; peace had brought unease and wariness. Yet here sat

Lily Hardcastle, drinking tea with Dot Barnes from next door.

'It's not the same any more, is it?' said Lily.

'It's not as bad now as he can't hardly walk,' came Dot's cross-purpose reply.

Another opinion, noted Lily.

'I ... er ... I don't know how to say it, Lily. No, no, I don't know how to say it.'

Lily paused, hand containing cake hovering halfway between mouth and table. 'Just say it,' she answered. 'Get it over and done with, Dot.'

'Just say it,' echoed Dot. 'Right, I will, I will.'

Lily's cake found its way back to the plate. She waited, watched Dot's face closely. 'Come on, love,' she wheedled. The men would be back soon and Lily had to know. Why, she wouldn't catch a wink tonight if Dot Barnes didn't cough up.

Dot drew in an enormous breath. 'I'm going,' she said.

Lily waited. 'Going where?' she asked at last.

'Away, love. I'm leaving him.'

The hostess sank back against the spindles of her chair. Hadn't she entertained the same idea only hours ago? Wasn't this wizened woman one of the very people in whose tragic footsteps Lily was following? Oh, she'd never been hit, but Lily Hardcastle felt just as squashed and hopeless as Dot plainly was. 'Where will you go?'

'To our Frank.'

'Your Frank?' Dot had Lily at it now, repeating, repeating.

'He's got a little general store up Bromley Cross,' said Dot, her spine straightening with pride. 'Saved up, he did, then got a mortgage on the house at the back of the shop. I'll be selling all sorts, Lily, selling all sorts.'

'Well, I am pleased for you, love.'

Dot took a great gulp of tea. 'There's a bit more to it,

Lily, a bit more to it.' She sucked thoughtfully on her dentures, ran a hand over thinning hair.

Lily set herself in waiting mode once more, watching as Dot drained her cup right down to the dregs. She glanced at the cheap clock on the mantel, hoped it wasn't running slow again.

'You know my Frank, Lily. Aye, you know him.'

'Course I do.'

'He's forty-two soon. Forty-two, Lily, and still a little lad to me. Shy, he is. I thought he'd never marry. Time and again I've told meself he'd always be a bachelor.'

'Aye, he's shy all right,' answered Lily encouragingly.

Dot shivered. 'Courting, Lily. Been courting about six month.'

'Right.'

'Lily?'

'What, love?'

'It's one of the Higginses.'

It was Lily's turn to gulp in mouthfuls of air. 'But they're only young, them Higginses, Dot . . .'

'I know.'

'And they're . . . Catholics.'

'I know.'

'And he's . . .' Lily jerked a thumb in the direction of Dot's house, 'he's . . .'

'He's a swine.' Dot completed Lily's sentence for her. 'He hates Catholics, especially the Higgins lot. Remember that time he threw stones at the statues during the walks? Then when Peter and Paul's church were set afire – that were him, Lily. So, I've had to tell you, because you live next door to him. When I go, there'll be murder. There will, there'll be murder.'

'God help us,' gasped Lily.

Dot's hand crept across the table and grasped one of Lily's. 'Frank's for turning,' she whispered.

31

'No!' In the silence that followed, a dropping pin would have achieved the same impact as a bomb. Turning was unheard of in these parts. Turning was a form of brain-washing, weeks on end of sitting with a priest while you learned a load of rules and promised to bring your kids up as Catholics.

'See, when Ernest hears, Lily . . . When Ernest hears . . .'

Lily agreed, though she tried to look on the brighter side. 'There's not much he can do, Dot, not with his leg.'

'I don't trust him,' declared Dot. She looked her neighbour straight in the eyes. 'You must have heard it all, Lily.'

'Aye, I have, love.'

'He battered my boys, too, long before you moved in. Years I've had. Years and years.'

'I know.'

'So I'm going. Aye, I'm going, lass.'

Lily gripped Dot's hand tightly, noticing that it was drier, harder even than her own. 'You can trust me, you know that. Anything I can do, just tell me.'

'I will.' Dot's eyelids blinked rapidly, a few reluctant tears squeezed out by the movement. 'When I've gone, I'll write to you.'

Lily shivered involuntarily. 'Hey – I've just thought – what about that lot across the road? How will they take it?'

Dot smiled through her sadness. 'They're thrilled to bits, Lily. They know their Rachel will be looked after and they're not bothered about the age difference, specially seeing as how he's turning. Aye, he's all right because he's turning.'

When Dorothy Barnes had returned to her own house, a place she was about to leave after going on forty-five years, Lily breathed freely at last. The thoughts she had entertained earlier in the day were suddenly not so wicked, not as unusual as she had believed. Women had had enough. As the world entered the second half of the twentieth century, females were beginning to think for and of themselves. After all, hadn't they managed well enough for six years while men had fought for king and country?

She prodded her pastry to make sure it was cooked, fetched a loaf, a knife and some butter. The difference between herself and Dot was that Dot hated her husband with a deep, quiet passion. For Sam, Lily entertained no such feeling. She didn't love him, didn't hate him, was able to tolerate the man as long as he brought some wages home.

Then there were the boys. Dot's two were long gone, one into the army then the Merchant Navy, the other into the pit, out of the pit, into a little general store in a pretty village. 'There'll be butterflies there,' whispered Lily, 'butterflies, flowers and birds.'

She found herself envying Dot, the woman she had always called 'poor thing', realized that she wanted exactly what Dot was moving towards – fresh air, country walks, a nice little job.

The front door crashed inward. 'It's only me,' yelled Sam.

It was only him. He said those same words every time he came home. Yes, yes, it was only him, miner, drinker, husband and father.

Lily picked up a large knife, held it like a dagger, smiled as she plunged it into golden pastry. If little Dot Barnes could find a new life, then anything was possible. Brown gravy trickled through the stab marks. Yes, there would be changes next door. And not before time, too.

Three

Sarah and John Higgins lived in happy, careless squalor with their eight daughters and a son they laughingly claimed to have kidnapped, as he was not of their blood. A meaty couple of average blond looks, they had combined to clone children of remarkable beauty and even, generous temperament. Strangely, this yellow-haired pair had produced dark-haired offspring, though each Higgins daughter was blessed with a fair complexion.

In a house with just two bedrooms, a parlour, a kitchen and a tiny scullery, they made their unorthodox living arrangements, ate while sitting, standing or lying down, went to school, went to work, sang and played until they faded into sleep. There were few quarrels, and any small skirmishes were always settled before bedtime, to make, as John put it, a clean sheet for the morrow.

Ranging in age from eighteen down to eight, the daughters were Rachel, Vera, Theresa, Eileen, Annie, Mary, Angela and Maureen. They were all the same, all pretty, with dark hair and flawless Irish skin, soft eyes in a variety of shades, and singing voices like a heavenly choir. Ambition was not a compulsory part of their schedule, so most of the girls passed effortlessly from school to mill or to serving in shops, happily, with no apparent resentment towards their parents, siblings or employers.

John and Sarah, the latter commonly known as Sal,

were inordinately proud of their daughters. Grief, whenever it floated to the surface on a sea of black beer, was attached to Peter, John and Patrick, the three sons who had failed to thrive, and Nuala, a baby girl who had been stillborn. The loss of their babies was a cross they bore stoically between them, neither blaming the other, each managing to remain in love with life, with wife or husband and with the children. Life was good and they were noisily grateful for the little they had this side of eternity.

In the front parlour, three beds were squeezed, two along the walls and one under the window. During daylight hours, these formed the basic seating arrangements, but were transformed into beds for the use of the four older girls, who took turns to sleep 'single,' then top and tail on a rota basis. The four younger occupied a pair of double beds in the larger of the two bedrooms, while their parents were squeezed into the smaller room at the back.

Thomas Grogan, whose unofficial name was Laughing Boy, slept in solitary splendour in the kitchen. He was special. Not only had he survived a bombing raid without so much as a scratch, he had taken the place of John and Sal's lost boys. Unlike the Higgins brood, he was blond, with a mass of curls and long-lashed blue eyes. Spoilt by too many women, he expected his own way and usually got it, though toys and games were few and far between in this impoverished household. He knew one thing; not for all the tea in China would he swap this loving, noisy family.

It was a Saturday night in September when John Higgins declared that war was about to begin. All were squashed into the parlour, some on beds, others on the floor. As usual, there was a jug of beer fetched from the outdoor licence shop, some chips to share, John's melodeon standing by for the singing. 'Frank came for her,' announced John gravely. 'So poor Dot didn't even have the time to collect all her things. She's away just now to the village to start a new life, and it's luck we wish her, indeed it is.'

The children were silent. They had heard the tales of Ernest Barnes's dislike for Catholics. And now, someone had told Mr Barnes that his son was about to become a Catholic in order to marry one. And that particular Catholic lived here in number 4 Prudence Street. Several pairs of eyes were fixed on Rachel, the intended of Frank Barnes. She sat in silence, a cloud of black curls surrounding a perfect, oval face. Although she had not begun to weep, her lower lip trembled slightly.

'I wonder who told him?' asked Sal. She touched her husband's arm. 'After all, doesn't everyone know what a bigot he is? It would have to be a troublemaker, so.'

'Sure he's not on his own,' replied John, 'for there are many Orange Lodgers who would enjoy causing this type of bother.' He looked again at Rachel, whose fiancé had just removed his poor, ill-treated mother from the arena across the street. 'Frank's a good man,' he said softly. 'Aye, no matter what the carryings-on might become, he will stand by both you and his mammy.'

Rachel closed her eyes, wished that it could all be over, that she might raise her eyelids and be up on the moors with Frank and his mother in that sweet little shop. 'Why do people fight about Jesus?' she asked. 'Isn't it all the same? Didn't Jesus come for the whole of mankind to open the gates?'

John smiled sadly. 'Ah, now there we have the pure truth. And we should all see it.' He remembered the ferocity of priests back home in Dublin, their insistence that only Catholics would enter the kingdom. 'Faults on both sides,' he declared, 'for aren't some of us as bad as some of them? We should fool them all and become fast friends, Catholic, Protestant, whatever.'

'True,' replied his plump, blond-haired wife. 'And there's none of us perfect.'

'Frank's dad will go worse,' said Rachel. 'If he hears Frank is on the turn – oh, God – he'll be out of his mind altogether.'

'Then he'll wear out no shoe-leather,' answered John, 'for his journey to madness will be a short one. Many's the time I've seen him demented. I recall him getting holy water, spitting in it then pouring it down the grid.'

'He put the Mother of God in his front window,' said Sal, 'a great big picture with glasses, a beard and a moustache. 'Twas a terrible sight, but.'

It began then, the rumbling seeds of laughter that pervaded this house on a regular basis. Sal rocked back and forth, young ones rolled about the floor, John opened his mouth and released a loud guffaw. The situation was made worse, of course, by the fact that their glee, attached to mental images of a bearded virgin, was monumentally naughty.

'Ah, 'twas a terrible thing,' moaned Sal, collapsing against her husband's shoulder, 'because, you see, it was a desperate painting to start with. In fact, I would go so far as to say . . .' She mopped at streaming eyes. 'That Mr Barnes did her a service, since she looked so much better in the guise of a man.'

The older girls fell about the beds in agony, while the younger ones continued to mix themselves up on the floor, arms and legs tangled as they pushed and pulled at each other. Even Rachel, worried as she was, managed to giggle. In the doorway, little Thomas Grogan laughed along with them. If he couldn't have his real mam and dad back, these were the very people he would have chosen for himself. The papers had been signed; he was now Thomas Grogan-Higgins and he was happy.

Ernest Barnes was on the floor of the kitchen. His inability to return to the vertical was the product of anger rather than a result of his bad leg. The bitch; the scheming, good-for-nothing piece of trash. He had married her, had stood by her, had kept her fed, clothed and warm until that damned horse had finished him. God, if he could just get his hands on her now . . .

Of course, she had denied all knowledge of Frank's intentions. Here she had sat in the very chair against which he leaned, oh no, she had heard nothing, oh no, their Frank had never said a word. Liar. She was a damned liar and he was no fool.

He closed his eyes and replayed the scene. Bert Mansell stood in the doorway, hat twisting in his hands. He came straight out with it, his face red with embarrassment. It hit Ernest deep in his guts, as if he had been kicked by yet another brewery animal. 'Our Frank?' he asked more than once, as if an echo would make the words sink into his numbing brain. This had to be wrong, had to be a mistake. A Barnes sinking into the abyss dug by popes and Irish idiots? Impossible.

'It's one of that lot from across the road,' concluded Bert. 'Eldest, Theresa or Rachel or some such daft name. Aye, the oldest, I think, nice-looking girl, works at Derby Mills.'

Dot put the kettle on.

'But . . . no,' stammered Ernest. 'He's forty-bloody-two, Bert. He's never been one for the women, more interested in saving up to get out of the pit.'

'Well, I've heard it's right,' Bert said, 'my missus is never wrong about these things.'

Dot poured hot water into the brown teapot.

Ernest stared hard at the back of her head, trying to enter her mind, almost. Did she have a mind? She had said very little during forty-five years of marriage, had scarcely screamed when beaten. In fact, it was the calm, the lack of reaction that angered him. She forced him to hit her, forced him to see red. Apart from the fact that she made meals and kept the place tidy, she wasn't much of a person at all, seemed to have no opinions, no ideas.

Bert Mansell hovered in the doorway. 'Bolton's at home,' he said. 'So ... well ...'

Dot stiffened. Although the movement was barely discernible, Ernest marked it, notched it up in his mind. Frank always visited his mam after a home match. 'Sit down,' he advised Bert, 'have a cup of tea and tell me all about it.'

Bert lowered himself gingerly into a chair, his eyes darting from Ernest to Dot and back again. Knowing full well that the news he carried would bring trouble, he believed sufficiently in the cause to see this through. No way could he have sat back and watched while Frank Barnes turned Catholic. Frank was of an Orange family, a long line of papist-haters. But Bert replied to Ernest's barked questions in monosyllables, fingers still clawing at the already tortured cap. All he wanted was to be outside when the balloon went up.

Dot made the tea, poured it into the solid silence that filled the room. Ernest never took his eyes from her. 'Well?' he asked as he lifted his cup. 'What's going on?'

'How should I know?' she replied.

'He tells you everything.'

'Frank's said nowt to me,' said Dot.

And in that moment, Ernest Barnes knew. She didn't fool him, not for a second. The trio drank tea in uncomfortable silence, then Frank arrived, his joyous cry declaring that Bolton had won and would surely get to Wembley soon.

Bert Mansell left the house as quickly as a hounded fox.

Frank took Bert's place at the table, looked at his parents, realized the significance of Bert Mansell's visit. 'All right, Mam?'

'Oh, fair-to-middling.' Her voice trembled as it hit the air. 'Aye, lad, fair-to-middling.'

Frank looked at his father, held his gaze. 'Get your stuff,' he told his mother. 'Go and fetch all you can carry, Mam, because I'm not leaving you here with this bad bugger.' He continued to stare into Ernest Barnes's eyes. 'You've hit my mam once too often and I'm taking her well beyond your reach.'

Ernest roared, leaned sideways, picked up one of his sticks and waved it across the table. Unafraid, Frank caught the stick with his right hand, scarcely flinching as the wood crashed into a coal-hardened palm. 'No more of that.' His voice was low.

'This is my house,' snarled Ernest.

'It was our home,' replied Frank, 'mine, our Gerry's and Mam's. This was where we came after a long day at school, the only place we had. When we got here, we had to tell Mam all our troubles before you came home.'

'Give over,' Ernest yelled, 'you sound like a flaming nancy boy.'

'Do I?' Frank wrestled the stick from his father's hand. 'Well, let me tell you what you are. You're a big bully, a stupid, nasty piece of work who gets a thrill out of hitting people and hurting them. I bled every time you strapped me for wetting the bed. Well, it's finished, done with, all of it.'

It was then that Dot spoke up. She stood in the kitchen doorway, a bundle of unironed clothing in her hands.

'Why won't you die?' Her voice, soft and gentle, did not fit the seemingly callous words it framed. 'While I've polished yon grate, while I've cooked and washed, I've prayed for you to die. All I've ever wanted was a life without you in it.'

Ernest found no reply.

'I've felt like killing you meself,' she continued, 'but it'd only have made a mess. I've cleaned enough of your messes.' She glanced at Frank. 'I thank God for him and our Gerry. Gerry enlisted in the army, joined the Merchant Navy, because of you, just to get away.'

'Rubbish,' shouted Ernest.

'You're the rubbish,' was Dot's retort, 'and ooh, I've waited long enough to tell you that.'

Frank threw the walking stick onto the hearth. 'You're going to be alone now,' he advised his father, 'because Mam will be living with us.'

'You and a bloody Higgins,' snapped Ernest.

'Aye.' Frank nodded. 'She'd make ten of you.'

'Papist shite,' spat the furious man.

Frank took an item from his pocket. 'Look,' he said, 'for counting prayers on.' He rattled the brown rosary beads. 'For the Our Fathers, the Hail Marys and the Glory Be's.'

Ernest tried to snatch the beads, but his fingers closed around fresh air as Frank pulled the rosary out of reach. 'I hate you,' he informed his father, the voice not quite as gentle as Dot's had been. 'For as long as I can remember, me and our Gerry hated you. You drove us to that.'

'Get away with your bother,' roared Ernest, 'you'd have been nowt without me.'

Dot pushed past her older son, placing her bundle of possessions on the dresser. 'Without you?' she asked. 'Without you, they would have had skin on their backs. Do you know they've both got scars?' She rolled up a sleeve to display black, brown and yellow bruising. 'See them? Well, you made them marks. But you have hit me and mine for the last time, Ernie Barnes. And if you need help, go to your lodge, see if any of your friends'll give a hand. As far as I'm concerned, you can starve to bloody death.'

She bundled her belongings into baskets, picked up her coat, walked out of number 5 for the last time. Both men heard the door slamming shut in her wake.

Frank eyed his father. 'You'll have to shape now,' he said, 'no Mam to be running after you all the while.'

'I'm a cripple – in case you hadn't noticed.'

'I noticed,' said Frank. 'At least it slowed you down a bit. And who saved you, eh? Who got the horse's head and calmed it down? Who risked getting a gobful of hoof? John Higgins did.'

'Well, he needn't have bothered.'

Frank inclined his head in agreement. 'That's what we thought and all. He should have left you, should have let the horse dance on you. But no. My Rachel's dad saved your life. A bloody Catholic came to your rescue.'

Ernest said no more.

When his son had left, he reached for his other stick, crashed to the floor and stayed there for a good half hour. He would get no tea, no supper. The fire would die down. His breathing became unsteady as he wondered how he was going to manage. For the first time in years, Ernest Barnes was truly afraid.

Slowly, he made his way through the panic attack. He had never been alone. He had gone from childhood home to this house, had not spent a single night in a place without other people. Of course, he could have managed had he not been disabled. Couldn't he? Could he?

It occurred to him then that he had seldom made a cup of tea, that he had never made toast, let alone a full meal with spuds and gravy. He had no idea about cleaning, polishing, ironing. The house would deteriorate until it became like Nellie Hulme's, an indoor rag-and-bone yard filled with grime and filthy clothes.

Self-pity took up residence in his mind. He did not deserve this, because he had worked hard all his life until that damned horse had bolted. Ernest Barnes had never sent his wife out to work, not until he had become too disabled to provide for her. She had taken up a few hours' cleaning, but their main income had come from interest on his savings and on the compensation paid out by the brewery. Who would do his shopping now? Who would make sure that he had the basics – bread, milk, butter, sugar?

Anger moved in then, red-hot and fed by bitterness. It fuelled him sufficiently to stand up, his hands shaking as he held on to the table. This was all the fault of them across the road, that teeming, senseless family whose members succeeded in being happy even on bread and scrape. Eight ragged girls, and his son was about to marry one, was training to be a Catholic. Oh, the shame of it – he would never live this down.

With difficulty, he retrieved his walking sticks. Normally, she would have fetched them, would have helped him up, all the time wishing him dead. That quiet, docile woman had been a traitor, an invisible knife poised and ready to plunge into his flesh. 'I've prayed for you to die,' she had said. And now, by depriving him of her help, she had condemned him to total uselessness.

He stumbled to the front door, opened it. The house opposite was quiet for a Saturday evening; well, he would disturb their peace soon enough. Stepping cautiously, Ernest Barnes crossed the narrow street, cursing under his breath each time his sticks made poor purchase on damp cobbles.

When he achieved his goal, the door was already open.

'So you've been told,' said John Higgins.

'You know I have,' came the terse reply.

'I got wind of you being told while I was up on the road,' said John, 'so I've been half expecting to see you.'

Ernest's leg felt as if it were on fire.

'Will you come in and sit?' asked John.

'No.'

'Then the mountain must be fetched.' John Higgins disappeared, only to return moments later with a chair. He placed it on the pavement, then stepped back into the doorway, a sentry set there to guard his castle.

Ernest sat. 'Are you telling me you knew nowt about my son and your girl?'

'No, I am saying no such thing,' replied John, his voice steady as a rock. 'Sure, we knew about Frank and Rachel, but we found out just today that you were about to learn the good news. He's a fine man.'

'He's a Protestant,' spat Ernest.

John decided to make no reply. His faith was simple; he differentiated between good and evil, but left room for all Christians to choose their own way through life and into the hereafter.

'She's too young for him,' continued Ernest.

'I've never thought age differences to be that import-ant,' answered John, 'and as for religion, had she wanted to marry out, we would have supported her.'

Ernest drew a deep breath. 'My wife has gone,' he stated baldly. 'She knows my opinion, and she has taken off with Frank, to live with him and your daughter, I suppose.'

John nodded. 'Aye, that'll be the truth of it.' He cast an eye over the man on the chair. 'This'll leave you in a merry pickle, I expect.'

'Nothing merry about it,' came the swift reply.

'You only need to ask,' said John Higgins.

It was then that Ernest saw red. Here he sat like a begging dog, unable to achieve level eye contact with a man who represented all he despised. 'You think you're so clever,' he said.

'Do I now?'

'Hiding this from me.'

John leaned an arm against the door frame. 'Can you imagine any one of us choosing to tell you, Mr Barnes? What sort of reception would we have got? My daughter is inside the house just now, quaking in her shoes—'

'So she has shoes?'

'She does, so.'

Ernest's rage was surfacing. He took one of his sticks and drove the end of it into John's stomach, pushing so hard that John fell inside the house, while Ernest, unsteadied by the ferocity of his own movements, crashed backwards onto cobble stones. The last thing he saw before losing consciousness was a crowd of Higgins faces peering down at him.

John stood up, his hands folded over a sore stomach. 'Ernest needs the hospital,' he told Sal.

Rachel wept quietly in the kitchen doorway. Although she loved Frank Barnes with every fibre of her being, she was beginning to wonder how much trouble she was bringing on those she loved. 'Oh, Daddy,' she wept. 'Is it worth it?'

John looked at his wife, at his poor-but-clean home, at the holy palms above the fireplace next to a framed papal blessing. There was a little font of holy water inside the front door, a small statue of the Infant King on the mantelpiece. 'It's worth it,' he advised Rachel. 'A good marriage is the best gift of all.'

Sal smiled at him. 'Thomas,' she told their adopted son, 'away now and fetch the ambulance for Mr Barnes. Dr Clarke will telephone for you. And tell the girls to put a blanket over him, or he'll be frozen stiff before he sees the hospital. Go with Thomas, Rachel. The rest of you – go out the back way for a while after you've covered up Mr Barnes.'

When they were alone, John sat next to his wife, took her hand in his. 'I'll never get to grips with this Catholic and Protestant stuff, all the persecutions and the sadness caused. But I looked into that man's face, Sal, and I saw a blind, boiling hatred for me and mine.'

'Frightening,' she answered.

'Tell me again, Sal – as if I don't know – why did Jesus come?'

She giggled like a child uncertain of her catechism. 'To save us,' she said.

'All of us?'

Sal nodded.

John squeezed her fingers gently in a fist that might have cracked a walnut wide open. 'Then the ambulance must be got,' he whispered, 'so that even Barnes might have a chance.'

Four

He woke in a bed, his head sore and bandaged, the bad leg burning, an angel leaning over him. Had he died? No, the angel was familiar, one he had seen many times before. Where was Dot? He would be needing his baccy and papers, clean pyjamas, decent food if his memory of hospital dinners served him right ... Dot. Oh God, where was she? She was a fixture in his life, a thread of continuity, something he saw every day.

She had left him. Memory flooded back into place, the surge causing his head to hurt even more. He had spoken to Higgins, had prodded him with a stick, thereby unseating himself. All those damned girls had crowded round him, then he had passed out. And he still had his problem. Who was going to look after him? A bang on the head might buy him a few days in hospital, lumpy porridge, lumpier mash and soggy toast, but what about afterwards? The angel was not smiling. She was simply staring at him, her gaze unflinching.

'Mr Barnes?'

Oh, God. Another flaming Irish Catholic, another voice that sounded as if it belonged in a musical box. He grunted a 'yes,' the monosyllable echoing in his skull. She lived at number 2, had a daughter who was reputed to be some type of genius. The trouble with these Irish types was that they were often endowed with an extraordinary beauty. She looked like something off one of those holy picture cards – all she needed was a halo and a bunch of flowers.

'I'm just now going off duty, so I thought I'd come and look at you. How's your head?'

'Sore.'

She nodded sympathetically. 'The ward sister said a neighbour of mine had been brought in. Well, I hope you will soon be feeling better.' This was one terrible man. Until his leg had been shattered, he had introduced misery into many lives. Magsy O'Gara prayed for patience, but could not offer much of a smile to the man in the bed. He had cold eyes, no expression in them, certainly no hint of remorse in those steely orbs.

Ernest cleared his throat. 'And I might as well tell you before the street does – my wife has left me, and my son is going to marry one of the Higgins lot.' He could not remember speaking to Magsy O'Gara before. As she lived at number 2, she was attached to all the din that came from the Higgins household. She had just the one child, as her husband had died before the papist breeding programme could get off the ground properly. Rabbits, they were. They should be marched en masse to a vet for neutering.

'Then I am sorry about you, Mr Barnes.'

He tried to lift his head from the pillow, failed. 'I don't want your pity,' he replied.

''Tis your situation I feel sorry about,' she said, the soft Irish voice lilting across the space between the two of them. 'Feeling sorry for you personally would be a difficulty, as you invite no concern and no friendship.' Well, she told herself, it was time somebody put the truth to him. He would have to ask for help now, would be forced to drop his guard.

His jaw slackened after she had spoken, but he offered no answer.

'Well, I'll be off,' she said now.

He considered his immediate needs. 'Will you fetch me some tobacco and papers?' he asked. He pointed to the bedside locker. 'There's a ten bob note in there.'

She retrieved the money, held it up for him to see. 'I will get your tobacco. Anything else?'

'No.' After a moment spent beneath that gentle, undemanding stare, he added, 'Thanks.'

'I'll be going, then.'

He didn't want her to go. He didn't know why he didn't want her to go. 'Are you a nurse?' he found himself enquiring.

'A cleaner,' she answered. 'I'm on extra hours today.' She eyed him dispassionately. 'Beth is cared for by my neighbour, Sal Higgins. After all, what difference to them is one girl-child more or less? I mean – they have so many already.'

He caught the benign challenge, did not rise to it. 'You lost your husband right at the end of the war. Couple of months later, it was all over bar the shouting.'

'That's right.'

If he had been capable of squirming, he would have squirmed. Ernest had never been so close to Magsy O'Gara before; she lived on the Catholic side while he was an inhabitant of the Protestant terrace in Prudence Street. Why was he bothering with her? And why did he feel so uncomfortable? She had the advantage – she was in a standing position while he lay flat and helpless – but it was more than that. She was so ... composed. In a way, she put him in mind of Dot, the woman whose failure to react had caused all the trouble at home. Women were devious; they drove men to drink and worse.

49

'But you have to remember that my late husband was only another Irishman, Mr Barnes.'

He shifted his gaze until it rested on a man across the ward, an aged chap with no teeth and very little hair. 'What time is it?' he asked now. The old chap was dribbling onto a bib tied round his neck.

'Time I was off to Mass,' she answered.

'On a Saturday?'

'It's Sunday,' she informed him, 'you have been unconscious for the whole night. That was quite a crack you took, according to the nurses. But you've been X-rayed and you seem to be in fair condition.' She paused, and her eyes twinkled slightly. 'That's a good, thick, Protestant skull you have there, Mr Barnes. If you will wave sticks at your neighbours, you'll be needing those strong bones. Mr Higgins is a large man.'

He attempted no answer.

'So, I'll be off to the early service at St Patrick's, Mr Barnes. Will I say a little prayer for you?'

Again, Ernest found nothing to say.

Magsy drifted away down the ward, stopping to chat with several patients on her way out.

In the doorway, she paused, turned and looked at Ernest Barnes. He was the enemy, yet she could not think of that pale, shrivelled and injured man as a foe. He had beaten his wife and his children; he was a deeply, radically unhappy man.

She came out of the hospital and breathed deeply. The smell of pine disinfectant, floor wax and human waste was cleared from her nostrils in seconds. She hated her job, but was glad to have work. In Magsy O'Gara's life, there was one aim – her daughter must not be a workhorse. Oh no, Beth would live to see better and easier days. To this end, Magsy O'Gara worked ceaselessly. If there was overtime to be had, she took it, and the powers were so impressed that she was under consideration for an orderly job. Orderlies, still dogsbodies, helped the nurses, cleaned patients instead of floors, and the pay was another sixpence an hour.

It was a fair stride from the infirmary to Prudence Street, but Magsy would walk home. Only in the filthiest weather did she allow herself the luxury of a bus ride through town and up Derby Street. She covered her head with a scarf, pulled up the collar of her coat and trudged towards the fire station. The weather was not particularly cold, yet she armed herself, covered as much skin as she could. Because Magsy had an enormous problem.

The problem was men. Men coveted her. Everywhere she went, she discovered a follower, a would-be suitor who wanted to ply her with drink, take her for a walk, take her home to meet his mother. At the age of thirty-one, Magsy still managed to look like a teenager. She had accepted this with equanimity for a while, but, after having been chased by a group of marauding youths, she had decided to cover herself up and keep her head down. William was dead; she wanted no other man in her life.

Well, it looked as if Ernest Barnes was in a fix. Scarcely able to walk unaided, he had finally been abandoned by that poor, thin little wife. He must have been in a bad temper to force himself to walk across to the Higgins house – his hatred for that particular family was hardly a secret in these parts.

After calling in at St Patrick's for early Mass and Holy Communion, Magsy soldiered on, striding past the open market towards Derby Street. His anger might have helped him to move, she supposed. And there again, he had probably wanted a word or two with John Higgins. A Barnes marrying a Higgins? Never! God, there promised to be some fair and not-so-fair fighting within the foreseeable future.

'Hello, love – sorry to bother you – don't I know you?'
She shook her head.

The man stepped out in front of her. 'Course I do, we live near one another.' He swallowed audibly, then took the plunge. 'I could take you to the pictures later on.'

'No,' she insisted.

He grinned, displaying a set of teeth almost too white to be true. 'I'm a stranger in a way,' he said, 'only I'm not, because I live nearly back-to-back with you, just a few yards away. We're neighbours. I'm Paul Horrocks.'

Magsy eyed him. Yes, she had seen him about. 'And I'm late,' she told him.

'No, you're Margaret O'Gara.'

She fought a threatening smile – she didn't want to encourage him. 'If you don't mind, Mr Horrocks, I have to fetch my daughter from my neighbour's house, then I must get her off to church.'

'Then I'll walk with you. Some funny characters about, you know. Never know who you'll bump into.'

Squashing the obvious reply, she stepped around him. He caught up immediately. 'I work for a builder,' he said. 'Bit of overtime this morning – the extra always comes in handy.'

Magsy tried to ignore him, but this was a man who refused to be sidelined. There he was, striding along, jaunty as a young pup, carrying on about bricklaying, plumblines and how to mix mortar.

'I'm tired, Mr Horrocks,' she said during a brief pause in the monologue.

'Oh, are you?'

She wasn't going to enter into details about double shifts, about saving up so that Beth might have extra books for proper schooling. It wasn't his business – wasn't anyone's except her own. 'Yes, I am exhausted, Mr Horrocks.'

'You can call me Paul.'

She inhaled sharply. Why should she have to put up with this sort of thing all the while? A person should be able to go about her business without being a target. 'I am tired,' she repeated, 'tired of this ... this type of behaviour.' She stopped, faced him. 'Leave me alone,' she said distinctly. 'I do not want to go for a drink, nor do I wish to visit the cinema. I have worked hard all morning and I need to get home to my daughter.'

He frowned. 'And what do you do in your spare time?'

Magsy raised a shoulder. 'I eat, sleep, look after my child.'

'And for fun?'

'I educate her.' She stepped away and carried on in the direction of home. All the time, she knew that he was still there, that he was following her, that he would persist until she reached her door. She squashed a disobedient bubble of excitement that rose in her throat, a feeling that caused her breathing to quicken slightly. He was just another of 'those' men, after all.

Paul Horrocks was not a man who gave up easily. He had fixed his eye on this young widow some months ago; it had taken every ounce of his will to finally speak to her. He had done that all wrong, too, sounding like a callow youth, did she fancy a night at the pictures. Beauty such as hers was not easy to approach, since it seemed so out of reach to the ordinary man. He had made a right pig's ear of it, a total mess. It was hard, too, talking to somebody who looked like she should be in the films instead of in the audience.

And there she was, a yard in front of him, all muffled up against intruders, her mind on the little girl, her eyes fixed resolutely on the path to home and the way towards her future. She, too, was possessed of determination. He caught up with her again. 'I'm sorry,' he mumbled. 'I never meant to upset you.'

53

'Forget it,' she advised. 'I have.'

'Don't say that,' he said, 'please don't.'

Magsy was shocked, not by what he had said, but because she had heard something in the words, a vulnerability, almost a fear. 'I don't mean to be rude, you know.'

He tried to laugh, but it came out all wrong, like a cross between a witch's cackle and the neighing of a sick horse. 'I know,' he managed, his voice higher than normal, 'it can't be easy for you.'

'It isn't.'

'I mean ... I mean you didn't ask to be born looking like a film star.'

It was Magsy's turn to laugh. 'Hardly a film star, although I do get more than my fair share of attention. But I am so sorry if I have offended you.'

He perked up. 'Then you will come out with me?'

They turned into Prudence Street. 'Thank you,' she said, 'but no.'

Magsy retrieved Beth from a tangle of Higginses who were playing cowboys and Indians, though all the cowboys were girls and poor Thomas was the sole Indian, his face caked in gravy browning, a few paper feathers in the blond curls. In the middle of total chaos, Sal sat on one of the beds knitting at a rate of knots. Magsy surveyed the scene before dragging a reluctant Beth out of the Higgins house and into their own.

The silence was a blessing. While Beth drank a cup of milk and chewed on a shive of bread and jam, while she found her rosary and missal, Magsy took off her work clothes and put them in soak. She sent her daughter to church, dressed herself in skirt, blouse and apron, made a fire, brewed tea and threw together a meal of eggs and bacon. When Beth had returned and the food had disappeared, when crockery and cutlery sat and waited for another kettleful of water, the pair got to work.

54

This was Magsy's other job and she took it very seriously. From the age of three, Beth had been reading and writing. Now nine, she played her part at school, never appearing too knowledgeable, though her private studies had now taken her far beyond her own mother's abilities. The child opened a book, grinned broadly. 'You got it, Mam.'

'Yes, I did indeed. I must take it back, though, because it's a valuable book.'

Beth opened the cover carefully, peeled back a layer of tissue. 'This is the nervous system,' she explained to Magsy, 'all the blue lines are the major nerves in our bodies. We have hundreds of miles of these. They allow us to feel heat, cold, pain and physical pleasure. We use them to distinguish textures, too. Otherwise, if blind-folded, we would not know the difference between a brick and a block of wood. Each sense adds to the others – sight, hearing, touch, smell and taste are all complementary to each other. The human body is amazing,' Beth concluded.

Magsy swallowed, wondered how on earth this child's emotional self was going to keep pace with her intellect. A stranger coming in would wonder what was going on. A nine-year-old lecturing an adult on the subject of physical pleasures? 'Like when we stroke a cat – that kind of pleasure?' asked Magsy.

Beth, already lost among diagrams, simply nodded. She had reached the part that explained physical movement, which also depended on nerves.

This was how it had become. Magsy still sat in on the studies, but roles had been reversed slowly, steadily, until she was now the student. But this system had its compensations, because, in explaining the intricacies of anatomy to her mother, Beth compounded her own learning by translating it and passing it on. She was going to be a doctor. 'If we lose our sight,' Beth explained, 'other senses become more acute to make up for the loss.'

Magsy nodded – she had heard about that.

'But the loss of nerves can be dangerous. We need to feel pain, Mammy. Pain is the first warning that something is wrong. It is a message to the brain asking for help.'

'Miss Hulme can see for miles,' commented Magsy, 'or so they say. It seems the deafness has made the eyes work harder.'

'Smelly Nellie,' murmured Beth.

There, thought a relieved Magsy, that was the child speaking. Inside the miniature adult, there remained a junior school girl who played cowboys and Indians, skipping rope, hopscotch and marbles. There was a huge collection of the latter in a jar on the sideboard. When it came to marbles, Beth O'Gara was legendary. Many boys in the area came begging for swaps, since Beth's collection of ballbearings in a variety of sizes was massive. A 'bolly' was worth at least three glass 'ollies' in the local barter system.

Magsy's eyes swept the room, taking in piles of books, a photograph of her dead husband, some ironing, a few bits of utility furniture. Every last penny after food and rent went into the improvement of Elizabeth O'Gara. Magsy was determined that her daughter would not become a mill-girl or a cleaner. Beth would have a proper job, one that carried respect and a decent salary. Oh yes, Beth would never wear an apron at work. A thought struck – surgeons wore aprons, but their aprons were not badges of slavery.

'Mammy?'

'Yes?'

'Who was that man?'

'Which man?'

Beth closed her book. 'You're blushing, Mammy.'

Magsy laughed. 'Ah, that'll be the heat from the fire.'

Beth was unconvinced – the fire was scarcely up and running. 'Don't try to wriggle off the hook – I saw you coming down the street with him.'

'Ah, that man.' Magsy turned away and put the blower to the flames. The blower, a square of metal with a handle at its centre, served to encourage flame to pull its way up the chimney, thereby enlivening the weakest of fires.

'I've seen him before,' continued Beth.

'Oh, have you?'

'Yes.'

Magsy carried on tending the grate. She had no idea why, but she did feel embarrassed, as if she had been caught doing something wrong. And she hadn't done wrong at all. 'We were walking in the same direction, Beth.'

'Yes. Yes, you were.'

The mother, feeling the child's eyes boring into her back, removed the blower, took up the poker and lifted kindling to allow in more oxygen. The trouble with having an intelligent daughter was that said daughter was always a couple of paces ahead, sometimes in the wrong direction. 'You have an imagination,' said Magsy, 'but don't let it run wild.'

'Paul Horrocks.' There was a giggle contained in Beth's words. 'Lives round the back with his mother. She is ill in bed and he has to do everything for her. According to Mrs Higgins, the poor man will never get married while his mother's alive.'

'Is that so?'

'Yes, Mammy.'

When Magsy turned round, Beth's nose had reburied itself in neurology. Beth always knew a great deal about the neighbours, as she spent time with Sal Higgins, who made everyone's business her business. Not that there was any malice in Sal . . .

'Do you like him, Mammy?'

'Read your book.'

'But do you?' The chin was raised. 'I won't mind. If you get married again, I'll be happy for you.'

'Holy St Joseph,' cried Magsy, 'can I not walk along a few paces without the banns being announced to all and sundry? You are a desperate torment to me, Beth O'Gara.'

'We couldn't breathe or eat without nerves,' came the reply.

Well, thought Magsy, thank the same holy St Joseph for that. The good thing about a genius was that she was easily drawn back into her chosen subject of study. Marry again, indeed. What would she be wanting with a new husband when no-one could hold a candle to Billy O'Gara? Such dignity, he had owned. Magsy had called him William, because that name had suited him. She carried the kettle through to the scullery, poured its contents into the enamel washing-up bowl.

The voice of genius floated through the doorway. 'He's had a lot of women after him, Mammy.'

Magsy scrubbed bacon fat from a plate.

'He is very handsome.'

Knives and forks clattered.

'Are you going to see him again, Mammy?'

A flustered Magsy appeared in the doorway between scullery and kitchen, a knife in her hand. 'Have you any idea about what I'd like to do with this?'

Beth grinned. 'You'd have to sharpen it first – that wouldn't make a dent in my epidermis. You'd be better with a scalpel.'

The special moment happened then, an event they shared on an almost daily basis. They laughed. The precious gift of shared humour was the most valued expression of their love. It had seen them through days with insufficient bread, no gas for light or cooking, little fuel for their fire. Always, always, they would be close.

'We'll get there, Mammy,' said Beth when the noise faded to a giggle.

'That we will, my love. Whatever it takes, however long it takes, we shall get you there.'

'Not just me, Mammy. This is for us, for both of us.'

Magsy smiled, though her eyes pricked. Beth would move forward, would meet her William – please God – and travel on along her own road. 'Just remember,' she whispered now, 'that you are my daughter. It isn't pride, Beth, but I know there is something in me and that I have passed it on to you. Yet whatever you do, it must be for yourself.'

'You gave me strength, Mammy. You gave me reading and writing, you gave me happiness and fun.'

'Even when there was nothing to eat?'

Beth closed her eyes against the sweetest pain. 'Especially then, Mammy, especially then.'

There was trouble in the street, a disquiet that passed itself along Nellie Hulme's spine until the hair on her scalp rose and tried to walk away. She didn't know what this sixth sense was or where it came from, but it was very much a part of her essence. It might have been best described as a tingling sensation, as if some kind of electric current switched itself on in her stomach, feelers spreading until her backbone was on red alert.

She had seen it all from behind the tattered remnants of her adoptive mother's curtains, had watched Ernest Barnes hobbling across the street to the Higgins house.

What a fall he had taken, too. Mother had explained to Nellie about Catholics and Orange Lodgers, but why hadn't all that ended? The war had altered things, surely?

Restless on that Sunday, she watched Magsy O'Gara waving young Beth off to Mass. An insomniac, Nellie saw most of what went on in the early mornings. Five o'clock, Magsy O'Gara had set out for work on the Sabbath. She had done about four hours, and was now sending her daughter off to church, to the eleven o'clock Mass, a long service with no communion. So Beth might have eaten, at least. In Nellie's opinion, the custom of denying food before communion was nothing less than barbaric, but at least she didn't hate Christians who chose to worship the Roman way.

Magsy had walked down with a young man from Fox Street, a personable character with good looks and a nice smile. Dressed in working clothes, he, too, had been called upon for Sunday work. Something to do with building, Nellie guessed, from the cut of his clothes. She smiled. Was this the beginning of a courtship? Oh, she hoped so. When she wasn't working, Nellie had a penchant for lurid love stories. Their bitter-sweetness reminded her of all she had missed, yet the same quality reassured her that life and love would go on for ever.

Nellie was still restless. A strange urge had come over her, a need that was just an almost impossible dream. Nellie wanted a clean house. No matter what she did, no matter how well she protected her materials, they stank – even though they went straight from the laundry to the customer, there was still a whiff of Nellie about them.

Her sense of smell was well developed and she wished that it would deteriorate. She had been quite happy with her haphazard life, but she had suddenly started to notice how filthy her house really was. The job of clearing it was too much for her, too much for ten men. Yet who could she get to help her? And there was no point in starting with personal cleanliness, as she would quickly revert to her original condition if she went to the slipper baths only to return to this unprepossessing place.

Nellie picked up a tin, its lid sealed against dirt. She would do this, she really would, because she wanted to, wanted to give something to the people across the street. Ernest Barnes might be in hospital, but Nellie's sympathies lay with the large family opposite, the happy band whose father had been at the receiving end of Ernest's stick.

She opened the door, looked left and right. It was such a short distance, yet a lifetime away. Nellie had never crossed the street. She had walked up it, down it, but never across it. Her parents had kept themselves very much to themselves, and Nellie had followed suit. But she stepped down onto the pavement and waddled over to the Higgins house.

Sal opened the door. 'Hello,' she said.

Nellie knew with a blinding certainty that she was not being judged, that this woman took folk as she found them. 'Toffees,' she mouthed, 'kiddies.'

Sal's face spread into a huge smile.

'Clean.' Nellie shook the tin, showed that it was closed.

'Come in?' asked Sal.

Nellie shook her head. Why should her filth infect a household that was already troubled?

Sal took the sweets. 'Thank you.' Her mouth moved all over the place as she sought to make contact with this deaf woman. 'Very good of you.'

Nellie turned and walked back to her hovel. She had done an important thing today. She had made contact with a nice woman and she had given sweets to children.

It was a giant step. Now, she needed cardboard boxes, sacks, tea-chests – whatever. An inch at a time, she would get this place right.

It took over half an hour to find the top of the dresser, but Nellie experienced a feeling of pure triumph when she discovered its surface. Slowly, very slowly, she would get to the bottom of things.

As she gazed at her blurred face in the dusty mirror, she suddenly realized the full extent of her intentions. The reason behind her recent activity had little to do with living conditions. Her heart bounced around in her chest like a kiddy's toy. She faced her reflection, faced the days to come. The decision was disturbingly sudden. Because Nellie Hulme was going to find out who she was and where she had come from.

Ensconced once more in her favourite chair, exhausted by her effort to clear that minute section of her cluttered home, she slept. The dream came again, a tall man, an elegant lady. This time, Nellie was inside a house, but the room was vague. It felt like a large room and it contained a great deal of furniture. There was a portrait over the fireplace, but the figure depicted was unclear. The lady sat near the window; she was sewing very quickly. The tall man was near the fireplace – he was seated and reading.

Plates clattered. Nellie left the room and found herself in a kitchen. A large lady was banging something on the table, probably dough for bread. Nellie could hear each crash as the woman pounded the mix. A dog barked. Outside, birds twittered in the trees, their conversation loud and quarrelsome.

Nellie ran through the doorway into that green world. The fields went on for ever, rising in gentle slopes towards a far horizon. She was so small that she could not look into the horse trough, even when she stood on tiptoe. A ladybird crawled up her arm, unfolded its wings and flew away. In her dream, the beating of the insect's wings was as loud as the flapping of a hen. Yes, there were hens, and there was a cockerel who made a terrible noise. Cows lowed. In a nearby field, they began to congregate, lining up like a row of people in a shop. They were going to be milked.

She woke, sweat pouring down her forehead, stinging her eyes. Those two people were her parents, of that she felt sure. They had given her away to the Hulmes because she had turned out sub-standard, deaf, non-speaking. Somewhere in this terrible house, there was a clue – perhaps the whole answer.

Every month, the money came, the amount increasing to keep pace, just about, with the cost of living. It sat now in a bank account, as Nellie had no need of it. In 1949, her income from lace-making had been over four hundred pounds, enough to buy the house in her dream. Why, if she could face the humiliation, she could easily afford a few cleaners to come in and mend this place. No. She had to do it herself. Whilst having no concept of what she was looking for, she knew that she would recognize whatever it was when she found it. Someone else might throw it away with all the other wreckage. After all, it was probably just another very old piece of paper.

Yes, the money was there, but money was not the issue; what Nellie wanted was to trace her own history, her background. To do that, she needed to be clean and respectable. The Hulmes, gentle, kind people, had been good to her. They had taught her to read, to count, to draw, paint and sew. They had loved her, had protected her from a world that was often cruel to a child who was different. But those two good people had told her nothing beyond the fact that they had chosen her to be their daughter.

Closing her eyes tightly, she tried to revisit the dream, to remember the sounds contained within it, but, as ever, she failed. Yes, it was time to find out the whole truth.

Five

Why did the little things get her down? Lily Hardcastle put the iron on the hearth and sank into a chair. In the end, it was the tiny details of life that corroded the surface, burning away till flesh and bone got wearied.

For a start, there was him and his nose. He'd never warned her before the wedding, hadn't bothered to tell her that he spent most of his time at home with a finger stuck up one of his nostrils. Sam Hardcastle was probably the world champion nose-picker, such a perfectionist that his wife was surprised that he had stopped short of removing brain tissue.

Lily shook her head and heaved a great sigh. Her husband ought to have cups and certificates all over the house, his name in the papers, a letter from the king. And Sam had become so absorbed in his hobby that his features seemed to rearrange themselves throughout these regular excavations, gob wide open, face like a fit, as Lily's mother had been heard to opine. At work, he mined coal; in his house he carried on mining, wiping each retrieved item on the cushion that supported him. Lily was tired of washing his 'crusties' off the cover. At least the deposits were mostly on just one side of the chair, as his second picking finger had been blown off in the war. Sam always used his little finger, just occasionally inserting a longer digit when that extra quarter-inch was required.

Danny, her eldest, had started to drink, although his attitude remained apologetic and he always tipped up money for his keep, bless him. He ate with his mouth wide open, did Danny. It was like sitting across from a miniature version of a cement mixer, contents rolled this way and that, a great deal of noise accompanying the process. She'd told him over the years that these performances rendered her sick in the stomach, and the lad had tried, but he couldn't seem to eat like a normal person.

Aaron. Oh God, Aaron. Where had she gone wrong at all? Aaron had feet. He hadn't always had them, but they had burgeoned in recent months as he strode towards manhood. She had bought a special bowl for Aaron's feet, and many pairs of socks, too. He was supposed to clean his feet straight away when he returned from school, though he seldom did. Whatever came out of Aaron's socks should be taken to a laboratory for analysis and given to the War Office to be used as an offensive weapon next time Germany kicked off. It would be like Napoleon's retreat from Russia, the enemy drifting away into oblivion, many never to be seen again.

History was interesting, thought Lily, who had started to pick up factual books from the library. Yes, and Aaron's feet produced something very close to mustard gas, of that Lily was certain. She never had to wonder where Aaron was – she just followed her nose.

Roy was still a kiddy, but Lily knew what was coming. Both the older boys had been blessed with teenage spots, though they had managed to stop short of manufacturing craters all over their faces. Roy had fiddled with his chicken pox until his skin had started to bear a strong resemblance to the surface of the moon. And there was something about redheads that made such blemishes more visible, probably because their epidermis was finer than the skin of most other folk. The red hair had come from Sam's side of the family, so Lily took no blame for that.

She was sure that other wives and mothers didn't sit here with a pile of ironing to complete and shopping to do, their minds fixed on feet, nose-picking, eating habits and teenage acne. She wasn't normal. Women loved their families instinctively – real women, anyway. They didn't loll about with a Woodbine, minds fixed on faults, thoughts reaching the point where they said, out loud, 'They're boring, that's the problem.' Lily had just said it, had heard the words coming from her own mouth.

Someone tapped at the back door.

Lily jumped up, threw the cigarette end in the fire, smoothed her apron. She had to look the part, even if it was all just an act. Women fettled. They were here to fettle, to keep the house nice, provide food, warmth and clean clothes.

Lily opened the door. 'Nay, lass, you should have just walked in, no need to wait.'

Magsy O'Gara stepped inside, followed Lily into the kitchen. 'Ironing,' she declared, 'don't you just hate it?'

Lily laughed as she pushed the kettle onto the fire. 'I'd sooner drink a cuppa any day of the week.' She was glad that Aaron was still at school, because there was a natural elegance to this beautiful young woman, and Lily could not imagine her tolerating the smell that accompanied her middle son through life.

After being invited to sit, Magsy placed herself at the table. 'Now, I hope you don't mind me coming.'

'No bother. I needed an excuse to leave that lot alone for a few minutes.' Lily inclined her head in the direction of clean but wrinkled clothing. She busied herself with cups and saucers. Magsy O'Gara might be poor, but she was definitely not the type for an enamel mug or a cheap pot beaker. And here was history in the making, a Catholic taking tea in a Protestant home!

'I was in the back street here,' Magsy began to explain.

'That's as may be,' replied Lily, 'but you can come to my front door any time you like.'

'Thank you.' Magsy accepted a slice of malt cake.

'Can't be doing with this Cat-lick and Proddy-dog business,' mumbled Lily. 'Look what it's done for that daft beggar next door. Dot's gone, you know.' And oh, how Lily wished that she had the courage to follow the woman who had always been known as 'poor Dot'. Well, Dot was poor no more, God love her. At least she had reaped some reward after years of drudgery and violence.

'I have visited him in the hospital.'

Lily froze, caddy and spoon in her hands. 'You what?' she asked, too shocked to stop herself.

'And glad enough he was of it,' continued the visitor. 'Sure, he's had not one single caller except for myself.'

Lily brought the teapot to the table. 'Mags,' she declared, 'that man has only himself to blame, I can tell you that for no money. Years he's laid into her. I've not enough Christian charity in my soul to go and see him on his sickbed.'

'I know he was cruel to her.'

'And the kiddies – when they were kiddies. Flayed their little backsides raw, he did. As for Catholics, he would have tarred and feathered the lot.'

Magsy sat back while Lily poured.

'Whatever were you doing in our back street?' asked Lily.

'Oh, it's young madam,' replied Magsy. 'lost a button off her cardigan while playing tig. Whoever caught her dragged so hard that the button flew off. She's a caution.

She's out there now still searching, thinks it may have gone down a grid.'

Lily swallowed a bite of malt cake. 'Isn't she supposed to be one of them child prodigies? Like Mozart?'

Magsy burst out laughing. 'Not quite, but she's blessed and cursed with an inquisitive mind, Lily. She's leaving me behind, but. It's all anatomy and physiology – clear as mud.'

'I read,' Lily said. 'I enjoy reading – it takes me out of myself, gets me mind going. Yes, I love books.'

'You do?'

'Oh yes.' Lily nodded gravely. 'I'm doing the French Revolution and the Napoleonic Wars. You know, he was only little, that Bonaparte, but look at the damage he did. And I've been having a go with that there Dickens. He goes on a bit, but he takes you there, pulls you back a hundred years. *Tale of Two Cities* was what dragged me into the Revolution.'

Magsy sipped at the thick tea favoured by people in these parts. So Lily Hardcastle was a reader and amateur historian. It was amazing what went on behind lace-curtained windows. Perhaps Beth wasn't so unusual after all. 'Well,' she said carefully, 'I came about a strange matter, Lily.'

Lily, eager as ever for gossip, leaned forward. 'Oh?' she said expectantly.

Magsy smiled. 'Have you heard no noise from next door?'

'Which side?' Lily asked, wondering whether Ernest Barnes had had the burglars in.

'From Miss Hulme.' Magsy placed her cup in its saucer.

'Well, she rattles about a fair bit.' Lily frowned. 'When she pulls a day's clinkers out of her fire bottom, I sometimes think me wall's going to cave in.'

Magsy laughed. 'That'll be her deafness – she doesn't know how loud she is. But it's not the fire she's tending. She has her kitchen window pushed right up, and there's stuff flying out into her yard at a grand rate of knots.'

'You what? Never.'

'It's true,' insisted Lily's unexpected guest. 'I've never seen the like except on the back of a rag-and-bone cart. There's paper, cardboard, clothes—'

'Oh my God,' exclaimed Lily, 'she'll have all the rats and mice on the move. What the hell's she playing at?'

'Not tig, that's for sure,' came the quick reply. 'You know what?'

'No, I don't know what.'

'I think she's having a clear-out, Lily.'

Lily blanched. 'Never.'

'Then why all the piles of rubbish in her yard?' asked Magsy.

Lily considered the question. 'Well – happen the house is full to the brim and she's started on the outside. I mean ... no. No, love. That place has seen neither sweeping brush nor mop since her mam died. Adopted, were Nellie. She got brought up clean, decent and Methodist. According to what I've heard, she were doted on. Then, when the Hulmes were dead, she started to let things slide. She'll not alter, lass, not at her time of life. She must be well past seventy, you know.'

Magsy took another bite of cake. 'Mmm,' she murmured, 'that's good.'

Lily all but preened. She was a fair hand at baking, though she didn't do it very often these days. Come to think, there were quite a few things she'd cut down on, like polishing and black-leading, brass-cleaning, bed-changing. Her heart wasn't in it any more. The house was clean and tidy, but it no longer sparkled. Like herself, it was losing its sheen. 'I wonder how Dot's going on?'

The wistful edge to Lily's words was not lost on Magsy.

'I mean, it's countryside up yon,' Lily continued, 'all fresh air and fields. Her Frank's got a little shop.'

'Yes,' said Magsy.

'When's the wedding?' Lily asked.

'Just a few weeks.' Magsy finished her cake.

'Dot'll be happy,' said Lily. 'She'll like that, nice little shop, their Frank settled and happy, decent place, no factory chimneys, no soot getting stuck to her curtains.'

Magsy reverted to the original subject. She could almost feel Lily's sadness, as if it reached out and touched her. 'We should find out about Miss Hulme,' she said now. 'All this sudden hard work at her age might kill her.'

Lily Hardcastle pondered. In a funny kind of way, the dirty old woman next door owned a sort of dignity, an aloofness that had come from many years spent alone. Magsy O'Gara was the same, just a little Irish girl with nothing to her name, few expectations, yet she managed to be a lady. Magsy wasn't dirty, but, like old Nellie, she was ... unusual. 'We can't just walk in,' said Lily eventually, 'and there's no use knocking.'

'I know.' Magsy pulled a silky skein of hair from her face. 'Lily, I can't leave her like that. What if she takes a fall? What if she gets a heart attack?'

But Lily remained hesitant. She didn't want to go pushing her way into the hell that was next door. The very thought of it made her shiver, as if someone was ice-skating over her grave. 'You go,' she said after a few moments' thought. 'You go, have a look what's going on, then, if you need me, come and fetch me.'

'Coward,' grinned Magsy.

In that moment, Lily realized how much she liked this young woman. It was as if they had known one another all their lives, as if the religious divide had never existed.

'Listen, you,' she said, 'I'm the one what has to live next door. She might turn on me.'

'Away with your bother,' answered Magsy, 'she's just a little old woman who needs a bit of help.'

'Aye, so were Dot,' replied Lily. 'Nobody tried to help her, did they? She was in more trouble than enough every day of her life.'

'Then let's not make the same mistake again.'

Lily fixed her eyes on a woman who still managed to look about eighteen, not a line on her face, a sprightly figure, eyes that shone with health. She was a worker, too, forever at the hospital, always looking for overtime. 'You're saying two wrongs don't make a right.'

'I am indeed.'

Sighing, Lily dragged an old cardigan from the back of a chair. 'Come on, then,' she ordered smartly. 'Let's go and get it over and done with. She might clout us.'

'Aye, she might.' Magsy giggled at her own attempt to speak Lancashire.

In the scullery doorway, Lily ground to a halt so sudden in nature that Magsy all but shunted into her back. 'I've just had a thought,' she exclaimed.

Magsy grinned. 'And it isn't even Christmas.'

Something about this remark found a giddy spot in Lily, and she started to laugh. It was a deep, almost manly chuckle that grew in strength until even poor Nellie next door might have heard it. She backed into the kitchen, pushing Magsy into reverse. They finished up at the table, each bowed over its surface, both on the verge of collapse. They could scarcely remember why they were laughing, because nothing very funny had happened.

'You ... er ... I think you had a thought,' managed Magsy, her voice trembling with the last vestiges of glee.

'Did I?'

'Course you did. You stood on my foot when you decided to come in here backwards.'

'Did I?' repeated Lily, the two words causing another few seconds of manic amusement.

Gradually, they calmed themselves. Lily thought her heart would burst with gratitude, because she hadn't laughed like that in years. They were like sisters, tuned into one another, one English, the other Irish, one Methodist, one Catholic, both blessed with a marvellous sense of the ridiculous. 'By,' said Lily when sufficient oxygen fuelled her lungs, 'I've not carried on like that since the war finished. You do me good, you do that.'

Magsy straightened face and spine. 'The thought?' she insisted.

'Eh?'

'Don't be starting again with me, Lily. 'Tis a desperate state I am in already. Share your thought, please.'

Lily Hardcastle pulled herself together. 'There's a clean room.'

It was Magsy's turn to be taken aback.

Lily, pleased by her coup, nodded vigorously. 'Our Roy went up her drainpipe a few days ago and he were that surprised, he near fell off and broke his neck. Back bedroom. All cloth, he says. Piled up on shelves.'

They stood in awed silence for several seconds. Lily, who had conveyed the information, was surprised by it all over again, as if saying it out loud had made it brand new. Magsy, who had lived opposite Nellie Hulme for some years, could not absorb the concept of any cleanliness behind those filthy windows. 'He's only a boy,' she said thoughtfully.

Lily inhaled deeply. 'There were something about his face, Mags. He were that shocked – it has to be true. She's making stuff up there.'

'And throwing stuff out down here.' Magsy pondered. 'I've had a thought, too. My Beth is the answer – send her to talk to Nellie. Beth has a funny little way with people – she could revive a corpse, I'm sure.'

The back door crashed inward. Roy, still slightly speckled by chicken pox, poked his head into the kitchen. 'Oh,' he said, a carefully arranged smile fading to nothing. 'Erm ... erm ...'

'He's up to something,' Lily said. 'See that left eyelid? It's twitching about like a monkey up a stick.'

'Erm ...' continued Roy.

'Three erms,' said Lily.

'We found it. Well, Beth found it.'

Magsy smiled. 'Thank goodness for that – all those buttons would have needed replacing had she not managed to find the missing one.'

'You what?' Roy asked, momentarily confused.

Lily knew instinctively that she was perched on the edge of something monumental. Roy's face was screwed into a relief map of South America, all ridges and dips. His mother sat herself in a spindle-backed chair, her breathing still short after all that merriment. 'Methodists don't swear,' she said slowly, 'but what the bloody hell have you been up to?'

Roy hadn't bargained for this. He had recruited the aid of Beth O'Gara, a pretty girl months older than he was, a great deal wiser than he was, and with a face that would melt the iciest heart. And here he was, on the brink of a new career, but Mam had a visitor.

'Beth says she's ... erm.'

Lily turned to Magsy. 'Is your daughter an erm?'

'Well, she wasn't when last I saw her.' Magsy bit down hard on her lower lip. She was not going to laugh. Whatever had reduced Roy to erming, it was terribly serious in his book.

'Roy?' Lily had that steely look in her eyes.

'Beth says she's pregernunt.'

Magsy closed her eyes. Too young to be pregnant or pregernunt, Beth must have been spreading her limited knowledge of anatomy and physiology all round the world.

'She can't be,' declared Lily, an edge to her words.

'She is,' insisted Roy, 'she's lumpy on her belly and thin everywhere else. You can see her bones.'

'Jesus, Mary and holy St Joseph,' muttered Magsy.

'Oh, I forgot – we found the button and all.' Roy threw this mitigating circumstance into the arena. 'It were nearly down a grid, right on the grating.'

It happened then. Announced only by a scuttering on scullery flags, a creature entered the room. Fastened to the animal by a length of clothes line, Beth O'Gara was dragged into the kitchen. 'Roy's right,' said the breathless child. 'This is a greyhound and it's going to have pups.'

Not a single word was spoken while the dog escaped from Beth's clutches to do three laps of honour round a very confined space. After these exertions, the bitch walked up to Lily and placed her head in a stiff and startled lap.

'She likes you,' cried Roy.

Beth remained in the doorway. It had taken at least ten seconds for Roy to fall in love with Skinny-Bones, as he had christened the unfortunate beast. But Mrs Hardcastle didn't seem so smitten by the canine. Perhaps she would grow to like her. There again, perhaps she wouldn't.

'This takes the flaming biscuit,' announced Lily.

'I bet she likes biscuits.' The hope in Roy's tone was dying fast. Mam had a mood on her, one that looked like staying for a while.

Lily looked down. A pair of frightened, hungry eyes returned the stare. The words 'Help me, please' were emblazoned across its features. A swollen belly announced the animal's condition, while bony protuberances spoke of hunger and neglect. 'She can stop till we find whose she is,' said Lily, thereby surprising herself and all other occupants of the room. 'Needs somewhere to have these pups,' Lily added, 'and you, our Roy, can do all the feeding and cleaning up, 'cos I've got enough on me plate.'

Roy could not say a thing. His throat was closed, while his chest filled up with a feeling he could not have named in a thousand years. He had a dog; soon, he would have a lot of dogs. Greyhounds were worth money – he had the potential to become a rich man. 'I can sell 'em,' he said at last.

Lily laughed mirthlessly. 'They'll be mongrels.'

'She's a greyhound,' Roy insisted.

'But the father could be anything,' said Beth. 'You have to have two greyhounds to have greyhound pups.'

Roy scratched his ginger thatch. This was all beyond him. But nothing mattered now. He had a dog, and that was all he needed. 'Can I give her some scraps?' he asked.

'Soak some bread in warm milk and water,' Lily advised, 'half and half. Give this poor thing anything stronger and she'll fetch it straight back up. Aw, it's a shame.'

Roy's shoulders relaxed. Mam was always on the side of the unfortunate. If Skinny had been any healthier, she might not have got a look-in at the Hardcastle table. He busied himself with bread, milk and water. When the sloppy concoction had been prepared, the dog all but inhaled it, eyes huge as she raised them from her empty plate. All the love and gratitude in the world came to reside in Skinny's face. She was home. She was safe, warm and ready to have her pups by a real fireside.

'Lily,' said Magsy, her voice wavering, 'if a dog could cry tears of joy, we'd be flooded.'

Lily blinked. 'Aye, well, she'd best behave. I don't want her taking washing off lines and dragging it about.' Oh, God, the expression worn by Skinny would have melted the coldest heart. And look, here she was putting a paw on Lily's knee. What had happened to her? Had she been a poor racer, had she got herself pregnant and been thrown out? 'I'll see you right, lass,' Lily said quietly. 'Only remember who's boss and you'll not go far wrong.'

The room relaxed, as if the very walls sagged with relief. The issue of Miss Hulme was not raised again. By the time they had settled the dog in an old wash basket containing a khaki blanket, no-one had sufficient energy to deal with anything further.

Magsy and Beth went home, while Roy Hardcastle went into the business of finding bedding for Skinny-Bones.

Half an hour and two more army blankets later, the bitch was ensconced in a corner of the kitchen. She had always been here; her memory of times past slipped away in the warmth that surrounded her. She was in the right place, the best place. And nothing else mattered.

Six

Hesford was a robust little village, its main street cobbled and flanked at each side by sturdy, square houses built of rectangular stones. On a slope that reached onward towards the mountains, its pavements were steep enough to warrant occasional steps, stumbling blocks for many a playing child, the curse of young mothers with prams.

There was just one gap in this monotonous arrangement, another square, a space containing Knowehead, a four-bedroomed detached house of Accrington brick. Most of its curtains remained closed, although it seemed to watch the road constantly from one particular upstairs pane, yet another oblong shielded by thick lace. Everyone knew about the shrivelled crone labelled Miss Katherine Moore – and God help anyone who forgot the 'Miss'. Like the sky, the birds and the weather, Miss Moore was always there, was threaded through the continuum of life, a supervisor, an onlooker who chose not to take part in Hesford's small daily ongoings.

She sat there when the new people moved into the shop opposite, watched the young bride in her full-skirted white frock, the groom in a suit too shiny to be new, his withered mother in winter coat and close-fitting blue hat. Change. Katherine Moore hated change. She hated most things, really, was a bitter person whose small view of the world kept her narrow, unaccepting.

'Bloody fool,' she snorted when she watched the new Mrs Barnes moving into the shop, 'marrying a man old enough to be her father.' Miss Katherine had never married; no man had come up to her rigidly set views of correctness, her idea of her own place in society. No mere mortal had ever pleased Katherine's father, whose temper had been unpredictable even on the best of days.

She sighed. 'And I am another fool.' The voice, unused to exercise, croaked its way out of a parchment-dry throat. There was no-one with whom she could converse. That stupid girl would be downstairs, no doubt, was probably entertaining one of those young yokels who sneaked up the path from time to time. 'I should have got out of here,' she muttered, 'should have left him to rot.'

But she hadn't gone, had waited, instead, for Father to die. Had she abandoned him, he might well have left his paltry legacy to a charity, a home for worn-out horses or foxhounds. Damn him, anyway. How much he had lost, how little she had received after years of drudgery, 'Yes, Father, no, Father, of course you are right, Father.'

Katherine had never owned a mother. Mother had died on the day of Katherine's birth, had left Father angry in his grief. In his turn, Bertram Moore had created an ill-tempered daughter, one who had grown up knowing little of love or forgiveness.

She turned her head and gazed at a blank wall. Had she been able to see through plaster and masonry, Miss Katherine Moore's eyes would have lighted on the roof of a mansion, a solid pile with seven bedrooms, servants' quarters and several acres of land. Father had imbibed it, had converted it to liquid – whisky, gin, brandy. Chedderton Grange was now a school for young ladies, a place where the daughters of the privileged enjoyed an expensive and thorough education.

As a daughter of the privileged, Katherine was angry.

Now in her seventies, she had enjoyed a limited period of learning dealt out by a series of governesses and tutors whose main function had been to bed her father or to join him in drink, depending on their sex and inclinations. Miss Farquar-Smith had left under a cloud and with a large belly; Mr Collins had finished up in hospital, had died of a bleeding ulcer caused by alcohol; Miss Bellamy, whose vices had embraced both of Father's hobbies, had been taken away in an ambulance, her demented screams rending the air as she was dragged on board.

And here sat the daughter of the landed gentry, a small servant girl her only companion, her days spent fastened to a window through which she saw little, enjoyed nothing. It was the unfairness of it all that drowned her spirit, though she congratulated herself on needing no alcohol to dampen her soul. Alcoholism ran in families, and she did not intend to follow in her male parent's unsteady footsteps.

The door opened. 'Ready for your dinner, Miss Moore?' asked the girl.

The girl was pretty in a rather loud way, large brown eyes, home-permed hair, the complexion coarsened by ruddy cheeks, a sure sign of healthy country living. Katherine noticed the insolence in her tone, a message that spoke volumes about activities below stairs. This one would be pregnant soon, no doubt, would pick names out of a hat until she decided which bumpkin she should trap. 'I am not hungry,' she replied.

'Cup o' tea, then?'

'Later, thank you.'

A slight raising of the servant's shoulder conveyed a nonchalant attitude. She had to go. Katherine sighed. Here she sat, three score and ten already achieved, with a few months added on for good measure. How many of these girls had she been through in recent years?

'But you've got to take your tablets,' wheedled Phyllis Hart. She wanted to be off, needed to grab a couple of hours before returning to tidy up Miss Katherine for the night.

'My arthritis is slightly better today.'

Phyllis could not have cared less. This miserable old devil deserved the pain – she never spoke a word of thanks, never offered a smile. In fact, if the biddy were to smile, her dried-up face might well snap into two pieces.

'I've got to get back to me mam, miss.'

Katherine nodded. The chit did not want to get to her home – she probably had an assignation with some spotty youth, a plan to give herself away yet again to anyone with the price of a chocolate bar. 'Then go,' she said.

Alone once more, the crippled woman picked up her sticks and dragged her aching body across the landing into a rear bedroom. From here she could see her back garden, was able to focus on the summer house. A wooden structure, it was built around a chimney breast of brick, so it was possible to keep a fire going on cool evenings. It had a porch all round, three rooms and a primitive kitchen. 'I'll do it,' she stated aloud. 'I shall make sure that the place is weatherproof, then I shall advertise.' She was sick to the core of feckless young women. It was time to hire someone more mature, a female who could be on the spot and on call at all times. She would advertise in the *Bolton Evening News*, would get a woman from the town. Said woman could live in the summer house – it could be furnished with bits and pieces from the attic of Knowehead.

Sighing, Katherine sank onto a spare bed. Her life was pain and pain was her life. The tablets took the edge off the misery, but only death offered a promise of complete release. Trapped upstairs within easy reach of the bath-room, she had not visited the ground floor of her own house for almost a year. Soon, it would be Christmas. Christmas would mean little but more misery, as the girl's visit would be brief, just a few sandwiches and a flask of tea to last all day. This was no way to live.

'You have two choices,' she informed herself. 'You can take all the tablets in one go, or you can hire live-in help.'

For a reason best known to her subconscious, she opted for the latter. The urge to continue alive in this valley of unhappiness remained strong even now. It was not yet time to die.

Rachel Barnes could not work herself out at all.

She had a wonderful new husband who would probably worship her for ever, a kind mother-in-law, a shop and a house with plenty of space, acres of space when compared to the hovel she had shared with her parents and siblings. Yet she managed to be lonely.

'You'll get used to it, love,' Dot had told her on several occasions. 'Everything takes time.'

Rachel wondered. There was something about a big family, she concluded, and she had taken it for granted for too long. How badly she had wanted her own room, how often she had needed to jump the queue for a quick morning swill in the scullery sink.

But she missed the music, the fights, the constant flow of emotions and ideas that emanated from her father, her mother, from the other girls, from Thomas, who was now Grogan-Higgins. There were few secrets in the Higgins household, because privacy was a luxury enjoyed by none when such a crowd lived in conditions so close, so crushed.

It was the silence, then. Even at work, Rachel's world had been noisy, the clatter of spinning mules, the shouting of comrades who, rendered half deaf by exposure to machinery, were boisterous when tramping homeward in the evenings. This place was so quiet. Even when the shop was busy, folk spoke in muted tones until they arrived at the front of the queue waiting to be served.

The shop was wonderful. It had two distinct sides – one for ironmongery, the other for general groceries, sweets, tobacco and newspapers. Frank looked after the hardware, while Rachel and Dot, firm friends from the start, worked opposite him at a long polished counter.

Behind the shop there was a large living room, a scullery and a washroom with its own toilet. Never before had Rachel or Dot enjoyed the luxury of indoor sanitary arrangements. Upstairs, three bedrooms and another bathroom completed the living quarters. Rachel and Frank had a large bedroom, while Dot, who had turned the second bedroom into a sitting room for herself, slept in the smallest, just space for a bed, a chest of drawers, a chair and a makeshift wardrobe with a curtain instead of a door. Dot, anxious not to interfere, lived a life as far away as possible from her son and his wife. She cooked, cleaned, worked in the shop, then listened to the wireless in her own room.

Rachel felt guilty. Christmas was almost here, and all she wanted was to be with Mam and Dad. There would be few presents, yet John and Sal would provide the yearly jigsaw, a puzzle of many parts that would take up the whole kitchen table for days, its presence forcing the family to take meals while perched on the edge of the beds in the front room. The melodeon would be on hand, carols would be sung, two chickens would be stretched to feed the whole happy band. Irish potato cakes, soda bread, pounds and pounds of potatoes, the favourite filler of many Irish bellies.

'This is your family now,' Rachel advised herself aloud

on several occasions. But it wouldn't be the same, could never be the same. She simply had to get used to it, and that was that.

Then she noticed the house across the way, was suddenly keen to know about the inhabitants, the lack of movement, and she stopped thinking about herself.

Phyllis Hart offered the story while buying two slices of boiled ham and a small Turog loaf. 'She's a miserable old woman,' the girl announced to a shop that was empty except for herself and Rachel. 'Has to take pills for her arthritis.' The girl sniffed. 'And she pays rotten wages, too.'

Rachel weighed the ham. 'Will she have Christmas with her family?'

'She hasn't got no family.'

'No-one at all?'

Phyllis raised a careless shoulder. 'Me mam says she used to be posh. They had a big house a few miles away down in a dip – you can't hardly see it unless you climb up on a roof, like. It's a school now.'

Rachel passed the merchandise across the counter, dropped money into the till drawer, handed out the change. 'So she'll be all alone on Christmas Day?'

'I'll go in to give her some dinner, like, but she doesn't want nobody, really. She just sits at that window all day.' Phyllis pointed across the road. 'That one there. She'll be staring at us now. There's not much happens round here what she doesn't know about. But she says nowt. Get blood out of a stone easier than words out of her, me mam says.'

Rachel decided that this was a shame. That very evening, while sharing a meal with Frank and Dot, Rachel announced her intentions.

'But you can't do that, love,' exclaimed Dot. 'From

what you say, she can't hardly walk. How's she going to get here?'

Rachel smiled sweetly at her husband. 'Frank can carry her.'

Frank dropped his fork, depositing a shower of pickled red cabbage in his hotpot. 'You what?'

'Carry her,' Rachel repeated.

Frank glanced from his wife to his mother, back to his wife. 'I can't go dragging a woman across the road,' he cried. 'She could have me up for assault.'

'Aye,' agreed Dot, 'and from what I've heard, she likely will.'

Rachel grinned, the width of her smile announcing that she was confident of her ability to twist Frank right round her little finger – plus five times round the block. She would be happy, she would. Anyone would be happy with Frank Barnes.

He tutted, lowered his gaze so that he might avoid that vision of perfection, clouds of dark hair tumbling to shoulders he had kissed, eyes of brightest sapphire, skin smoother than silk. And the way she responded, uninhibited, joyful, unselfish. He knew that he was beginning to blush . . .

'Frank?'

He studied his plate. 'What?'

'She shouldn't be on her own, not at Christmas.'

Dot tried not to smile. She knew that these two were enjoying each other, though she did her best not to listen to the sounds created by lovemaking. Let them be like this for always, she begged inwardly. She knew that Rachel was about to get her own way, but she would offer no further counsel.

'Please,' Rachel begged.

Frank plucked up his courage and faced her. She was

a right little madam, cheeky, outspoken, adorable. There she sat, a finger placed in the centre of a plump lower lip, her eyes riveted to his face, a smile pulling at the corners of her mouth. 'I'm having nowt to do with it,' he announced with the air of a man who pretends to be in charge. 'If you want her here, then get on with it. But I'm not carrying nobody.'

She had won. Rachel picked up a shive of soda bread and dipped it in gravy. She would deal with the details later, would persuade Frank to help her with Miss What-ever-her-name-was. As she finished her food, she made up stories about the old woman, imagining her aban-doned at the altar, or engaged to someone who had perished at the front in the First War.

Dot picked up the dirty dishes and went to fetch apple crumble from the kitchen. As she poured custard into a glass jug, she wondered briefly about Ernest. He would be alone at Christmas, she supposed. Happen that would teach him a lesson, she pondered as she carried the pudding through. There'd be nobody for him to scream at, no target for his sticks. But no, folk like her husband didn't learn lessons. They marched in orange sashes, threw stones at Catholic statues, defiled churches, hated their neighbours.

Back at the table, she shared out the pudding. 'Thanks,' she said quietly.

'What for?' asked her bemused son. 'You made the food, Mam.'

'For letting me live here – both of you.'

Rachel's laugh, as light as any crystal chime, floated through the air. Frank, his eyes wet, grabbed his beloved mother's hand. 'Don't mention it,' he answered, 'because we're kind to old ladies at Christmas – aren't we, Rachel?'

The laughter ground to a sudden halt. 'Dot's here for

always,' she answered solemnly. 'She's not come just for Christmas.'

Dot picked at her crumble. If she got any happier, she would surely burst.

Ernest Barnes had decided to be heartbroken. As a result, the neighbours had started to be good to him. Also, since he was now without a skivvy, he was forced to push himself onward, thereby discovering that he remained quite strong in spite of his disability, that he could get down the yard, could manage to boil potatoes and vegetables, was able to cope with most things with the exception of shopping.

His shopping was done by Magsy O'Gara, an Irish Catholic with a no-nonsense attitude to life, a beauty whose features deserved committing to canvas. Too young for him and from the wrong side of the religious divide, she walked in and out of his life on a daily basis, was beginning to disturb his sleep. He was tormented by dreams of her, nightly scenarios in which he took the upper hand, in which he was young and whole again.

He lived for the unmistakable sound of her footsteps in the narrow hall, could tell immediately when Lily Hardcastle took it upon herself to become a poor replacement for the younger woman. Magsy floated; Lily plodded.

In spite of his growing affection for Magsy, Ernest refused an invitation to spend Christmas with her and Beth. To use a Catholic as a servant was one thing, to break bread under her roof another matter altogether. Orange could not sit down with green – that was one of Ernest's extra commandments. And yet . . .

Well, he would see her, because she had promised to

plate a Christmas dinner and fetch it across for him. He had refused an invitation from the Hardcastles, too. He felt uneasy in the presence of Lily Hardcastle, because she looked at him 'funny', as if she remembered Dot's screams, as if she saw right through him, as if she knew that the poor abandoned husband he pretended to be did not really exist. Well, she didn't matter; all that he needed was to see Magsy O'Gara on Christmas Day. That would be the best present of all. In fact, it would probably be his only present.

Lily Hardcastle had always taken Christmas seriously, but the lethargy which had visited her since September was still upon her. She couldn't be mithered with it. However, guilt sat heavily on her shoulders, so she relented quite late in the day, made a couple of puddings, a cake and some sticky toffee. Roy was a beggar for toffee, as were these daft bloody dogs whose presence made the house smaller than ever. She shoved the toffee in a tin, stuck almond paste on her cake and threw a couple of three-penny bits in her puddings.

Lily eyed the youngest of her three sons. 'Listen, you,' she said, 'you have to get rid of these pups. I keep falling over them – they're getting in me road.'

'They're only six weeks, Mam,' came the plaintive reply.

'Seven,' she snapped. 'I should know, I've had to live with the little buggers. Now, get rid, or they go to Vernon Street.' Vernon Street was where dogs went when nobody wanted them.

Roy sighed dramatically. There were only four pups, all male, all healthy enough, but he did not know where to begin when it came to disposing of them. Beth O'Gara had been right – she was always right, that one – Skinny's babies were nothing like greyhounds. They had big feet for a start, dinner plates as Mam called them. Their heads were out of proportion with their bodies, while their tails were like bits of string, straggly and fraying at the ends. Nobody would like them. Like any decent father, Roy adored the offspring, but he tried to view them objectively and had to conclude, however reluctantly, that these were not things of beauty.

'I want them gone by Christmas,' she continued, 'they've already ate three socks and the peg rug.'

Roy looked at the evidence, holes in the rug Mam had pegged from old clothes. 'We needed a new rug any road,' he mumbled.

'And I need a week in Blackpool, but I won't get one,' replied his mother.

He sighed again, waited for the lecture to continue.

'Anyway,' added Lily, 'Mags says Beth can have one.'

Roy grinned broadly. That was nearly the same as keeping a puppy, because he would see Beth most days. Skinny was staying, but she had to have an operation to stop more pups being born. Mam had an operation jar on the mantelpiece where she saved for the vet's bill. Mam wasn't as hard-hearted as she pretended to be.

'Can we keep one?' he begged.

Lily rounded on him, a large knife clutched in her right hand. 'Now, listen here, you,' she chided. 'I've kept me promise and she's had her pups. They're weaning, Roy. They want meat and biscuits – I can't hardly afford to keep Skinny, never mind the others. Now, get out of this house and start fettling. There must be some crazy so-and-so out there who wants a pup for Christmas.'

He picked up the least ugly of Skinny's brood, placed it under his coat and dragged his way out of the house. Argument would be futile, because Mam was right – the Hardcastles could not afford to feed more than one dog.

He tried not to look at the trusting little face that peeped out from his jacket, blinked back tears as a tongue licked his throat. This was the fattest pup, its markings lopsided, a black patch surrounding one eye, another ink-blot right in the middle of its mostly white back.

He sat on the step and wondered where to start. The O'Garas were having one, so that left three. Who could manage to look after Spot properly? Who would care enough for the little creature? And he wouldn't cry, no, he definitely would not cry.

A hand touched his shoulder and a familiar smell assaulted his nose. It was Nellie-Next-Door. 'Hello,' mouthed Roy.

She bent forward and stroked the little dog's head. The boy was near to tears and Nellie knew why. 'Me,' she said, though no sound emerged from her mouth. 'Me.' It was a sudden decision, but she stood by it. There was enough money to keep a houseful of little dogs – and a bit of company would be nice.

Roy's brain went into top gear. She wasn't fit to have one of his puppies, wasn't clean, even if she had started sorting her way through the wreckage. It stank, did Smelly's house. And she ate daft stuff, would give daft stuff to Spot. He clung to the little dog, his mind scuttering about all over the place, thoughts colliding, worry making him stupid.

'Me,' she repeated.

Well, there was another way of looking at this, Roy told himself. Number 1 might not be the poshest house, but it was next door. Spot and Tinker – the pup he had assigned to Beth O'Gara – would be right on his doorstep. He would be able to keep an eye on them both. And anyway, there was such kindness in Nellie's eyes that she would surely do her best for Spot.

Nellie handed him a pound.

Startled, he shrank back. A whole quid? For a mongrel?

The large woman nodded vigorously and pushed the money into Roy's pocket.

He gulped, then drew the shivering pup out into the cold December air. 'Spot,' he said.

'Spot,' she repeated silently.

For the first time in his young life, Roy Hardcastle actually thought about Nellie Hulme. Being deaf must have been horrible. She couldn't listen to the wireless, never heard anybody knocking at her door, had to lip-read at the pictures. She had no husband, no children, no company. She lived every day the same, sewing or whatever in that upstairs room, walking to the chip shop, visiting the cinema or the library. He had never worked out why she went to the cinema, because she couldn't hear anything. Yet he did know the answer, yes, of course he did. There were other people at the pictures. At the pictures, she felt normal. Nobody liked her because she smelled funny, but she paid her money to watch the film and became the same as everybody else. He handed over the puppy and tried to smile.

Nellie held the creature, felt its warmth, was pleased that it did not turn away from her. Humans objected to her; this little fellow would love her no matter what. Her own affection was born in that moment, in the instant when the tongue licked her chin. She had a dog; she had a companion.

In the past three months, Nellie Hulme had made considerable progress inside her hovel. Piles of newspapers, old clothes and broken furniture had been removed by Charlie Entwistle, the rag man from the end house. The narrow hall was all but cleared, while Nellie's living room now boasted an area of ground clear enough for linoleum to be visible.

She placed Spot in a box, knew that he was whimpering, saw the little mouth opening and closing as he fretted for his mother and his three brothers. Poor little mite – he was probably hungry. After removing the pastry from a pie, Nellie cut up the meat and fed the dog crumb-sized morsels of beef.

Spot's eyes widened. This was all suddenly very promising – good food, a box to himself, a nice hot fire burning in the grate. He yawned when his stomach was full, accepted his lot with the equanimity born into dogs of mixed breed. He had a good home – what more could a puppy want?

Nellie stroked her pet until he slept, smiled when he 'ran' in his dream, wondered how newborn animals could possibly manage to dream. It was bred into them, she decided; it was race-memory, was handed down through the ages, passed from dog to dog right back to the Stone Age and before. Like the first wolf brave enough to approach humanity, this puppy had come in from the cold to warm himself at a caveman's fire.

If this little mite knew exactly what he was, then she, too, had the right to know. Like Spot, she experienced dreams; unlike Spot, she had no idea of her own identity. A room, a garden, a man, a woman. Birdsong that eluded her during hours of wakefulness, a man's voice, a woman's laugh – Father, Mother? And the other thing, the nightmare whose edges had begun to touch her troubled soul when dawn approached, a nameless fear that made her sweat.

So far, she had found nothing here, no birth certificates, no adoption papers, no clue. Yet this tiny creature with its white and black coat seemed to embody hope.

More important than that, Nellie would have company this Christmas.

Magsy O'Gara opened her front door. She knew who it was before actually seeing the handsome square-jawed face, startling blue eyes, the shock of near-black hair that seemed to scream for a comb. Oh, he was screaming, all right, was becoming a nuisance, so persistent, almost desperate.

'Hello,' he said.

She folded her arms and leaned on the door jamb. 'Hello. Again.' She spaced the two words carefully, deliberately.

'I just wondered . . .' His voice tailed away.

'You do a lot of wondering,' replied Mags.

Paul Horrocks bowed his head. He felt like a child who had been sent to the head teacher's office for some small playground misdeed. 'Well, it's Christmas soon,' he advised the doorstep.

'I had noticed.'

He raised his eyes and forced himself to look at her. She was the most beautiful woman on God's earth. 'I thought you might like to join me and Mam,' he said. 'Being as you and young Beth will be on your own.'

'We shall have each other, Mr Horrocks.'

'Paul.' It was like dragging blood from a stone, he decided. Magsy had the voice and face of an angel, yet she was as stubborn as the average mule. 'But you've no family,' he added.

'Beth is my family and I am hers.'

'You're Irish,' he told her, 'and I am from Irish stock – my mam comes from Mayo.'

'Does she now?' Why should I make this easy? Magsy asked herself. 'And how is that pertinent?' she asked.

Pertinent. Here she came again with the big words. 'Irish usually have big families and they get together at Christmas.' His words tailed away, as if they died beneath her steady gaze.

'Then Beth and I are atypical,' she replied.

This was hopeless. He wished with all his strength that he could drag himself away from this impossible female, that he might set his sights elsewhere, but she was like a drug on which he had come to depend. 'I'm a good cook.' This last statement stumbled from his lips like a challenge.

'So am I.'

Hope blossomed – perhaps she would invite him to come to her house? He waited, but she offered no more words.

Magsy, who had decided some weeks ago that enough was enough, stepped onto the pavement, causing Paul to back away while she closed the door in her wake. 'This has to stop,' she informed him, the tone gentle. 'I have no wish to offend you, but your attentions are not welcome, Mr Horrocks.'

'Why?' he blurted before he could check himself.

She smiled. 'Why is the sky blue? Why is the rain wet? I have no answers to those questions either. They are just facts of life, you see. And another fact is that you are beginning to annoy me.'

He drew a hand through his hair. 'It's such a waste,' he managed after an uncomfortable silence. 'You shouldn't be alone.'

'I have a daughter.'

'You know what I mean.'

Magsy nodded slowly as if considering her next words. 'Mr Horrocks.' Her tone wore an air of deliberately applied patience. 'I had an excellent husband. He died. William is irreplaceable.'

'But—'

'But nothing, Mr Horrocks. You have no claim on me. I have given you no encouragement and have made you no promises. This is my life; this is the way I have chosen to live. Now, it is cold and I want to get back to my ironing.' She turned, opened the door and walked back into her house.

Angry and confused, Paul Horrocks walked away. Like all beautiful women, Magsy O'Gara knew her power, was well aware that he had fallen under her spell.

Magsy closed her eyes and pressed her back against the wall. Would he never give up? And what was it about herself that attracted men in droves? Didn't God understand that she would never remarry, that no-one could ever replace her wonderful William?

'Was it Paul Horrocks again?' asked Beth when her mother entered the kitchen.

'Yes.'

'It would do no harm,' Beth began, 'for you to—'

'No,' snapped Magsy. 'Do not interfere, Beth.'

Across Prudence Street, in the house known as number 5, Ernest Barnes watched the young man trudging homeward at the pace of a reluctant schoolboy. 'Not good enough,' Ernest whispered. 'She needs a man, not a boy.'

After uttering these words, he staggered to a mirror and stared at his own reflection. He was a very old man. And she was a very young Catholic. And his hair needed a trim . . .

Seven

The trouble with having a bright child was that bright children understood a little too much and a little too little. In spite of her great capacity for learning, Beth remained immature, emotionally unable to cope with adult life and all its complexities. Engrossed in the Korean War, she had begun to concern herself about America's relatively new but terrifying arsenal.

Magsy shook out a tablecloth and sprinkled it with water in preparation for ironing. 'It won't happen,' she said for what seemed like the tenth time.

'How do you know?' was the next question.

'Because Mr Attlee was reassured by President Truman that—'

'Mother!' cried Beth. 'Mr Chamberlain had a piece of paper promising that there would be no war.'

Magsy began to iron the best cloth. Christmas loomed and she still was not ready. 'Beth,' she sighed, 'there will be no atom bombs dropped on Korea. Truman is not a liar – Hitler was, I'm afraid.' Why couldn't Beth just look forward to getting her puppy? Why all this fretting? Magsy, who knew the answer to her own unspoken question, pursed her lips and carried on ironing. No matter what she said, her daughter would continue to speculate about radiation sickness and the unfairness of mankind.

Beth, who had taken to having nightmares about war, was not convinced. She had been reading about Hiroshima, about people who were still dying slowly, about newborn babies who were malformed. 'There's no cure,' she said sadly.

Ah, well. Magsy pressed Irish linen, worried about her chicken, worried about being forced to work for part of Christmas Day, worried about Beth worrying about atom bombs. Would the chicken stretch to feed Ernest Barnes? Should a good Catholic mention to a priest that she would be cleaning on the holiest of feast days? Probably not. She folded the cloth and stood the iron back on its plate in the hearth. People who worked in hospitals were exempt – as were priests, of course.

'You still miss Daddy.'

'Of course I do.' Right. Now where was this conversation going?

'Paul likes you.'

Ah, destination achieved in one move. 'Beth, I do not want to talk about Mr–'

'Paul. He said we should call him Paul.'

Magsy leaned against the table and stared at the photograph of William. He took centre stage on the mantelpiece, halfway between Beth as a baby and a framed certificate from the king.

Beth followed her mother's gaze. 'May his sacrifice help to bring the peace and freedom for which he died,' she read aloud. 'So, if the Americans drop atom bombs on Korea, my dad's sacrifice will have been for nothing.'

'Beth?'

'Yes, Mam?'

'Would you ever shut up?'

'Yes, Mam.'

Magsy grinned. 'There's a good girl. Now, put the kettle

on and we'll have a nice cup of tea. No Paul, no atom bombs, just a drop of milk, thank you.'

Ernest wiped the brooch on a bit of chamois, polishing the silver filigree until it shone like new. Neglected in a drawer for several years, the metal had blackened, had been as dark as the pearl it surrounded. This was Mam's black pearl. It had been passed down from Grandma, was old and possibly valuable.

He paused, placing the jewellery on the table. Was it right? Should he be giving this precious item to a Catholic woman? Better than leaving it for Dot, that traitorous so-called wife, or to the Higgins floozy, who had taken her and Frank away. No, this would look right bonny pinned to the breast of Magsy O'Gara. She wasn't the usual run of Catholic, was a hard worker, had confided in him about her ambition to become an auxiliary nurse at the infirmary.

'I'm going daft in me old age,' he advised his reflection in a small shaving mirror. God, he wished he were twenty years younger. But he didn't look too bad, considering. The barber had been to cut his hair, and he was getting about a bit better, was even managing the odd step without the aid of sticks.

He packed the brooch into a little box, then wrapped the box in red tissue. Closing his eyes, he called to mind her face, that perfect oval surrounded by hair so clean, so blonde, those blue eyes, lips that were naturally pink ... oh God, he was like a stupid kid. His heart, banging like the big bass drum at an Orange parade, missed a beat, settled again.

Using the wraparound fireguard for support, he heaved himself up and practised walking without sticks. Slowly, painfully, he passed the rocking chair, reached the understairs coal store, turned, went back to his seat at the table.

He was almost ready. Soon, he would venture outside, would get up to the road, would catch a trolley into town. At Moor Lane bus station, he would find the Hesford terminus ... At this point, his thoughts became confused. Why did he need to get to Hesford? To show her. Yes, that was the reason. To show them both that he no longer needed them, that wife and son were surplus to requirements.

All was well. Ernest Barnes would walk again, would hold his head high. And Magsy O'Gara was wonderful ...

Well, at least all the puppies were spoken for.

Lily stood in her back yard, listened as Nellie breathed her way to the lavatory, the large woman's steps interrupted every time she came to a pile of rubbish. Rubbish? There was enough for a tip, enough for landfill where the houses had come down during bombings. Charlie Entwistle had sent several rag carts over recent weeks, but the heaving and clattering had continued to disturb Lily's short rests. She would sit there with the Bolton paper, cigarette lit, cup balanced on the fireguard, then Nellie would kick off again, chucking all kinds of debris into her back yard.

Tinker, the puppy intended for Beth O'Gara, began to chew Lily's shoelace. She lifted him gently with her foot, the movement absent-minded. They had made a right mess between them, this lot. And Skinny, their doting mother, had lost interest now that they were weaned, leaving them to get up to all kinds of mischief. Next door, Spot barked. Well, the other three were promised and would be gone in a few days.

'Come on,' she bade the dogs. 'Inside before you start

another war.' They had a habit of answering Spot-next-door, and Lily had had enough yapping for one day.

Inside, she finished icing her Christmas cake, flattening the white coating with a palette knife. She would stick a ribbon round it later, would balance a plastic snowman and a Father Christmas on the surface. It was the same every year, same figures, same ribbon, same routine.

'What is the matter with you?' she enquired of her reflection. 'You've as much shape as a melted caramel, you dozy bugger.' It was as if the life had begun to drain out of her – and it wasn't just her body, either. Her mind was going on strike.

Skinny, ever-hopeful, hovered near the table looking for scraps. 'And you can lose yourself, too,' she advised the animal. 'Costing me a fortune – and I've to pay to have you doctored.'

Skinny crawled under the table. Sometimes, it was best to take the line of least resistance.

Lily lit a Woodbine and sat by the fire. Ever since Dot Barnes had escaped, Lily's restlessness had increased. She wanted to get out of here, wanted a fresh start, a new life, something to look forward to. But she had nothing to run away from had she? Sam never hit her, never started a row. How could she walk away? How could she blame nose-picking, sweaty feet, open-mouth eating and scabby spots? What sorts of reasons were they for a God-fearing woman to use as justification?

Lily sniffed. 'I mean, I'm not perfect, am I? Why should I be different?'

She didn't resent Dot, but she envied her. That bad bastard next door deserved to be on his own, while Dot, poor soul, deserved a better life. 'Ooh, I wish I could walk away,' she muttered. 'But I'd only be fretting over me guilt.'

The front door opened. 'Are you there, Lily?'

Lily smiled. Dot's leaving had opened many doors – not just Lily's. Sal Higgins from across the street had become a regular visitor, a welcome one. 'Come in, Sal.'

Sal strode into the room, a plate of buttered soda bread in her huge hands. 'I thought we'd just indulge ourselves, so,' she announced. 'This is still warm, so we mustn't eat too much of it. Away, now, get the kettle on.'

Lily did as she was told, her heart lighter now that the large Irishwoman had taken up temporary residence in her kitchen. Things could have been worse. A lot worse.

The house across the road still looked dead.

Rachel Higgins-as-was, now Rachel Barnes, turned to the mirror, smoothed her hair and made sure that her coat was fastened properly. Frank had bought her some new Christmas clothes – a pretty blue-grey suit in wool, a navy coat, some gloves, a bag and shoes. She was so posh. After receiving an answering smile from her reflection, Rachel went down to the shop to elicit the approval of her mother-in-law. 'My Christmas outfit,' she cried, swivelling on the spot. 'He's good to me, is your son, Dot. See how nice I am going to look at midnight Mass this year.'

Dot stopped her shelf-stacking. 'Eeh, love,' she murmured, 'you favour one of them models in a magazine. No wonder our Frank's proud of you.'

Rachel grinned. 'Good enough for Miss Katherine Moore, do you think?'

Dot sniffed. 'Aye, too good. Too good for her, from the sound of things. Aye, you are that.'

Dot would never lose the habit of repeating herself, thought Rachel. It was as if she needed to double-underline all her expressions in order to convince herself that she deserved an opinion. Ernest Barnes had done a lot of damage here. 'Should I wear a hat?' asked the younger woman.

'To walk across the road? I should flaming cocoa.'

'Flaming cocoa' was as bad as Dot's language got these days. 'I want to be proper,' said Rachel.

'Aye, well, I wouldn't stir meself over being proper for her, not from what I've heard.'

Rachel laughed. 'It's Christmas and we have to be Christians.'

'I know all about Christians.' There was an edge to Dot's tone. 'I lived with one for long enough. Aye, I did. Long enough, too long and that's for certain sure.'

Rachel nodded. 'I know, love.'

Dot picked up a bottle of Camp Coffee Essence and placed it with its brothers on a shelf. Turning to face her daughter-in-law, she asked, as casually as she could, 'Will I be able to come to that midnight Mass? I mean, I'm not a Catholic.'

'All welcome in God's house, Dot.'

'I'm not saying I'm for turning, like, but I want to have a look at what goes on. It's a mystery.' She nodded. 'Aye, it's all a mystery.'

Rachel picked up her handbag. Suddenly nervous, she patted her hair again.

Dot allowed herself a tight smile. She had lovely hair, did Rachel. Not for her the universal rule of waves to the ear lobes, then pin-curls into the nape. Rachel allowed her tresses freedom, let the dark locks cascade down to her shoulders, no clips, no slides, just a side parting in that slightly wavy sheet of silk. 'Ye're bonny love,' she proclaimed, 'too bonny for that owld woman. She'll look at you and be jealous. Then, if she says she's coming for Christmas dinner, we'll all have indigestion for the next twelve months.'

Rachel giggled. 'Aw, remember she's got nobody.'

Another sniff made its way up Dot's nose. 'Some deserve to have nobody. Your father-in-law's got nobody, so will you bring him up here for Christmas Day?'

'No.' The dark head moved emphatically. 'Because Frank wouldn't let me.'

'So think on,' answered Dot. 'You are swapping one bad so-and-so for another, that's all. Only difference is that Ernest were bad to us, while her across the road hurt other people.'

But Rachel was determined. She blew a kiss to Dot, then stepped outside into the clean frostiness of country air. It was lovely up here. She could see for miles across to the east where the Pennines began their sweep towards Yorkshire. The moors, crisped and whitened by hoar, were sectioned into many shapes, each farm marking its bounds by hedges and dry stone walls.

Yes, she was lucky. She had a fine man, a lovely ma-in-law, a business that gave her life purpose and dignity. No longer subjected to the deafening clatter of machinery, no longer living in the shadow of factory walls, Rachel was enjoying many kinds of freedom. And, as time went by, she missed her family less and less. Not that her love for them had diminished, but contentment grew within her, helping a healthy young mind to embrace with gratitude all that she had been given.

It was happiness that drove her now in the direction of the unknown, because she wanted to share her new-found joy. No, she could not help her prejudiced father-in-law, but perhaps she might melt some of the iciness with which Miss Katherine Moore had apparently surrounded herself.

As arranged, Phyllis Hart opened the back door of Knowehead. She looked at the prettily dressed visitor, then widened the gap to allow Rachel into the kitchen.

'Don't know why you're bothering – her's in a filthy mood,' announced Phyllis cheerfully. 'Her's chucking things. Mind, she's no good at chucking, what with her arthritis.'

Rachel gulped. 'Oh,' was all she managed.

'Eeh, don't worry,' said the girl, 'her won't hit out at you, like. It'll be me what gets it for letting you in.'

Rachel's eyes travelled round the room. It wore a film of neglect, as if it had not had a proper bottoming in months – even years. Everything was in its place, yet none of it sparkled. It was plain that this young madam did not stretch herself unless pressed.

'Follow me.' Phyllis led Rachel into the hall. 'Second on the right,' she advised, 'and try not to wind her up. I've already cleaned the carpet – bloody soup and boiled egg everywhere.'

With her heart in her mouth, Rachel climbed the stairs. The house smelled musty, as if it had been left empty for a decade. Wallpaper was stained and scuffed, while paint-work looked as if it needed a good scrub or a new coat all round.

She tapped on the door.

'Go away,' rasped a voice. 'I've had enough of you for one day, Phyllis Hart.'

'I am not Phyllis.' Rachel's own voice emerged high-pitched and wavery. 'I am Mrs Barnes from the shop across the road.' Without waiting for a reply, she opened the door and entered the room.

The woman was seated on a chaise longue, legs stretched out, a blanket spread over her lower body. Thin to the point of emaciation, she was not a pretty sight – iron grey hair scraped back, face lined, brownish eyes clouded by age and pain. She stared at Rachel, the eyes quickening as she cast them over the young woman's attire.

'I just . . .' Rachel's voice died, so she covered the pause with a cough.

'I don't want any diseases,' snapped the householder. 'Don't bring coughs and colds in here, please.' The girl was dressed neatly, but in clothes that screamed off-the-peg, no real style, just a set of loose covers for a youthful body. Katherine placed her in a category she termed 'poor-but-proud', then looked at the face. This was a stunner, yet the owner of these looks had no awareness of her power. Yes, she was decent and boring, probably. 'To what do I owe the pleasure?'

'It's . . . er . . . well . . . it's nearly Christmas.'

'Indeed.'

'I was wondering if you wanted anything.'

Katherine Moore tilted her head to one side. 'All I need has been purchased, thank you.'

'We have the shop across there . . .' Rachel pointed to the window, 'and we wondered—'

'If I need anything, I shall send for it.'

Rachel decided that this was a losing battle, yet she struggled on. 'No, I was meaning – would you like to come for Christmas Day dinner?'

Katherine frowned. 'And why would I do that?'

Rachel raised a shoulder. 'Just because it's Christmas, I suppose.'

'Ah.'

'The season of goodwill, Miss Moore.'

'Really?'

'Yes – love thy neighbour – all that sort of—'

'Love thy poor, spinster, crippled neighbour – is that it?'

Rachel frowned. Now she could see what Phyllis Hart meant. 'I was told that you are a bitter woman, Miss Moore.' God, had she really said that? She felt the heat rising in her cheeks, yet something prompted her to continue. 'I am here as a new neighbour, not as the representative of some charity,' she added. 'Take it as you will, Miss Moore – I shall trouble you no longer.'

'Wait!'

Rachel, who had turned to leave, responded to the sudden strength in the old woman's tone. She stopped in her tracks, then counted to ten before facing the dragon again. 'Yes?' she asked, patience etched into the syllable,

'Sit.' Katherine waved a stick at an armchair.

The young woman fixed a pair of flawless eyes on the crone in the chaise. 'Why? Why on earth should I want to spend one more second with someone as selfish and as rude as you are?'

Katherine picked up the gauntlet. 'As you wish, then.'

Rachel knew full well what was afoot here. She had dealt with teachers similar to this, nasty old women who resented youth, who laughed when girls were forced by poverty into the mill. Knowing that she had a fine brain, Rachel Higgins had left school at fifteen, had gone into one of the Derby Mills, had worked like a sweating pig for eight hours a day. But she was out of there now, was as good as anyone. Without taking her eyes from the shrivelled occupant of the chaise, Rachel Barnes seated herself.

'You are a beautiful woman.'

Rachel nodded – she had no need to deny her own looks.

'So why are you here, then?'

Again, Rachel shrugged. 'I am from a large family. We were brought up to look after one another. An upbringing like that leaves a mark, Miss Moore.'

'So it would seem. Now, why do you want a miserable creature like myself to grace your table?'

Rachel found no answer.

'You need to satisfy some urge to be charitable, is that it?'

Again, the visitor maintained silence.

'I do not leave my house. Movement causes pain, so I keep it to a minimum.'

Rachel lifted her chin. 'But you will seize up even more if you don't try to move.'

Katherine Moore sighed heavily. If only people understood the sheer agony of arthritis! On a whim, she decided to confide in Rachel, mostly because she needed to talk to someone in order to achieve her goal. 'There is something you might do for me.'

The younger woman inclined her head.

'It's that girl, you see,' continued Katherine, 'she is utterly and absolutely hopeless.' When no response was forthcoming, the rusty voice raised itself. 'I have a summer house in my garden – wooden – but sturdy and quite warm, as it is built around a central stone chimney. There is, of course, no bathroom, but the facilities here in the house can be used by the occupant. And there is an outside lavatory.'

Again, Rachel nodded.

'I need someone to live there.'

The visitor saw the sense in this. 'That sounds ideal, Miss Moore. So you are letting Phyllis go?'

'Yes – but do not tell her that.'

'Of course I won't. But what do you want me to do for you?'

Katherine plucked at the blanket with a clawlike hand. 'You may know just the right person.'

Rachel rifled through her list of acquaintances, came up with no immediate answer.

'The pay will be good,' added Katherine, 'but I do not want a young person. I would much prefer a woman who is clean but needy.'

Rachel guessed that whoever applied for this job would have to be very needful. Miss Katherine Moore was possessed of few social skills, was as tactful as a bull in a china shop. 'What about somebody with a child?'

The old woman shook her head, the small movement causing her to grimace with pain. 'Well, I suppose if one must employ a mother, as long as there is just one child – one well-behaved child – I might take that into consideration.'

Rachel rose from her seat. 'I'll ask around,' she said. 'Now, if you refuse to come for a meal, may I bring the meal to you? One more plate won't make any difference.'

Miss Katherine Moore attempted a smile. 'Very well. And I have . . . enjoyed meeting you, Mrs Barnes.'

'My name is Rachel. Good afternoon.' She left the room, closing the door quietly in her wake. Phew. What an ordeal that had been. She began to walk away.

'Rachel?'

She stopped, breathed deeply, retraced her steps, poked her head round the door. 'Did you call, Miss Moore?'

'I did.' There followed a short silence. 'I want to thank you,' said Miss Katherine Moore.

Dumbfounded, Rachel could move neither backwards nor forwards. She stared into rheumy brown eyes, saw a glimpse of moisture. Had she, Rachel Mary Higgins-as-was, made a difference? Had she rushed in, a fool in the wake of reluctant angels? 'You are most welcome,' she stammered.

'I know,' came the reply. 'And that is why I am thanking you.' The tone changed. 'Send that fool of a girl up, will you? I need a hot drink and my medicines.'

'Right, Miss Moore.'

'Katherine. And tell no-one beyond your immediate family about this meeting, if you please. I cannot afford to have my reputation as local harridan tarnished at this stage.'

Rachel inclined her head. 'Whatever you say ... Katherine. Always the dragon, eh?'

'Exactly. Always the dragon and forever breathing fire.'

Rachel closed the door. She had just touched real loneliness, complete solitude. And suddenly, she thought of Nellie Hulme – poor old Smelly Nellie in her silent, isolated world. 'Never mind, Rachel,' she told herself as she descended the stairs, 'just do your best, like Mam says. Make a difference where you can. Where you can't, just pray.' Yes, tonight she would say an extra decade for Nellie Hulme, then another for Katherine Moore.

Nellie Hulme had fallen head over heels for the daftest dog in Christendom. Spot was just feet and ears, all points between thin and bony, a coat of white fur doing little towards covering a skeleton that was frighteningly fine. The black patch over one eye lent him a look of rakishness, as if he were planning something dramatic – perhaps piracy on the high seas.

She spent ages just looking at him, watching him as he chewed bones, clothes, shoes, books and anything else that happened to grace his path through life. How had she lived without him? Why hadn't she realized that love came packaged like this, with a wagging tail and soft, liquid eyes that showed a soul filled with generosity and unconditional affection?

Still busy with her clearout, Nellie had found that the pup had his uses. Whenever Charlie Entwistle sent a cart to collect rubbish, Spot told her. He did this by running up to her and pulling at her clothing. He knew that she was deaf. Quite how he knew she could not work out, but within days of moving into number 1, the little dog became her ears. She had started to cook, too, was always making a stew or a pie to share with Spot. He liked a bit of liver and was passionately fond of carrots, so Nellie had begun to eat better and to walk further, was becoming a familiar sight on Deane Road, ball in one hand, red lead in the other, a proud Spot trotting along by her side.

It was quite a hike to Haslam Park, but Nellie achieved it at least twice a week, making do with a quick march around the streets on other days. Soon, she would get to the park every other day, thereby exercising herself and the dog simultaneously.

The main problem was clothes. Within a week of acquiring the pup, Nellie noticed that her skirts were suddenly loose around the waist, that she could bend and stretch, that her breathing was easier. Lace-making was abandoned for a while, as she needed to take in a few garments.

She noticed the smell of herself then, when she started to work on clothes that had never seen soap or water. Spot didn't seem to mind the pong, but Nellie found herself restless and needful. The slipper baths were only a few hundred yards away, but how could she possibly go there? To be fit to go to the public baths, she would need to have a bath . . .

How? She was still far too big for any standard zinc tub – how could she hope to clean an expanse as big as she was? It was a puzzle and no mistake. She knew that the dog shared her bewilderment while she put clothes to soak in a bucket of Acdo. He stuck a paw in the bubbles, looked quizzically at his mistress, then yawned and fell asleep.

She scrubbed the clothes three times, then set them to drip in the hearth. The fire burned all day while she heated water and filled the bucket at least twenty times. With painstaking slowness, she washed one leg, then the other, one arm, then the other. She lifted rolls of fat and cleaned crevices where her skin, broken down by decades of sweat, was red, rough and sore. Wrapping towels round a broom, she scrubbed her back, amazed at how exhausting this whole process became.

When her hair was dripping wet, she let out a huge sigh and dropped her corpulence into a ladder-back chair. Right. She had clean clothes, new towels, a loofah, a sponge and some lavender soap. For Christmas, she would furnish her living room, would get Charlie-at-the-end to remove all this stinking upholstery. Tonight, Nellie Hulme would walk up Derby Street to the public baths. Like any other customer, she could present herself as ready for a good soak, because now she smelt of lavender and talcum powder. It was time for Miss Helen Hulme to reclaim her membership of the human race.

Spot grinned at her. Plainly of the opinion that all this activity had been a great source of amusement, he licked his owner's fragrant hand. It was an interesting life – and there was a stew in the oven . . .

Paul Horrocks was not happy.

He had visited Magsy O'Gara, had waited on street corners for her, had bought flowers, chocolates and even a silk scarf. She wasn't interested. She wasn't interested in anyone, because she was still in love with a man who had been dead for years. How could he compete with a ghost, with the idea, the memory of a person who, according to his widow, should be canonized?

A handsome face looked back at him from the over-mantel mirror. He was not a proud man, was not self-obsessed, but he recognized his own good points. He was square-jawed, with bright blue eyes and a shock of dark, wavy hair. His height was six feet and some inches; he was broad without being fat, firm without being over-muscled. What the hell did she want? Had he been unemployed, a drinker, a breaker of the law, then he might have understood her hesitancy, her reluctance to step out with him.

Lois watched her son. He was up to something, was spending far too much time grooming himself, forever looking in mirrors, shaving, combing his hair, staring into space while eating, missing what she said, ignoring her.

Lois Horrocks was not a woman to be ignored. Used to being the centre of her only son's universe, she felt abandoned, as if he had already left her to her fate. A sufferer from several illnesses, Lois had been housebound for some years, had finally finished up under the stairs in the kitchen, head at the taller end, feet tucked underneath the lower steps. Here she ate, slept and waited, bed pushed out of the way of general traffic, parlour saved for the visitors who seldom came, the patient warm, safe and at the hub of matters. She waited for company, waited for Paul to return from work, waited for her neighbour to warm up food, to help her onto the commode, to wash and clean her poor, pain-racked body.

'All right, Mam?' Paul turned from the mirror.

'Oh, I see. Remembered I'm still here, have you?'

How could he forget? Ever since the abdication of his father, Paul had been in charge here. Dad had died deliberately – of that Paul Horrocks felt sure. After helping his already crippled wife upstairs, Tommy Horrocks, still fully clothed, had stretched out beside her on the bed, had given up his spirit, eyes wide open, a slight smile stretching lips that had expressed displeasure for some considerable time. Oh, Dad – why couldn't he have hung about until his son had managed to escape?

'Of course I remember you're still here.' How could anyone fail to notice? She was so fat that she seemed to ooze out of her nightdress, great rolls of flesh overhanging the high collar, at least four chins cascading down onto tea-rose flannelette, pork sausage fingers clawing at a woven quilt, facial features clustered together in a sea of white lard. Mam was as ugly as sin. 'I've not forgot,' he replied tersely.

'I might as well be dead for all the notice you take of me. You're forever preening, carrying on like a bloody parrot.'

He attempted no answer.

'Cat got your tongue?'

Paul raised a shoulder. 'I reckon a cat would go for the full parrot, not just its tongue.'

She shook her head, causing her bloated cheeks to quiver. 'Clever, eh?' Sarcasm trimmed her tone. 'Who is she? Who's at the back of all this film star stuff?'

'What film star stuff?'

She laughed mirthlessly. 'Carrying on in front of mirrors all the while, titty-fal-lalling about as if you're going on the flaming stage. There's got to be a woman at the back of all this.'

He stared at her. 'Mam, I'm thirty-two.'

'And I'm fifty-five. What's that got to do with the price of fish?'

'Time I was wed,' he said.

This was a moment Lois had dreaded for a long time. He was a good-looking lad, more handsome than his father had ever been, certainly better looking than anyone on Lois's side of the family. So far, she had been lucky, as Paul had never stuck to one woman, had enjoyed a series of short liaisons with females who had not impressed him sufficiently for marriage. But this was a different kettle of kippers altogether. The lad was smartening up, was clearly out to leave a mark. 'Who is she?' repeated Lois.

'Nobody.'

She sniffed. 'Well, that's a lot of bother for a nobody. I've never known anybody go to so much bother for nobody. She must be something special, this nobody of yours.'

Paul sank into a chair. 'It's all right, she's not interested in me,' he said quietly. 'I'm not good enough for her.'

Immediately, Lois's hackles rose. 'Not good enough?'

He shook his head.

'Why not? What's wrong with you?'

'Nowt.'

'Nowt? It must be summat if she won't take you on. Who is she?' The idea of someone having the audacity to reject her son was not a comfortable one. She needed to hang on to him, was terrified of losing him, yet she could not bear to think of him being judged sub-standard. 'Who is she?' she asked again.

Paul's shoulders drooped. He ran a hand through tousled curls, shook his head slowly. What did it matter anyway? 'Magsy O'Gara,' he answered eventually. 'She lives in Prudence Street, has a daughter called Beth.'

Lois rooted around in her mind. 'But she's a Catholic. I remember Bertha next door telling me about her. Didn't her husband get killed in the war? And she has a daughter, one who's supposed to be clever.'

'Aye, that's her.'

Lois pondered. 'She's a Catholic,' she repeated eventually.

'Makes no difference to me,' replied Paul.

'Well, it should. You don't want to be getting yourself tied up with a Holy Mary. Remember I used to be one till I met your dad and turned Methodist. They're all rosary beads and Latin, no sense to them at all.'

Paul raised a shoulder.

'It's her what's not good enough for you,' pronounced Lois. 'Catholics are no good to nobody.'

He lit a Woodbine.

'You know that bothers me chest.' To demonstrate her displeasure, she coughed and placed a hand at her throat.

Paul took another drag, then docked the cigarette, placing the remainder of it behind his ear.

'She works at the infirmary,' stated Lois. 'Cleaning up.'

'I know. But they're going to let her do orderly work, like an assistant nurse.'

'Very nice, I'm sure,' replied Lois. 'So she'll go from dirty floors to dirty backsides – I wouldn't call that promotion.'

He stood up and walked out of the room. No matter what, he was stuck with his mother. Even if Magsy O'Gara had decided to care for him, he would have been unable to commit himself. Who would want to live with this? Which woman in her right mind would volunteer to dedicate a lifetime to the care of Lois Horrocks?

'And I can't leave her,' he advised the back gate. 'I am bloody trapped as fast as a rabbit in a gin, tied down and bled dry.' He resented his situation, was suddenly angrier than ever. There had been one or two girls who had interested him, but no-one like this, no Magsy O'Gara. She tormented him in dreams and in reality, was the first and last item on his life's agenda, was fast becoming his goal. 'I love her,' he breathed quietly, 'and God knows I wish I didn't.'

It was the way she held herself, the way she walked, spoke, smiled, laughed. It wasn't just a craving, a sexual need that wanted assuaging. No. It was her, the full package, ups, downs, in sickness, in health, until death . . . He could not bear the thought of her dying. As for Mam – Mam would probably outlive everyone, would creak on and on like an oil-starved gate.

He wasn't wishing his mam dead – of course he wasn't. It just seemed unfair that he should be crippled by his mother's rheumatism, by her inflamed veins, by her thick, sluggish blood. Yes, she was not the only one held down. All his mates were settled and married, many with children and homes of their own. And here stood Paul Horrocks, shirtsleeves rolled under a starlit December sky, his core frozen by ice, by Mam, by the indifference of Magsy O'Gara.

It wasn't fair. He hadn't asked to fall for an Irish Catholic with a child in tow, didn't need this kind of bother in his life. There were three or four women who wanted him, but he couldn't have cared less. He had to make life fair. On Christmas Eve, Magsy would doubtless be busy with the child, the one person in whom she had invested all her faith, hope and love.

What had he to lose? Nothing – less than nothing, really. It was time to tackle Magsy yet again.

Eight

Paul Horrocks nipped his Woodbine, then stuck the remaining inch behind his right ear. No, that would not do. Remembering his destination, he took the cigarette end and pushed it into his pocket. Magsy did not like smoking.

It was Christmas Eve. The black, star-sprinkled sky promised a cold night with no blanket of cloud to protect a naked earth. He shivered, wished that he had dared to wear his old army greatcoat, regretted that vanity had got the better of him. She had to listen to him, had to give in. There was nothing wrong with him, nothing to which she might reasonably object. Except, of course, for the fact that he was not William O'Gara.

Just before reaching number 2 Prudence Street, he panicked and hurriedly relit his Woodbine. He was in love and scared to death. Was love meant to be like this? Was he supposed to be afraid, to act like a teenager, to want to run away from and towards her all at the same time? Whatever, he was almost broken in two – one half of his mind urging him on, the other side telling him to run for the hills, over the hills and into Yorkshire if necessary.

Then there was Mam; oh yes, there was always Mam.

The cigarette died on the ground, crushed beneath his foot. Determined not to be a coward, he advanced on her door and rattled the knocker. But his sails deflated when she opened it almost before he had finished announcing his presence.

'Yes?'

God, she was the most beautiful thing on the planet. He pulled at a collar that was suddenly tight. 'Er . . .' he achieved finally.

Magsy folded her arms. She had much to do before midnight Mass and this fellow was becoming a plague. 'What?' she asked.

Paul dug deep in his pockets. 'I . . . er . . . I bought these at that Catholic repository shop,' he managed. 'I'm not a Catholic myself . . .'

'I know that.'

'But . . . well . . . they were nice and I thought you might take them up to church tonight.' He paused for breath. 'They're rosary beads – pearl ones – a set for you and one for Beth.'

'They have to be blessed first,' she heard herself saying. Oh, why could she not be civil? 'It's . . . it's just a Catholic thing.'

'Oh.'

'I shall get them blessed as soon as possible. And thank you so much for thinking of us, Mr Horrocks, but–'

'Paul.'

'Mr Horrocks,' she continued, a determined smile painted on her face. 'You should not be spending your hard-earned money on me and my daughter. I know you have a sick mother to care for and a house to keep, so–'

'I like you,' he blurted.

Magsy took a step back into her tiny hallway. 'Please don't,' she said quietly.

He turned his face away, offering her just his profile as he continued. 'I didn't ask to feel like this about you. I don't even want to feel like this. I'd rather have a bad cold or a dose of flu, to be honest. This is one bloody illness I could do without, thanks very much.'

Magsy bowed her head. She knew what this confession had cost, as few men in these parts opened up their hearts so freely. 'I am very sorry,' she told him. 'But I do not have the same feelings for you, Mr Horrocks.'

He swung to face her once more. 'Can you not give me a chance? Can you not just walk out with me a few times, see how we get on?'

'No.'

'Why?' His voice raised itself. 'Am I not good enough? Am I ugly, too poor, or is it just because I'm not a Catholic?'

Magsy shook her head. 'None of those reasons applies,' she answered. 'I simply do not intend to become involved with anyone, so this is not meant to be personal.'

Visibly uncomfortable now, Paul Horrocks stepped away from her. 'I have tried to get over this,' he told her. 'God knows how I have tried. But it's ... it's got the better of me. And I know I shouldn't be telling you this ... it gives you a sort of power over me ... but you're the first and last thing on my mind every day.' He swallowed. 'And I don't know what the hell I am supposed to do about it.'

She could feel his suffering, could see it in the slope of his shoulders, in hands that would not lie still. 'I did not wish this illness on you ... Paul. I haven't encouraged you – not consciously, at least. But I am a one-man woman, you see.'

He bit his lower lip so hard that he tasted blood. 'He's dead. I am sorry about that, but it's the truth. And believe me, if I could stop caring about you, I would.' Desperate now, he glanced skyward, as if seeking divine intervention. 'I have never, ever loved a woman before, Magsy.'

She did not know where to look, what to say, how to

extricate herself from this uncomfortable scenario. Beth was out, was across at the Hardcastles'. As from tonight, the puppy known as Tinker would be claiming a place inside number 2 Prudence Street. 'You had better come inside.' She turned sideways to allow him into the house, her head filling immediately with fear. Whatever was she thinking of? No, no, he would not attack her, surely?

In the living room, she sat at the table and waited for him to place himself opposite. 'Look,' she began, 'I don't know why you have fixed on me, Paul. There are many lovely girls in Bolton, so surely you should be looking further afield?'

He stared at her. Gaslight flickered on her hair, making her almost ethereal, angelic. Her hands, delicate and long-fingered, were folded on the white linen tablecloth. She had poise, self-possession, intelligence. A perfect nose led his attention down to full lips, but he could not look at her eyes. They were blue, bright blue, with flawless whites and long lashes. No, he was unable to meet her gaze.

'Would you answer me?' she asked.

'You know the answer,' he replied rather tersely. 'This is not something we choose, is it? What do you want me to do? Line 'em all up along Churchgate like they did at the old cattle market? Prod 'em with a stick till I find the best beef cow?'

A smile flickered on her lips, but she managed to contain it.

Paul saw the temptation, squashed his own urge to grin. If he could make her laugh, he was halfway there. 'All I want is a chance,' he said.

'I'll think about it,' she said after a long pause. Perhaps, if he got to know her, he would love her less. 'Now, I must ask you to leave, as Beth will be home very soon and she ... she interferes.'

He stood up. So, Beth was an interfering sort, was she? And from the way her mother had spoken, Paul guessed that Beth was likely to be on his side. That was another possibility, then. Yes, he would work on the child and on Magsy's humour.

'I hope you have a lovely Christmas,' Magsy said.

Lovely? With Mam parked in the corner, a small chicken between two, no chance of a decent night out, Christmas Family Favourites and the Billy Cotton Band Show on the Light Programme? And, at the end of it all, a cold bed and a lonely heart. 'Thanks,' he managed, 'and the same to you and Beth.'

When he had left, Magsy let out a great sigh of relief before placing herself in front of the overmantel mirror. She touched her hair, smiled, tilted her head this way and that. Whatever was the matter with her? Why should she care how she looked? He wasn't even a Catholic and he most certainly was not William.

William. He was not coming back, was he? There was no more William and there could never be another like him. So, what was a person supposed to do? Settle for less, make do with whatever was available? A second adult with an income would make life easier in one sense, but did she want more children?

Tut-tutting at herself, she turned from her reflection and picked up the small parcel left behind by Paul Hor-rocks. Rosary beads. In buying those, in choosing rosaries, he had paid his respects to her religion. He was a good man, a kind man, and ... And she had to go across to number 3. Ernest Barnes would be waiting for her, hair combed flat, stick leaning on the fireguard, lust in his eyes. 'This is Christmas Eve,' she reminded herself, 'so go and do the decent thing, Magsy O'Gara.'

She picked up a bag filled with small delicacies and made her way to the door.

In the street, Paul Horrocks stood under a lamp post. He was talking to another man, was whiling away the minutes before going to face his crippled mother. Yes, he was yet another human who lived with human miseries. Sighing, Magsy went to do her Christian duty. Sometimes, being a Catholic was not easy.

His heart missed a beat when the door opened. She was here. Every fibre of Ernest Barnes's being was suddenly alert, and he hated himself. How many times had he berated his sons for talking to Holy Romans? He was an Orange Lodger, a man whose hatred for Catholicism was a legend in his own lifetime. And yet ... and yet here he was, doddery, old, a couple of hundred in the bank, head over heels with a pretty face.

She came in and placed a bag on his table. 'Just a few mince pies and a very tiny Christmas cake, Mr Barnes. Oh, and I sliced you a bit of my ham for a sandwich.'

He fixed her with his eyes, wished her gone, wished her in his arms.

Magsy, pretending not to notice, chattered on about the puppy, about tomorrow's dinner, about the weather. The effect she had on men was annoying, to say the least of it. Here she stood, just minutes away from the previous encounter, another male gazing intently at her face, her body ... She did not wish herself ugly, yet she did not like this, either.

He cleared his throat. 'I want to thank you for all you've done for me. There's a parcel yonder – behind you – on the dresser. Open it.'

With hands that suddenly trembled, Magsy opened the package. Inside, she found the brooch and a book for Beth. The book was too childish for her daughter, but

Magsy thanked him. 'I cannot accept the brooch,' she stammered uneasily.

'It was my mother's and I want you to have it. Dot never liked it any road. Come to think, she never liked my mam, either.'

Magsy placed the brooch on the table. 'No,' she said softly. 'I don't want any thanks and I don't need presents, Mr Barnes. Without wishing to appear ungrateful, I must decline to accept.'

She was bright, especially for a Catholic. Her English, softened by the brogue, was perfect. Ernest concluded that Magsy was not just a pretty face and a wonderful body – she was also extremely well read. 'I want you to have it.'

'And I refuse to take it,' she insisted.

The challenge was there. This was a strong-minded woman, one who would stand by her principles no matter what the temptation. Her beauty was startling, and she was aware of it. They were all like this, the pretty ones, in charge, wielding a power that left men shaking in their shoes.

'I shall leave the brooch here, Mr Barnes.'

Fuelled by temper, Ernest rose to his feet. After many hours of practice, he could now manage a few steps unsupported. When he reached the other side of the table, he stopped just inches away from his visitor. 'I could give you a good life,' he said.

Magsy shivered and leaned back against the dresser. Shocked to the core, she saw his hands reaching out to touch her.

'I'll look after you,' he continued, 'and the kiddy – I'll look after her and all.' Gently, he touched her waist, a thumb straying upward in search of softer flesh.

She was unable to speak. His eyes, narrowed by desire,

contained a coldness that she had never seen before, not at such close quarters, at least. His reputation was dreadful, though his bigoted anti-Catholic activities had lessened now that age precluded him from indulging his hobby.

'I just want to look after you,' he continued.

Magsy swallowed a lump of fear, then opened her mouth and screamed.

Startled, Ernest stumbled backwards against the table. He righted himself clumsily, then hit her hard across the face. 'Stop this hysterical carry-on,' he ordered.

She stopped. Her cheek stung from the blow, but she was no longer afraid, because she could hear signs proclaiming that help was at hand. After a perfunctory knock, the front door flew open and Paul Horrocks marched into the house. His long legs covered the area between front door and kitchen in three or four strides. 'What the hell are you doing?' he yelled before dragging Ernest away from Magsy. He threw the man into a fireside chair, then stood over him. 'If you ever, ever touch her again,' he jerked a thumb in Magsy's direction, 'I swear to God I'll separate you from your breath, you bad bugger.'

Magsy, her legs suddenly deprived of substance, sank into a straight-backed chair. She shook so violently that she bit her tongue and began to weep noiselessly into her hands.

Paul continued to glare at Ernest. 'She's too good for keeping company with you. Get your own flaming dinners.'

Magsy did not know what to do. She could not go home like this, because Beth would be there any moment with Tinker, her puppy. Also, Magsy's legs were continuing to refuse to co-operate with her brain; she could not stand up, yet she could not continue to sit here in this room, in this house, with this dreadful old man. Deliberately, in an effort to stem the urge to vomit, she dropped her hands, opened her mouth and inhaled deeply. She must stop crying and must not be sick.

Paul continued to stand over Ernest Barnes. 'We all know how you treated your wife.'

'Shut your gob,' yelled the seated man. 'It's nowt to do with you.'

Paul shook his head as if in despair. 'Nowt to do with me? Nowt to do with me that you plagued Catholics round here, that you spoiled walking days, that you threw stones at church windows?' He leaned forward until his face almost touched the old man's. 'Listen, you. Any more trouble and I'll put you in the morgue, never mind the infirmary. I'm glad your Frank got out of here.'

'Frank?' spat Ernest Barnes. 'Frank?' He laughed, though there was no merriment in the sound. 'He's nowt a pound, our Frank, not worth a bloody second thought.'

'He's worth ten of you,' answered Paul.

'Is he now?'

'Aye, he is – and so's your wife. I hear they've got a lovely shop up Hesford way, a good living and a nice place for Dot's grandchildren to grow up in. As for you, you're a bitter, twisted old wreck – and I don't mean just your body. You'll never see your grandkiddies, because Frank'll have enough sense to keep them away from you.'

Maggie let out a shuddering breath. 'Leave him, Paul,' she advised quietly. 'Don't get yourself into trouble because of that desperate creature.'

Paul straightened. 'Did he ... did he touch you?'

She shook her head.

'Why would I touch a bloody Mick?' roared Ernest.

'Because you think you can,' came the reply. 'Because you think women are there for your amusement and your comfort. Am I right? Aren't they there to wash and iron and cook and for your other bodily needs? Well, let me put you straight, because I'm one who has to do all that for himself and for a sick mother. I could have found a slave, I suppose, but no, I—'

'You work for a Mick,' spat Ernest.

'Yes. Yes, I do. I work for Pat Murphy, and a fairer man I've yet to meet, so smoke that in your pipe.'

Ernest stared into the startling blue eyes of this cocksure young man. Aye, he thought he knew everything, did Paul bloody Horrocks. 'I'd sooner starve than work for an Irishman,' he said now.

'Then you're an even bigger fool than I thought,' answered Paul, 'because a sensible soul would choose work over starvation any day of the week.' He turned to Magsy. 'Come on, let's be having you out of here. This isn't a healthy place for a young woman, so you'd best stop away in future.'

She dragged herself up, using the table for support until Paul came and led her out of the house.

Ernest Barnes leaned back in his chair, eyes closed tightly against the memory of his own stupidity. Why had he done that? Why had he tried to make a play for a woman young enough to be his daughter, an Irish immigrant, too? He had been mad, deranged, ready for the funny farm.

But Magsy O'Gara's face was still there, imprinted on the inner surface of his eyelids, burnt into the flesh like an indelible tattoo. He hated her, missed her, needed her. Tomorrow, she would not come. His heart was a lead weight in his chest, hopeless, no bubble of joy rising unbidden in expectation of tomorrow. He did not want tomorrow. And whose fault was this? Whose?

Bloody Dot, that was who. Bloody Dot with her martyred air and those sly looks she thought he had never noticed. But he had noticed, oh yes. They had been corner-of-the-eye jobs, small flickers under those age-shrivelled lids, quick darts expressing pure poison. She had hated him, had hated his mother, had brought all this on by tormenting him. Wife? She had never been a bloody wife, would never have made a wife in a thousand years.

He fumbled down the side of his chair, retrieved pen and paper, scribbled a note. Then, in accordance with a pre-arrangement with Lily Hardcastle, he tapped the poker against the wall three times. Three times meant Roy. Young Roy would take this note to Charlie-at-the-end. Charlie Entwistle had offered several times to take Ernest out, so a ride up to Hesford was a distinct possibility. Aye, it was time to get a few things straight.

Nellie Hulme's parlour sparkled. In fact, it was so clean that it looked surprised, firelight dancing excitedly on newly polished surfaces, the mirror winking, gaslight glowing warmly from wall-mounted mantles. There was a new three-piece suite in green, a carpet square, a dark red rug in front of the hearth. And then there was the picture.

It was a photograph in sepia, one she had overlooked. How grateful she had been to Charlie Entwistle when he had returned it to her after finding it while removing one of her many mounds of rubbish. It had been secreted between the leaves of an old magazine, and Charlie had brought it back to her.

She stirred the embers with a shiny new brass poker, smiled at Spot who lay curled in a padded wicker basket, then she closed her eyes and slept, the photograph resting on her belly, hands folded over the pleasant scene.

They were there in the dream, the two people in the photo. A tall man and a shorter, pretty woman, a garden behind them, birds flying, birds ... singing. But, after a nap lasting just seconds, Nellie opened her eyes and sat bolt upright. There was another factor, a black edge to the dream, a feeling that she was moving away from trees and grass towards . . . whatever, it was menacing.

She had to concentrate on something else, something ordinary, had to kill the panic in her chest. Yes, the walls needed decorating. She intended to get the whole house papered and painted in the spring, but she had to be content for now with stained walls and a cracked ceiling. So much had been achieved, including new clothes and a brand new self, a person who washed each day and went to the slipper baths every Thursday, a towel rolled in a basket containing sweet-smelling soap and a tin of Johnson's Baby Powder.

What was the threat in that dream? What dire event would shatter the pleasant interlude in a lovely garden? Whatever it was, it crept a little closer every time she slept. And, if she could 'hear' while asleep, why was she unable to catch sound in her conscious mind? Was it sound? The thing that happened while she dozed, that extra dimension, was that noise, was it really birdsong?

She studied the photograph for what seemed like the hundredth time. Such a pretty young woman, such a handsome man. Yes, she had 'heard' them too, him laughing, her singing. Singing. How could a deaf person know how song sounded? Yet she did know, but only when she was asleep.

How many times had she woken with a start, only to find that she could recreate none of the qualities of sound? Yet in spite of having no recall, no ability to reshape in her head what she had found in sleep, she owned this certainty that she had experienced sound. Perhaps she was going mad. Perhaps a lifetime of silence was finally driving her to the edge of sanity.

She laughed at Spot. He had risen from his cot, had

found his over-long and stringy tail, was chasing it round in an eternal circle. Yes, that was it. Like Spot, she was turning, turning, following a dream that came and went. It was probably a figment of her imagination. Yet no, here sat the evidence, two people printed on thick paper, the pair who haunted her every night.

The dog stopped his whirling, stood still as stone, then ran excitedly towards his mistress, the barking reaching her only by means of what she could see – that opening and closing mouth, the tension in his ribcage as he attracted her attention. Nellie knew that this little chap understood her deafness, because he had trained himself in just a few days to warn her of the comings and goings of mankind. As ever, he leapt up and touched her knee, waiting for the titbit that was always his reward.

Nellie walked to the window, saw a distraught Magsy O'Gara weeping on the shoulder of a fine-looking young man. What had upset this usually calm woman? Ah well, perhaps she would remarry. He looked a fine enough chap, well-defined features, a smart jacket that looked rather thin for December. Yes, it was time for Mrs O'Gara to start again.

It was none of Nellie Hulme's business, so she closed her new curtains and went to put the kettle on. A bit of toast and marmalade would go down a treat, then it would be time for Spot's walk.

Lily had put Beth O'Gara in the front room. Confused almost to the point of madness, Lily was running around like a screw-necked chicken, flapping, panicking, unable to settle. They were all ill. Roy had gone down first, then Sam, then Aaron, then Danny. And Ernest Barnes was knocking on the wall, was sending the signal for Roy, and

Beth was waiting for the one remaining pup, and there had been a scream from next door, then, to top it all, the beef tea was bubbling too fast.

Lily deposited Tinker in Beth's lap. 'Now,' she said, her mind racing, 'go next door and see what that bad owld bu– what Mr Barnes wants. And don't come back, love, because there's summat nasty in this house, like germs or a fever, so get gone. Tell Mr Barnes as our Roy is took badly, so he won't be coming in to see him. Then get yourself home, shut that door and stay in. Do you understand me, love?'

Beth nodded. There was an hysterical edge to Mrs Hardcastle's tone, a rise in pitch that spoke volumes about the woman's state of mind. 'Is there nothing I can do?' asked the child.

'You can get gone and be safe. Oh, don't go to church and tell your mam not to go and all. I know it's Christmas, but I think this is that there influenza or some such fancy illness. All right? Go next door, see what he wants, then get home.'

Beth dragged the little dog on his new red lead. Tinker did not like the lead, so he progressed down the hall on his rear, eyes wide with surprise when he was picked up and dumped on the pavement.

'Right,' said Beth, 'let's get this straight before we start. You are the dog and I am the boss. The boss is the one at this end of the lead, and the dog is the one at the other end. I walk, you walk. You can do as you are told, or you can go through life with a sore bum. Do you understand?'

Tinker scratched his ear and yawned.

Beth watched her mother as she disappeared into number 2, Paul Horrocks behind her. Now, that was a good thing. Another good thing was that Beth was standing in for Roy, who was ill, so Mam and Mr Horrocks would have a few minutes together.

The dog adopted the line of least resistance and followed his new mistress into number 5.

Ernest Barnes looked up and glared at Magsy O'Gara's daughter, the supposed genius child of a soldier and an Irish immigrant. 'What's that bloody thing doing in here?' He waved his stick at the dog.

'He's mine,' came the succinct reply.

'I never asked whose it was, I just want to know what it's doing in my house.'

Beth sighed. 'He is with me,' she said.

'Where's Roy? I knocked for Roy.'

'Ill in bed,' answered Beth.

'Well, what about the others?' He didn't want this child in here, couldn't bear to think what she might say if she found out he had upset her mother.

'They're all ill except Mrs Hardcastle,' explained the child.

Ernest handed her the note. 'Push this through Charlie Entwistle's letter box,' he demanded, 'and don't bring that dog in here again.'

Beth took the note, taking care not to come into contact with Ernest's hand. She didn't like him, didn't want her flesh to touch his. She glared at him levelly. 'Did my mother scream before?' she asked.

He raised a shoulder. 'I never heard no scream.'

'Well, Mrs Hardcastle thought she did,' replied the child, 'and so did Skinny, because she started barking.'

'Likely some kiddies laking,' said Ernest.

Beth, who understood the old Lancashire term for play, placed the note in her pocket. 'It didn't sound like laking to me, Mr Barnes.'

She was the same as her flaming mother, he concluded. So bloody sure of herself, so confident. 'Get gone,' he blurted, 'and shove that note through Charlie's door.'

Beth picked up her puppy and left the house. It would

be a long, long time before she set foot in number 5 again. She went next door to the end house and posted Ernest Barnes's message through the letter box. Mr Entwistle's house was in darkness, as usual. Even on Christmas Eve, the man would be down at his yard, separating wool from cotton, iron from lead, would be counting his money, retrieving anything of value. His house was reputed to be filled with antiquities thrown out in error by the people of Bolton.

She glanced up the street towards her own house, wondered whether Mam would start to be nice to Mr Horrocks. The giddiness hit her then, a sudden wave through her head, a feeling that seemed to match the movement of the tide coming in at Blackpool beach. It passed in a second, so she decided to walk her dog round the block. He had to be trained, and she might as well start now.

It took two ambulances to shift Lily's family. Sam and Roy went in the first, Aaron and Danny in the second. The clanging of bells disturbed the whole street – even Ernest Barnes stood at his door and watched while the Hardcastles got carted off.

Advised to stay away from the hospital, Lily re-entered her house and sat in silence while the shock melted from her bones. They were going into an isolation unit. Nobody knew what the disease was, but the ambulance men had worn masks while carrying Lily's menfolk out of their home. The doctor might have said something about trying penicillin, but Lily wasn't sure.

So this was what happened to women who wanted their freedom. She had wished this upon them, had made it come about by her resentment. Such dreadful symptoms, too, vomiting, coughing, fever, delirium. And now she had what she wanted. No Sam to pick his nose, no Aaron to stink the house out with his feet, no Danny to churn his open-mouthed way through Christmas dinner.

Then there was Roy, poor little Roy who had gone down first with this filthy illness. He was right out of it now, was burning up and talking a load of nonsense, eyes glazed and fixed, lips cracked, wet hair plastered to his head like a dark red cap.

'Why didn't I get it?' she asked the chair opposite, the seat in which her husband usually rested after a day down the pit. And it had come on so quickly, too, man and boy toppling one after the other, pains in limbs, sweat-beaded brows, then the delirium. Was it typhoid? There had been talk of that, something to do with imported corned beef. But they hadn't eaten any corned beef just lately. And what about the others, those who worked with Sam and Danny, kiddies who were in Aaron's class, in Roy's class? Was this going to turn into an epidemic?

The door opened. 'Lily?'

It was Magsy O'Gara. 'Stop where you are,' yelled Lily. 'They've got summat and it could be typhoid.'

There followed a short silence. 'Are you all right?' was Magsy's question.

'Aye, I am the only one what is all right,' replied Lily.

'Only my Beth's gone missing.'

Immediately, Lily's spine was rigid. 'She came for the dog, love. Then she went next door to do a message. Eeh, that was over an hour ago, Mags, because I went for the doctor, then I waited for the ambulance men, and . . .' Oh, God. Roy and Beth had spent a lot of time together lately, training pups to walk on leads, encouraging the dogs to go outside to perform their toilet. 'Aye, it's well over an hour,' she concluded, her heart banging in her chest.

'Paul Horrocks is looking for her,' shouted Magsy.

Lily jumped up and pulled on her coat. 'Get home,' she said, 'wait there in case she comes back. I'll go out and search for her.' It was too late to worry about spreading germs. In her heart of hearts, Lily already knew that little Beth had the same illness as Roy, that the child was in trouble.

Then she heard the noise. It was an unearthly sound, something between a roar and a screech. Without hesitation, Lily ran out of her house, down the yard and into the back alley. There she found Nellie Hulme, two little dogs at her feet, the unconscious Beth in her arms. Nellie was crying, screaming, howling. In all the years she had spent in Prudence Street, Lily had heard no sound from Nellie. 'Wait,' she ordered, her mouth wide so that Nellie would get the drift.

Yes, it was far too late to worry about germs and quarantine. Lily dashed back through her house and dragged Magsy inside. 'Back street,' she said breathlessly. 'Nellie's got her. Go on, hurry up.'

Lily forced herself to sit down while Nellie and Magsy carried the child into her kitchen. The two little dogs greeted their mother with a joy that seemed inappropriate on this occasion. When Beth was stretched out on the horsehair sofa, Nellie sat down at the table, tears streaming down her face. She had carried Beth for two blocks, had found the child in a frozen heap, the already loyal Tinker lying on top of her, as if offering his warmth to the sick girl.

Lily sighed, weariness and misery etched into the sound. 'Get the ambulance,' she advised Magsy. 'Go up to Dr Clarke's – he'll sort it out for you.' She watched the Irishwoman, who seemed frozen to the spot. 'Magsy,' she yelled, 'get gone, because there's talk of typhoid.'

Galvanized by this statement, Magsy fled from the house, Lily's front door slamming in her wake.

Lily studied the cleaned-up Nellie, watched the face of a woman who seemed truly grief-stricken. 'You'd better go,' she mouthed. 'All my lot's in hospital.'

Nellie nodded, stood up and took hold of Spot's lead. 'Write a note if you want anything,' she mouthed. She pointed to Spot. 'Get me if you need me. He tells me. He'll tell me if you come.'

Lily kept a close eye on Beth after Nellie had left. The child's breathing was rapid and shallow, while twin spots of colour on her cheeks advertised fever raging beneath the skin. Was this going to be like the plague all over again? Lily had read about that, had learned that the fire of London had been the killer of that particular epidemic. Oh, God, she felt guilty. 'I'm selfish,' she told Skinny and Tinker. 'I prayed for change and it looks like I'm going to get it.'

Absently, she fed the bitch and the pup a few scraps from the beef tea meat. She covered Beth with a shawl, gave both dogs a dish of watered-down milk, brewed tea for herself.

The third ambulance arrived just as the doctor and Magsy walked into number 3. Lily sat by the fire, the two dogs held in close so that they would not interfere in the work of the masked men. Like Lily, Magsy was told to stay away from the hospital and to report any symptoms of her own which might develop.

Paul Horrocks arrived, his square jaw dropping as he entered the house unannounced. 'How long has she been like that?' he asked Magsy, a hand pointing towards the stretcher on which Beth lay. 'She was all right, wasn't she?'

Magsy shook her head. 'She seemed all right, but it's plain that she wasn't.' Her whole life lay on that stretcher. Without Beth, Magsy would have no reason at all to continue alive. When Beth had been removed from the house, when the bell announced the ambulance's departure, Magsy walked to the door.

'Shall I come with you?' asked Paul.

Magsy shook her head. 'No. Thank you, but I want to be alone just now.'

When Magsy had gone, Paul placed himself on a kitchen chair. 'Can I get you anything?' he asked.

'No,' replied Lily.

'We've some brandy at home.'

'No,' she said again.

He inclined his head. 'What the hell's going on? Beth only came for her dog.'

'Nellie must have found her unconscious,' said Lily. 'Walking her puppy, I should think.' She raised her head and looked him full in the face. 'They're talking about typhoid.'

'Good God.'

'Aye.' She turned her face to the fire. 'Ever since Dot Barnes got away – no – before that – I've been fed up. I even took to talking to meself in yon mirror.' She lifted a limp hand and pointed to the overmantel glass. 'I wanted to get out of here, Paul. I wanted it so bad … and bad's the word. All I could see in front of me were years of drudgery here and up at the pub. I kept imagining living out yonder where Dot's gone with her Frank and young Rachel. It's as if I were jealous of her.'

'But you're not like that, Mrs Hardcastle. Stop blaming yourself. You've enough trouble without hitting yourself with a big stick.'

'It should have been me,' she said. 'If anybody deserves typhoid fever, it's not my kids and it's not my husband – it's me.'

'Rubbish,' he answered.

'And you shouldn't be here, neither. It's catching, you know. You touch summat they've touched, and you could be dead in days. So get off with you, Paul, and give my regards to your mam.'

He had no intention of going home. No way would he leave Magsy O'Gara by herself on Christmas Eve, the beloved daughter in hospital, not even the pup for company. 'Will you hang on to Tinker?' he asked.

'Course I will. Go on, love.'

He went. He would call tomorrow, just to make sure that Lily was all right. But for now, Magsy needed him.

It was plain that Magsy wanted no-one. When his knocking brought no response, he let himself into number 2 and searched the house from top to bottom. She was not there.

He sat by a dying fire, his mind rushing about like a mad hound. He knew where she was, oh yes, he knew, all right. Without her darling Beth, Magsy would shrivel and die like an autumn leaf. She had gone to the infirmary, of that he felt sure.

Right. He stood up and drew a hand through unruly hair. It was time to call in a favour, time to appeal to the good nature of Pat Murphy. First, he must see Mam, explain what had happened, then he needed to get a van or a wagon from Pat. He would force Magsy to come home ...

An unbidden smile visited his face. Trying to imagine Magsy being forced into anything was not easy. She was a woman of guts and determination and that was why he loved her. However, he could only try ...

Nine

When Paul Horrocks reached the infirmary, midnight had arrived. He drove Pat Murphy's van up the side of the hospital, noticing as he passed the front entrance that a fracas had developed. He saw a couple of policemen, at least two nurses, then a blonde head that was definitely familiar. The mother tiger had arrived, it seemed, and was unwilling to depart before determining the condition of its cub.

He parked the vehicle, took a deep breath, dashed to the infirmary's entrance. Magsy was muttering and sobbing like a woman unhinged. Her hands were twin balled fists, while tears flooded down her face.

'You can't stop here,' a constable was saying.

Magsy seized his arm. 'That is my child. They have to allow me to be with her . . .'

The second policeman tutted loudly. 'Isolation means isolation, Mrs O'Gara. Even on the ordinary wards, you can only come in at visiting times. You can't go upsetting sick folk and them what's supposed to look after them.'

Paul pushed his way into the small group and took hold of Magsy's shoulders. 'Come with me, love,' he bade softly. He could feel the hysteria shuddering through her body. 'Carry on like this and you'll be ill yourself.'

'Tell them,' she implored, 'tell them I can't live without

her and that she can't live without me. She can't die, because she's going to be a doctor.'

He made secure eye contact with her. 'Magsy, love, if they let you into isolation, you'll come out with all sorts on your clothes. Can't you see that? These lads and lasses are only doing what's right. Now, do you really want to spend the night in a prison cell? Do you? Because that's where you'll finish up if you don't give folk a bit of peace.'

Magsy held his stare. 'But where will I go?'

'Come with me,' ordered Paul. 'Now. This minute, before I ask a doctor to knock you out with something or other. This is no way to behave.'

She continued to gaze levelly into his eyes. Something about this man reached out to calm her. He was dependable, trustworthy. Putting herself into his care would do no harm at all. 'I don't want to go home,' she said eventually. 'I know I can't see her, but I have to be near her.'

'We're not going home,' he told her. 'We're camping out.'

'In this weather?'

'That's right.' He spoke now to the policemen. 'You'll have to forgive her, I'm sorry. Beth's all she has in the world. She lost her husband in the war – this is the last straw for her.'

One of the two nurses wiped a tear from her eye. 'We do understand,' she said softly, 'because I'd be just the same if it were my daughter. But we have to have rules, you see, otherwise we couldn't do our jobs. Magsy knows the rules, because she works with us.'

Paul led the weeping Magsy round the corner to the back of the van. He opened the doors. 'Right – there's your bed, so lie down.'

She crawled in, placed herself on an old eiderdown, allowed him to heap blankets on her. When he stretched out beside her, she felt not the slightest fear. With a sureness that cut through all the grief and confusion, Magsy knew that this man would never, ever hurt her. He understood, realized that she had to stay here. Sitting or lying in a van in the grounds of a hospital might have seemed insane, but he accepted her craziness.

'Next door's looking after my mam,' he said. 'Now, get to sleep. If I catch hold of you, it's only for warmth – I've no plans for rape.'

'I know that.'

'How?'

'I just do.' She closed her eyes. 'Paul, what's she got?'

'I don't know, love.'

'And all the Hardcastles, too. She's spent quite a bit of time just lately with young Roy.' A shuddering breath made its way into and out of cold-stiffened lungs. 'God help them all,' she said.

'Go to sleep, love.'

'William used to call me that.'

'Then I'll try to stop.'

After a pause of at least a minute, her sleep-slowed voice reached him. 'I don't mind,' she said.

There came a light tapping at the van's back door. Paul struggled inelegantly out of his nest of blankets, crawled along, opened the van. 'Oh, hello,' he said.

The nurse gave him two steaming cups of cocoa and a plate of toast. 'Just to warm you up,' she whispered, 'and I suppose it's no use wishing you a happy Christmas.' She sniffed back a sudden need to weep. 'Look after her.'

'I will,' he promised.

And he did. He forced her to take small bites of toast, got half a cup of cocoa into her. When she finally slept, he remained at her side, senses tormented by her proximity, his mind firmly fixed inside the hospital in which her daughter lay. The question of touching Magsy was never on the agenda. He slept with her, held her, wiped away the tears.

For this woman he would do almost anything. Her grief affected him beyond words, as he could find no language to assuage it. Whenever she woke, he simply stroked her hands until fitful sleep arrived once more; he soothed her as one would instinctively calm an animal or a human infant in distress.

Morning found them huddled together, awakened once more by a little nurse who brought tea and bacon sandwiches. She imparted the news that there was no change in Beth, no change in any of the Hardcastles. The illness had not yet been identified, but several others from the Deane and Daubhill area had been admitted during the night.

'It's an epidemic,' said Magsy.

'Looks like it,' Paul replied.

'If she dies . . .' The rest of her sentence was lost in a bout of weeping. There was no possibility that she could face life without her daughter.

'Try not to think like that,' he said.

'I can't help it, Paul.'

While they picked at the sandwiches, he found himself wishing that he could be in Beth's place. If only he could make the swap, he would lay down his life for the sake of this woman's happiness. So this was love, then. It was not just a physical need, was more than a meeting of minds. Love was an instinct that depended on no particular sense.

'Why her and not me?' she asked.

'It happens, Magsy. Let them find out what it is, then they can shift it.'

'She was unconscious.'

'I know.'

'You could have fried eggs on her face.'

'Yes.'

They walked together into the hospital, requested and were given permission to use toilet facilities just off the reception area. In the ladies' room, Magsy watched the pale ghost in the mirror, wondered what had happened to yesterday. She remembered the fun of packing parcels of books, most bought secondhand from a market stall, Beth's giggles as she had wrapped Magsy's gift. Where was yesterday? How could life change so suddenly, so easily?

Paul warmed his hands on a radiator. It was Christmas Day and Mam was all on her own except for Bertha next door. Bertha next door was about as much fun as a burning orphanage, all downturned mouth and snide gossip. Yet he could not abandon Magsy at the infirmary.

He joined her at the front desk. 'Any news?' he asked.

Magsy looked at him. 'Not yet. But isolation's nearly full. And they want us out of here in case we are carriers of whatever this thing might be.' She straightened her shoulders. 'She would want me to go home. We can do nothing here.'

So she was talking sense at last. 'Yes, she would. And we have been asked to leave, anyway, in case we pass the disease on.'

They left the hospital grounds and drove in silence through town and up Derby Street. As he reached Magsy's door, Paul spoke for the first time. 'You'll be on your own.'

'No, I won't. I'll be with Lily.' She turned and looked at his profile, saw that his chin was darkened by new growth of beard. He was kind. He was a good friend. 'Thank you,' she said, 'you have calmed me. I had better go and cook now.' She considered the idea of planting a kiss on his cheek, decided against it, opened the door. It was time to think of practical things. The dinner intended for Ernest Barnes would go to Nellie Hulme. 'Go to your mother,' she told Paul, 'and I cannot thank you enough.'

When Magsy was back inside her house, she placed all the Christmas gifts in a cupboard. From somewhere within herself, she had found a strength bequeathed to her by generations of starved Irish cottagers, a will to survive no matter what. Enclosed in that determination was a special seed, a small plant that seemed to take root of its own accord. Beth would survive. With a certainty for which she would never account, Magsy O'Gara knew that her daughter was not going to die.

When the simple dinner was prepared, she washed her face, combed her hair and went across to visit Lily. Quarantine was senseless – everyone in this street had been exposed to whatever raged in the infirmary's isolation unit.

She walked into Lily's house, only to find that the housewife was sitting beside a cold grate, no sign of food, no attempt to keep warm. 'Lily?' It was plain that the woman had not washed, had not combed her hair, had not taken as much as a cup of tea.

'Oh, hello.'

The bitch and her puppy leapt gladly at the visitor; a morning of silence and hunger had not pleased them. Magsy found them some scraps, then squatted in front of Lily, rubbing the woman's cold hands. 'Come on, love.'

'Eh?'

'Over to my house for a bit of dinner.'

Lily blinked, her eyes dull and empty.

'I shall bring Nellie as well. If I knock, Spot will fetch her.'

'Roy's puppies,' said Lily.

'Yes.'

The older woman's mouth opened wide and she

howled like a wild animal baying at a full moon. She railed against the Almighty for allowing the illness, at mankind for carrying it into her home, at the world for being a cruel place. But, for the most part, Lily Hardcastle's anger was directed at herself. 'I prayed for change,' she howled.

'We all do that,' replied Magsy.

Lily continued to berate herself, crying out about nose-picking, smelly feet, spotty faces, folk who ate with their mouths open. 'It were all getting me down, then Dot went, then I wanted to go, then I knew I couldn't. I hate this place and my job and everything, so God has repaid me. He's made me watch this, Magsy. If I could be ill, I wouldn't suffer in my head, because I wouldn't know anything. So He's making me eat my words.'

'God isn't like that,' said Magsy.

'Then happen the devil heard me,' cried Lily.

Magsy made all the right noises, yet she knew that Lily's anguish was unreachable, that this poor woman would not respond to reason. Having been in this state so recently, Magsy understood that no amount of argument would serve to calm Lily.

Someone knocked at the front door. 'I'll go.' Magsy abandoned her weeping neighbour to allow Nellie Hulme into the house. The old woman waddled up the hall, her arms filled with gifts. These she deposited on Lily's table. 'No fire. This house is cold,' she mouthed at Magsy before approaching the weeping woman. Nellie, too, was close to tears. 'Come,' she said, pulling at Lily's hands, 'come and see.'

Lily allowed herself to be dragged to her feet. Nellie led the way, a reluctant Lily behind her, while Magsy brought up the rear. They entered Nellie's house, both visitors gasping when they saw how neat and clean it was. Lily was so startled that she forgot to cry as she looked at the furniture, the new rug, a spotless hearth where a fire burgeoned. 'It's . . . clean,' she stammered.

Spot threw himself at Lily, pleased to see the one who had been there right at the beginning of his life. He fussed, yapped, then did a lap of honour round the three women.

Nellie took them through to her kitchen where a black-leaded grate boasted new polish. Flames danced across the room, falling on a table whose cloth was exquisite. 'I made dinner,' Nellie mouthed proudly, 'but upstairs first. I show you.'

'Would you ever take a look at that cloth,' exclaimed Magsy. 'I swear that's hand-made and worth a fortune.'

But Nellie was ushering the pair of them towards the stairs. When they reached the top, the deaf woman turned and beamed at them. 'My secret,' she said.

Lily already knew the secret, as Roy had seen it, but her breath was taken away when she entered Nellie's back bedroom. It was spotless, gleaming, had obviously been kept in this state for years. The walls were lined with rolls of linen in white and ecru, while shelves bore piles of completed items. A work table was spread with dozens of bobbins, most in pairs identified by beads, small bells, wooden cubes.

'Good heavens,' exclaimed Magsy.

'Roy climbed up the drainpipe,' said Lily, 'and told me about this.'

Nellie showed them letters from the households of gentry, barons, dukes, princes, Buckingham Palace. Magsy wandered across to look at a fan on a wall, its lacework so delicate that it almost required magnification to see the detail. Letters from the mothers of debutantes were also pinned to the wall, as were requests for table linens, collars, chair covers. 'Bloody hell,' Lily exclaimed, 'her does this for royalty.'

'She does indeed,' said Magsy quietly. She thought about the old lady, given up for adoption due to deafness, isolated by that same condition, depressed to the point where she had cared naught for her appearance, for her diet, for the state of her home. And here was a room filled with beauty, the island on which Nellie had marooned herself with silent deliberation, a place filled by books, pricked-out patterns, the cushions on which those patterns were executed.

Magsy turned and made eye contact with Nellie. 'Beautiful,' she said.

Nellie nodded. 'Always hope.' The two words, perfectly framed, emerged soundless from her lips. 'This is my hope, mine.' She hit her breast with a closed fist. 'You must never stop the hope, because it is all we have.' She spoke perfectly, yet soundlessly, the words accompanied only by the rasping of her breath. An expert lip-reader, Nellie Hulme had practised for many hours while standing in front of a mirror.

Magsy threw her arms as far as they would go around Nellie, who, in spite of recent weight loss, was still a hefty woman. Lily joined them, and they hugged like children in the street, a band of humanity joining in tearful confusion. Nellie's tears were almost noiseless, but Lily made up for the absence of sound, her whole body heaving as she broke her heart once more.

They separated, each woman sniffling and patting at nose and eyes with a handkerchief.

'You've worked hard,' Magsy told Nellie.

The deaf woman nodded. 'They say I was born on a Saturday,' she mouthed.

'So was I,' exclaimed Magsy, 'and Beth was, too.'

'And Saturday's child works hard for a living,' said Lily, the words fractured by sobs.

Nellie led them downstairs and served up a lunch of

chicken portions cooked in red wine – 'I found a book in the library,' she explained soundlessly – with roast potatoes, parsnips and a selection of vegetables. Lily did her best, but emotions were still too raw for her digestive system to accept much food, though Magsy, strangely calm, did justice to the feast, even accepting a second bowl of trifle.

Nellie cleared the table. While she was in the scullery, Lily spoke. 'Well, she's turned over a new leaf. Cooking, cleaning, going up to the High Street baths every Thursday.'

Magsy sipped at her coffee. 'More than a single leaf, Lily. This is the whole encyclopedia up-ended. From somewhere, Nellie has taken courage. Imagine living in a silent world, though. How must it be never to hear music, never to listen to a play on the wireless? Very lonely. I am glad to see that her life has taken a turn for the better, that she seems positive now, full of a kind of joy, I suppose.'

'Dog's done her good,' replied Lily.

'It started before the dog.' Magsy placed her demitasse in its saucer. 'It was something to do with the big clear-out. What prompted that?'

Lily lifted a shoulder in a careless gesture. 'God knows.'

'He does indeed.'

The older woman sniffed to announce a change of subject. 'What if they die?'

'Don't think like that. I know in my bones that Beth will come through. Never ask me why or how, but I am sure that she is going to survive.'

'I don't feel like that,' said Lily. 'There is no way of being sure that any of them will come out of that infirmary – except in boxes, of course.'

'Then have faith, find hope and pray for them.'

But Lily's faith seemed to be taking a holiday. She had

never been an avid churchgoer, was one who attended christenings, weddings and funerals, although her parents had been regular worshippers. For Lily, God was an idea, sometimes a good idea, too often a bad one. 'Where's your God now?' she asked. ''Cos I think mine's in Blackpool, top of the tower in a Kiss-Me-Quick hat. I can't find Him, Mags.'

'Will we go and look along the Golden Mile, then, Lily?'

'Too bloody cold. I don't want me feet frozen off, thanks.'

So there was still humour. Where there was humour, there was a chance for sanity. 'We can do nothing.' Magsy's hand reached out to cover Lily's. 'Nothing practical, that is. There is even a possibility that these streets may be cordoned off in order to contain whatever this is. We can't visit, can't sit with our loved ones, can't watch over them. We have to wait.'

Lily pondered. 'I'm no good at waiting. I have to be doing.' She cupped her chin and gazed thoughtfully at the remains of Nellie's trifle. 'I liked the war. It was good doing something useful, making bullets, having a proper job. I loved it in munitions, Magsy. Then ... then it was all over and they came home.'

'Of course they did. Well, most of them.'

Lily wished that she could bite back her words. 'I'm sorry, love.'

'Ah, no bother.'

'What I meant was that here we are, back to cleaning pubs and hospitals. That were a good job I had, you know. I got to be in charge of a whole section, me and Elsie Shuttleworth – her that lives on Fox Street – her husband's a postman.'

This was the longest statement Magsy had heard from Lily, so she kept quiet.

148

'Now, it's back to women's jobs, isn't it? Jobs not good enough for men. We get to clean and serve in shops – if we're lucky. Aye, it's a man's world.' She nodded thoughtfully. 'I think the end of the war meant the end of me. I'm back to being nobody now.'

'Everybody is somebody, Lily.'

'Somebody? Is cleaning up sick and snot the sort of job you'd give to a somebody?' Lily sighed heavily. 'Aye, in them Emblem Street sheds, me and Elsie Shuttleworth were in charge of more than forty people. We turned out enough stuff to blow half of bloody Germany into kingdom come. And now?' A sad smile visited her lips. 'Now, Elsie's back to carding cotton and I swill up after filthy men.'

'Yes, I know,' replied Magsy, 'but the forces had to have something to come home to.'

Lily was not listening. She was ploughing a careful furrow towards her own reasons, her own guilt. 'So I've ... resented getting back to normal. My own family got on me nerves, Magsy. That day-to-day grind, everything the same, cook, shop, wash, clean the house, clean the pub. I've lost all heart. So I started imagining – pretending, like – a different life, a fresh start.' She gulped noisily. 'They weren't in my imaginings, Mags. When I was thinking and hoping, I was on my own.'

Magsy waited.

'So when this happened – it was as if I'd brought it on.'

'Well, you didn't. You didn't give them the germs, Lily.'

'No, but I wished it on them.'

'You can't blame yourself.'

'Just watch me,' answered Lily. 'Because I will always blame my selfishness. Sometimes, it's best not to dream, because your dreams might come true and do a lot of damage.'

It was hopeless, decided Magsy. Whatever was said, Lily would continue to believe that she had put her own men into the isolation unit at the infirmary.

Nellie waddled in with cheese and biscuits. An ever-hopeful Spot placed himself on sentry duty beneath the table, his stomach groaning in happy anticipation of scraps. The three women ate and drank coffee in silence, each immersed in her own thoughts. Christmas was a family time, but each had just the other two for company.

After the meal, Nellie led them through to her front room and showed them the photograph. She mee-mawed the words, 'My mother and father, I think,' then poured three glasses of port wine. Raising her own glass, she toasted them with more silent words. 'To you and yours,' she mouthed.

Magsy's strange calm stayed with her throughout the whole day. Lily managed to contain her panic, while Nellie, tired after the meal, slept in her fireside chair.

'Funny how she snores,' commented Lily. 'You can hear that all right, yet she can't make a sound when it comes to words. And fancy her making all that stuff all these years. Aye, she's a dark horse, is Miss Nellie Hulme.'

'We all have our secrets,' said Magsy.

Lily turned to stare at her companion. 'Is your secret Paul Horrocks?'

'No.'

Lily thought about that. 'Well, happen he's that much of a secret that you haven't even told yourself about him.'

Magsy found a strange yet undeniable sense in Lily's words. There were two levels at which a person functioned, led by reason on the one hand, by emotion on the other. Between these two elements there was a no-man's land, a chasm that could not be crossed until a bridge appeared of its own accord. Was it possible, then, to be drawn to a man in spite of one's own better judgement?

Ah well, none of that mattered just now. Beth was possibly fighting for her life; Beth would win through. How did she know that? Because that self-constructing bridge had spanned the gulf again. Paul Horrocks? He was a different territory, one to which she had not yet sent an expeditionary force.

When Nellie woke, she led her two companions through the mysteries of lace, showing them books containing pictures of bobbins, beads, pillows, pricked-out patterns. They drank more port, more tea, talked about the epidemic.

When her visitors had left, Nellie took Spot for his walk. She was well pleased with her day's work, was proud of all she had achieved.

Nellie Hulme, spinster of the parish, was a housewife at last.

Ten

Sarah Higgins, usually known as Sal, was a contented soul. Mild-mannered, kind, a 'goodly' woman, she expected little from life and was satisfied with her situation. She had a good husband, eight beautiful daughters and an adopted son on whom she and all the other females in the household doted unashamedly.

It was Christmas Day in the year of Our Lord 1950. Everyone had been to Mass, all had taken Holy Communion, the dinner had been acceptable, small gifts had been joyfully distributed, the melodeon had been played, each member of the family had sung, the jigsaws were well under way and the world was well.

Magsy and Lily had gone in to Nellie's, so that had turned out well, too. Dead were the days of Catholics on one side, Protestants on the other. Only Ernest Barnes kept the old grudge – and what a wiping his eye had taken, for hadn't his son upped and wedded the lovely Rachel, daughter of this very Catholic household?

Sal gazed into the flames. Opposite her, on the bed beneath the front room window, John Higgins played with Maureen, the youngest of eight daughters. Well, she was the youngest just now, but Sal had reason to believe that another was on the way. This suspicion she nursed contentedly, although childbirth had never been easy and she had thought that her childbearing years were done.

During an otherwise happy marriage, Sal had lost three sons and one daughter, yet she never questioned the will of God. Peter, John, Patrick and Nuala had not been a part of the Maker's plan, but this one would survive.

John looked across and saw his wife smiling, recognized the way she was sitting, hands folded over her belly, a half-smile tugging at the corners of her mouth. 'Another?' he asked.

She laughed. 'Another stout?'

John shook a finger at her. 'You know what I mean, Sal.'

'I think so.'

'Then there's a good reason for us to take just one more jar of the black stuff.' He frowned. 'Well, God spare Beth next door and all those poor souls from Lily's house. Is there any news?'

'No.'

''Tis a plague of some kind,' he said sadly. 'There are more sick from up the road, you know. I hear they're planning on taking over a whole wing of the hospital. They say it's some kind of flu.' Like his wife, John accepted with equanimity the possibility of another child. Rachel had gone; surely they could squeeze in another little one.

Sal sighed. She had been watching over her brood with the eyes of a hawk, was forever feeling foreheads to see if they were cool, was doling out cod liver oil and malt by the shovelful, had bought a supply of Fennings' powders just in case. The thought of children dying was not one she wanted to entertain, so she did what she always did – her best. Once her best was done, she reverted to type, singing, playing with Thomas and the girls. She was not a natural housewife, though the place was never filthy. Sal provided her family with food, enough clean clothes to get through the week, but any cleaning in the house was a surface job, the quick flick of a cloth, an occasional scrape of a broom. Bed-changing scarcely happened, as this family slept all over the place, some upstairs, some down, Thomas in the kitchen. Bedtimes meant catch-as-catch-can, each sleepy child grabbing for sheet, quilt and blanket.

Sal had discovered early on in her married life that putting things away was the best she could achieve, so she tidied up every day, washed dishes, made meals. Cooking for eleven people was a chore. But, including Thomas, there were only ten now, as Rachel had gone away with Frank. The ninth natural child was still a mere cluster of cells, but Sal knew with complete certainty that this would be a fine, healthy boy.

She accepted a mug of stout from her husband, slapped his hand playfully as he touched her cheek. Her eyes remained fixed on him as he continued his game of tiddlywinks with Maureen, who was now eight. Angela, Mary and Annie were in the kitchen with Thomas, their voices muted as they concentrated on jigsaw pieces. The older girls, Eileen, Theresa and Vera, were upstairs trying on cheap new shoes and dresses. As for Rachel, she was the best off of all, was up on the moors with a good husband and an excellent mother-in-law. 'We are lucky, so,' Sal told her husband.

A shiver trickled down John's spine. 'We are,' he agreed.

'God spare us to continue so fortunate,' she whispered.

'Amen to that,' answered John. But the ice in his spine remained.

Rachel was wearing her Christmas finery again as she set off across the road, a platter of food in her hands. She had bought the oval plate specially, as Katherine was probably unused to the thick white pots in Rachel's own house. There was a napkin, too, one Rachel had made from the best section of an old sheet, the initials K and M embroidered neatly into a corner. This small offering was to be Katherine's Christmas present, and Rachel was proud of her handiwork.

She swung the gate of Knowehead inward and walked along the side of the house. As arranged, Phyllis Hart had left the key under a brick to the right of the back door. When Rachel rose with the key in her hand, a small movement caught the periphery of her vision. This was not a fox or a squirrel – it was something else, something ... wrong. It was an out-of-context presence, a human, Rachel decided. She stared into the rear garden for a few seconds, then shook her head and walked into the kitchen. She was becoming fanciful, had been rather jumpy since getting the message from Mam. Rachel and Frank had been ordered to stay away from Bolton, as many were in hospital after coming down with some strange disease.

This would be the first Christmas away from Mam and Dad. What if they became ill? What if any of her siblings got lifted into hospital? What if ... ? Rachel placed Katherine's dinner on the kitchen table and berated herself inwardly. What-iffing would not get her anywhere. She set the tray with Katherine's silver, tutting when she had to use a tea-towel to scrub away water stains. Phyllis Hart deserved sacking. How could anyone allow such beautiful cutlery to become so shabby?

It happened again. While Rachel polished a knife, something caught the corner of her eye and she shivered involuntarily. It was that funny little house, she decided, the place in which Katherine intended to install her housekeeper. Someone was in there. He or she probably felt safe, as Miss Moore lived in the front of the house called Knowehead. Was it Phyllis Hart with one of her many boyfriends? Surely not. Even a heathen as bold as Phyllis would be with her family on Christmas Day. Who, then? She placed the dinner on the tray, then turned to scrutinize the back garden.

There was nothing to see, yet Rachel knew with an unwavering certainty that the little wooden house was occupied. No smoke emerged from the central chimney, no lace curtain twitched, yet the place screamed of habitation. 'It'll be the Irish in me,' she said aloud. 'I'll be seeing a crowd of leprechauns and hearing the Banshee any minute now.'

She carried the meal upstairs, noticing for the umpteenth time how grimy the house was. She was the only one, apart from Phyllis, who was allowed to visit Miss Katherine Moore. She often read to the old lady, had even opened up to her, had made her smile when she told tales of her 'rumbustious' family and the trouble they had endured at the hands of Frank's father. Miss Moore, originally shocked to find herself in the company of a Catholic, was now beginning to ask questions about the faith, was begging to read the *Catholic Herald* and other publications produced by Roman Catholic presses.

An expert now when it came to tray-carrying, Rachel pushed open the bedroom door. 'Happy Christmas,' she cried.

Katherine smiled through her pain. How wonderful life had become since the arrival of Mrs Rachel Barnes. She lit up the room every time she entered, made marvellous sandwiches from home-cooked bread, was not averse to a bit of chatter over a glass of wine. 'I wish you the same,' she replied, 'and thank your mother for recommending that medication from her chemist. My joints feel slightly looser already.'

'Good, I am pleased to hear it.' Rachel placed the tray

on a tallboy then brought the mahogany stand, a wonderful piece of equipment that opened up to reveal something that resembled a stool, but with a webbed top. Onto this she placed the tray, dropping its sides so that the tray formed a circular table. With a flourish, Rachel removed a domed cover to reveal her dinner. 'There you go. You have goose and vegetables and roast potatoes. Leave that saucer on top of the pudding dish to keep it warm.'

Something stung Katherine's eyes. She blinked rapidly, refused to allow tears to fall. For one thing, she did not wish to damage her own reputation; for another, she hated the idea of upsetting this new friend. 'That looks wonderful.'

Rachel sat down. She wanted to say something about the summer house, yet she knew that she could not. This was a very old lady whose frailty forbade Rachel to speak. And it was Christmas Day – oh, Frank would have to deal with the matter. Once Frank had been to the summer house, Rachel could then decide what was best.

'What about your own dinner?' asked Katherine.

Rachel laughed and patted her stomach. 'All eaten,' she answered. 'One more mouthful and I would burst.'

Katherine ate. Both were becoming used to these companionable silences. The old woman could not imagine how she managed to eat while Rachel watched, yet she could, so she had stopped questioning herself regarding the issue. 'My initials,' she cried as she patted her lips with the napkin.

'I made that for you.'

'Thank you.'

'It's only a little thing, but it's your Christmas present.' She noticed how Katherine placed her knife and fork together when she paused, that the eating implements had little space between them. Eager to learn manners, Rachel no longer allowed her own cutlery to rest akimbo on her plate at home. Should she ever be called upon to eat 'posh', Mrs Barnes intended to know her Ps and Qs.

'I have a gift for you,' announced Katherine. 'It is on the dressing table over there.' She waved a thin hand in the direction of that piece of furniture. 'I had it sent up from town, so I guessed the size. The shop will change it for you if it is not suitable.'

Rachel fetched the parcel, reseated herself, peeled away the covering brown paper. Inside, she found a box with the words HELEN DUBARRY printed on its top in gilt letters. Helen Dubarry. Nobody got to wipe their feet on that shop's doormat for less than five pounds. 'Oh,' she sighed.

Katherine marked this as one of the most pleasurable moments of her life. Her own heart beat faster as she watched the young woman's facial expressions. So this was how it might have felt had she ever had a child. It would have been a girl, of course. Oh yes, had Miss Katherine ever married, there would have been just the one child, a female.

Rachel lifted the silk and lace blouse from its nest of pure white tissue. 'Oh, sweet Jesus,' she breathed before checking herself. Katherine would never say that, would never take the good Lord's name in vain. 'I am sorry,' she stammered, 'but I never in all my life owned anything so absolutely gorgeous. If you hadn't that arthritis, I would hug you.'

Katherine smiled inwardly. Occasionally, she caught traces of the Irish in Rachel – not in the accent, rather in the choice and arrangement of words. 'You are most welcome to the gift, Rachel,' she said. 'If anyone can do justice to silk, you most certainly can. You have a rare beauty, my dear.'

Without the slightest embarrassment, Rachel peeled off her clothing and tried on the blouse. It was white, with pearl buttons up the front and a collar of snowy lace that fastened just below her throat. Like a child, she ran to the cheval, angling the mirror until it contained her whole self from top to toe. 'This is . . .' She swallowed hard. 'This is a lady's blouse,' she managed at last. 'It is the most beautiful blouse in the world.'

Katherine smiled and continued to enjoy her feast. For the very first time, she realized that the greatest pleasure lay in watching the joy of others.

Rachel knew instinctively that she must not mention value. A gift was a gift whether it cost a shilling or ten pounds. Or twenty, she thought as she swivelled for a view of her back. To refer to the cost of this sumptuous blouse would constitute a breaking of a code of etiquette that had developed without words. 'Thank you,' she said. 'It's lovely.'

'I hear that skirts are going to lengthen,' said Katherine. 'They were abbreviated by necessity, by the war. But if you care to look in that wardrobe, you will find a good dark grey suit on the left hand side. I think I used to be about your size – and you may find someone to make it over for you.'

Her breath shortened by such generosity, Rachel declared herself capable of making any alterations. She opened the wardrobe door and found herself face to face with materials she had never imagined to be within her reach. There was cashmere, linen, tweed, silk. Below the clothing, shoes of the finest leathers were arranged like soldiers on parade, not a single man out of line, every corporal and private perfectly placed as if waiting for a sergeant's command. The poor woman had been tidy to the point of obsession.

'I liked good clothes,' said Katherine, her voice almost plaintive. 'Reduced to wearing loose dressing gowns now,' she added.

'But you may get better,' protested Rachel.

'And pigs might fly,' came the quick answer.

Rachel turned. 'Are you going to finish that dinner?'

'Yes, Mother.'

The young woman noticed the twinkle in rheumy eyes. 'I want that plate to shine.' She delivered these words in the soft brogue used by her own parents.

The suit was magnificent. As she studied it, Rachel realized that her new clothes were not so wonderful after all. Yes, they were, because they were from Frank, but oh, what a difference. The grey skirt, cut sharply and accurately, was fully lined. Even without a wearer to fill it out, this clothing hung well, as if designed by an engineer, a scientist rather than an artist.

'Good clothes speak for themselves,' remarked Katherine. 'They require no explanation and few embellishments.'

'Yes,' gulped Rachel.

'And they span years. A classic is a classic and is always adaptable.'

'You have good taste.' Rachel tried on the jacket and it fitted perfectly.

'Dubarry provided the taste – I was just the clothes-hanger,' replied Katherine. 'One of the advantages of money – not that I ever had a great deal – is that a person can buy good taste. Three suits and a dozen blouses can get a woman through a whole season.'

Rachel had never owned a suit – or a costume, as the working classes termed a skirt and jacket. The blue wool she currently wore was the first complete outfit in her wardrobe. It was still pretty, still comfortable, but would she become spoilt now? Would she measure everything against this brief glimpse of couturier items?

'Borrow whatever you like, but keep the suit.'

Manners were forgotten. 'I couldn't. It wouldn't be right.'

'Why is that?'

Rachel pondered, found no immediate reply.

Katherine laughed. 'Is it right to give the moths a feast, to leave good cloth hanging there for years on end? Look at me, Rachel. Look at me.'

Rachel responded to the order and faced her benefactor squarely. 'Yes?'

'I was a tall woman for one of my generation – about five and a half feet. Now, I am small, because my bones are bent. I am three stone lighter than I was in my heyday. Can you imagine me tripping around the town in a designer suit? Those clothes would drown me now. The pain of getting into them would floor me for a week. So, take that classic grey suit home and keep it. Everything there is yours, but leave the rest here so that I shall have the pleasure of helping you to choose an ensemble.'

The younger woman dashed a tear from her cheek.

'And do not disappoint me by becoming silly. Half of those clothes were never worn, because I was locked in with him towards the end of his life. Then, not long after he died, my own pain started.'

'Your father?'

'Oh, yes, my father.' Katherine grimaced. 'Now, be off with you so that I might enjoy my pudding in peace.'

'Thank you,' whispered Rachel. On a whim, she crossed the small space and planted a kiss on top of the old lady's head. 'Katherine?'

'Yes?' The monosyllable was thickened by emotion.

'Who ... who bathes you?'

'The girl and I manage a bed-bath between us. Why? Am I malodorous?'

'Not at all, but ... I was thinking. If I could lift you into the bath, the hot water might ease the arthritis, thaw you out a bit.'

'A thought,' agreed Katherine, 'as long as you don't drop me.'

Rachel giggled. 'I might, you know. After all, if I killed you off, I would have a wonderful wardrobe.'

They stared at one another for several seconds, each knowingly poised on the brink of the next phase in this rapidly improving relationship.

'I can see the headline now,' said Katherine at last. 'Old lady killed for her Dubarry collection.'

'Would they let me go to the gallows in my new suit?' asked Rachel, not a trace of emotion in her tone. 'And before I start planning, do you have any jewellery of worth? We could sell it off and extend the shop, you see.'

Katherine drew in her lips. 'You are a horrid girl.'

'Yes, it's the way I was dragged up. And mind you don't choke – there are silver threepenny pieces in my pudding.'

'That would solve your problem,' replied Katherine. 'Different headline. Old lady chokes on neighbour's kindness.'

Rachel reached and placed a hand on Katherine's shoulder. 'Don't you dare die,' she said softly. 'My grandparents are all in Ireland, so I shall probably never see them. Consider yourself adopted, Miss Katherine Moore.'

When Rachel had left, grey suit and silk blouse held carefully before her like the Crown Jewels, Katherine allowed her tears to flow. For the first time ever, she felt love – not just from herself to another, but flowing in her direction, too. This under-educated Irish child-bride was her equal, her match. The pain and joy of love were too much for a neglected woman, so it poured down her face until she became too tired to weep.

The pudding, though cold, was excellent. And life, so near to its end, was worth living at last.

Frank Barnes felt like something out of a very bad film, the sort of entertainment offered in serial form on Saturday afternoons to hordes of screaming schoolchildren. And Rachel, who had refused to listen to orders, was creeping along behind him. Behind Rachel and also in defiance of advice, Dot Barnes brought up the rear of a group termed by Frank 'the Lancashire Keystone Cops'. The three of them were acting so furtively that anyone who braved the elements on this Christmas night, any sane person who might catch a glimpse of the guilty-looking trio, would immediately fetch a constable.

He turned and looked at his wife. 'Stop here,' he said, though he knew she wouldn't.

'Sshhh,' hissed Rachel.

He pointed to the back door of Knowehead. 'Mam, keep Rachel near that door.'

Dot sniffed. 'No,' she whispered determinedly, 'we are in this together.'

'Three flaming Musketeers now,' bemoaned Frank. 'I don't know why I'm bothering. There's nobody in yon hut.'

'Well, there was,' said Rachel, 'and it's not a hut, it's a summer house.'

Frank shook his head incredulously. Because of his wife, whom he adored with a passion, he was trespassing, was creeping about like a criminal in the grounds of a poor old woman who had also fallen under Rachel's spell, was in the company of a wife he needed to protect and a mother he had already removed from danger. God, he needed his head seeing to.

They made their way along the side of the house, through the garden and up to the door of the summer house. 'It's locked,' declared Frank, relief plain in his tone.

'Push,' ordered Rachel firmly.

He pushed and the door shot inward, taking him with it. Breathless, he stood in total darkness before striking a match.

'There's nobody here.' It was plain that Rachel was disappointed.

What had she wanted? Frank wondered. Jack the Ripper, a burglar with a swag-bag, the Gordon Highlanders complete with pipes and drum? 'What are you doing now?' he asked as Rachel overtook him. She was a minx, this one. From a predominantly female family where everyone made up her own mind, she was wilful, spoilt and absolutely determined. He loved her to pieces and felt that she might charm rabbits from their burrows if she put her mind to it.

Rachel lit a small candle on the stone mantelpiece. 'It's nice here,' she said. There was a table, some chairs, a little sideboard and a picture of a ship hanging crookedly on the chimney breast. She righted the latter item, then pointed to the table where a newspaper was spread, some greaseproof paper screwed up in its centre. 'See? Somebody has been here.' She carried the candle to the table. 'That newspaper's got last week's date on it – Friday. So there has been a visitor.' There was triumph in her voice.

Together, they made their way through the little single-storey house, bedroom, kitchen, small closed-in porch round the back. They found cigarette ends in a cracked saucer, crumbs on a mattress, an old shoe under the bed. 'I told you,' said Rachel.

'I know you did,' replied Frank. 'You've been telling us since half past three.'

'Quarter to four,' argued Dot. 'I remember looking at the clock when she gave us that fashion show.'

Frank sighed heavily. 'Can we go home now?'

Rachel concurred. 'Right, but we need to get Katherine a housekeeper as soon as possible. Whoever's coming in here wants chasing. He should have more respect for somebody else's property.'

'How do you know it's a man?'

Rachel awarded him a withering look that was wasted in the dim light. 'No woman would leave newspaper and sandwich wrappings on a table.'

'Nellie would,' said Dot.

'Even Smelly Nellie's cleaning herself up,' answered Rachel. 'No, this is a man's doing.' She extinguished the candle and led the way out. 'Be quiet,' she admonished, 'we don't want to be frightening her.'

Frank muttered under his breath as he led his household homeward. What did it matter? If some tramp was spending the odd hour in an empty hut, what harm was he doing? Nobody else lived in the place, nobody was losing out. Rachel was so fiercely protective of Miss Katherine Moore – why? 'I don't know why you bother,' he said as they reached the shop.

'I know you don't.' Rachel rounded on him in the doorway. 'Money's not everything,' she informed him loftily.

He unlocked the door. 'I never said it was.'

'And I never said you said it was.'

Oh heck. This was looking as if it might turn into one of Rachel's circular arguments, three times round the flaming block, meet your original opinion on the way back.

Inside the shop, Rachel sat on the customers' chair. 'She has never had any love. Her mam died giving birth

165

to her, then her dad was as much use as a flat rolling pin. He drank everything except water and he never took any notice of her. All she has now is that house and a bit of pride.'

'More pride than sense,' interposed Dot.

'More pride than a family of lions,' added Frank.

'That's as may be,' Rachel insisted, 'but when you've lived in a house without love—'

'We have,' said Dot rather sharply.

'You loved your sons.' Rachel folded her arms and tried to look stern. 'It's not your fault that your husband turned bad. And you protected your lads. There was nobody to protect Katherine, so she's grown a suit of armour. And so thin,' she said sadly. 'I've seen more meat on a Good Friday than what she has on her bones.'

Frank sniffed a drip of moisture, declared himself to be frozen stiff, went through to the house to brew some tea.

'Give over worrying,' urged Dot.

'There's somebody living in that summer house, and—'

'And that's as may be,' interrupted Dot, 'but you've no responsibilities there, Rachel. Look to your own. Aye, look to your own and don't be mithering over her.'

But Rachel could not help herself. Did the unwelcome lodger know about the key under the brick? Was he in the house, was he going to hurt Katherine?

She followed Dot into the back, closed the door, tried to close her mind. But the images would not go away – greaseproof paper, an old shoe, the Bolton newspaper. It needed sorting out, and Rachel was the man for the job. She had to be, because no-one else cared.

The scream that tore its way out of Sal Higgins's chest ripped through the December air. She stood in the scullery doorway, a child in her arms, mouth opened wide, breath misting as it hit crystals of frost in the freezing atmosphere.

John raced through the house, pyjamas flapping as he ran towards his wife. Sal never screamed. Even in childbirth, she had borne the pain stoically. She had accepted the deaths of her babies, had kept going for the good of her family, was not one for great displays of emotion. 'Sal?' he yelled. 'Sal?'

But she was halfway down the yard, ancient slippers skidding over a layer of ice. She shook the child in her arms. 'Breathe,' she shouted, 'for God's sake, breathe.'

John reached her, stopped, looked at the kiddy's face, white, cold, as frozen as marble in a churchyard. 'What . . . ?' he began.

'Deep sleep,' she chattered. 'Gone into a deep sleep, John. I keep shaking him, but he won't wake.'

John felt as if the life was draining out of himself, too. He steadied himself against the wall that separated the Higgins yard from the O'Garas', legs turning to rubber, knees quaking, bare feet burning in a patch of frost. This was unbelievable. The child had been quiet over Christmas, but there had been no discernible fever, no warning, no symptoms.

'Shall I take him in?' Sal asked.

'Yes.' John pulled himself together. 'Put him on his bed, love. I'll send one of the girls for the doctor.' Thomas Grogan-Higgins was dead. The pallor of his face approached blue in colour – the child had been gone for several hours.

Sal wrapped the little body in blankets and placed it gently where she had found it not five minutes earlier. 'He's gone, hasn't he?' she mumbled.

'Yes.' John pulled her into his arms. 'There was nothing you could do, love.'

'I know that.'

He lifted her face. 'Sal, it's not our fault.'

'No.'

'Poor soul must have had a weakness.'

She began to shake, tremors sweeping through his body, too, like a small earthquake, a warning of devastation yet to come. They clung together, neither noticing when doors flew inward to allow Magsy O'Gara into the house.

Magsy stood for a moment at the foot of Thomas's narrow bed. She turned on her heel and went into the front room where the Higgins girls sat, most crying, all wordless. 'Stay here,' she advised before returning to the kitchen. Yes, he was dead. That poor baby soul whose parents had been blown to kingdom come had now joined them. Magsy prayed, hands clutched into her breast, head bowed against the vision of that perfect, unmarked little body on the mattress.

When her prayers were finished, Magsy O'Gara set to, placing paper and kindling in the grate, finding bread, jam and margarine. Like all women before her, like most yet to be born, she did what women do in the face of death – she warmed and fed the living.

After jam sandwiches and milk had been delivered to the girls, Magsy waited to see whether John or Sal would speak, but neither did. They continued to stand in the centre of the kitchen, no tears, no words, just a lump of humanity joined together in the face of this new storm.

Magsy went back to her own house, picked up hat, coat, scarf and gloves, looked at her pale face in the mirror. 'Beth,' she muttered, 'oh, Beth, not you, not you.' It had happened to Thomas. Thomas had been the one to pay the price. Guilt rushed into Magsy's head, the emotion powerful enough to colour her cheeks. It was as if Thomas had been a token payment of some kind, the one who had done the dying for everyone. 'He may not be the only one,' she reminded herself.

Even so, as she set out to fetch the doctor, Magsy O'Gara continued to know that Beth would survive. In that certainty lay her only chance of sanity.

Eleven

Little Thomas Grogan was buried with his parents in the Catholic section of Tonge Cemetery.

He had done his job, thought Magsy as the tiny white coffin was lowered into frost-hardened earth. Thomas had achieved what generations had failed even to approach – he had brought Christians together. The church had been bursting, Catholics, Methodists, members of the Church of England, all crushed together, no grouping, no sectarianism, just people of all ages, all creeds, salt water pouring from their eyes, a copy of the Requiem Mass shaking in every pair of hands.

Magsy stood with Lily and Nellie, listened while the Irish priest made his farewell to a boy who had lived such a short life, whose parents had been lost, whose happiness had been extended by the thoroughly good Higgins family. Sal, who had spoken scarcely a word since the boy's death, was motionless throughout the burial. Sal had a special place inside herself, an area of which Magsy had caught brief glimpses in recent days. She was possessed of a shut-down mechanism, a facility she had used, no doubt, when her own babies had died.

Magsy put an arm round Nellie, whose tears were accompanied by the textureless sounds produced only by the deaf, no particular level to the noise, no cadence, just primitive howls. Nellie made enough audible fuss for everyone, because while most held their grief back, Nellie could not hear her own din.

Nevertheless, this horrible day was not without its good side, because the boy in the coffin had been a catalyst, a small element whose qualities had been vital to this particular formula. He had injected his tiny presence into the equation, had now disappeared without trace, solidarity and unity his priceless legacies.

Lily clung to Magsy's arm. Her husband and boys were still alive, while Thomas, who had displayed no particular symptoms of Asian flu, had died from inhalation of vomit, had choked in the night. Lily felt dreadful, was still as guilty as sin. Wishes should never be made, because they might just come true. She had desired change, was enduring change, while her menfolk remained isolated in hospital. And now, an innocent child had been taken and . . .

'Lily?' Magsy pulled at her sleeve.

'What?'

'Stop it. Stop it now.'

Did Magsy O'Gara read minds, was she capable of entering a person's thoughts?

'They will be fine,' continued Magsy in a whisper.

Lily inclined her head and said a silent prayer. Beth was certainly all right. Beth was in a tiny single ward now, was able to talk to her mother through glass, was eating, beginning to read again, was becoming restless.

'They'll be home,' said Magsy.

'Aye.' But there was no conviction in the response.

'They will. Now stop this, Lily, despair is a sin.'

Hiding a deadly misdemeanour that refused to be lifted from her sorrowful soul, Lily straightened her spine and watched while the Higgins family dropped soil onto the coffin of their adopted son and brother. John was in the worst state, features screwed up against unbearable misery, nose red with weeping, a handkerchief dabbing the wet from his face. Sal just went through the motions, a strange half-smile on her face, a mask concealing emotions that probably went too deep to be allowed an airing.

It was finished. The child's earthly remains had been returned to his birth parents, so that was that, the cycle completed long before it had run its course. 'We never know the day,' mumbled Lily.

'That's sure,' agreed Magsy as she made a hurried Sign of the Cross, 'and we don't dwell on it. Come on, now, we are having a bit of a warm in the Prince Billy, then it's off to hospital again, see how they all are.'

Lily pondered. 'But the Billy's a Protestant pub, Mags.' Protestants? Bloody heathens, more like, toilets like pig pens, washbasins filled with all kinds of filth.

'I know.'

'Catholics don't often go there.'

'I know.' Magsy steered Nellie towards the gate. 'All the more reason to go there today, then, for hasn't young Thomas opened the doors for everyone?'

'I suppose so.'

'Suppose nothing,' said Magsy through clenched teeth. ''Tis a fact. I have never been in a public house since ... since William died, but I shall go to this one now. Thomas has made a point and we shall learn from him.'

The pub was packed. The usual lunchtime drinkers found themselves wedged in a corner, most too respectful to intrude upon the dark-clothed interlopers. This was clearly a funeral party, and mourners always deserved respect.

Sal sat alone in a corner, her eyes fixed on an untouched half of black stout. The same expression remained on her face, corners of the mouth slightly upturned, the eyes unseeing, ears plainly closed against all that went on around her. Nellie placed herself opposite

Sal, pushing a small sheet of paper across the table. On it Nellie had written, *I am sorry and I shall pray for you.*

The Irishwoman made no move.

Nellie reached into a capacious handbag and drew out a tissue-wrapped item. She slapped Sal's hand. 'I made,' she mouthed. 'For you, I made.' With that unwavering certainty she had gained via her four heightened senses, Nellie homed in on this woman's misery. Sal Higgins had to be dealt with.

Sal fixed her gaze on Nellie. Smelly Nellie was no longer smelly. She was smart and clean in her dark navy coat and matching hat. 'Hello,' said Sal, 'nice to see you.' Had Nellie's ears been capable, she would have noticed the lack of expression in her companion's tone.

But Nellie did not need to own the ability to hear. Sal's strangeness was plain – the woman was in deep shock, had retreated into a safe place where nothing and no-one could reach her. 'Open,' commanded Nellie, her lips over-working the word.

Sal continued mute and motionless.

Nellie knew about noise. For well over seventy years, she had lived in a world where noise was a factor from which she had always been excluded, yet she had watched often enough while others responded to it. With slow deliberation, she lifted a large glass ashtray and crashed it onto the table's surface, her mind marvelling when the item survived the assault intact and without a single chip. She set it back in its rightful place and waited.

The Prince William was suddenly as still as the long-dead man whose name it had taken. Hands froze in mid-air, beer pausing on its way to owners' mouths. Cigarettes dangled from lips, regulars ceased chuntering – even Sal looked up.

Nellie held Sal's gaze, a hand reaching for the parcel she had offered. Slowly, the deaf woman removed the tissue to reveal an item of stunning craftsmanship. 'No sleep,' she mouthed. 'Made it.'

People nearest to Sal's table crowded round. It was a missal, black leather, its covers bound again in finest cream lace, a crucifix at the centre, Thomas's name beneath. The leather showed through the open pattern, a perfect contrast of these two natural and beautiful materials. Sal reached out and touched the book. 'Sweet Jesus,' she muttered. 'Oh my God, that is wonderful. You made that for me, Nellie?'

Nellie nodded. 'For you, for Thomas.'

Sal looked at his name and knew that it had been no nightmare. He was dead. Laughing Boy with his wide smile and blond curls had really gone and this was proof, his name across a missal. 'John!' she screamed.

And it was over, final, complete.

John collected his weeping wife and led her home to face what lay ahead. As he reached the door, he turned to Nellie Hulme. 'Thank you,' he said.

Drink flowed, regulars spoke with Catholic intruders, darts came out once the grieving family had left. Domino games began in the snug, everyone relaxed, pork pies were handed round.

Nellie smiled to herself, picked up her bag and left the pub. She grinned all the way home, because it had taken just two orphans to break down the barriers of religion. One had gone to his Maker, the other, well over seventy, still struggled to discover who she was. Yes, the lacework had been hard and hurried, but it had been well worth the time and effort.

She reached home, steeled herself against Spot's greeting, made tea, fed the pup, settled down in front of a newly lit fire. She had plans for the Higgins family, though the blueprints remained vague just yet. But she would do something – oh yes, she would. Lily Hardcastle was in the picture, too, but that was another uncertain area.

She settled back, feet warmed by the fire and by Spot's body. He plucked a lot of stockings, but that was a small price to pay for the comfort offered by the young dog. Oh, that rug was a lovely colour, such a rich red...

Red was not a good colour, no no. She was asleep, yet not asleep. Someone screamed. There was red everywhere, a great deal of red, wet red ... blood. Was she asleep? If not, why and how did she hear that noise, that ... that dying? Red, red, everywhere red. And the man turned and looked at her. The doorknob was so high, almost too high to reach. A small thing screaming. Louder, louder and the bigger scream and the rug was red – she should have bought green or blue or any colour but red...

Nellie's eyes opened so suddenly that she had to blink quickly. Five minutes, she had dozed. Five minutes, yet a lifetime. It was a nice rug, it was. But perhaps green would have been an even better colour...

Ernest remained the exception that proved the rule.

People from the mean streets hereabouts had neglected chores, had abandoned work, had ignored their religious divisions on this sad day. Oh, he had watched the damned fools as they had walked past his house, a grey-black sea of people off to church – to a Catholic church – to say farewell to the Grogan boy. The trouble with folk these days was that they had no principles, no sense of their own identity. It was easier in the old days – Catholics were rubbish and Orangemen were superior – so what had gone wrong?

'Do-bloody-gooders,' he muttered under his breath when he saw the grieving parents entering their house.

His hatred for the Higgins family had not abated. His intention remained to get up to Hesford and have it out with bloody Dot and bloody Frank. He wanted an explanation, would get one if it killed him and the rest of them, too. How had she dared to leave? She had walked out after years and years of work, his work, his striving to put food on the table and coal in the grate. Well, he would pay back the lot of them even if it took every last ounce of his strength.

He was walking better, was practising for several hours a week, could now get halfway up Prudence Street without losing balance or breath. Soon, Charlie Entwistle would take him up to Hesford to visit the household of his younger son and that beautiful bride.

He grinned, picked up his sticks and walked away from the window. He was doing very well. With her brood in hospital, Lily Hardcastle no longer helped, but Ernest had made an arrangement with a local grocer who delivered, while Charlie Entwistle had become a regular visitor. Yes, good old Charlie was not averse to carrying home a bag of fish and chips or a couple of chops from the market. To hell with Dorothy Barnes. Ernest was doing a grand job without her. But she would pay, by God, she would.

Magsy came back from the hospital with her step lightened considerably. She was filled with joy and hope, because her daughter was improving to the point where she was becoming difficult.

She stirred the fire, set the kettle to boil, sank into the rocking chair without pausing even to remove her outer clothing.

Beth had started to demand books, had delivered a diatribe on germs to a very young doctor who had waited for Magsy.

Laughing out loud, Magsy relived the scene.

'Excuse me?'

She turned in the corridor and looked at him, a small man with spectacles and earnest features. 'Yes?'

'Your daughter is an unusual girl.'

'I know.' She didn't bother with details, just stood and waited while he shuffled his feet. Like many men of his age, he became tongue-tied in the presence of Magsy O'Gara.

'Wants to be a doctor,' he managed after a pause of some seconds.

'Yes, she does.'

'I've seen you before,' was his next comment.

'I clean here.'

'Ah.' He rearranged his stethoscope and fixed a look of insouciance to his face. 'Very bright – extraordinary medical knowledge. Er ... Beth, I mean. In fact, I would go so far as to call her a prodigy.'

Magsy acknowledged that statement with a nod. 'At this point, I am more concerned with her medical condition than with her knowledge. Is she better?'

'Oh, yes. Very mild case, very strong constitution. She is a credit to you, Mrs ... er ... O'Gara.'

'She is a credit to regular cod liver oil and malt, doctor.'

'Erm ...'

Magsy was getting tired of the ers and the erms. 'When will she be home?'

'Soon.' He drew a hand through his hair, tried to make the best of a very thin show. 'Just a few more days, until we are sure that she is no longer infectious.'

Magsy felt like dancing up and down the green-floored corridor, but she damped the urge. 'Thank you,' she said.

He stepped closer. 'Where did she learn?'

Magsy lifted a shoulder. 'From books, of course.'

'Library books?'

'Among others, yet.'

His brow knitted thoughtfully. 'She should get the best, you know, should be educated properly.'

Magsy smiled at him. 'She will be. She will get into grammar school, and from there to medical college.'

'Catholic?' he asked.

'Why?' countered Magsy, an edge to the word.

He shrugged. 'Ah well, the good nuns. They don't exactly go mad on the sciences, you know. Science is not quite ladylike, so emphasis tends to be mostly on the arts. The best you could do would be Bolton School, somewhere non-denominational, or private. There is a school not too far from here – no boarders – where each child is treated as an individual. Very good teachers. They take on only gifted girls, then cater for each particular need.'

Magsy had never considered that aspect. She had done her best to prepare her daughter for a free place at the local Catholic grammar school, but had never really thought about Beth's needs. All she knew was that her daughter would want maths, English, ancient and modern languages, general science and a smattering of other subjects.

In the privacy of her own home, Magsy O'Gara now faced what the doctor had said, but she found no answer to the problem. Bolton School, the best for many a mile, was not the place for a Catholic girl. There were free places at this mainly fee-paying school, but Magsy was Catholic to the bone. 'You are prejudiced,' she informed herself out loud. 'All very well for you to invade a Protestant pub, but look at you now. Afraid of what the priests might say?'

The private school mentioned by the doctor was beyond consideration, was as out of reach as a full moon. That was a place for the daughters of businessmen, folk with real money and cars and whatnot. 'Bolton School,' she murmured. Perhaps Beth might get permission from the bishop to go there. Magsy could explain that Beth needed good science facilities ... But no. The clergy would not be amused by such a request. What, then?

A knocking at the door put a stop to Magsy's wonderings. She sped down the hall and allowed Rachel Higgins – now Barnes – to step into the house. 'Rachel. Come in – I have the kettle on.'

Rachel sat at the kitchen table. Grieved by the death of her adopted brother, she sat still for a while, waited until Magsy had poured two cups of tea. She sipped and swallowed, decided to get straight to the point. 'How's Beth?'

Magsy grinned. 'Up to no good, Rachel, driving the doctors out of their minds, telling them how to do their job.'

'Ah.' Rachel allowed herself a little smile. 'So she's on her way back to normal, then. She will be needing a lot of fresh air now that she's over the worst. So she's tormenting them?'

'She is, and God help them.' Magsy placed her cup in its saucer. 'I am so sorry about Thomas.'

'Yes.'

'That was a terrible blow.'

Rachel nodded as if attempting to clear unpalatable thoughts from her pretty head. She would have to get back to the shop soon, as she had left her mother-in-law to cope alone with the grocery side of the business. 'I met Katherine Moore,' she began, 'lives opposite the shop in a big house. She needs help.'

'Ah.' Magsy waited for more.

'She gave me this suit and I made it over.'

'It's lovely,' said Magsy.

Rachel launched into the tale of Miss Katherine, holding back none of the truth, yet emphasizing the fact that

Miss Moore's bark was worse than her bite. 'She's lonely,' Rachel concluded, 'and Phyllis is useless.'

Magsy pondered. 'And I would be living in a shed?'

'It isn't a shed – it's a summer house built around a big stone chimney. And the garden's nice and big, too.' Rachel omitted to mention the fact that the summer house seemed to have an occasional occupant – that would be dealt with now that the funeral was over. 'Come and meet her – you have nothing to lose.'

Magsy's brain shot into overdrive. 'The air's very fresh, then?' She looked at Rachel's skin, glowing with health in spite of her despondency.

'It would be the making of Beth, Magsy.'

With her mind still working furiously, Magsy thought about the future – a change of school for Beth, how would she get to Bolton when she passed for the grammar, was there a church? 'When does this woman want to see me?' she asked.

'Any time,' answered Rachel. 'Just call at the shop and I will take you across and introduce you.'

When Rachel had left, Magsy made a bit of toast and continued her ponderings while she chewed absently on the frugal meal. Her head was like a sponge that had soaked up too much water, full, saturated, no room for further expansion. She couldn't just up and leave, could she? She was due for promotion at the hospital, would be working in an area that might be termed medical, no more sweeping, mopping, polishing. Beth was happy at school, though she could afford to be better challenged – would a village school be an improvement, would it be Catholic, did Catholic matter?

But the fresh air, the chance for Beth to run free in the countryside, no mills, no smoke, little traffic. Oh, God, why was life so complicated?

As if to underline that question, a voice greeted her. 'Hello? Magsy?' It was Paul.

She set her plate on the fireguard. 'Come in,' she invited wearily. Yes, there was him, too, the eternal suitor, a man for whom she might even develop feelings if she wasn't careful.

He entered the room. 'Oh, I am sorry I missed the funeral,' he said.

Magsy shrugged. 'Tell Sal, not me. Sorry,' she added, realizing that her voice had been sharp.

'I have told her.' He lingered in the doorway, the now familiar smell of sand and cement wafting over to greet her. She tried a smile for size, rejected it because it did not fit her mood. 'Sit down, Paul.'

He sat. 'What is it?'

So she told him, outlined details of the job and the location, gave him her worries and misgivings, saw a trail of varying emotions tracking across his features. She saw fear, relief, concern and the usual affection in his eyes.

When she had finished, he processed the new information before replying. 'Think of Beth,' were his first words.

'I have. I am thinking of Beth.'

His knuckles tightened on the table. 'She needs the air, Magsy.'

It was then that Magsy realized that she was in real trouble. The man cared so much that he would allow his own wishes to be put aside for the sake of her daughter. Loving such a man would not be a difficult task. Oh dear.

'But schools?' she asked.

'Never mind schools,' he replied. 'Beth will get there somehow. You know I don't want you to leave, but we have to think about the greater good. Anyway, you could well go up there and decide you don't like Miss Moore. There is no decision to make, Magsy, because you can see only half the picture. Go and meet her – I'll borrow a van and run you up there on Sunday.' He grinned. 'After Mass, of course.'

'Of course.' She returned the smile. He already owned a small corner of her heart and was moving in on the rest of that territory. Why was he so ... so nice? 'You are good to us,' she told him.

He chuckled softly. 'I'm a good man, Magsy. My mother would try the patience of every saint. Sometimes, I could choke her. But I don't, because I am a good man.'

'Yes.'

His expression changed. 'Will you love me back one day, Magsy O'Gara? Will you?'

She made no reply, opting instead for a long look straight into his eyes. If he failed to read what her soul showed, then he was not the right man after all.

With his heart turning somersaults, Paul Horrocks did what he knew to be the right thing. He lifted cement-coated fists from the table, lifted the rest of himself from the chair. She was saying it, was allowing it to flood from those incredible eyes until it filled the space between herself and him. She had affection for him, was unafraid to show it.

He cleared a throat that seemed as stiff as the cement he had mixed only hours earlier. There were things to do – supper for Mam, some washing, the arrangement to borrow Pat Murphy's van at the weekend. And he would buy that second-hand motorbike advertised in the newspaper, because Hesford was a few miles out and he didn't need to be waiting for buses every time he wanted to visit this delightful, adorable woman.

'Go and look after your mam, Paul.'

'Right.'

She shook her head in pretended dismay. 'What am I going to do with you at all?'

He bit his lip, swivelled and left the danger area. He didn't know what she was going to do. Whatever, he could scarcely wait to find out.

Twelve

Rachel discovered quite by accident the identity of the intruder. She decided to sweep out the summer house, went across armed with broom and dusters, found herself in the presence of a man she recognized, a figure familiar all over Hesford and its spread-out environs. He was famous for his eccentricity, was renowned for being a contradiction in terms, for this was the educated tramp.

Startled by her sudden entrance, the man leapt to his feet, removing his ridiculous bowler hat as soon as he achieved a vertical position. He straightened his short spine, smiled and nodded in her direction.

Rachel, one hand to her throat, leaned on the broom for support. He was not dangerous, she told herself sharply. This man favoured widowed and spinster ladies, was gardener and odd-job man for Hesford and for other villages north of Bolton. All he ever wanted was a couple of shillings and a hot meal. When questioned about his place of residence, he always gave vague replies, mentioning a brother up on the moors, an out-of-the-way house with no address, a smallholding with a few hens and some vegetable plots.

'Why are you here?' she asked eventually.

'Shelter from the storm, ma'am,' came the answer in what Frank always called a gobful-of-plums voice.

'There is no storm,' she replied.

'Where there is humanity, there is always storm.' He placed his hat on a rickety card table. 'For a shilling and a hot meal, I shall clean this place for you.'

'For Miss Moore,' she corrected him rather sharply, noticing how his eyes narrowed at the mention of the woman who owned this property. 'She is going to let it to a housekeeper.'

'Then God help any such housekeeper,' he replied, 'for Miss Moore is not known for her generous nature.'

Rachel eyed him. 'Why are you here?' she repeated.

'I am sheltering from frost, Mrs Barnes. And I am doing no harm, surely? Perhaps my mode of existence would not suit everyone, but I am careful to occupy places that are not needed. When the housekeeper moves in, I shall remove the summer house from my itinerary.'

'Are you homeless?' she asked.

'My home is wherever my hat and cane rest,' was the smart answer.

Yes, his cane. He was famous for that, as well. It was a sturdy item, silver-topped and with a monogram engraved into its spherical handle. There was no doubt that the strange creature had received good schooling, and no-one could ever work out why a man of letters had chosen such a haphazard way of existence. 'So you have no brother on the moors?'

'That is correct.' Bright blue eyes twinkled in the weather-beaten face. 'I am a man of mystery.'

In Rachel's opinion, a man of mystery would be younger, taller, more of a Gregory Peck. This little fellow was not much bigger than James Cagney, slightly too plump for his moderate height, rather grizzled around a chin ill-served by blunt razors and a lack of hot water. She liked him and she couldn't quite work out why. Perhaps it was his cheek, the sheer gall of an older-than-middle-aged person who slept where he chose, worked when he liked and talked like someone educated at Eton.

He was almost laughing at her. 'Can't work me out, eh, Mrs Barnes?'

Rachel felt the colour rising to her cheeks. 'No, I cannot work you out, Mr Smythe.'

He tapped the side of his nose with a strangely clean index finger. 'Nor can I, I assure you. I could have been almost anything, you know. But being a nothing is something.'

'Is it?'

'Oh, yes. And, very soon, I shall be a nothing who has become a something.'

Rachel leaned her broom against the wall. 'How do you work that out? And be grateful that I am of Irish stock, Mr Smythe. A background like mine gives me a huge insight into the meaning of nonsense.' She nodded slowly. 'Yes, there is nonsense in my blood. Nonsense is my second language.'

'And you are extraordinarily fluent in it.'

'Of course.'

He smiled broadly. 'I am to be published,' he said. 'Very soon, the first Peter Smythe will be for sale in book shops. It is a tale of a travelling man, one who chooses not to be bound by the laws of society. I have studied humanity for many years, you see.'

She thought about that. Something told her that this man was no liar. It was easy to believe that he had written the story of his life and of all those who employed him.

'Miss Morgan typed it up for me,' he said, 'but was bound to secrecy. In return, I have cared for her garden free of charge for several years. Give and take, you see.'

'So, you will buy a house with the proceeds?'

Peter Smythe threw back his head and laughed. 'Goodness, no,' he announced merrily. 'Why would I need a house? Who wants that kind of responsibility? No, I shall carry on much the same, shall be living as I do now, within reach of all that is rightfully mine.'

She raised a quizzical brow.

'The world belongs to all of us,' he explained.

Rachel picked up the brush and thrust it at him. 'Right, Mr Author. Clean this place and, in return, I shall bring you food and money. I suppose you would call that a fair trade?'

'Indeed.' He bowed stiffly and took the implement from her. 'You are a free spirit,' he informed her.

Rachel walked to the door, turned. 'Tell my customers that,' she advised, 'since I seem to be on call twelve hours a day.'

He pointed to the grimy window. 'Out there is all yours, yours for the taking. But you have chosen bricks, mortar and safety, predictability and boredom.'

'Security,' she insisted.

He bowed again. 'As you wish.'

Rachel went outside and wondered whether she ought to tell Katherine about her non-paying guest, but he was harmless enough, a crank who had written a book, a tramp who valued the open road and the ability to sleep when he liked, where he liked. No, upsetting Katherine would be pointless.

In a few days, Magsy O'Gara would come to be interviewed about the housekeeping position. Rachel laughed aloud. She could not imagine Magsy being interviewed by anyone. It promised to be fun, because both Katherine and Magsy were proud and stubborn women.

Ernest groaned loudly. Climbing into Charlie Entwistle's truck had not been easy – in fact, without the help of the rag-and-bone man, Ernest would never have made it.

Charlie jumped into the driver's seat. 'All right? Ready to face the missus?'

'Aye,' answered Ernest, still breathless after his exertions.

Charlie, a man of few words, was bemused by this situation. It was nothing to do with him, but he could not understand his neighbour's desire to see Dot again. It had become plain over the years that the man had disliked his wife. Even Charlie, who spent most of his time out of the house, had heard enough of the violence. Still, he had promised to do the favour, and he was a man of honour. 'Ready for off, then, Ernest?'

'Yes.'

Charlie started the engine and pulled away. The truck needed a good run, so this was as good a way as any of burning the dust out of the system.

They left the town behind and began to climb Tonge Moor, the road that led north to several villages. Even here, on a road that was densely populated, Ernest noticed that the air smelt different, was cleaner and fresher. Oh yes, Dot had fallen on her feet, it seemed. So had that bloody Higgins girl with all her airs and graces. He still seethed inwardly when he thought about a son of his turning Catholic, all that bowing and scraping to plaster statues and holy pictures, fingers dipped in so-called holy water, Signs of the Cross, Stations of the Cross and enough saints' days to fill a calendar twenty times over. Well, Ernest would have his say at last.

Hesford was beautiful – even the jaundiced eye of Ernest Barnes noticed the quaintness of the village. His blood boiled when he thought of Dot enjoying these views of the moors, the openness of it all, that crystal sky, all this invigorating air.

Charlie helped him out of the cabin. When he had

righted himself, Ernest stared hard at the shop, a double-fronted affair with the word BARNES printed over the door, still fresh and new-looking. One window announced GROCERIES, the other HARDWARE. It looked like a thriving business. Oh yes, they were thriving, all right, while he lived on a measly bit of pension and interest on pathetic savings scraped together throughout years of self-denial. He had fed and clothed them all, he had put bread and meat on the table, so it was time for them to look after him.

Charlie Entwistle, who seldom took much notice of folk, marked the expression on his neighbour's face. Uneasy, he stepped forward. 'Do you want me to help you into the shop?'

'No,' came the barked response. 'I do this on my own.'

He straightened, made sure that his cap was on right, then walked into the doorway. A woman with a basket stood back to allow him in, holding the door for a man she probably saw as a poor old cripple. Well, if everybody had their own, this shop was his by right, because he had raised the man who owned it in the legal sense.

The shop was empty. He parked himself on the customers' chair and waited. The bell that had announced his entrance had also proclaimed the exit of the woman with the basket, so the shop's staff were probably in the back of the house, unaware of their very special patron.

He gazed around well-stocked shelves, saw little notices on items that were still rationed, breathed in the smell of earth clinging to locally grown winter vegetables. The place was a gold mine.

At the other side, ironmongery was stacked in boxes, nails, screws, putty, hammers and chisels. There were buckets, clothes horses, scrubbing boards, possers, brushes, dusters, lamps, kettles, pots and pans. Although

Hesford was not a huge place, this shop probably provided for residents of several other villages, so it would prosper, no doubt.

The inner door opened and Dot stepped into the shop, a large box of apples in her arms. She walked round the counter to place this on the floor with other produce kept on the customers' side, bent, stacked the box, then turned to face the customer. 'Hell—' The rest of the greeting froze in her throat.

'Hell's about right,' snapped Ernest. 'Hell's living on your own while your family pikes off to new pastures.'

She backed away into the gap, slamming down the hinged barrier that separated staff from customers. 'What do you want?' she asked, her tone shrill.

'I only want what's mine.'

She breathed hard against the need to vomit. 'There's nowt of yours here.'

'Oh aye? How do you work that out?'

Dot inhaled again. 'Our Frank saved for this. He did without for years until he got the down-payment and a mortgage.'

'And who kept him while he saved?'

'He kept himself.'

'Right. And who kept him till he could afford to rent that room? I did. I bloody kept him – and I kept you – and the other one.'

She gripped the edge of the counter, tried to hold on to her sanity at the same time. Was nowhere safe? Would she never escape completely? 'That's the way it works,' she told him. 'We look after our kids, then they grow up and look after their own kids.'

'And you. They look after you.' His eyes narrowed. She looked a damned sight better than she had in Prudence Street, was clearly doing well out of this arrangement.

'That's your fault,' she said quietly. 'They had to bring me away from you, because they knew that you would kill me in the end.'

'Rubbish,' he roared.

The noise brought Rachel into the shop. She stood for a few seconds in the doorway, then leapt forward, placing herself between Dot and the seated man. There was a counter separating them, but the man was armed with his sticks. 'Get out of my shop,' she ordered clearly.

'You what?' He rose to unsteady feet and raised a stick. 'Your shop? Your bloody shop, you bloody whore?'

'That's a lot of bloodies.' Rachel knew that her tone was annoyingly cool. 'I am not a whore, Mr Barnes.'

'Where's my son?' he demanded. 'I want nowt to do with women. Let's have a bit of sense spoken – fetch Frank.'

Rachel allowed her eyes to travel down to Ernest Barnes's waist, then up again until they met that wild, ugly face. 'My husband is out at the moment. He should be back in about half an hour, but he will not welcome you. In fact, he will bundle you out in two shakes.'

'Your husband.' These two words were hissed between narrowed lips. 'You fooled him into marriage, seduced him.'

Rachel nodded calmly. 'You should see a head-doctor, Mr Barnes. There's a new department at the hospital for people with mental illnesses.'

He snapped. In an instant, one of his sticks made hard contact with Rachel's cheek and she fell sideways, arms flailing in a vain attempt to save herself. Tinned fruit and Nestle's Cream toppled down, a dozen or so tins unseated by Rachel's arms.

Dot tried to catch Rachel, failed, saw her crumpled in a heap on the floor. And it simply happened. Where fear had lodged, a bubble of fury rose in the chest of that thin, meek woman. She strode around the corner, lifted the mahogany flap, dragged the stick from his trembling hands.

She beat him repeatedly, mercilessly, forced him to the ground where he crawled like a dog towards the door. Again and again she brought the stick down on his back, her breathing even, her aim true and straight. With a strength that denied and defied her size, she forced him to the door just as it opened.

'Oh, God.' Charlie Entwistle had crashed the door into his neighbour's head.

Dot fixed her gaze on Charlie. 'This pile of rubbish you fetched up here from the slums – stick it back on your cart,' she ordered evenly. 'No point weighing it in, 'cos I can tell you now it's worth nowt a pound.' She allowed herself a slow breath. 'Now, listen to me, Charlie Entwistle. If you bring that load of shite anywhere near my shop again, I shall sue you. You knew what he wanted, you knew why he was here—'

'I didn't—'

'Then you're dafter than them horses that used to pull your carts. How many years did you hear him beating me and my lads? Eh? And shut your gob, there's a number nine trolley bus coming.'

Charlie gulped. The biggest shock had arrived not with Dot's turning on her husband, but with her language. Shite? He had never heard that from a woman's mouth before. His gaze wandered to the back of the shop. Rachel Higgins-as-was had struggled to her feet. Blood poured from a split lip.

On the floor, Ernest groaned. 'I'll get you for that, you bitch,' he managed.

Dot's lip curled. 'Oh aye? You and whose army, you stupid owld cripple? Now get gone before I fetch a constable.'

When Charlie had removed her husband, Dot threw the sticks into the street. She closed the door and leaned her head against cool glass for a second or two. Her whole body shook, while the urge to vomit was almost overwhelming.

'Dot?' Rachel could not believe what she had just seen and heard. 'Dot?'

'You all right, love?'

'I think so. I'll just go and fetch the first aid.'

Alone in the shop, Dot staggered to the chair and sat down. Every ounce of that fury-stoked energy had drained from her body. As the adrenalin left her blood, she began to shake uncontrollably. But her mind remained unnaturally cool.

She heard Charlie Entwistle's engine starting, listened while gears meshed and the nightmare visitor was pulled away from the shop. He had found his way here, would always find his way to wherever she was. And what would Frank do when he found out, when he saw the marked face of his beautiful wife?

Rachel would deal with that, would stop Frank doing anything rash. But what about next time? Could they live like this, waiting for him to come again? No, they could not and would not.

Dorothy Barnes dragged herself up, was grateful for the lack of customers. She went to a mirror that advertised Monk's Custard, flattened her hair, prepared herself to go and tend her daughter-in-law's wounds.

And the decision made itself as she stared at her own face in that little glass. Like the man from the council who cleared rats from slums, she knew what her next task would be.

Dorothy Barnes was going to kill her husband.

*

Magsy, dressed neatly in a charcoal grey coat and matching hat, waited for the arrival of Paul Horrocks. She was nervous, yet she could not work out why. Yes, she could. There would be a decision to make, and life was hard enough without having to implement great changes. No, she didn't have to travel in a new direction – nobody could force her to alter her course through life. They could stop here in Prudence Street. Once Beth got out of hospital, they could both step back into the old routine, Beth at school, Magsy at work. There was promotion coming up, another sixpence an hour, a respectable job assisting nurses. But . . .

There it came again. But. But was a word that altered many a life. The But was Beth. Bolton was not the healthiest of places – the death of the wee mite next door had illustrated that fact well enough. Mill chimneys poured their smoke from morning till night, many factories now doing evening shifts right up to nine-thirty or ten o'clock. When the sun could be bothered to shine, it gave forth a brownish-purplish light, its rays refracted through layers of soot and grime. Whereas up on the moors . . .

She pulled herself up, tried to stop thinking at this point, because she knew nothing about up on the moors. As Paul had said, without knowledge, a person was powerless, unfit to decide. Paul. He was another factor . . .

Magsy sat down, sat on her thoughts. If only her mind would be still for a while, she might just be able to get on with life. The New Year had seen itself in, bells had proclaimed a fresh start, Beth was due home any day now. 'Let the year decide for me,' she told her handbag, 'because I am too tired for it.'

Paul let himself in, hands cupped as he blew warm air into them.

'You should wear gloves,' she chided gently.

'Can't drive in 'em. Are you fit?'

She remained where she was while a small thought grew. Yes, she could do it. Slowly, she stood up and walked to the Utility sideboard, opened a drawer, pulled out a cardboard box. 'Here,' she said, 'take these.'

He opened it, gasped in amazement.

'William was a chauffeur for a while. The owner of a mill bought him those. They don't slip on a steering wheel.'

He stared down into the opened box, breathed in the moment and the scent of leather. This was a big thing, an enormous thing. 'Are you sure?'

She nodded.

He pulled string-backed kid gloves onto his hands. This was more than just a gift; this marked the beginning of Magsy's letting go of her dead William. He tried to minimize the intensity of this second by smiling broadly at her, but the wetness in her eyes told all. Yes, she was saying goodbye – not to him, not yet, but to a man she had adored. 'Shall we go?' he asked.

'Drive on, Rupert,' she replied.

'Rupert?'

'In a library book.' She sniffed back a tear. 'The chauffeur was Rupert.'

'Bit posh for a servant,' he offered.

'Yes, I thought so, too. A Rupert would never learn his place, would he?'

Would Magsy? wondered Paul as they went out to the van. He could not imagine her bowing and scraping to the gentry, doing exactly as she was told. 'I've bought a motorbike,' he told her as they pulled out of the street. 'So I can visit you up yon.'

Magsy squashed a grin. Even if she had emigrated, he would have visited her, would have found his way to the other side of the world. And that didn't annoy her any more. In fact, she felt rather pleased to be in receipt of such affection.

Oh, well. Time to face the dragon, the future, the decisions. 'Why buy a bike now?' she asked. 'I haven't gone yet.'

'But you will,' he forecast. 'I'd bet me new gloves on it.'

She looked at William's gloves and smiled faintly. Something told her that William would have liked this man, would have wanted him to have his things. 'Like I said before, drive on, Rupert.'

Rupert did as he was ordered.

Katherine, too, was nervous. Dressed in her best housecoat, she half-sat, half-lay on the chaise, hands plucking at an open-weave blanket, mind darting about like an aimless butterfly. That girl had been and gone, had delivered very limp toast and a runny egg for breakfast. Lunch would be brought by Rachel, that fine young woman who had now become Katherine's only friend.

And what a mess that man had made of Rachel's face. If only Katherine had her health and strength, she would have visited him. Rachel had refused the offer of a lawyer, had told Katherine about Dot's actions. It was probably time to meet Dot, too, because that meek little woman had found the strength to deal with the bully. Oh, well, there was today's encounter to be dealt with first.

When Rachel led Magsy O'Gara into the bedroom, Katherine was almost dumbfounded. They were like positive and negative, two beautiful women, one dark, the other fair. Bolton was a dirty industrial town, yet neither of these people had suffered by living in it, perfect skin, bright eyes, shining hair.

Rachel introduced the two, then went down to make tea.

Katherine eyed the visitor. 'So, what do you think of Hesford?'

Magsy, too, was nearly tongue-tied. 'Lovely,' she managed eventually.

Katherine pointed to a chair, waited until Magsy had seated herself. 'I am not easy,' she began.

Magsy produced an absent nod.

'I am not liked.'

'Rachel likes you.'

'She is unusual.'

'So am I.'

'Yes, I have been told that. Rachel sings your praises very loudly and very often. You live next door to her family, I understand.'

'Yes.'

'So. Tell me about yourself.'

Magsy squirmed in her seat, put herself in mind of a child dragged before the headmistress for some misdemeanour. 'I am Irish, a widow, have one child and I work at the infirmary.'

'Which information tells me nothing.'

The visitor did not know what else to say. She was not in the habit of granting confidences to a total stranger. 'I can cook, clean, wash and iron. My cooking is plain, but nourishing. I am strong enough to carry you to and from the bath and I would have you living downstairs if at all possible. You should look directly at life, not from as great a height as this.'

Katherine pondered the final comment. Was this woman criticizing her attitude? Was she accusing her of looking down on the world in more ways than one? 'There is no bathroom downstairs,' she replied at last.

'Then get one put in.'

Katherine tried not to smile. It was almost as if this young woman knew that shares had picked up, that Katherine's broker had made quite a profit on investments. 'When can you start?'

This question caused Magsy's back to become ramrod-straight. 'Er . . . there is much to consider.'

'Is she out of hospital?'

'Soon.' Right away, this woman had found the hub of the matter. Well, at least she understood the priorities, then. 'She is my life,' Magsy said quietly.

'And she is brilliant, or so I am led to believe.'

'Yes. Yes, she is.'

Katherine nodded. 'Bring her to see me. Now, I ask you to leave me alone for an hour, as there is an idea I must think about. Go and look at the countryside – that young man will take you, I am sure.' She inclined her head towards the window. 'Are you going to marry him?'

Flabbergasted, Magsy froze at half-mast, her body rising from her seat. 'No,' she spluttered.

'Well, we shall face that when it comes,' Katherine said, almost to herself but not quite under her breath.

On the landing, Magsy all but shook herself. This was unreal, a dream, a nightmare, a terrible confusion. The village was wonderful, the harridan seemed sensitive up to a point, there was Rachel in the shop just across the way. But schools, churches? When could she start? She didn't know whether she was coming or going.

Rachel smiled from the bottom of the stairs. 'She got you all mizzled, has she?'

'Yes.'

'Then she likes you. If she hadn't liked you, she would have thrown you out in under ten seconds.'

'What a comfort.' There was sarcasm in Magsy's words. Sometimes, it was best not to be liked.

The summer house was lovely, even in winter. Rachel had lit a roaring fire and was plainly keen to influence Magsy in favour of taking the job. 'It's lovely,' she bubbled, the words emerging from a scabbed lip. 'There's fields and hills and lovely people—'

'He wants killing,' stated Magsy baldly.

'Who?'

'Your father-in-law.'

'Oh, him. Well, Frank would have done the killing, but I managed to hold him back. And that Paul Horrocks – he is head over heels with you, Magsy. He could live here too, and—'

'One bedroom.'

'Ah.' Temporarily deflated, Rachel soon recovered. 'You could rent a cottage with what he earns—'

'There's his mother—'

'And you could all live up here. Magsy, you'll be paid eight pounds a week with all found – free coal, free food, no rent. You could build another bedroom on...' She stopped, saw the confusion in her friend's face. 'Sorry, Mags. I know you have a lot to think about with Beth and all.'

Magsy allowed a tight smile. 'And I'd be grateful if you would stop marrying me off, Rachel. Yes, I like Paul, but there's nothing settled or sorted, so stop carrying on about him. This is all a very big thing.'

'Sorry.'

Magsy turned to the window and looked out. The moors, blue-green in the frost, drifted skyward towards Yorkshire. Here and there, farmhouses and outbuildings had settled into folds, looked as if they had been born there.

And, in that moment, Magsy O'Gara knew that she was home.

Thirteen

Nellie Hulme was getting scared, but she didn't fully understand why.

It was the dreams, of course, but she wasn't getting any nearer to the source of the redness. It was wet, was probably blood, yet she could not quite home in on it. So why was she frightened? Was the answer going to be murder?

In the dream, she was walking, but small. Everything went on above her head and she reached a lot for door handles, for a doll on a table, to peer over the lip of a horse trough. Grass was high – was it grass, or was it a crop of some kind? Barley? The house had a balustrade around it, stone pillars that were fatter in the middle than at the tops and bases. She often stood and peered through at a long garden with rose beds and patches of lawn.

There was a yard, cobbled. Sometimes, she slipped because the cobbles were wet. At other times, they were baked by the sun, so she did not dream the same day every time. These dreams were a diary of unremembered time, a period from long ago that had quit her conscious mind, yet the pictures remained seared into her subconscious. She had no control. Asleep, she was a victim of this circular, endless and seemingly pointless drama, a play with no conclusion, no real form, no plot.

She stabbed brass pins into the cushion, made another

stitch, stabbed again. This set of antimacassars would go to Chatsworth, to the Devonshires. Somewhere, she had a photo of Chatsworth, very grand, it was, a beautiful place owned by beautiful people who paid her well and who always took time to write letters of thanks.

A balustrade. Places like Chatsworth had balustrades and stables and a fountain. Now, where had that fountain come from? She wasn't asleep, wasn't dreaming, yet that fountain had just spurted all over her dress ... yellow dress ... black, shiny boots, tight-buttoned, small feet. Her heart quickened and she drew a series of short, panicky breaths.

Lace-making abandoned, Nellie leaned back in her work chair. She could sense Spot snuffling outside the door – he was not allowed in the lace room. There was a proper bedroom now, the one across the landing, as Nellie had not wanted to ruin her new front room furniture by sleeping on it. Spot used the bedroom, too, often curled up in a box on the floor, occasionally under the bed-clothes on her feet, a breathing, furry hot water bottle.

A doll's house. She dropped the pair of idle bobbins, left them swinging from the cushion in her lap. Yes, a doll's house in a corner, dark, not clear. Bruin? Where had that come from? A bear, dark brown, one eye loose? It was coming, it was coming and she was not ready for it. Yes, she was, because she had to be.

But there was no more and she could not force it.

She went downstairs, Spot leading the way with his tail on double time, head down as he concentrated on his balance. There was just one cupboard untouched, the one filled with Mam's knitting and sewing patterns, the final bastion of Nellie's history in this little house. Mam had been a good woman, had knitted and sewn all Nellie's clothes, had taught her to read, write and count, had given her the ability to read lips, to crochet, to knit.

She put the dog in the yard, set the kettle to boil, opened Mam's cupboard to the right of the kitchen chimney breast. It was packed to the top with all kinds of stuff. Mam's final piece of knitting was still there, musty and faded now, a green cardigan she had been making for herself. Sad, Nellie closed the doors. Why hadn't her parents told her who she really was? And why was it suddenly so important? What was she going to do with a house that had balustrades, stables, a fountain?

For today, she had had enough remembering. Time to cook, time to walk the dog, time to stop worrying. Until next time.

Sal recovered remarkably well after the death of her adopted son, taking each step carefully, minding her health, eating fruit and vegetables, always aware of the child she carried inside her belly. But her mind was taken off her own condition when she noticed the state of Ernest Barnes. With a bandaged head and legs stiffer than ever, he was walking like a man near death. She watched him as he bent to pick up his bottle of milk, saw agony in the shape of his body – he must have taken a fall.

Poor Lily Hardcastle had given up on Ernest. She did her cleaning job, then went to the hospital twice a day, once for the afternoon visiting session, again in the evening. Her family remained in poor shape, the youngest lad with some sort of brain fever, one with pleurisy, another with pneumonia, her husband suffering from an unsuspected heart condition that had shown up with the flu.

So Ernest Barnes had been left to his own devices, his sole visitors the delivery boy from the grocery, then Charlie Entwistle. The latter was such a slave to his business that he was available infrequently, so Sal decided to take the bull by the horns. It was the neighbourly thing to do. Magsy next door had been involved in some argument with Ernest at Christmas, and now Sal remained the last possibility.

She lifted a small pan of home-made soup and walked across the street. It was time to bury the hatchet, because this man was alone and ill. Without bothering to disturb him by knocking, she pushed the front door open. 'Mr Barnes?' When no answer came, she made her way along the dark and narrow hall until she reached the kitchen.

He was sitting by the fire, a bandage slipping down over one eye, the other eye almost glowing as it lit upon the visitor. 'What do you want?' he snapped.

Sal Higgins placed her soup on the table.

'I asked you what do you want.'

'I brought you some soup. And I could sort out your bandage.'

He grunted, pushed himself further back in his seat so that he would look taller, more substantial. 'I want nothing off you,' he told her, 'nothing from you and your sort.' Charlie did the bandage. Charlie was no expert when it came to first aid, but he was, at least, an Englishman.

'My sort?'

'Catholics.' The word was spat, as if it had tasted bad while being manufactured. 'Especially bloody Micks.'

She leaned against the dresser. 'Isn't it time all this foolishness came to an end?' she asked. 'We buried our boy just days ago. The Prince William was full of Catholics – my husband chose that pub on purpose, just to make the point.'

The one eye continued to glare at her. 'What point?'

'That we are all the same.'

He laughed mirthlessly. 'The same? Are we hell as like the same. Ask the bloody Black and Tans about Dublin and the bother they had with your lot. Ask all them who've been victims of the IRA. They'll tell you we're not the same. There's half of you can't even bloody read and write when you get here – you should stop over there with all the other stupid bastards.'

Sal tutted under her breath. 'Saints preserve us – we are in a bad mood today, aren't we?'

He wanted to hit her. Had his strength not been removed by his own so-called wife, he would have chased this Irish sloven from his house. She needed a damned good wash for a start – and her hair hadn't seen a comb today. 'Oh, get back over the street and carry on breeding – that's all you're good for, bloody brood mare.'

She shook her head slowly. 'I pity you,' she told him, 'because you are a blind fool. My husband saved your life–'

'Well, he needn't have bothered.'

Sal smiled grimly. 'At least we agree on one point, Mr Barnes, because your life is not worth John's trouble. You are a nasty, mean and spiteful man. We know that you scarred both your boys and that your wife is safe now only because of your son and my daughter.'

'Aye, well, I sorted her out,' he replied.

'Dot is beyond your reach,' insisted Sal.

'I'm not talking about Dot,' he shouted. 'I'm talking about that flaming girl of yours – she's the one I sorted out. Giving me cheek, telling me I wasn't allowed in my own son's shop – I marked her card for her. And her face. So put that in your pipe, missus. And get out of my house – now!'

Sal blinked a few times. 'So you have been to Hesford?'

'I have.'

'And you struck my daughter?'

'I did.'

She played with the idea of tipping the soup over his

head, decided against it. This was good food and her girls would enjoy it. Instead, she simply stared at him, her eyes never leaving his face during what felt like an eternity. It was a childish game, but she was determined to stare him out.

In the end, he lost the fight, because his one good eye became tired.

'So who did that to you?' she asked.

'Never you mind,' he answered darkly.

Sal picked up her pan. 'One day, you are going to wake up dead, Mr Barnes. So many people hate you that you will be killed sooner or later. Do not for one moment imagine that you will be missed. In fact, the funeral will be attended just by yourself and whoever digs the hole.' She was trembling now, because behaviour such as this was not in her nature.

'Oh, bugger off,' he said quietly.

Sal looked up at the ceiling, then back at him. 'I never noticed until today just how ugly you are. Yes, to be sure, you have a most unfortunate appearance. Well, this is New Year, a time for a fresh start, for goodwill and kind wishes. So, I wish you all the worst, Mr Barnes. You have hit a child of mine and God will repay you. Before this year is out, you will be dead.'

He shivered. Was this another Irish gyppo, the sort that sold pegs door to door, tell your fortune for a shilling? But the cold clung to his spine, even as he shouted, 'Rubbish,' at her disappearing back.

The front door slammed.

He tried to stand up, but the pain in his back was too intense. He should see a doctor, though how could he own up, how could he admit that he had been reduced to this by a woman the size of two penn'orth of chips? Oh, yes, he could see it now – the flaming doctor doubled up laughing because Dot had given him a hiding.

Yes, he had been hard on his lads, because he hadn't wanted them growing up like a pair of nancy boys, two big girls softened by a mam who knew nowt about what it took to make a real man. Well, a bloody good thrashing never did anybody any harm, did it?

He thought about that, realized that the belting he had received from Dot had done harm. But that was different – she had taken advantage while he had been on the floor. She hadn't knocked him down, not really ... Yes, she had ...

How long would it take him to recover? And would Charlie Entwistle run him up to Hesford again? And if Charlie wouldn't take him, who would? God, his back was sore.

He managed to stand, then staggered about, toasted some stale bread at the fire, spread it with butter and cheap plum jam. Dot would have the best jam, of course, a nice jar of strawberry or Golliberry, all thick and dripping off the edge of the slice. Tinned peaches, plums, apples fresh from the orchard, boiled ham, back bacon, spuds straight out of the ground. He hoped she would choke on it, that they would all choke.

When his pint mug was drained of tea, he settled back to sleep, arranging cushions to support his aching spine. Now, he could dream. And his dreams were of revenge.

Magsy poured a second cup for Sal. 'You shouldn't have gone. He tried to grab me on Christmas Eve.'

'And you should have told me. I knew you'd had a row, didn't realize he had made a play for you. And why didn't you tell me about what he did to Rachel?'

Magsy sighed and lowered herself into the chair opposite her visitor's. She was pleased about Sal's pregnancy, though she wondered whether another girl might make matters worse, since it was clear that the good woman expected a replacement for Thomas, a healthy boy, one who would thrive. 'Rachel said you had been through enough with – well – enough just lately. She made me promise. And she will not be left with a scar, I'm sure about that – though God knows Ernest Barnes would have marked her if he could.'

'I should hope she won't have a scar, indeed.' Sal polished off a slice of Magsy's delicious apple pie. With that alacrity of mind for which she was famous, she launched into a different subject. 'So, what are you going to do?'

Magsy raised a shoulder. 'I don't know. I went back after an hour – just as she had ordered – but Miss Moore muttered something about holidays and not being able to contact people – I am to go again soon with Beth. She insists on meeting Beth.' Magsy's feelings went from soaring hope to deepest gloom whenever she considered the size of the decision she was required to make. It was like being on a ride at the fair – up, down, round the bend. If only she could turn off her own mechanism for a day or two.

'Understandable. She would want to make sure that your daughter's no tearaway, so. But Magsy, how do you feel in yourself about the whole thing?'

How did she feel? Oh, God, she wanted so badly to live in that pretty village, even in that hut of a place that was called a summer house. Yes, she was filled with ideas of gingham curtains, summer evenings, lamplit winters, bread baked in the fireside oven, walks, Beth running free in that clear air, Tinker frolicking by her side—

'Magsy?'

'I don't know.' She glanced down at Tinker, the little

dog who continued to pine for his young mistress. 'There's the question of schools and church and the bus service to Bolton.'

'And the question of your daughter's health. Rachel goes to church – just a little place, but a church all the same. Priorities, Magsy. Getting Beth well has to be top of the list. And Rachel says the money's good and all found, nothing to pay out. Think of the books you could buy for young Beth.'

Magsy made no reply. Miss Katherine Moore was up to something, had been making telephone calls during that hour when Magsy had toured the house and the garden. What, though? And was she going to be a good employer? How would Beth feel about a move? Would she do as well in a village school and was there a Catholic school and … she gulped. Did Catholic matter? She had heard that question before, probably inside her own head.

'So, you're to go for Beth tomorrow.'

'Yes.'

'They'll be glad to see the back of her.'

'Yes.'

Sal rose to her feet, chair scraping loudly as she pushed it backwards. 'Sure, I might as well try to have a conversation with the fire-back. You complain about your daughter being vague, but I can see where she got it.'

'Sorry, Sal.'

Sal reached out and touched her friend's shoulder. 'Away with you, for I shall miss you something desperate, yet I want you to go. It's for the best – ah, you'll be grand.'

'Will I?'

'You both will, and–'

The front door slammed inward, its handle making sharp contact with the wall. The two women froze, waiting for God alone knew what, yet no further movement was detected.

'Who's there?' shouted Magsy.

'Only me,' came the quiet reply.

'Come in,' called Magsy.

A bedraggled Lily Hardcastle walked into the kitchen, hair all over the place, coat unfastened, face bloated with weeping.

'Sweet Jesus,' murmured Sal.

'I didn't know where to go,' said Lily. 'The house is so empty.'

Magsy guided the new arrival to the best rocker in front of the fire. The woman's hands were like blocks of ice, the coldest Magsy had ever encountered. She rubbed life into fingers so white that they were taking on a tinge of blue. 'Where on earth are your gloves, Lily?'

'Eh?' The eyes focused on Magsy.

'Your gloves? And your scarf?'

'I don't know.' Lily inhaled a few times. 'See, I would keep on dreaming – butterflies and birds – things I wanted for me. And I carried on about nose-picking and smelly feet – as if I'm perfect, like. God didn't hear me, but the devil did.'

Glances passed between Sal and Magsy, the former remaining with Lily, the latter picking up the teapot to pour a cup for this very distraught and chilly woman. But Lily was too far gone to hold the cup, dashing it away when Magsy guided it to her lips. 'It's my fault.'

Magsy stood up. She and Sal could only watch while their neighbour rocked back and forth, repeating the words that proclaimed belief in her own guilt. For several minutes this behaviour continued, that dry, hoarse voice making the statement, 'It's my fault.'

Magsy turned to Sal. 'Someone died, I think,' she mouthed.

'What shall we do?'

The younger woman thought about doctors, about

Lily's sister who lived just streets away, rejected those ideas. For the rest of her life, Magsy would wonder how she had known the answer; she even played with the concept of a minor miracle. Whatever the reason, whatever its source, none of that mattered in this vital moment. 'Get Nellie,' she said.

'Nellie?'

Magsy nodded. 'She understands ... things.'

Sal pondered for a few seconds, then went across the street to disturb Spot, that little dog who had become the ears of Miss Nellie Hulme. For the life of her, Sal would wonder at Magsy's decision to nominate Nellie as the one who would put things right.

Magsy waited at the table, her eyes riveted to Lily. Tinker tried bouncing up and down, licking Lily's hands, but the mantra continued, that same statement repeated over and over.

Nellie arrived, her loud breathing audible long before she entered the room. Sal, who had a meal to prepare, went next door, leaving behind the message that she would return if summoned by a knock on the wall.

Magsy wrote on a piece of paper, *We think someone has died, but we cannot get sense out of Lily.*

Nellie read the words, then took the nearest dining chair and parked herself next to Lily. She sat for several moments, eyes straining to get the drift of her neighbour's words.

Magsy scribbled *It's all my fault,* passed it to Nellie.

The deaf woman placed a hand on Lily's shoulder, made eye contact with the grieving woman, her other hand coming up to cup Lily's chin. Chanting and rocking stopped.

Magsy stepped out of the picture, stood near the sideboard and waited, aware, after a few seconds, that she had been holding her breath. Why? Both these women were deaf now, one clinically, the other shutting out all sound in a world that had suddenly become unacceptable.

It all came out then, every syllable enunciated clearly. Sam had suffered a heart attack, had died in the night. So here she sat, poor Lily Hardcastle, three sons sick and her husband dead. Magsy took a handkerchief from the pocket of her apron and mopped her streaming eyes. So this was it. This was what happened to people who lived in dirty towns where the air was filled with smoke and grime. How lucky she had been, because Beth had survived.

People were still going down with this new plague; the isolation unit was filled to capacity and there was talk of closing the hospital to all except urgent cases. Those awaiting surgery would wait longer, their wards taken up by the victims of Asian flu. Doctors, nurses and cleaners were ill, the service was stretched almost to its limits . . .

Lily continued to talk, her voice cleared now by the need to communicate with the deaf. Yes, Nellie had been the answer. And Beth's future lay in the countryside. Sal had been right – survival first, education lower down the list. The decision had made itself.

Dot was clearing out the yard in preparation for a good swill with hot water and Lanry. The thing about a food shop was that cleanliness was vital, so the yard got bleached every other day. It was cold, so cold that she shivered as she opened the back gate. And there he was, that funny little man with his stubbly chin, daft bowler hat, scruffy bow tie at his throat, an over-large overcoat hanging from his shoulders. No, she would not laugh. He had twinkly eyes and a lovely smile – and he was well respected hereabouts.

'Mrs Barnes.' He removed his hat as if it had been the feathered variety favoured by cavaliers.

'Hello, Mr Smythe. Cold enough for you?'

'I don't mind the cold,' he replied, 'so allow me to clean that yard for you. All I ask is a meal.'

She rewarded him with a smile. The cleaning of the yard was the worst job, one she had volunteered for. She was grateful to Frank and Rachel, and this was her way of showing that gratitude. 'Fair enough,' she replied cheerfully. 'Will sausage and mash do you? And I've a bit of apple crumble left over from last night.'

'Nectar.' He took the rubbish from her hand and stacked it in the alley.

Dot wrapped her thick cardigan tightly around her slight frame. This was an easterly wind – how did the man survive in this weather? 'Did you have shelter last night, Mr Smythe?'

He nodded. 'Miss Morgan has given me a small caravan on her land. I am too old now to take my chances with the weather, so that very kind lady gives me a roof and a supper each night. I am blessed in my friends.'

He meant it. Here was a man of education, one who had spent his life on the road, a spirit unencumbered, a person who found no task too menial, one who worked hard for his crust. The nicest thing about the educated tramp was that he appreciated everything – a flower for his buttonhole, a bag of toffees, someone's cast-off clothes, a cup of tea. Yes, he was grateful and he said so.

She made lunch, wondering all the time about Peter Smythe. Who was he really? Had he done all that university stuff – Oxford, Cambridge – had he fought in a war? Where was his family? He sounded ... not London, no, because London had its accents just like Manchester and Liverpool. He sounded like somebody on the wireless, a BBC Home Service type of voice, no accent at all, a clean voice, perfect. Yes, he could have read the news with no bother at all, because Peter Smythe spoke the King's English.

'Funny way of life altogether,' she told her potatoes as she creamed them, 'walking about for years, no proper home. There's no brother in the hills, 'cos he told our Rachel. People don't just happen, they get born. I wonder who owns him?'

As both Frank and Rachel were working in the shop, Dot invited Peter inside for his meal. Someone had trained him, she thought as she watched him removing his shoes in the doorway. Or had he always known not to wear dirty shoes inside a house? And he washed his hands so thoroughly at the kitchen sink.

He ate slowly, like a person who had never known hunger. His manners were perfect – in fact, Dot wondered whether she ought to have given him a napkin.

'Cheese?' she asked when he had finished his crumble.

He smiled. 'A little to take away, if you please.'

Dot smiled too. He was well known in these parts for wanting a little to take away. Should she ask? Could she?

She parcelled up some Cheddar with three slices of buttered bread and passed the gift to him. He was standing by his chair, hat in hand, the famous silver-topped cane leaning on the wall beside him.

'Can I ask you a question?'

'Certainly.' Again that courtly little bow.

'Where are you from?'

He pursed his lips for a moment. 'Do I have to answer? I must plead immunity, Mrs Barnes, from some questions.'

'Sorry.'

'Enough that I am here, dear lady, that I might clean your yard several times a month and that you will reward me with food, warmth and kindness.'

Dot felt like something that had been walked in on a shoe. She repeated her apology.

'No matter,' he insisted, 'for human curiosity is at the root of all we value – literature, art, music, medicine. Let us just say that the life I have chosen fits me like a glove, for I have written my magnum opus and it is to be published quite soon. I learn a great deal about people, you see, about how they think, who they are, where they fit, why they need to fit.'

'And you don't need to fit, Mr Smythe?'

He chuckled. 'Of course I fit – we all do. Without me, the hedges and lawns of Hesford, Bromley Cross, Harwood and so forth would be overgrown. I mend walls and fences, paint doors and window frames, tend animals out in the fields. Just like everyone else, I am another piece of the jigsaw. Place me correctly and I shall fit.'

She understood. 'I fit now, but I didn't fit down yon with him lashing out all the while.'

'Exactly,' he answered, 'and this is the man who visited you at the weekend? The one who marked the young Mrs Barnes's face?'

She nodded.

'You had a bad marriage. I am glad you got away.'

For a reason she could never have explained in a month of Sundays, Dot found herself delivering her life to this person. She didn't mind spilling her history and her feelings to this stranger, because she felt as if she had known him all her life.

'You were squashed,' he said when she had presented the outline. 'And not just physically. He took away who you are, damaged those you were designed to protect, kept you a prisoner.' He sighed and shook his head sadly. 'A prisoner does not have to be in jail, Mrs Barnes. All it takes is a wedding band and a man whose only chance of leaving a mark is by beating those he is supposed to love. That is a sad character.'

'He's not sad,' Dot protested vigorously. 'He's just evil.'

'Evil,' mused Peter Smythe. 'And who created him?'

What did this man mean? 'His mam and dad, I suppose. His mam were a tartar. Never left us alone, always calling round at the house and criticizing everything I did. She'd no love for any of her grandchildren and they didn't reckon much to her, come to think. Then, when she died, she left me a brooch. Silver, it is, like woven, with a black pearl in the middle. Black like her heart. I would never wear it.'

She sat down again and Peter joined her. 'Come on, tell me the rest,' he urged.

Dot swallowed. 'I can't sleep. He's crippled, got knocked down by a carthorse years back, but he managed to get up here, Mr Smythe.'

'Peter.'

She smiled absently. 'I'm Dorothy, Dot for short. Anyway, he got here. He's bad enough for anything, that one. Hates Catholics, Jews, anybody who looks a bit foreign. Just hates everybody. But mainly, he hates me.'

'I see.' He waited. 'Go on.'

She studied the man, didn't understand why she trusted him so completely. 'I want him dead. Isn't that awful? I shan't rest till he's dead.'

Peter shook his head thoughtfully. 'No, that is not so terrible. You fear for yourself, your son, your daughter-in-law—'

'And for any grandchildren I might have.'

'I see nothing wrong in that,' he said carefully. 'In the animal kingdom, rogues are often sought out and killed by the majority. You see, I know from what you have said that your husband is not going to change. I tried to guess what had made him so bad, but I was not about to excuse him – I was merely interested in what makes him tick.' He paused for a moment. 'I collect people, you see. Butterflies would be easier, but people are my hobby.' He drummed his fingers on the table. 'May I visit him?'

Dot's spine was suddenly as stiff as a ramrod. 'You what? Why would you want to go and do that?'

'For my next book,' he answered. 'I intend to write one.'

'Well, I–'

'I am adept at explaining my sudden appearances, Dorothy. I cannot call you Dot – it sounds like a mark on a page.' He gripped one of her hands. 'You are more than that.'

She smiled ruefully. 'I am changing. I used to say everything twice – people said that was because I had to convince myself that I was worth listening to. Well, I've nearly stopped that. I like my life, Peter. I love it up here, the shop and everything. And he just turns up out of the blue and up-ends me.' She retrieved her hand and beat her breast with it. 'I can't let him do it again.'

'No.'

She bit down hard on her lower lip. 'Five, Prudence Street. It's off Derby Street, not far from the Tivoli Picture House.'

'Leave it with me.' He stood up. 'I must finish the yard.'

'What will you . . . ?'

'Don't ask, Dorothy. Let us just say this – I came into this world an accident. I never knew my father, but Mother told me that I was special. She educated me herself, and I must say that she made quite a good job of me.' He laughed. 'No colleges or universities for me, you see. She gave me everything. Now, I have told you more than I am willing to impart to most people. Keep my secrets and I shall keep yours. Do not ask any more. I have a yard to clean.'

And he was gone.

Dot sat until it was her turn to keep shop. He was a funny one, all right, was Peter Smythe. Yet she would have trusted him with her life . . .

Fourteen

Nellie took Lily under her wing. Apart from night time, Lily became a permanent fixture at number 1. They had the two dogs for company, and Nellie's quiet suited Lily, because she had little to say and much thinking to do.

Danny was recovering from pneumonia, though he would not go back into the pit for months, if ever. Aaron, whose pleurisy was also clearing, was a shadow of his former self, but, with warmth, care and decent food, he might be back at school after Easter, his last term as a child. But Roy was different.

With his chicken pox faded, the lad had developed another rash, something far more sinister than the usual childhood illnesses. Dark red spots had appeared all over his body, the angry marks of blood stirred beyond reason and almost beyond human endurance. These marks were the outer sign of an inner turmoil grim beyond belief, because the poor little lad had meningitis.

She had brought it on. By resenting her position, by being unhappy about tolerating what every other God-fearing housewife endured, she had wished her menfolk out of existence. Sam's death had been both blow and relief – if one had to die, then it should be a parent, not a child. But Roy? Would he be taken, too? Surely the price had been paid?

Lily had a book about the disease, one she had picked

up in the library. The covering on the brain became inflamed, then the spine was affected. Blood poisoning went hand in hand with this illness and those who survived sometimes suffered after-effects. Oh, God spare him from brain damage and loss of limb. Poor balance and depression they could cope with, but please, not fits, not a little boy in a wheelchair . . .

Nellie whipped the book from under her neighbour's nose. 'No,' she chided soundlessly, 'stop. Come.' She led Lily upstairs into the lace room. 'Sit. Watch.'

She had made a contraption the likes of which Lily could not work out. Thoroughly puzzled, she allowed herself to be pushed into a chair, then she watched the deaf woman as she went through a very elaborate rigmarole. On an old padded chair seat, Nellie had fixed a pattern, huge, gargantuan when compared to the delicate items around the room.

'Lace,' said Nellie. She proceeded to twist wool and bobbins, using nails instead of pins to secure each stitch. 'Watch,' she ordered every ten seconds.

Lily watched. She watched for well over half an hour, saw the twisting and turnings, the impaling of each loop as it was formed. What the hell was Nellie up to at all? There was a funeral in a few days, and here they sat like two kiddies playing cat's cradle, daft patterns in green wool, twist, turn, pull one, push one, pin it, cross it over . . . 'What?' she asked when the bobbins were pushed into her hands.

'You,' ordered Nellie. 'Your turn.'

Lily's chin dropped so suddenly that she thought her face would split in half. What the bloody hell was going on at all? 'I can't do that,' she mee-mawed, the words exaggerated. 'This is not for me, Nellie.'

Nellie frowned. 'Do it.'

'Bugger,' muttered Lily under her breath.

Nellie shoved a piece of paper under her neighbour's nose and Lily read, *Right. You need money to look after the boys so you can't go to work so you can make lace and I will pay you. Is your eyesight good?*

Lily blinked. She had good eyesight, but lace? Another piece of paper appeared. *And if you can crochet and knit we can sell things on the market. I have a deaf friend who has a stall.*

It was hopeless. For a start, complicated explanations were never easy when the recipient was deaf. Lily picked up the paper, wrote, *I can sew clothes but I can't do lace, Nellie.*

'Yes, you can,' mouthed the lady of this much improved house.

Well, there was no use arguing with a woman as stubborn as Nellie Hulme. Deaf she might be, stupid she certainly was not. And she was right, too. When the boys came home, Lily would be needing work, the sort of work she could do at home. But what was she doing sitting here with a load of nails and wool when she was a woman in mourning? Nellie was magic, it seemed. She made everything calm just by being here, just by being Nellie.

Nellie left the room and Lily found herself gazing down at a pricked paper pattern, four pairs of bobbins and some green wool. God. Where to start? She wound the wool round a nail, wound another pair of bobbins, made a hole in the windings and thrust a nail in. That was it, more or less. Wasn't it? Ah, no. Nellie's wool had gone the other way – that way – no …

Several minutes later, Lily had produced a wonderful mess. There were nails everywhere, while a bulky mass of confused wool lay impaled upon the cushion. She was sweating. A husband to bury, and here she sat, confused, dazed and hating the colour green with a passion. Now, if she had pushed the wool twice round the first nail, happen it might have come out – ah. She could see where she had gone wrong. Nellie was coming. Lily could hear those heavy footfalls on the stairs.

Nellie looked down at the mess. She picked up the paper and pen, wrote laboriously, tongue protruding from a corner of her mouth. Lily waited, a child from Standard Three who knew that her report would be bad.

The note read, *Yes, a good try, so after the funeral we do some more and you will be my apprentice.*

The apprentice looked up, saw kindness and goodness in Nellie's eyes. This deaf woman was splendid, she was the best. She reached out and took a hand that was plump, yet thinner than it had been. 'Thanks, Nellie,' she mouthed. The tears flowed, streamed everywhere, damping the green wool to a colour even more hideous. He was dead and she could never bring him back. Roy was unconscious, the other two were still poorly.

But Nellie was here and now, was solid, was 'talking' about making tea and toast. Outside the door, dogs were snuffling, each waiting for the mistress, each ready for that walk. Nellie mattered, by God, she did. Because Nellie made a difference.

And that, concluded Lily Hardcastle, was the true secret of life. Each person was here to make a difference – and not all wool was green.

Beth was quieter than usual. She took the news about Sam's death well, but her brow knitted when she heard about the Hardcastle boys. She drank milk, chewed on a biscuit, broke off a bit for her delighted dog. 'I might not be a doctor,' she announced when her snack was finished. 'I might go into germs instead.'

Magsy lifted the iron and placed it on the table. So

now Beth was planning a career in medical research. She would probably go through teaching, law and several other possibilities before reaching adulthood. 'How are you feeling now, sweetheart?'

Sweetheart shrugged. 'I've been better for ages.'

'Yes,' agreed Magsy, 'I think they kept you in for the entertainment value. Weren't you telling them how to do their jobs?'

'No, I wasn't. I just made suggestions. Anyway, I think scientists are far more important than doctors, because they find the germs. Doctors just try to mend people, but scientists can discover the trouble before everybody starts dying.' She paused for thought. 'Poor Roy.'

'Yes, we must pray for him.'

'Is it menin . . . What's it called?'

'Meningitis.'

'Hmmm. Well, I hope he gets better. I shall look after him when he comes home.'

Magsy pressed a sheet. It was best to get things over quickly with Beth. The child did not respond when a subject was skirted – no, Beth wanted facts, the truth, the whole truth. 'I was thinking of a move,' she began.

The child frowned. 'A move? Where to?'

'North. Into the countryside. I thought we might go up together tomorrow and take a look. It's beautiful up there, just what you need to get those roses back into your cheeks.'

Beth stood up and looked through the window. She had always lived here, could not imagine living anywhere else. Why was this happening now? 'Is it because I've been ill? Is that why we have to move?'

'Partly, yes.' Telling lies to Beth was useless. Sometimes, it was necessary to minimize information, but direct untruths never went down well. Anyway, Magsy was no good at lies. Had she sat an exam in deceit, she would have failed spectacularly. 'We don't need to go up there yet. Paul will take us.'

Beth swung round. 'He's nice.'

'Yes.'

'Visited me twice.'

'I know.'

Beth sat down again, a hand straying to pet the ever-present Tinker. 'Is he your boyfriend?'

Oh, God, not again. This one would have Magsy married in two shakes of a lamb's tail, papal blessing, nuptial Mass and the massed bands of the king's guards. 'He is male and he is a good friend.'

'With a motorbike.'

'Yes, but we shall travel to Hesford in a van. I am not getting on one of those things and there is no sidecar, so forget it. It would not carry the three of us.'

Beth pondered. 'He could visit us on his motorbike, then.'

'Yes.'

'And you'd let him?'

'Yes.'

Beth sighed happily. 'That's all right, then. Shall I make some toast?'

Magsy turned to dash a tear from her eye. She thought back to a time not too long ago when she had not been able to visit this precious girl, when she had feared the sort of complications now suffered by poor Roy Hardcastle. People died from influenza. How lucky she was to have this child, this wonderful, troublesome girl who, today, possibly for one day only, was going to become a leading microbiologist.

'I love you, Beth,' she whispered.

'That's all right then, because I love you, too. How

223

many slices do you want?' She picked up the toasting fork and got on with life.

Lois Horrocks was furious. Her several chins wobbled with anger as she spoke to her son. 'You know I don't like them things. Bella Eckersley's lad's like a bloody cabbage now, brain gone after he went under that tram. You've done it on purpose. You've done it so as I'll die and you'll have nowt to worry about.'

For a woman about to die, Lois had a lot of energy, her son thought as he watched and listened. She didn't like motorbikes. She didn't like girlfriends, work mates, pub mates, any kinds of mates. She didn't like cheap sheets on her bed, chip shop dinners, tripe without onions, wool next to her skin. She didn't like Dick Barton on the wireless, being on her own, didn't like visitors.

'I'm sick to death with worry,' she concluded.

'I can tell,' he answered, knowing that irony was lost on his mother. She wanted him to bring the money in, look after her, stay in the house with her for ever. Yes, she wanted it all her own way and nobody else's way mattered.

'You'll be killed,' she shouted.

'Then there'll be nobody to look after you.'

She opened her mouth, closed it, kept the response inside.

'Is this going to be my life, Mam?' he asked.

'I never asked to get crippled,' she moaned.

He hadn't asked to become unpaid nurse, cook and bottle-washer, but he made no comment about that side of things. 'I want a life, Mam,' was what he said after a pause. 'I want a wife, children, a house of my own.'

'You want Magsy bloody O'Gara.'

'Yes. Yes, I do.'

She puffed and panted, pulled herself up against the pillows. 'And the bike's for her, I suppose.'

Paul shrugged lightly. 'Not particularly, no. It's for getting me to work and up to Hesford if needs be. She doesn't like motorbikes, either, so it's not for her to ride.'

'Who do you know up Hesford?' was the next bullet from her gun.

'Nobody yet.'

Clearly frustrated, she closed her eyes for a second before beginning again. 'Why would you want to go somewhere where you don't know nobody?'

He couldn't be bothered. What was the point of explaining the truth to a woman who was so self-centred that she chose to understand nothing unless it affected her own comfort? She had ruined Dad's life and was now attempting to spoil her son's.

Paul turned on his heel and went out into the yard. Wishing his own mother dead was not nice. Even if Magsy did agree to have him, he could not impose his mother on her, on Beth. He lit a cigarette, made a smoke ring, watched it disappear as surely as Magsy would after meeting Lois Horrocks.

He closed his eyes and imagined the scene, Magsy cooking, Lois refusing to eat, Magsy changing shitty, wet sheets, Magsy trying to move the mountain that was Lois. Yes, she would be doing that at the hospital if she stayed and took promotion; yes she might well be performing such tasks for the woman in Hesford, but that was paid work, chosen work. Whereas . . .

'I am stuck,' he told the wall quietly. He was glued to Lois, umbilically fixed, impaled, welded. He could not simply go off and leave her to die, could not impose on the goodwill of neighbours. 'Are parents our fault,' he mused, 'just as we are theirs?' No, it was not supposed to be like this. He should have been married by now, married and with a couple of children.

Today, he was taking Magsy and Beth up to Hesford for Magsy's second interview. The woman would take her on, he felt sure. Anyone would employ her, as she was diligent, honest and caring. And cheap. Yes, this was a rich man's world. Beth needed the air, Magsy needed the money, he needed Magsy and was very fond of the child, too.

He murdered the cigarette end under a heel, took a deep breath, went back indoors. It was time for plain speaking, time for his opinion to matter.

She glared at him. 'Having a tantrum, were you?'

This woman, who had given him life, plainly believed that she had the right to remove that life from him. He cleared his throat. 'Right. I want you to do something that you have never managed before, I want you to shut up and listen.'

Something in his voice, the quietness of it, the strength behind the softness, made her squirm. Was this the moment she had dreaded all her life? She snorted, but said nothing.

He launched straight in. 'Mam, I think you are the most selfish, ungrateful woman on this earth. I know you are ill, but you gave up far too soon and now, because you can hardly walk, you expect me to be at your beck and call except when I am at work.'

She blinked rapidly, opened her mouth, shut it.

'If Magsy will have me – and I am intending to wear her down – I will be getting married. If I have to turn Catholic, I don't care, because I will do anything she wants. That's love. That's real love, Mam, something you don't know about.'

He shook his head in despair. 'Magsy is going for a job in Hesford. She needs the countryside for the kiddy – she's only just out of hospital. Now, I don't know what I can work out, but if she will have me, you are not living with us. You would spoil my marriage within a week and I won't have that.'

Lois pressed a hand against a rapid heartbeat, but she maintained her silence.

'You'll be living on your own,' he said. 'I'll pay Bertha to do your meals and keep you clean, because I wouldn't ask anybody to deal with your moods for free, but you will have to shift yourself from yon bed and start trying. If it kills you, that's not my fault. I've been stuck here long enough. Even if Magsy won't have me, it's time I was off. There's plenty of work down London way after the bombings, houses being built all the time.'

Her mouth was suddenly as dry as blotting paper. She wouldn't have been able to speak even if he had allowed it. Her chest felt tight and her hands tingled. He was killing her. He was murdering her as surely as if he had put a pillow over her face.

'I'm going now.' His tone was conversational. 'I am driving to Hesford with Magsy O'Gara and her little girl. We will be eating in a café, so I've left you some tea and ham butties. Bertha will come in at three o'clock. If you want the wireless on, get out of bed. I know you get out of bed when I'm not here, because I've seen stuff moved when Bertha hasn't been in.' He pulled on his coat. 'If Ernest Barnes can manage without Dot, you can do without me, Mam. See you later, but I don't know how long I'll be.'

Alone, she shivered in the warm room. She would be stuck here for going on five hours now, fastened to this room, waiting for Bertha. He had taken a day off work for

Magsy O'Gara, would never get time off for his own sick mother. Well, if he wanted to pike off to London, there was nowt she could do about that.

As for Magsy flaming O'Gara, Lois would put that one straight, oh yes. It was time to meet that bloody woman. With nothing to lose, Lois Horrocks put her thinking cap on. It was time to take that cow by the horns.

Beth, wrapped up warmly in coat, hat, scarf and gloves, stood at the top of Hesford Brow and scanned the countryside. It was all frost, silver in the low sun of winter, fields spread like carpets as far as the eye could reach. Hollows became rises, smoke streamed in straight lines from farmhouse chimneys, brave birds swooped and lifted, wings spread across a sky whose blue was not believable, the kind of colour that comes straight from an infant's paintbox, no refinement, just solid bright sapphire.

Magsy stood with Paul, her arms folded against the chill. They should have brought the pup. She could imagine Beth running wild here, her dog chasing the scent of rabbit and hare, silly ears flapping as he bounded across moorland. 'She likes it,' Magsy whispered.

'Anybody would,' he replied.

'I do,' she admitted, 'though I'd like to know what Miss Moore is up to. The other day, she told me to come back in an hour, so I did, but she was just in a bad mood because she couldn't get through to somebody on the phone.'

He nodded. 'They get selfish.'

'Who do?'

'People who are stuck in the house. My mother is as selfish as they come.' He sighed. 'It's a mess, Magsy. Half of me tells me I can't leave, then the other three-quarters tells me to go.'

She giggled. 'That doesn't add up.'

'I know.' He clapped together hands covered in William's driving gloves. 'It's a bugger and it has never added up, not since my father died.'

Magsy sensed his pain, decided to change the subject. 'We'd better get madam fed, because she's lost enough weight.'

Paul touched her arm. 'Leave her a minute – she'll never starve, Magsy. Your Beth knows what she wants, when she wants it, and she's not afraid to ask for it.'

Magsy laughed. 'You noticed.'

'I did. She is definitely her mother's daughter.'

If Magsy had one qualm about leaving Prudence Street, it was attached to this man. He was solid, kind and ... and just there. He made no demands, never took liberties, was interested in Beth, he worried about the child, played with her, talked sensibly to her. Was Magsy falling in love? Was she finally abandoning William?

As if reading her mind, he said, 'Do what's right for you and her, Magsy. Don't worry about anybody else. I will come and visit you both, so you'll still be in touch with the old place. And there's Rachel, Frank and Dot just over the road.'

'Let's visit them,' she suggested. 'We've still got well over half an hour before we are expected at Miss Moore's house. Yes, we can call in at the shop, see how they're getting on. We can buy stuff to eat while we're there.'

Of course, they were not allowed to buy. As soon as everyone had finished exclaiming over Beth and how well she looked, the adult guests were ushered through to the kitchen where Rachel set to with bread board and knife to make sandwiches for everyone.

Beth stayed in the shop with Dot and Frank, leaving Magsy and Paul to chat with Rachel.

Rachel had a gleam in her eye. Magsy caught sight of it, but kept quiet. Was this young woman pregnant?

No, it was something else altogether. Dot had an admirer and Rachel was full of it, glee almost spilling from her eyes as she spoke in a near-whisper. 'He's going to show her his worts.'

'His what?'

'That's what I said at the time,' giggled Rachel. 'I think they're wild flowers or weeds or summat. The pair of them's going to frolic hand in hand through Bluebell Woods – when there's some bluebells, like – and he's all for introducing her to his fox.'

'Sounds serious,' said Paul, his tone matching the words.

Rachel fell across her cutting board, while Magsy, almost in pain, held a scarf over her face. 'Stop it,' she pleaded.

'He's nice,' Rachel managed, 'at least five foot four and with a bowler hat. He lives in an old propped-up gypsy caravan on some land belonging to another girlfriend – Miss Morgan.'

'Lovely,' said Paul.

Magsy hit him. 'Behave,' she chided.

'I am behaving,' he said mournfully. 'I am taking this seriously. Young love, old love – it's always wonderful.'

Rachel righted herself and waved a carving knife at Paul. 'Where did you find him?' she asked Magsy.

'Near the bins,' came the stern reply. 'The corporation refused to shift him.'

The door opened and Dot's face insinuated itself into the resulting gap. 'You all right?' she asked, bemused when this question attracted gales of laughter.

'I believe you know a man who knows a fox, Dot,' said Paul.

Dot blinked. 'Oh, don't be listening to Rachel. She's got me courting.' When this statement brought forth even more silly laughter, Dot gathered her shattered dignity and left the arena.

Rachel regaled them with the tale of the educated tramp, colouring in grey areas with shades collected from her own imagination. 'If he was a bit taller, he'd be OK, only he looks like a tall dwarf, if you know what I mean. But he's very polite, knows what knives and forks are for, never drops his aitches. Frank's mam's certainly going up in the world.'

Paul shook his head thoughtfully. 'No, if he is so short, she has to be going down, surely?' He rubbed his bruised arm after taking a second blow from Magsy.

Rachel became sober. 'Sorry to hear about Sam Hard-castle,' she said, 'and those poor sick boys. Lily must be out of her mind.'

'I've put her with Nellie,' explained Magsy. 'And Nellie's got her tatting. It's funny, but they're right together, like a pair of sisters. They go shopping, share the cooking – Lily only goes home to sleep. Mind, she spends a fair time at the hospital, so that breaks her day up. My rosary's worn out with praying.' She smiled at Paul. 'Yes, the one you bought me.'

Rachel placed sandwiches on the table. Oh, these two were right together. They each knew what the other was thinking, and they acted daft. Daft mattered; daft was what kept a marriage going. Still, she had better stop with all this matchmaking. 'So, you're going to see Katherine?'

Magsy nodded, her face suddenly grim. Not often afraid, she had to admit to a degree of trepidation in the area of Miss Katherine Moore. 'She is up to something. I know I have met her just once, but she's a planner. I wonder what it is?'

Rachel, who knew what it was, kept Katherine's secret, just as she had promised. 'Don't worry about her, Magsy. Once you get to know her, she's all right.'

'I hope so.'

Rachel fetched Beth from the shop and they ate a hurried lunch of cheese sandwiches followed by some of Dot's Victoria sponge. Then Beth was forced by her mother to wash hands and face, then to comb her hair. 'Why?' moaned the child. 'I'm not even dirty.'

But Magsy, who suspected that Miss Moore might spot a minute speck of dirt from a distance of a hundred yards, insisted on this cleansing.

Paul decided to stay where he was – there was no point in lingering in the lorry's cab while he was able to sit in a warm kitchen. 'You'll be all right,' he told Magsy before she led her daughter across the road.

Then he kissed Magsy very lightly on the cheek. 'Go get 'em, tiger,' he whispered.

Blushing, Magsy O'Gara left the scene, a giggling Beth in tow. That had been a nice kiss. And she was smiling.

Fifteen

Lily Hardcastle began to appreciate Nellie's persistence with the lacework. It was hard and frustrating, especially when Lily had to start on the smaller stuff, but it kept her focused. More than once, she had thrown the lace-pillow across the room, but Nellie, that ever-patient saint, had simply laughed, strange, high-pitched sounds emerging from an uncontrolled larynx. Nellie was the best thing that had happened to Lily in many a month.

They walked together into Wilkinson's funeral parlour, Nellie's breathing loud in the hushed atmosphere of this quiet place. It was Nellie who led the way, following the black-suited undertaker into the back room where Sam lay in his demob suit, hair combed, face shaved, a tiny smile on his lips.

Lily grabbed Nellie and clung on to her. Would Roy want to live without his beloved dad? Would Roy get the choice? And why had she made so much fuss about a bit of nose-picking? Oh, God, it wasn't fair. Sam had done his best; even with his drinking, he had never got abusive. She should have appreciated him when he was alive, should have loved him enough to put up with that one small habit.

'All right,' mouthed Nellie. She tapped her ample breast. 'Me here. I look after you.'

For Nellie, that had been a long speech, one she would

normally have delivered via pencil and paper. Lily dredged up some courage and kissed her husband good-bye, just a small peck on a cheek as cold as any head-stone. And it was done. This was more important than the funeral, because this was a personal farewell.

They left the building, Lily drawing breath for what seemed the first time in minutes as they stepped out onto Derby Street. They turned left for town, not bothering to wait for transport. Just lately, they had taken to walking, usually with two dogs in tow, Skinny the mother and Spot the son.

They passed the market place and walked down the slope to the hospital grounds. Aaron and Danny had both been declared out of danger, so it was Roy's ward that they visited first. Nellie wrinkled her nose against the smell of disinfectant; Lily, much of whose life had been spent here in recent weeks, scarcely noticed the scents – they were part and parcel of her daily routine, as familiar as the smells from home.

He lay on his pillows, face bleached white, hands loose on a yellow cover, hair as bright as ever. Yes, that red thatch looked far too cheerful when compared to the rest of him. Lily sat and stared at him, just as she always did.

Nellie moved to the other side of the bed. She picked up one of his hands and began to stroke it, gentle move-ments from wrist to fingertips, the exercise repeated many times. From her lips, a small hissing sound emerged, a noise of which she could not possibly have been aware.

Lily found her own eyelids becoming heavy. It was that special Nellie-magic again, the gift this woman had been awarded in place of her hearing. She was such a tranquil soul, was able to lull her daft puppy to sleep in moments, even when the young dog was in one of his tearaway moods.

Lily leaned forward, placing her head on the pillow

next to her son's unnaturally still face. No matter how hard she tried, her eyes would not remain open.

She was woken by a completely different sound, one she would not have recognized in a month of Sundays. 'Mam? Mam?' Whose was that quiet little voice? She sat up.

'Mam?'

'Oh, my God,' she moaned, looking across at Nellie. She would never be sure, yet Lily felt in her bones that a miracle had happened during those moments of sleep, because Nellie Hulme's face was different, as if someone had turned on a light behind the eyes.

'Mam?'

'Yes, love?' Lily's voice cracked.

'Where's me dog?'

Lily's tears flowed, Nellie joined in the weeping, a nurse arrived, declared her intention to fetch a doctor. 'Your dog's fine, love. She's had her operation and she's all right.'

'Skinny,' he said.

There was nothing wrong with his brain, then. He looked half-dead, his lips cracked and dry, eyes still sunken, wrists thin, skin transparent, but every little chicken pox scar had disappeared, as if God had taken an iron, had smoothed him out. 'Oh, Roy,' wept his mother. No matter what, Lily would hope for nothing from this day onward. A widow, she would accept her lot with equanimity, would strive to make life as easy as possible for Sam's boys.

'Me dad?' he asked.

Nellie placed a hand on the boy's head. Again, that small noise came from her mouth, a sound that reminded Lily of steam escaping from a simmering kettle. Roy slept. Lily did not know whether to laugh or cry. He was alive. Her youngest baby was going to be all right.

The doctor arrived. 'He woke?'

Lily nodded. She nursed a truth that would never be accepted by medics, a fact of which Nellie herself was probably unaware. Nellie Hulme was a healer. No matter what any doctor said or did from now on, Lily Hardcastle would always be certain that Miss Nellie Hulme of Prudence Street, Bolton, Lancashire, had saved the life of Roy Hardcastle.

They went then to visit the other two boys. It was time to tell them that Roy was improving, that their father would be buried tomorrow. Yes, it was time to move on.

Rachel led Magsy and Beth into the bedroom.

Miss Katherine Moore looked considerably better than last time, eyes a little brighter, a glimpse of mischief in those rheumy orbs. 'Well,' she declared, 'so this is the famous genius daughter. Are you a genius?' she asked Beth.

'I am very clever,' the child replied directly, 'always top of the class. But I don't know whether I am a genius, because I don't know what a genius is. Except for Albert Einstein. He's a real genius.'

'Ah. So you are modest, then.'

'I don't know,' answered Beth. 'If I think something, I usually say it. What's the matter with you? Why are you lying down? Are you ill?'

'Arthritis. But your neighbour sent me some medicine and it has made me rather better.'

'Good,' said Beth before wandering off to the window. 'You can see the shop from here,' she remarked. 'We had sandwiches there.'

Rachel made a quiet goodbye before returning to her job. She would have liked to stay, but this was an interview, so it was private.

Magsy sat opposite Miss Moore. She folded her hands in her lap and watched while Katherine fell in love with Beth. She wasn't surprised, because Beth was loved universally.

'Do you like school?' asked the old lady.

'It's all right, but I learn more at home.' She swung round. 'I was going to be a doctor, but I might be a scientist now.'

'I see.'

'Albert Einstein did sciences. He could have done anything, but he chose science. He's old now, still clever, though. They asked him to be a president in Israel, but he said no. The only thing he did wrong was helping with atom bombs, but we all do something wrong. It's just that his wrong thing was bigger than other people's wrong things because he's more important than most of us.'

Magsy squashed a grin. If Katherine Moore wanted a lecture, she had sent for the right child. It occurred to Magsy then that she had never said the words uttered so often by other parents – 'She didn't half show me up' – because Beth fitted anywhere and everywhere. Wherever Elizabeth O'Gara landed, she would do herself and her family proud.

'Would you like to go to a different school, Beth?' Katherine asked.

Beth lifted her hands in a gesture of acceptance. 'I'll have to if Mam decides to come and live here. This is too far from Daubhill, so I've got to change schools.'

Katherine took a sheet of paper from a small table next to her chaise. 'This is a special school, Beth. It happens to be in a house that used to be mine, Chedderton Grange. It's just for girls, very clever girls. The school keeps in touch with universities, because some of the girls are too advanced for the teachers and work has to be set by professors. Every child has her own tutor, someone who

237

will find the right work, the right things to read. It is a very new idea. Would you like to go there?'

Magsy's heart lurched. Chedderton Grange? Where had she heard about that? Ah yes, she remembered, that funny little doctor of Beth's – he had mentioned it. But it was expensive, well beyond the means of ordinary folk. Ah. Katherine Moore was being very clever, was finding a way to ensure that Magsy would take the job. Cunning. Yes, very clever.

Beth took the page from Katherine's hand and studied the content. 'I'm not eleven,' she said, 'I'm ten. It says here they take girls from eleven years of age.'

This one was ten but about to turn forty, thought Katherine. 'They'll snap you up. They owe me a favour or two, you see. They got that house very cheaply and I think they will be happy to waive a part of the fee.' She turned to Magsy. 'This child has to be dealt with. At the Grange, each pupil has a learning schedule to suit her own needs, which is why they take only the best. It is not a boarding school, so Beth would still live with you.'

Magsy, unusually lost for words, merely nodded.

'They have physics,' Beth pronounced, 'and chemistry, not just general science. Tennis in the summer, too. And the house is so pretty.' She passed the brochure to her mother. 'Is there a uniform?'

'No,' replied Katherine. The school believes in the individual, so it does nothing that seems to conform. As long as you are decently dressed, no-one will notice you.'

Beth clapped her hands in delight. 'So, even if you're nine, you still get proper work?'

'Yes, they will aim for you to reach your full potential.'

Magsy decided it was time for her to speak. 'Is that the telephone call you were trying to make the other day?'

'Yes. Rachel told me of Beth's brilliance, so I thought I would try to get her into the Grange.'

Magsy considered that. 'And if I don't take the job?'

Katherine made no reply, but the challenge was there in her eyes. With so much offered to Magsy's precious daughter, the decision was already made. 'I have written out a list of my requirements,' said the old woman instead, 'my day-to-day needs, foods I like and dislike. Rachel Barnes has been lifting me in and out of the bath – she will show you what to do.'

Magsy dropped her chin for a moment and considered her situation. 'Beth?' she said after some thought. 'Would you go downstairs while I talk to Miss Moore?'

Katherine straightened as far as her aching bones would allow. A pang of something approaching fear paid a brief visit to her chest. She had wanted the mother; now that she had met the child, she wanted the pair. How her life had opened up since the advent of Rachel Barnes and her family. Now, here sat the embodiment of a more comfortable future, a life that might be bearable, at least. Had she overstepped the mark?

Magsy waited until her daughter had left the room. 'You should not have done that, Miss Moore.'

She had overstepped the mark.

'To offer something to my daughter before discussing it with me is a low blow.'

'Below the belt, Mrs O'Gara?'

'Well below, and well beneath your own dignity. Now, she wants the school, the books, the chances.'

'And you do not want those things for her?'

'Of course I do. But the concept of the school should have been mine to consider, not hers. The point is that you have quite deliberately placed me in a cleft stick, because if Beth does not get to that school, she will blame me. You have ensured that I will accept the position.'

The old eyes narrowed. 'So you do not want the work?'

'I wanted the choice to be mine and yours. In fact, I had already decided to accept, because I know now that Beth's health is more important than her education. We live in an industrial town and the air is far from clean. Here, life would be better for her.' She considered her next words. 'I am now inclined not to accept, because you have shown yourself to be manipulative.'

Katherine drew in a sharp breath. This was a strong character, an immovable force. She should not have mentioned Chedderton Grange. The card she had thought of as an ace had turned out to be just a joker. There was nothing more to be said, because the woman was furious. Magsy O'Gara did not shout, did not frown, but the ice was there, a coldness that would have measured well below freezing point on the Fahrenheit scale. Was it too late? Should she offer a little more money? Probably not. This Irishwoman was not purchasable, was proud beyond pounds sterling.

Magsy gazed into a pair of eyes that were old but intelligent. The will of Miss Katherine Moore promised to be unbending. What was to be done? 'If I do decide to work here, you will never again use my child as a pawn in your game of life. It is unfair and despicable. She is her own person. I am grateful for your proposal, but it was made in the wrong company.'

There was no more to be said.

Katherine could only sit and watch as her visitor left the room, a feeling of disquiet in her wake. Had she been possessed of X-ray vision, had she been able to see beyond that closed door, she would have been encouraged. Because Magsy O'Gara was leaning against the wall, her eyes closed in silent prayer.

The job was already hers.

*

There was more wool and cotton in this bloody cupboard than in Yorkshire and Lancashire put together. In the end, Lily finished up with a suitcase full of patterns and three paper bags overflowing with materials.

Behind Lily and breathing very heavily, Nellie Hulme scrutinized everything that came off those shelves. Mam had not been a lacemaker, but there were some wonderful crochet instructions, so she saved several, piling them up on the table for future reference and further investigation. If she could get Lily crocheting, there would be saleable items on the agenda soon, things that could be sold on the outdoor market in Bolton.

Balanced on a chair, Lily pushed her hands into the cupboard's deepest recesses, hoping against hope that she would make contact with no lower life forms. Thanks to Skinny and Spot, the rats had moved on to new pastures, but there was still the odd mouse, some silverfish and the occasional stubborn cockroach. As for spiders, well, Lily hoped they had all hibernated, because spiders sent her running a mile.

She stopped for a moment, thought about Roy, Aaron and Danny, all improving, none of them well enough for home yet. They had not attended their father's funeral, though the two older boys knew that Sam was dead. The job of telling Roy was not something she relished. And she missed Sam, would always miss him. Had she loved him after all? And did it matter? Loving or not loving – neither would bring him back.

Nellie prodded Lily's leg and made her get down. They sat together at the kitchen table with mugs of tea and Eccles cakes. The silence really suited Lily, because it gave her the chance to be herself even when she was in company. As long as she was doing something, she managed to limp through the days, the hospital visits, the difficult yet fascinating business that was lacemaking.

Nellie's hand suddenly grabbed Lily's. For a moment, Nellie looked as if she might be choking, eyes bulging, mouth opening and closing, small, bubbling sounds escaping from her throat.

'Nellie?' Although she knew that it was useless, Lily found herself screaming the name.

'See,' mouthed the older woman. 'See.' She pushed a document into Lily's hands.

Lily looked at the old newspaper clipping, just a photograph, grainy, faded, a picture of a house.

'Mine,' breathed Nellie, 'my house.'

'Oh, I see.' It was a grand place, steps up to the front door, low pillars making a balustrade, large windows, lions couchant at the top of the stone flight. The photographer had captured some of the garden, too, had stood back to include flower beds, lawns, a fountain. So this picture had been locked in the sewing cupboard for years.

Nellie closed her eyes and willed it to happen. Closer and closer it came, not always while she was asleep, sometimes when she was making lace, sometimes while she nodded by the fire. Red, bright red. Before she could remember properly, she would have to reach the red, accept it, wade through it.

But that was her house. The item had been clipped from a newspaper, probably by Mam. So Mam and Dad had known Nellie's true identity all along – why, otherwise, would Mam have kept this photograph folded amongst knitting and crochet patterns? And the money – that came from somewhere.

Nellie didn't need the money any more. After years of working and saving, she probably had enough to buy that house, lock, stock, barrel and furniture. Yes, she had to find it. Opening her eyes, she grabbed back the cutting, scrutinized it, looked for clues. Nothing. The house could be anywhere. This was a place where she could hear. She had heard. If she went back, would she hear again? Was the house still there? It was old, probably eighteenth, even seventeenth century. Oh, she knew nothing about houses . . .

Would she never hear again? The red was the thing that had taken away her hearing. Birdsong. Yes, light, like . . . like blue, pale blue. She found herself smiling.

'Nellie?' Lily leaned forward. 'Nellie, love?'

Sounds were colours. The man's voice was brown, the woman's gold. Birdsong was blue, a cow's lowing seemed grey, sad. And red was . . . red was screaming. Red was a wide open mouth and pain and anger. Red was shock. Red was the end of hearing . . .

'Nellie?'

'Red is dead,' she mouthed.

'Oh, Nellie . . .'

And the smiling turned to tears. 'Red is dead,' the deaf woman framed repeatedly.

Lily didn't know what to do. 'Tell me,' she said.

Nellie brushed the wetness from her face with an impatient hand, then grabbed pencil and paper, wrote furiously for a few minutes.

Lily picked up the page.

Lily, I was born in that house. I could hear then suddenly I could not hear. Something terrible happened. When I am asleep I go back to that house. The birds sing. In the dreams I can hear. Now all I know is that sound is like colour, but I can't really remember it when awake. Lily, I have to find that house. I have to find the red, remember the red.

Lily replied in writing, asked Nellie what she meant about the red.

The answer was very stark. *Blood* came back.

'You think there was blood?'

The deaf woman nodded. 'A lot,' she mouthed.

Blood. Had Nellie seen a murder? Was it possible for somebody to go deaf from shock? Well, perhaps this all made sense. Nellie had been adopted by the Hulmes, whose circumstances had been comfortable – so it was possible that Nellie's family had set aside money for the rearing of their deaf daughter. 'Do you still get money?' she asked now. 'Apart from what you get from lace, I mean.'

Nellie nodded.

'Where from?'

The old woman raised her shoulders. She did not know. The money came to the bank from a Manchester solicitor. She had written to ask about the source, had been informed that certain investments had been made in her name and that he simply sent on the proceeds. An accountant had been mentioned by the bank, but he, too, had had little to say about the matter.

Lily sipped at her cooling tea. She had seen Nellie's bank book – it had been open here on the table just days ago. Nellie had thousands saved, so she wasn't wanting to find this house in order to sell it. No. The poor woman was genuinely trying to discover who she was and where she came from. 'Don't worry, love,' she said carefully, each syllable separated so as to be readable. 'We'll get there.' She would look after Nellie Hulme no matter what. And Nellie Hulme would look after her, of that she was very sure.

Ernest opened the back gate to find a strange little man in a bowler hat. 'Were you knocking?' he asked.

'Do forgive the intrusion. I found this outside your gate and wondered whether it might belong to you.' He help up a rather disgraceful scarf. 'It is in need of some repair, but I thought it could have had sentimental value.'

Ernest leaned on his sticks. The item displayed was of no value whatsoever, sentimental or otherwise. In fact, he had seen better on Charlie Entwistle's rag lorry, but this weird fellow was holding it as if it had come from the same box as the flaming Crown Jewels. 'Nowt to do with me,' said Ernest, 'and anyroad, it's a woman's thing. There's no woman here any more.' He went to close the gate.

'I, too, am a widower,' sighed Peter Smythe. 'My wife passed away last year.'

Ernest pulled the gate wide again. 'Ah, well, mine buggered off not long since, went of her own accord. Mind, she were useless, so it's just as well. Can't be doing with women under me feet.'

Peter tutted sympathetically. 'Some people have no gratitude. That happened to a friend of mine, an Orange Lodger. His lady wife went off with a Catholic. The humiliation sent him wild. Sad to say, he is in the process of drinking himself into oblivion.'

Ernest found himself interested in this creature. He clearly knew what was what, anyway. 'You from round here?' he asked.

Peter shook his head. 'No. I came to see my long-lost brother, but I learned today that he has passed on. However, I seem to have found some work – odd jobs and so forth – so I shall stay in the area for a while.'

Ernest was rather short of company. Charlie visited infrequently, while the women of the street scarcely bothered with him. Not one for whims, he decided to indulge himself for once. 'You might as well come in,' he said. 'No use keeping me stood up here gabbing all day – I've a bad leg.'

Peter removed his hat and followed Ernest into his dark and dingy home. He waited until Ernest had settled himself by the fire. 'Shall I make some tea?' he asked.

'I'd not say no,' replied Ernest tersely. He watched while this funny little chap messed about with caddy, teapot and cups. 'Odd jobs, you say?'

'Yes. I work for the slightly better off, the sort who can pay for a little gardening and so forth. Since my wife passed away, I have been glad of the freedom to move about and work where I please. Of course, your liberty is curtailed by your leg. How did that happen? Is it a war wound?'

Ernest thought about decorating himself in lies and glory, but opted for the truth. After all, this man might well talk to the neighbours. So he told the sad tale of the brewery horse and of John Higgins's coming to the rescue. 'Then me son ups and marries the bloody man's daughter, gets himself a shop in some village up yonder. And takes his mother with him – my flaming wife. I've been stuck here on me own ever since, trapped by this leg, nobody to give two hoots whether I live, die or go mad.'

'Terrible,' said Peter.

Ernest found himself warming to this intruder. 'Never a second glance, mind you, the day she walked out of here. Picked up all her clothes – and I bought her only the best – and buggered off, just left me here to rot. See, there's no reasoning with women, specially them what mix with Catholics.'

Peter sipped his tea and tut-tutted whenever Ernest left a pause.

'I even went up to plead with her, but would she listen? Would she bloody hell as like.'

'Most unreasonable,' commented Peter.

'I wouldn't care, but she were kept like a queen here, only the best for Dot. She had as much housekeeping as she wanted, good grub, decent clothes, a jug of Guinness from the outdoor every Saturday night. I even paid for her to go to the pictures. I couldn't go, oh no. I had to stop here with me leg.'

Peter made more noises of sympathy.

Warmed by sweet tea and his subject matter, Ernest was emboldened. 'I followed her.'

'Did you?'

'Oh, yes. Like I said, I pleaded with her, got nowhere. So next news, I gave her down the banks a right telling off. I can tell you that for no money. Frightened her halfway to death, I did.'

'No more than the woman deserved, I am sure.' Peter stood up and lifted his hat from the dresser. 'I shall go now,' he said, 'and thank you for the tea.'

Disappointed, Ernest sank into his chair. 'Well, you know where I am now. Name's Barnes. Call any time you're passing.'

Peter smiled. 'I shall, Mr Barnes. I most certainly shall. By the way, I am Peter Smythe. Good day to you.' Then he left as suddenly as he had arrived.

Ernest grinned. He had met a new friend and he intended to make good use of him.

Sixteen

June was always a beautiful month, but the June of 1951 was spectacular. Flags and paths baked in the ever-present sun, gardens demanded water, grazing animals slowed, sheep all but screaming to be shorn, cows ambling home-ward like sleepwalkers, their only motivation a need to empty swollen udders.

Magsy was reasonably content in her work. The old woman was demanding, arrogant, occasionally unkind, but she did experience a great deal of pain, so Magsy left room for that. Now that the rhythm of the day was established, the job was manageable and the living conditions were good.

The house was finally organized in general terms. There was a bathroom downstairs and Miss Moore was settled in one of the front living rooms. Everything was clean, each room had been decorated and the old lady was cared for at last. Occasionally, Magsy missed the bustle of town, the markets, the chattering among staff at the infirmary.

But there were benefits, of course. Beth was receiving an excellent if somewhat unconventional education, they were well fed, decently housed, the countryside was available at all times. With Tinker, they walked the moors, explored woods, visited other villages. The summer house was comfortable, if rather small, and Miss Moore had furnished it well.

At three o'clock on a Monday afternoon, Magsy took her siesta in the rear garden of Knowehead. Above her head, the canopy of an old apple tree gave her shade, while birds hopped and hovered, their twitterings softened by the day's heat. She was happy. Never one to shun work, she had thrown herself wholeheartedly into the improvement of Miss Katherine Moore and was pleased with the results. The woman was even wearing dresses and shoes, was walking a little, had begun to put in some effort.

A small sound disturbed Magsy's musings. She opened her eyes to find the lady of the house sitting beside her on a rustic bench, an item cobbled together out of rough planks. 'Miss Moore,' she exclaimed.

'No fuss,' snapped the new arrival. 'Stay where you are and say nothing. It took me over fifteen minutes to get here, but I am here and I need to rest for a while.'

Flabbergasted, Magsy obeyed the order. If Miss Moore had decided to walk, then she must be left to get on with it.

'You may have to carry me back inside,' said Katherine after thirty seconds of silence. 'This lawn is beautifully kept. Does that funny little man do the garden now?'

'Yes.'

'Peter Smythe?'

'Yes.'

Katherine closed her eyes and allowed the sun's natural heat to warm her bones. How long was it since she had managed to come into her garden? Oh, how wonderful the sun felt, how wonderful it was to be alive. Her bones ached, but she still had her mind, still had Magsy and Beth, so many things to be grateful for.

Magsy waited. There had to be a reason for this change in behaviour, this supreme and painful effort. What was going on in that over-active head?

'Is the summer house adequate for you?' asked Katherine eventually.

'Yes, thank you.'

'Would you not be better with a bedroom each?'

Yes, something was going on here.

'I understand that the Smythe man has an arrangement whereby he sleeps in an abandoned caravan. That can hardly be satisfactory.'

Wheels turned in Magsy's head. 'He is a gentleman of the road, Miss Moore.'

'I know that.' There was an impatient edge to the voice. 'I also know that he used the summer house before you and your daughter came along. I have never been completely immobile, so I did notice what was going on in my own garden. So, whatever his attitude to life, the summer house must be sufficiently bohemian for him to live in. I shall put him there.'

Put him there? Katherine Moore plainly treated life like the games of chess she played with Beth, pieces to be moved, a king, a queen, but mostly pawns. She had probably been working up to this for a while.

'Four empty rooms upstairs here,' the old woman continued, 'sufficient space for you each to have a bedroom, two further rooms and a bathroom. We could make the bigger room into a drawing room, the smaller into a kitchen. You would be far more comfortable up there.'

Magsy processed the information. Yes, she and Beth would be comfortable in the house; they would also be available. Ever since the incident at her second interview, Magsy had tried to keep Beth away from her employer. They played chess on Fridays, but, for the most part, Beth lived and worked in the summer house. The bedroom was small, especially with two beds and Beth's bookcase and desk, but they managed.

'So the decision is made?' Magsy turned to look at Katherine.

'Beth tells me that you store your clothes in the porch, as there is no space in the bedroom.'

'That is not a problem. After the slums of Bolton, the summer house is a palace.'

Katherine knew that she must tread carefully. 'Because I now live downstairs, your accommodation would be completely separate from mine. Your hours would be the same, but, should I fall, there would be someone in the house to help me.'

Magsy sighed. In Katherine's head, the documentation was signed, notarized, passed by parliament, sealed, now delivered. 'I shall speak to Beth,' she said.

'Speak to a ten-year-old? She will go where she is put.'

Magsy bridled. 'As you have taken care to mention yourself, Miss Moore, Beth is no ordinary child. And remember, you had reservations about Tinker, even though he was to live with us in the summer house. There would be a large dog in Knowehead – have you considered that?'

'I have.' Katherine loved Tinker. A mess of a dog, he seemed to understand her needs, her pain. He never jumped at her, was always apologetic about entering her room, yet he came whenever he could, visited each time doors were left ajar. 'The dog is no trouble,' was all she chose to concede. 'So, that is my decision. I leave you to make yours.' She rose painfully.

'Shall I help you?'

'No.' The agony was dreadful, but Katherine fought to conceal it. Determined to get the O'Garas into her house, she had to make the best of herself. Racked with severe pain, she made her slow way towards the french windows, surprised when Magsy appeared by her side. 'I can manage,' she snapped.

'That is a load of old blarney,' replied Magsy. 'You are

transparent in more ways than one, Miss Moore, thin as a garden rake and determined to have your own way at all costs. Now stand still and do as you are told for once.'

Katherine stood. This robust Irishwoman had a way of carrying her that minimized the pain, so she gave herself up into the care of another stubborn and determined person. 'You and I are the immovable force and the irresistible object.'

'We are locked horns,' replied Magsy as she swept up the ridiculously lightweight Katherine. 'This will always be a fight, you know. We are both controllers.'

With the walk completed, Magsy placed Katherine on her chaise. 'Cup of tea?' she asked.

'Later, thank you.'

Magsy left her employer and walked back into the garden. Ah well, it was going to happen. There was sense in the suggestion, and Magsy would minimize the contact between Beth and Miss Moore. She grinned to herself. There were three of them, three determined souls. Beth would make her own decisions. She would hurt no-one, would disturb no-one. But, at the age of ten, Beth had her own very decided way of dealing with life.

Whatever, the destiny of the O'Garas was inextricably linked with the woman indoors. Time for a little snooze before Beth got home. Beth would be for the move. And there was little that Magsy could do, because it would be two against one.

She settled into her deckchair, a smile still playing at the corners of her mouth. Understanding Katherine Moore was not difficult. With no family and few visitors, she was making the best of her allotted time. It would all work out, Magsy felt sure. And there was still Paul. Yes, thank God, there was still Paul.

*

He stepped back from the bed, a hand to his throat, guilt almost choking him. He hadn't meant to kill her, no ... no! But she wasn't breathing. 'I didn't mean it,' he sobbed, 'honest, Mam, I loved you.' He wouldn't have stayed otherwise, would he? But how many times had he challenged God, fists balled, head bent in that back yard, why, oh, why was he fastened to her?

'Mam,' he whispered. 'Mam?'

She was as still as a broken millstone, had been a millstone, his albatross, his burden. Her lips were turning blue, while her grip on the woven quilt had slackened. It had been quick, at least, he told himself. But he remained beyond comfort. No matter what sort of person a mother was, she was still the source of life; the source of his life was now extinct.

The room was hot and oppressive. He staggered to the table and dropped into one of the four chairs. Doctor? Ambulance? Minister? Undertaker? All of the above? What was he supposed to do now? Oh, he was competent when it came to anyone else's difficulties, but this was beyond him. A ciggy might help. With hands that seemed to belong to someone else, someone with a nervous disease, he managed to light a cigarette. He had killed his own mother.

How many times had she screamed at him, 'You are killing me'? How often had she begged him to use a knife, which would have been quicker? She had seemed bent on continuing for ever, a bane, a chore, a nuisance, but she was gone now.

He flicked ash in the general direction of the fire. A tidy man, he would never have thought of tossing cigarette ash about the room, but he was not himself today; today, he was a man who had killed his own female parent.

He remembered how her colour had changed just

before the fit had taken over, how white she had become, how sweaty. The whole room had seemed to shake. And it was his fault, because he had forced her to swallow those pills. 'For God's sake, Mam,' he had yelled, 'stop messing about and get them down you.' Those painkillers had killed more than pain . . .

Honour thy father and thy mother, the bible said. That law had kicked in with Moses and it still applied. 'Stop it,' he said aloud, 'stop it. You stayed with her, you did your best.' Well, it was time to face the music. With arms almost as heavy as his heart, he dragged on a jacket and prepared to fetch the doctor. The nightmare had to be tackled. Mam was dead and gone. And, in the strictly legal sense, Lois Horrocks had died a natural death.

Danny was a good lad. He had gone back to the pit in Westhoughton, but for less money, as he was now a surface worker. His chest, though improved, was judged insufficiently sound for face work, so he counted, graded and supervised the collection of every piece that came up from the depths.

But, more important than that, he had taken over where Roy was concerned, had told the lad about Sam. Lily's gratitude knew no bounds. She was determined to be an excellent housewife and mother now that her boys were out of hospital. She would value them, care for them, would do her best to make sure that they had decent lives. In pursuit of that objective, she worked hard with Nellie, her lace skills improving no end, her knitted garments sent for sale on the outdoor market.

For the past few months, Lily's lads had led a very different and somewhat unusual life, because they now had two mothers. Nellie might have been deaf, but she was tender, appreciative of help. She was no longer smelly, and her house was clean, newly decorated right through.

The whole Hardcastle/Hulme family made its way to the High Street Baths every Thursday, separating only when divided by gender, female to the left, male to the right. Afterwards, they always met outside the slipper baths, then Nellie treated them all to ice cream sodas at Drinnan's Parlour.

Roy's recovery was slow, as they had been warned to expect. Nellie was amazing with him. In spite of her affliction, she read with him, mouthing the longer words, breaking into syllables any that proved too difficult for the lad. She painted with him, made models, played soldiers, walked with him and the dogs.

So the Hardcastles had two homes now. They slept in number 3, ate in number 1 and number 3, dashing from one place to the other depending on menus. After a while, Lily found that she actually enjoyed widowhood, took pleasure from being the only adult in her household. She was the boss, yet not the boss, because Danny became a father figure, while Nellie was closer to her than any of her real sisters.

Nellie was content for the most part, though nights were still filled with dreams of that other place, that garden, the stables and horse trough, the fountain whose trickling she heard only when she slept. The red was still there, was still waiting to claim her, but she continued to back away from it, waking each time the big, bold colour tinted the edge of her subconscious. So … loud? … it was, so frightening, dominating, terrifying.

She had done nothing about the house in the photograph. The same element that feared the red made her hang back, as if the truth might prove too much to bear. Apart from that, she was happier than she had been in her whole life. She had three adopted nephews, a wonderful adopted sister, and more reasons than most to want to continue in this vale of tears.

It was Monday afternoon. Lily had gone off to the market with some crocheted babywear for the stall, Danny was at work, Aaron and Roy at school. She mused about her plans for Aaron. The influenza had left him rather weak, so she had set out to find work that would suit the lad. Her deaf friend on the market was ready to retire; Nellie's idea was that Aaron would take over the stall. Nellie had a contact at the Society for the Deaf, many of whose members were skilled in craftwork. Aaron could sell their products, would be out in the fresh air, which situation would serve his health better than would a position down a mine or in a factory.

Pleased with herself, she put the final touches to a massive tablecloth, folded it, placed it in the bag for the Chinese laundry. Although her house was now clean and tidy, she still preferred her pieces to be washed before delivery, as many of them took weeks to perfect and they were all handled for hours on end during preparation.

She left the lace room to find that Spot was carrying on something daft outside the door. 'Silly boy,' she mouthed.

But the dog refused to be quietened, which fact indicated that he was trying to tell her something.

She descended the stairs, walked to the front door, opened it.

Across the street, Sal Higgins staggered, her form doubled over, her mouth opened in a perfect O.

Nellie shut Spot in the house and hurried across. It was plain that Sal was suffering and was having difficulty standing up. Nellie dragged her into the deserted house and forced her onto the bed beneath the front window. The woman was in labour. Although Nellie had never dealt with a birth, instinct came to her rescue, told her that there was no time to fetch a doctor or a nurse. She removed Sal's undergarments and saw that the infant's head was already crowning.

Sal screamed so loudly that Magsy's replacement at number 2 put in an appearance. She assessed the situation, announced her intention to fetch the midwife from Fox Street, then left the scene.

Nellie took a deep breath. She had to be calm, had to deliver this child safely, must not panic. She grabbed Sal's hand. 'Baby coming,' she mouthed. 'Very good.'

The baby came. Nellie held him, made sure that the cord was not twisted around the little neck, framed the words that told Sal that she had a fine, big son. The umbilicus was rather beyond Nellie's comprehension, so she placed the infant in a towel and watched ... and watched ... and hurt ...

The red came. It was not profuse, but it was red, a steady stream that edged its way out onto Sal's mattress. And this time, Nellie was swept into it, had no choice in the matter. The room darkened, changed, became another time, a different place. This was the big house, the one in Mam's cupboard, photograph curled with age, grey, grainy, unclear.

She was small, so small that she could scarcely reach the handle on the door. But she persevered, finally managing to push open that large, heavy wooden barrier. And there it was. Red, everywhere red. The man was shouting, but she could not move. 'Go,' cried Daddy. 'You have a sister, now go.'

But she remained riveted to the spot.

A terrible scream came from the red, then another noise, high-pitched and breathy. A new baby, a new life, a sister. The baby screamed and the red screamed and the red stopped screaming. He scooped up the new baby and placed it on a table in a blanket. There was a woman there, a servant or a nurse, but she was unclear, not known to Nellie.

The red was Mother and Mother was no more.

In both times, Nellie blacked out and hit the floor. Just before she fainted, she heard the baby screaming. It was her sister; yet it was not her sister . . .

Pain, oh God, such pain. Shapes, mouths, great black holes making the pain, teeth biting on the pain, tongues shaping it, making it worse, better, bigger, smaller. Lily. Lily giving pain, Aaron, Danny, Roy, Spot, Skinny, pain and pain and *pain*.

Lily sat on the edge of the sofa. 'Nellie?'

Oh, please stop the hurt!

'Nellie?'

The pain was in the shape of Lily's mouth. The real agony came from Spot and his mother. Red, red, the red had gone, but the agony remained, here, real and now.

'Nellie?'

That was her name. She recognized the shape of her name, but no more than that. There was huge discomfort beyond the window, outside the house where life continued, where Sal Higgins had just given birth.

So. The red had been her own mother, her birth mother, bleeding to death. The man was her father. The newborn was her sister. And if this was hearing, Nellie begged God with all her heart to take it away from her again. Where were the birds, the lowing cows, the gentle trickle of that fountain, the soft breezes in the trees? Hearing in the dreams had not been like this. Although her concept of dream-hearing had been vague during waking hours, she could not recall it being frightening until it reached the red part.

Lily stood back. 'Danny?'

'Yes, Mam?'

'Fetch Dr Clarke. Unless I'm very much mistaken, I think your Auntie Nellie can hear again. Tell the doc she's been passed out for well over quarter of an hour, then get him here. Aye, something's happened and this one can hear again, so can we have a bit of hush?'

While she waited for the doctor, Lily sat and held Nellie's hand. 'You'll be all right, love. No matter what it takes, I'll make sure you're all right.'

It was not all right, it was all wrong. The words were the correct shape, but voices hurt, scalded her head, made it sore. Then there was another thing, a heaving thing, almost black, dark. It was her own breathing. Sharp things, bold, purple, happening all the time – was that the clock? Mam's clock. Mam was dead and Mother was dead, so what about the sister?

Air made noise. Air moved, was not silent. It was too much. She placed her hands over her ears and forbade them to work. She would never sleep again, would never rest. How did the hearing sleep? How did they shut out all this disturbance, all this agony?

By the time the doctor arrived, Nellie was wild-eyed and her stomach had begun to heave. She vomited, lay back, her face bathed in sweat. There was no peace, no relief. The enemy had invaded her territory and she was defenceless.

He took her pulse, watched her face. 'You say she can hear? She has always been deaf.'

'No,' said Lily, 'she spoke about dreams. She remembered hearing and could hear in a way when she was asleep – birds singing – she wrote it all down for me.'

'So she suddenly went deaf?'

'I think so,' answered Lily, 'and that was why she got adopted, I'd say. They gave her away, Dr Clarke.'

The woman's heart was racing. 'I think we'll have her

in the infirmary for a day or two, see what's what. We don't want her having a heart attack. How long has she been like this?'

'Since she delivered Sal Higgins's new baby.'

'Ah.' He stood up. 'Shock of some sort, I'd say. Let the experts look at her. Now, don't worry,' he advised Lily. 'You have had enough on your plate, so stay calm. Miss Hulme will be cared for.'

By the time Nellie was removed from her house, her appearance had decayed until she resembled an insane person, somebody from a nasty film, the sort who should be locked up for the rest of her life. Lily went with her. Guilt struck again, because Lily knew that the absence of this woman would hurt her more than the death of Sam. As they drove away, she patted Nellie's hand. 'Don't you fret, love, I'll get that new tablecloth up to the laundry and I'll look after your lads.' Yes, they were Nellie's lads, too.

Nellie cried. The vehicle was loud, almost red, so terrifying. Monstrous clatterings went on outside the ambulance, crudely interwoven colours from the primary end of the palette. It was invasive, cruel, nasty. There was no space for thought, no escape, no comfort. 'Lily,' she mouthed, 'help me.'

But no-one could help. Nellie Hulme, now cursed with the gift of hearing, had entered the reality of her nightmare. She gave herself up into the pain and passed out of consciousness.

Peter had never been summoned into the Presence before. He waited outside the front living room of Knowehead, bowler twisting nervously between very clean fingers. He had washed in Dot's kitchen behind the shop, had shaved, had even allowed Dot to find a shirt of Frank's that was not too grossly large for him.

Why was he so afraid, so shaken? She was just another woman, another unwed female who needed his help. According to rumour, she had started to walk again, just a few steps, just into her own garden. It seemed that Magsy and Beth O'Gara had changed Katherine Moore, had managed what no-one had achieved before. Through them and through Dot's daughter-in-law, the crone had finally begun to show a degree of humanity.

Magsy came out of the room, held the door wide for him. 'Go in now.' She smiled. He had not been told about the summer house, as that was Miss Moore's business, but Magsy wished that she could keep an ear to the door. Peter Smythe was a character, one who would not easily wear the guise of one of the old lady's chess pieces. More locked horns, she thought as the door closed behind him.

He studied Katherine, so frail, thin, almost translucent. But the voice was strong. 'Sit,' she commanded.

He sat without thinking, would not have dreamt of disobeying.

She stared at him, unblinking, eyes hard and cold. 'You work in my gardens.'

'Yes.'

'Why? I have never met you before, of course, though people hereabouts say that you have clearly had a decent education, so why do manual labour?' The eyes twinkled for a second. 'They say you "talk proper".'

'Yes, I was taught by my mother, though I trained for no particular occupation. She was an educated woman, so I speak as she did.'

'Very good,' she replied absently, 'and I feel I must congratulate you on the way you have dealt with my land, especially the garden at the rear. It was quite a wilderness. I was beginning to feel that I had invented England's first true jungle.'

He relaxed slightly. 'I know a great deal about plants and their habitat. And I study people.' For a reason he could not understand, he did not mention his writing. 'People fascinate me,' he added.

'I have heard about your book,' she told him. 'I have also heard that you are living in a caravan.'

He bridled slightly. What business of hers was that? His mode of living had been chosen. He did not want to be tied to a house. Even this short stay in Knowehead was making him feel claustrophobic.

'Will you buy a house when your book makes money?'

'If it makes money,' he replied. 'No. I do not have the desire to own a property.'

She nodded wisely. 'But you do not mind using other people's properties?'

'No. The world belongs to everyone. I consider borders and boundaries to be in direct conflict with nature.'

'And money is of no interest to you?'

He shrugged. 'I believe in inheritance. But I never knew my father. Mother lost him before I was born; thus I had nothing to gain from my predecessors. My way of life may seem strange to you, but I am happy with it.'

'So your mother was widowed?'

'Yes,' he replied after a short pause.

The pause was noticed and Katherine identified him as illegitimate. This was, indeed, an interesting man. Something about him made her feel as if she had known him for ever. Like herself, he was eccentric, was ploughing his own furrow. 'You used to live in my summer house.'

He made no apology. 'Yes, that is the case.'

'Now, a caravan?'

'Yes. Miss Moore, if my book were successful, I might

buy a horse to tether between the shafts. Then I could move house on a regular basis.'

Katherine loved the sound of that, indulging herself for a few moments, imagining the freedom, the sheer joy of travelling aimlessly through life, a gypsy, a liberated spirit. Without arthritis, naturally. 'The summer house is yours, if you wish. No rent, just tend my garden and take the accommodation as payment. I shall also supply you with coal to heat the place and oil to light it. I may have electricity put in eventually, but not just yet.'

He swallowed. He loved that summer house, had written much of his prose and some of his poetry in there, while the light had lasted. 'I don't know what to say.'

'Then say nothing, just nod for yes.'

He nodded.

'Then that is settled, Mr Smythe. The O'Garas will be moving into the house – they are to use the upstairs rooms. I am not sure yet of the date, but we shall inform you. Oh, one more thing.'

'Yes?'

'I demand a free and signed copy of your book. Do we agree?'

'Certainly.'

'And Mrs O'Gara, my housekeeper, may need you to help occasionally in the house. Will that be satisfactory?' There was tiredness in her tone now, and an air of dismissal accompanied the words.

'I shall be glad to help, Miss Moore. And thank you.' He rose. 'I shall not shake your hand, as that might cause pain.'

'Ask Mrs O'Gara to come in, will you?' said Katherine. 'Tell her I need one of the blue pills, Mr Smythe. I have enjoyed our conversation. Goodbye.'

He left her, found Magsy in the kitchen, told her about the blue pill. 'She suffers greatly,' he said.

'I know. But she is trying, Mr Smythe, is making an effort to move.'

'You and Rachel have given her reasons to live. And, speaking of living, I am to have the summer house. It was a royal edict from the one who must be obeyed.'

Magsy laughed, picked up a bottle of pills. 'She is not bad, you know. Yes, the pain is awful and yes, her father treated her abominably – that is the main reason for her bitterness. But you know what she has done for my daughter?'

'I do, yes.'

'She is manipulative, insensitive, sometimes cruel. But underneath, there is a gold side to her. Sometimes, I find myself almost liking her. Hers has not been an easy life. She has no-one of her own, but she has chosen me, my daughter, Rachel and you to be a sort of substitute family.'

'Then she is privileged,' he laughed, 'since most of us are given a family and have no choice in the matter.'

He left the house and stood in the garden that was his own creation. Lawn, flower beds, herb patch, raspberries, lettuces, radish, rhubarb – all of these were his own work.

Yes, it was time to settle down. The summer house was probably the nearest he would come to true domesticity. He was home. And he had to go now, because Dot would be waiting to hear the tale.

Seventeen

The small room was cream, a colour more peaceful than white. White could be stark, too bright for new ears. Oh, what was she thinking of? Were her senses so welded together that sound would for ever be coloured? But at least the fear was receding, while those terrible nightmares were now consigned to her past.

She wore pads over her ears, was protected as well as possible from the bustle of this very busy hospital. She had been suffering from hysteric deafness. No-one had come across an hysteric deafness that had spanned so many years, so Nellie was an object of kindly interest. Her doctor was a warm-hearted man, one who treated people with illnesses of the brain. Nellie, who needed no surgery, who fitted no set of particular symptoms, was being treated for her reaction to restored hearing.

So that little child, the one who had rested her chin on tables, who had been too short to look inside a horse trough, had gone deaf because of shock. Her subconscious mind had chosen to go deaf. Dr Christian, a gentle man whose character suited his name, had guided her through a process that had taken many weeks. She had been witness to her own mother's death, had heard the screams of the dying, the cry of the newborn. And her brain had simply closed down the hearing department, had decided not to leave little Nellie open to any similar shocks.

When Sal Higgins had given birth, the sight of blood had triggered something in the depths of Nellie Hulme's head. The first sound she had heard had been the cry of Sal's baby son. Redness had swamped Nellie, had drawn her back to that other time, to the death and the birth she had witnessed in infancy.

Some noises got through lint and cotton wool. There was the clanking of the cleaners' buckets, loud laughter, the clatter of the dinner trolleys. But it didn't matter any more. Nellie no longer shrank into herself when sounds reached her – she was even beginning to use her new-found ability, was learning to foretell the progress of life outside her little room. Hearing might even be useful once she got the hang of it. Speech – ah – that was a different matter, a whole new dimension.

Every few days, another layer was removed from the padding. Noise soaked through more easily each time the protection was lessened. Soon, she would have to face the pain and the joy of hearing, would be taken outside by Lily and the boys, would re-enter the land of the truly alive.

Dr Christian came into the room, mouthing, 'Hello, Nellie,' as soon as he had her attention.

'Speak,' she said. Talking was funny. She had discovered her vocal chords while sobbing, was having trouble getting them under control. Dr Christian had told her not to worry about that, had explained that she heard herself from inside her head as well as from the outside. She would learn, he said firmly.

'Ah, so you wish to hear my dulcet tones?' he asked, smiling broadly. 'Carry on reading my lips, Nellie. Separating sounds comes much, much later. Every voice is different. Soon, you will know who is coming long before you set eyes on them.'

'All right,' Oh, God, would she ever be normal?

He sat beside her, moving a pile of books and some knitting from this second chair. 'Nellie?' He made sure that she was looking at him. 'Today, we uncover your ears and take out the earplugs. And I have a treat for you. Are you ready for this?'

She nodded.

'Say yes.'

She said a bright blue 'yes', rather sharp, jagged.

He made a beckoning motion towards the door. Nellie turned to see that it was half open, that a nurse stood there with a large object in her hands. It was a gramophone. Nellie had read about those, knew that they produced music and that some music was judged to be beautiful.

The nurse placed the item on a table, then removed Nellie's bandages. 'Hello,' she said to the new ears.

'Hello,' answered Nellie, the tone still sharp blue.

The girl walked to the table, her footfalls softened by crepe-soled shoes.

'Music?' Nellie asked.

'Better than that,' answered the doctor.

The room was suddenly filled with Nellie's dream, the good part, the best and blessed part. Birds. She closed her eyes, but fat, heavy teardrops pushed their stubborn way under tight lids and down her face. Mother sewing, Father smoking a cigar. The trees were high and so green, waving, moving gently against a sky of brightest blue. Horse trough, kitchen table too tall, standing on tiptoes, hands grasping a chair. Oh, dear God, who was she?

They twittered and warbled, chirruped and cheeped, these little creatures who were taken for granted by the hearing population. Nellie felt as if she were floating, as if she had been lifted physically out of the room and into a time that was neither past nor present; she was visiting eternity.

The record stopped and she opened her eyes. 'Birds,' she said, dashing the tears from her cheeks.

'Birds,' he repeated.

She copied his voice until her own was a reasonable facsimile.

The doctor nodded towards the nurse. 'Music now, Nellie. Written by a man who went deaf. He wrote it but could not hear it towards the end of his life. He was the other way round, Nellie, lost his hearing and could not find it again.'

'Sad,' she said.

He found himself almost envying Nellie, because she would hear the sixth symphony for the very first time. Would she know rhythm? Would she enjoy the form, the patterns created by this great master? How would she feel?

At first, it was just noise, just another new thing, a series of golden, pain-free sounds that rose and dropped like a bright waterfall. She looked from doctor to nurse, wondered what she was supposed to be feeling. So she closed her eyes, forbade distractions. And it simply entered her, became one with her blood, with her cells, with her very foundation.

'It had to be Beethoven,' he mouthed to the nurse. Mozart would not have been right, too many fiddly and twiddly bits, not enough flame. And so it was that this young doctor had the privilege of watching a very old lady as she fell in love with one of mankind's greatest products. The only trouble with Beethoven was that he had not lived for ever, that he had not written more before silence and death had claimed him.

The three of them sat through the movements, doctor and patient on chairs, nurse perched on the bed. The two professionals watched as Nellie's hand came up to her mouth, knew that her pores had opened to receive all the power and beauty of this huge maestro. To hell with medicine, Dr Christian thought – not for the first time. In this case, beauty was the cure.

It ended. Nellie opened her eyes in a different world.

'How was it?' the doctor asked.

And she responded in the only way she knew, with the words that described perfectly what she had just heard. 'It was a rainbow,' she replied, the syllables distorted by creaky vocal chords.

And the nurse wept.

The funeral had been over and done with weeks ago, but the lethargy that had descended upon him refused to lift. There was no life in Paul Horrocks, no joy, precious little movement. He worked, came home, ate, slept, woke, did all the same things as yesterday. Life without Mam was peaceful, silent, full of guilt.

It was August and he had not seen Magsy O'Gara since the end of June. He thought about her, knew that he was not good enough for her or for anyone, because he had wished his mother dead, had forced upon her the tablets that had choked her.

He sat and smoked endlessly, not bothering to read a newspaper, too lethargic to pay attention to the wireless. When someone rattled the door knocker, he could not stir himself to answer. He needed no-one, wanted no social contact, was closed for business.

'Hello?' The voice travelled up the hall. Bugger. He had forgotten to lock the door.

Lily Hardcastle walked in. 'Paul,' she exclaimed. 'At last. I've been trying to catch you in. Have you been out a lot?'

'Yes.' He hadn't been anywhere except to work, but he hadn't opened the door in days.

'So.' She parked herself opposite him. 'Did you hear about Nellie getting her hearing back? And Sal Higgins having a little boy?'

He shrugged listlessly.

Lily studied him. 'You'd best shape yourself. Your mam would go mad if she could see you sitting here now needing a shave and your socks full of holes.' What had happened to him? 'Have you got a new lady-friend?'

'Eh?'

It was like talking to the fire-back. 'I said have you got a new lady-friend?'

'No. Why?'

Lily closed her eyes as if praying for patience. There was something very wrong here. This creature in no way resembled the smart young man who had passed through Prudence Street on a regular basis. 'Listen, you,' she ordered sharply, 'I've come because Rachel was visiting her mam and dad. She came to the infirmary with me to see Nellie and she said Magsy O'Gara's worried about you.'

'Oh.'

'Oh? What do you mean, "oh"? I'll bloody oh you in a minute, Paul Horrocks. What's happened? You used to be up and down Tonge Moor Road on that there bike like sugar off a shiny shovel. What's the matter? Have you given up?'

Slowly, he turned to look at the woman who had blossomed since her husband's death, a woman who was becoming a lacemaker, a producer of garments, the head of a household. He told her, let it all pour, about Mam, about imprisonment, about wishing Mam dead. 'I knew I'd never be free till she died. Then I killed her.'

Lily remained mystified. 'She died of asph– choking, didn't she? What did you do? Strangle her?'

'No.' Paul elaborated, opened his chilled heart, confessed the wishes he had nurtured. 'I prayed for her to die,' he concluded, 'and she did.'

Lily drew a hand across her mouth, inhaled deeply. 'Same here in a way,' she admitted after a pause. 'Only it were me husband and me kids.' And she told the long tale of Sam and his drinking, of Danny following in Sam's footsteps, of Aaron's feet, Roy's chicken pox. 'All I could see were me in a mirror, me old, me worn down, me never catching a glimpse of a bloody butterfly, me, me, flaming me.' She beat her breast in time with the last four words, looked like a Catholic doing a *mea culpa*. 'So, when they all went down with that illness, it were my fault, because I wanted to be on me own.'

Paul threw the cigarette end into the fireplace. 'You didn't give them the germ.'

'I know that now.'

He stared into the near distance. 'I gave her the tablets.'

'Why?'

'To shut her up. They worked.'

Lily leaned forward. 'Tablets for what?'

'For pain. She said she couldn't swallow, but I made her, held the cup of water to her mouth. And she died.'

Lily inclined her head pensively, raised it again. 'Did you mean her to die then, when you gave her the pills?'

'No, but I was mad at her. She was always moaning, too hot, too cold, would I smoke outside, not enough milk in her tea. She had pain in her legs, so I gave her the two tablets early, half an hour early, just so I could get out of the house and see Magsy. She always kicked off when she knew I was going up to Hesford.'

'Magsy is missing you. And like I said, you listen to me, Paul. I felt as if I had killed Sam. I wanted to get away from him and I am away from him. So I know what you are going through and I know there's no need for you to go through it. You didn't kill your mam. She were on borrowed time, any road. The only reason she lived as long as she did were because you looked after her all them years since your dad died.'

His eyes filled and spilled. 'I hated her sometimes.'

Lily smiled. 'Aye, well, we all hate somebody sometimes. Sam drove me mad, pinching the housekeeping, rolling in drunk, no thought for what we were going to eat when he'd spent up. But I didn't kill him and you didn't kill Lois. So frame yourself before you finish up where Nellie is.'

He sobbed quietly. 'Explain to Magsy, will you?'

'No, I bloody won't. Do it yourself. She thinks you've abandoned her. Living in the house with Beth and that woman, she is, and Dot's boyfriend's in yon shed. Now, get fettling before I lose me rag altogether.'

'Thanks,' he managed.

'Don't mention it. Now, you sit here thinking your way through all that's gone on, then stick it on the fire and burn it, because it's a load of rubbish. You did your duty and more. Then, when you're nearly human again, get on that motorbike up to Hesford. You'll be losing her. She thinks you're not interested any more. And straighten your face, it looks like a smacked bum.'

The woman was right, he was not a bad man. When she had left, he did as she had suggested, went right back to his childhood, endured the scoldings his mother had administered, sat fishing by the Irwell with his dad, went conkering in the woods up Bradshaw with his pals. When he reached recent years, he lit another cigarette and waded straight in, Dad's death, Mam's increasing dependence, her demands upon his time.

Lois had been terrified of Magsy, because she had recognized the real thing, had sensed that her only child had started to drift away on a cloud of adoration. And here he sat, sorry for himself, blaming himself because of that one simple action, for the pills, for being in a hurry, for being alive and normal.

'Better shape up,' he advised himself aloud, 'because she's beautiful and noticeable. You'll lose her if you don't get a grip and visit her.'

He found his shaving stuff, scraped his face, washed, went out to buy a newspaper. Lily Hardcastle had saved his bacon, and he would never allow himself to forget that.

Rachel was fuming. Frank reckoned that if she didn't cool down, she was going to be in need of a chimney on her head, a vent to allow smoke and steam to evaporate from her brain.

'How dare he?' she asked, eyes blazing. 'How dare he write here begging for – no – demanding money? After all he did to your mam and to his kids. I don't care if he starves to death, there's no need for this kind of nastiness.'

Frank put an arm round her shoulders. 'Stop it, love. Remember you're carrying our baby and stay calm.'

'Calm?' she yelled. 'Why should I be calm? He says here that he'll be satisfied with two quid a week and any food we can spare from the shop. Shall I order some oysters and caviar?'

'Rachel—'

'No.' She dragged herself away and reached for her

coat. 'I'm getting the bus,' she announced, 'and I shall go and see Mam and Dad, then I might just pay a visit to your father while I'm down there. If you won't put him straight, then I will.'

Frank was a gentle soul, hardworking, quiet, one who wanted a peaceful life. After leaving home and abandoning his mother, Frank's goal had become this, his own business where the air was fresher, somewhere to raise a family, a place where Mam could live out her days in tranquillity. But he slammed his foot down. 'No. You are not going to see him. He will lay into you and you are expecting a baby. No need to walk into trouble. I'll do it.'

Rachel eyed him. He would do it? Would he? 'When?'

'What?'

'When are you going?'

'Not today, I've orders coming. Then I've to go and see about that van.' He intended to buy transport to enable him to deliver supplies to outlying farms and hamlets. 'It'll wait,' he said. 'Tomorrow or the next day.'

'Tomorrow never comes, Frank. Every day is today, but tomorrow is always a different day.' She knew this man well. He would have walked the Great Wall of China to avoid trouble. 'He will never leave us alone. Your mother jumps every time that shop bell rings – he's ruined her life.'

'I know.'

'Well, Chamberlain knew, and look where it got him.'

Frank allowed himself the luxury of a tight smile. 'Oh aye? And who are you? Winston Churchill?'

'No,' she replied hurriedly, 'I'm your wife and I'm having your baby. We've got this place up and running, but we still take no wages. Every penny needs ploughing back in, especially with that van coming. This baby won't be cheap – they need all sorts, do babies. He'll never stop. The day will come when he'll be back here waving his sticks at his own grandchild. He wants dealing with now, today.'

But Frank remained firm. He took Ernest's letter from her and placed it in his pocket. She was different now, shorter in temper than she had been. It was something to do with pregnancy, he decided, as Rachel had become more volatile in this, her third month. 'Just leave it, love,' he advised, 'because no good will come of you barging in on him. That's what he wants – you'd be playing into his hands. Now, upstairs and rest – that's an order. Mam will take over in the shop, so get your head down.'

She eyed him. Yes, even the quiet ones got a bit difficult at times. But her blood still boiled. She went upstairs and lay on the bed, eyes wide open, hands on her belly where her precious baby grew. So much to protect, so vulnerable, so loved. Well, it had to be done. He was going for his van and Peter Smythe could look after the ironmongery. Rachel would visit her father-in-law today; she was a grown woman and she could make her own decisions.

Dot and Peter stared at each other. Their friendship had blossomed to the point where they were easy together, where secrets became shared knowledge, where comfortable silences were the norm.

'She'll go,' whispered Dot. 'Sal's kids were raised like that, frightened of nobody, especially the bigot I married.'

Peter was nonplussed. There was one small secret he had nursed alone, one fact he had failed to share with Dot Barnes. She did not know that he had visited her husband, was unaware of the fact that Peter was beginning to get the measure of Ernest Barnes. 'Well, we shall be needed here to mind the shop. Can you prevent her from going?'

'I can try,' she answered, 'but I'd have to put me foot down good and hard, Peter. She's a clever lass, is Rachel, pretty determined, too. Hang on.' She strode off upstairs to deal with young madam.

Rachel sat up when her mother-in-law entered the bedroom.

'Now,' began Dot, heart in her mouth, 'if you go piking off down Prudence Street, I'm coming with you. Sorry I overheard you and our Frank talking, but you'd have needed to be deafer than poor Nellie Hulme were before she got the cure, because you were shouting that loud. So stick that in your pipe, Rachel, love. When our Frank goes looking for a van, you'll stop here if I have to get Peter to tie you to a chair. And if you still want to go with the chair fastened to your bum, then I'll come with you.'

Rachel sat up even straighter. She looked at the small woman who was her mother-in-law, that sweet, gentle soul, plumper now, less grey about the face, a twinkle in the eyes that sang of moorland walks and good living. And Rachel began to laugh.

'What have I said now?'

'Nothing.' Rachel hugged herself and rocked to and fro.

'I'm serious.'

'I know,' came the broken reply. 'It's just . . . oh . . .'

'What?'

'Who'd have thought that you would get so fierce?'

Dot put her head to one side and thought about that. Fierce? She wasn't fierce, she was just sensible. 'That's my grandchild you're carrying, so you can carry it away from that bad bugger. Right? Am I getting through to you?'

'Yes, Mother.' Rachel dried her eyes.

Dot grinned. 'I like that. I like Mother – it's posh.'

Rachel flicked her hair. 'I am posh. I'm being dragged up by Miss Katherine Moore, so what do you expect?'

'Oh...' Dot shook a fist in mock anger. 'I expect you to rest and do as you are told. I'll fetch you a cuppa later on, so get that head on the pillow and sleep.'

'Yes, Mother.'

'Stop it.'

'You said you liked it.'

'I do, so stop it.' Dot closed the door and went downstairs. Frank and Peter were in the shop, the former showing the latter some details attached to the business of selling hardware. Dot placed herself behind the grocery counter and started stacking shelves. Demanding money. She flicked an angry duster across the Black and Green's shelf and over to the Horniman's. With bloody menaces. There were a few spaces, so she pushed some more quarters of tea into the gaps. He wanted shooting.

'You all right, Mam?'

She looked at Frank. 'Yes. Now don't pay over the odds and make sure it runs proper, that there van.'

'Yes, Mam.'

Dot glared at her son. 'Don't you start.'

'Start what?'

'Never you mind. Get gone and buy that van. But only if it's worth the money.'

'Yes, Mam.' He left the shop just before the duster flew at the door. Dot retrieved it and walked back to reclaim her rightful place in the world.

'Dot?'

'What?'

'Are you well?' Peter asked innocently.

'I am. So don't you kick off, either.'

Peter scratched his newly barbered hair and got on with the business of pricing saucepans. The ways of women were wonderful to behold, but he was learning when to keep his mouth shut.

Katherine noticed the unhappiness of the young woman who tended her. It was caused, of course, by the absence of a certain man on a motorbike, one who had been a regular visitor during Magsy's stay in the summer house. He had stopped coming and Magsy's face grew sadder by the day.

She was tidying Katherine's room, and the slope of her shoulders caused the lady of the house to speak up at last. 'Bring Rachel across,' she suggested, 'and let us have another fashion parade.' After a great deal of tucking and hemming, the two young women were in possession of several decent outfits from Katherine Moore's wardrobe.

'She's expecting,' replied Magsy, 'thicker round the waist. Anyway it's too hot for dressing up.'

Katherine sipped her tea. 'Then would you rather have a dressing down? Because, Margaret, if you do not change your facial expression, we could be in possession of several cracked mirrors and fifty years' bad luck.'

Magsy stopped and sat down. 'Oh, Katherine.' It had taken Magsy quite a while to agree to the use of Miss Moore's forename, while the old lady categorically refused to call anyone Magsy. 'That sounds like a cat or a pet rabbit,' she had declared. 'No, Margaret is a beautiful name, good enough for the king's younger daughter, good enough for us.' So Margaret it was.

'May I be plain?' asked the older woman.

'Are you ever anything else?'

Katherine laughed. 'Margaret, go and get him. Please, I beg you.' She waited for an answer, received none. 'When I was young – yes, I was young, you know – there was a man.' Her face softened. 'A fine, handsome man,

278

broad, brown-haired, tall, humorous. My father was well pickled, soaked in brandy, a complete disgrace. But the young man didn't mind, offered to help me with him, became the only person allowed into the house.' She nodded, a sad smile playing on her lips. 'He was not good enough.'

Magsy waited. This woman seldom spoke about the past.

'He loved me, Margaret, offered to marry me. But why should the daughter of Bertram Moore tie herself to a labourer?' She closed her eyes. 'He was not good enough, not good enough. All these bitter years, I have insisted that he was unsuitable.' She lowered her voice. 'I know what it is to desire a man. I know the pain and the loneliness and the heartbreak. All these years, until Rachel broke into my life, I have told myself that I did the right thing.'

Magsy swallowed. This was costing Katherine Moore a great deal.

'So I stayed alone. Margaret, get a stepfather for that wonderful girl, a partner for yourself. He loves you.'

Magsy crossed the room and sat on a stool beside the chaise. Something had happened between herself and Katherine just recently. The relationship had settled, had become comfortable, pleasant. They liked the same books, the same wireless programmes, the same foods. And they loved the same child. Katherine had invaded Beth's life and Beth adored her. She was the grandmother and sage, the *aide-mémoire*, the listener, the talker, the friend.

'Marry him,' whispered Katherine.

Magsy smiled. 'And where would we live?'

'Here to begin with, then – who knows? I shall not last for ever.'

The idea of Katherine Moore's death did not please

Magsy O'Gara. This wise and difficult woman was probably enjoying these years, because she was finally allowed to flower, to relax and be herself, her real, human and vulnerable self. 'He has not proposed to me.'

'He will.'

Magsy sighed heavily. 'Will he? The last thing I heard was that his mother had died. Since then, nothing.' She touched the old lady's hand. 'I swear one thing to you, Katherine, that I shall be here with you until your end. What you did for Beth has been the making of her. She is finally allowed to express herself without being called cleverclogs by her classmates.'

The school was delighted with Beth. She was advanced well beyond her years, yet her eagerness to learn and her ready admission of her limitations endeared her to staff and pupils alike. Also, she was fussed over, had become something of a mascot, as she was the baby of Chedderton Grange, the youngest ever girl to pass the entrance with an A grade.

'Beth deserves it,' Katherine said, 'and you deserve some time off. Get the bus. Go to Bolton. Be there when he comes home from work.'

'No.'

'This is the middle of the twentieth century – are you planning to remain demure? Visit your other friends, make him a small part of your itinerary.'

Magsy pushed a hand through sweat-damped hair. 'All right. I shall leave a note for Beth – she's playing tennis, by the way – and she will see to your needs until I come home.'

Katherine smiled broadly. 'Wear the cornflower blue, that little dress of mine that you made over. Borrow my good leather handbag and the silk scarf. Go on. Go away, I am too tired for your fussing.'

Magsy planted a kiss on the wrinkled forehead. 'Yes,

Grandmama.' Then she dodged away from Katherine's weapon, a rolled newspaper that whipped through the air.

Yes, it was time to go and find him.

Eighteen

Alone, Katherine picked up Peter Smythe's newly published book.

He had delivered it only this morning, had handed it in to young Beth at the front door. A slim volume of some two hundred pages, it was entitled *The View From Up Here*, with a plain cover in white, black and gold. Well, there was little else to do. Beth had not returned from tennis, while Margaret, fussy and almost breathless in the cornflower blue dress, had set forth for Bolton in search of her young man.

She settled back on down-filled cushions, opened the book and began a fascinating journey through the life of a man who had never settled, whose origins were uncertain, who took what was offered, asked for little, worked when necessary. As she made her way through the early pages, Katherine encountered the real Peter Smythe, a self-made wit and gentleman whose written prose was as perfect as his delivered English. This was, indeed, a man of mystery . . .

Katherine woke as Beth entered the room, pink and damp after several sets of tennis. 'Beth,' she said, 'you should take a bath. Must you get so hot?' The child's fair skin looked as if it were glowing from the inside.

'I won,' cried Beth, 'and Angela Corcoran is older than I am.' She placed her racquet on the floor. 'Where's Mam?'

'She has gone to Bolton to visit friends.'

Beth sat on the stool next to the chaise. 'Will she see Paul?'

'I expect so.'

'Good.' Beth blew a strand of hair from her face. 'She has been miserable without him. I think that she didn't know she loved him until he wasn't here any more.'

What a concept for a child to express. Katherine removed the threatening smile from her own face. Living with precocity had its delightful moments. 'Did you go into school?' Although these were summer holiday weeks, Chedderton Grange never closed its doors to pupils. There was always at least one member of staff available at weekends, while two or more were present during holidays. Learning never ceased, so school never closed.

Beth nodded. 'I did photosynthesis, but some of the words were too big and I need to look them up.'

'Ah.'

'It's exciting. It's about how plants eat. Mr Smythe was telling me about it – they need light, air and water. Is there anything to eat?'

Katherine waved a hand at a biscuit barrel. 'Two only. Your mother has left salad for us.'

'Yuk.' Beth pulled a face.

'Now, when you eat lettuce and watercress, you will be eating things that have, in their turn, eaten photosynthetically. This is called absorbing your work.'

Tinker came in, leapt on Beth, stopped dead, then licked Katherine's hand. The old woman never ceased to marvel at this dog, because he had always been aware of her infirmities.

When Beth and Tinker had demolished the biscuits, the latter lay in the doorway, as this was the coolest place, while Beth rattled on about photosynthesis and excited molecules. When she spoke of the sciences she adored, her whole face lit up like a Christmas tree.

'Beth,' implored Katherine, 'please go and bathe before we eat. At the moment, you resemble cooked meat. I shall be eating you with a spot of horseradish.'

The child laughed. 'No, mint sauce. Mam sometimes calls me her pet lamb.' She dashed off to cleanse herself.

Katherine smiled and shook her head. She could not imagine life without Margaret and Beth, would not allow herself to remember life before Rachel. Out of the bowels of the Hades below, from mean streets guarded by mill walls, from that huge, industrial town, these wonderful people had arrived to colour her days.

Rachel was practical, beautiful, seemed to have been hand-made for business, for contact with the public. Margaret was quietly clever, a reader, as practical as Rachel, but with a hint of academia about her. Beth – oh, Beth was just wonderful. From a mating between a soldier and a pretty woman, this rare product had emerged, beautiful, talented and brilliant beyond words.

The brilliant-beyond-words child put her head round the door. 'Katherine?'

'Yes?'

'Can I use some of your nice smelly powder?'

Again, Katherine squashed a smile. 'You may. Can implies that you have the physical ability to use the talcum. May tells you that you might, that you have my permission.'

'Oh. Right. Thank you.' Beth went off to soak herself in water, bath oil and all she had learned today.

Katherine picked up the book again, smiled when she read about some of the idiosyncracies of Peter Smythe's clients. There was the widow with seventeen cats, a spinster who wore a hat at all times, rain, shine or when seated at her table. Another lady talked her cows into giving more milk, yet another old maid chased every man who came within a mile.

Then, she met herself. There was no name, but she was the featureless face at a window. Startled, she placed a hand at her throat. There she was, invisible, bitter, daughter of a drunk, her eyes welded to a pane of glass through which she observed life, though she never entered it, never entertained it. This had been written before the advent of Rachel, long before Margaret and Beth had entered Katherine's house and heart.

She inhaled deeply, put the book down. The matter was scandalous, almost libellous. She had not been identified by name, but everyone in these parts would surely recognize Miss Katherine Moore, daughter of the father from hell, bitter spinster crippled with arthritis, one who criticized others while protecting herself from their barbs by remaining hidden and unavailable.

Her hand, already on its way to the telephone receiver, creaked to a halt. No. If she made a fuss through her lawyer, that would exacerbate matters, would draw more comments, closer attention. She would talk to the man, by God, she would. If only ... if only she could walk to that summer house. No, she had to think. There was no point in rushing in, because she had not yet worked out what to say to Peter Smythe. The old pride reared its head – how dare anyone, let alone a tramp, write about Katherine Moore, daughter of the Moores of Chedderton Grange?

Democracy, came the answer. No names, no proof, though this was definitely her. Yet she had smiled while reading about others in the book – would people smile about her? Would they? This was probably another nine-day wonder and she should not allow it to affect her. He had provided her with this book, wanted her to read it, was waiting for her reaction. Well, she intended to play him at his own game. Let him wonder whether she had bothered to read it.

She placed a bookmark between the pages and waited for Beth. After their meal, the two of them could enjoy an unscheduled game of chess. To hell with Peter Smythe; he was, after all, a mere employee, a gardener.

Yet the subject rankled for the rest of the evening and Beth triumphed in the games.

Magsy O'Gara caught sight of herself in the window of Gregory and Porritt's. She looked good, looked great, in fact. The shoes were of kid, navy to match the handbag, the dress was an understatement in cornflower, while a loose silk scarf of blue and white completed the crisp outfit.

As she passed through town, heads turned – women as well as men stopped in their tracks to look at her, and she found herself smiling. For how long had she done the exact opposite of this? Years and years she had spent in hiding, clothes loose and black, a headscarf concealing remarkable hair, shoes flat and heavy, head down, always down as she made her way home to safety. And safety had been a photograph of a dead man and a certificate of thanks from the king. Oh, William. She had loved him, still loved his memory, but it was time to move on, time to make a life for herself, for Beth, also for Paul.

She kept her head high as she walked up Derby Street, answered shouted greetings, was pleased when people told her she looked pretty. She was pretty. She had always been pretty, should make the most of herself before life closed in and made her old.

Prudence Street looked mean and narrow, the Kippax Mill at the bottom, Kershaw's close to the house in which she and Beth had lived. How had they survived the din of that, the smoke that poured even now from tall brick nostrils whose supposed superiority sullied a sky that was duller here, dirty, clouded by filth? King Cotton, saviour of the north, killer of thousands – God, what was that monarch doing to these people and why had she never noticed before?

But here in the grey shadows, children played, housewives sat outside on old chairs, pigeons pecked in an everlasting search for crumbs between those filthy cobbles. Dear God forbid that she should ever be forced to live here again.

She stood opposite the dwelling she had occupied so recently, wondered anew at man's blind acceptance of conditions imposed by the real kings, the Bank of England and its stock exchange. Beth would never live in a place like this, would earn her way out by sheer hard labour at her books.

She opened the door of number 1 and stepped inside Nellie Hulme's newly decorated home. 'Hello?' she called.

Lily Hardcastle clattered down the stairs. She was pink in the face after the exertion of learning new patterns in the lace room. 'Magsy,' she exclaimed, 'you look beautiful.'

Magsy hugged Lily. 'Where's Nellie?'

Lily folded her arms in an attitude typical of a northern housewife who pretends to be angry. 'You might well ask,' she replied. 'I've been asking myself the same question this past hour. She went down to the market to help our Aaron. He's left school and he's going to sell stuff – that deaf stallholder's retiring – so Nellie's with him. Or so she says. But she'll not be educating nobody, Mags, oh no, she'll be listening to things. She found trains last week.'

Magsy sat down and smiled encouragingly. 'I see.'

'Well, I wish I could see. She were terrified of all sorts

when she first got her hearing back, but that didn't last. Oh, she's wanting adventure now. Her'll be stood on that bridge at Trinity Street waiting for trains. They rattle about underneath her and she gets covered in all sorts of muck.'

The visitor nodded. 'It's all a novelty to her.'

Lily sniffed. 'Aye, well, that's as may be, but I'm stuck here with two dogs, a dinner to make and fourteen napkins in ecru wanting finishing for some Scottish lord on an island up yon.'

Magsy laughed. 'But you're happy.'

Lily grinned. 'Ooh, Mags, we're like sisters, in and out of one another's houses all the while. See, she still struggles to talk, but she manages to tell my lads off. It's as if she's another mother for them.' She slowed down, perched on the edge of a chair and studied her visitor. 'So, what brings you down here?'

Magsy raised her shoulders. 'Just thought I'd have a wander, see how you are.'

'Right.' Lily cleared her throat. 'Have you seen anything of Paul Horrocks?'

'No.'

The monosyllable contained sadness, Lily thought. 'Lost his mam.'

'Yes.'

Lily did not want to say that she had called on Paul Horrocks, so she jumped up to make tea. 'I'll put the kettle on. Sal's little lad's doing well, but she never takes her eyes off him. You'd best go and see her after, she'd expect that. Ernest Barnes still pulls faces at them across the street. There's another Catholic family in your old house. Would you like a ginger biscuit?'

While Lily rattled about, Magsy realized how much her life had changed. This house was tiny and oppressive. Even with new paint and wallpaper, it was dingy, almost claustrophobic. At Knowehead, she and Beth had a big sitting room, a bedroom each, a bathroom and a kitchen. Windows opened to admit fresh air, not this soot-laden rubbish breathed in by the poor of Bolton. There were night-birds, owls, nightingales, there was peace, sunshine, a good, fresh breeze. No hooter sounded, no clogs rattled by in the morning, no chimney belched into the clear sky.

Lily brought the tea. 'Are you all right up there with that owld battle-axe?'

Magsy giggled. 'Ah, she's very kind to Beth and she is in a lot of pain, Lily. Once I got to know her, I found her quite decent.'

'And Dot's all right?'

'A different woman, she is. He came up and clouted Rachel, you know, that creature from number five. Then he wrote demanding money – Rachel is furious. But Dot has blossomed, she really has.'

Lily sat down and sipped her tea. 'When Dot got out, ooh, I envied her. I wanted to get away, but this is where I was put, Mags, so I have to get on with it, God help me.'

Nellie came in, thinner, hatless, wreathed in smiles. With a croaky voice, she greeted Magsy before apologizing to Lily. She had been standing under the Town Hall clock waiting for it to strike. As it struck only four times throughout the hour, she had needed to stay for a while to get the full chime. 'I have heard it before,' she explained, 'but I wanted to be near it.'

Lily sent a knowing look to Magsy, an I-told-you-so expression.

Nellie rattled on, consonants fairly clear, vowels often distorted, excitement making the delivery even worse. She had heard newspaper sellers, horses, singing emerging from a pub, the tooting of several horns and the whistling of trains. The horses' hooves were purple, apparently, like the ticking of a clock but with more blue in the mix.

Lily thrust a cup into Nellie's hands. 'Here, drink up and shut up, for goodness' sake.' She glared at Magsy. 'It's like dealing with a five-year-old on Christmas morning, ooh-ing and ah-ing over every new thing.'

Magsy laughed. It was lovely to see Nellie so alive, so excited. In her bones, Magsy knew that Lily shared Nellie's excitement, that all who truly cared for Nellie Hulme appreciated her happiness and her confusion. Yes, Nellie was a child again and it was wonderful to behold. 'You can listen to the wireless now,' she said.

Lily bridled again. 'Have you tried making lace to the signature tune of Dick Barton, Special Agent? I tell myself I won't let it get to me, only you start rattling on without realizing it. Then she has the Home Service plays on, murders and all sorts. I wouldn't care, but she talks back to the wireless.'

'Practising,' said Nellie.

Lily ignored the interruption. 'And she sings, all on the one note, like, sounds like a cat howling in the night. Poor dogs go out of their minds, they don't know what to make of it.'

The afternoon sped away, borne on the wings of idle gossip and friendly banter. Magsy left, visited Sal Higgins, exclaimed over the new baby, talked about Dot, the dreadful Ernest and life in Hesford, about Frank's intention to buy a van, about Katherine, Beth, Peter Smythe and the cost of living.

After a small feast of bread and Lancashire cheese, Magsy left the Higgins home and walked round the corner to Fox Street. It was six o'clock and Paul would be home. With each step, her heart beat faster, but she maintained her outward coolness as she knocked on his door. There was no reply.

Bertha stuck her head into the street. 'He's gone out, love, said he were borrowing yon van of Murphy's. Didn't want to go on his bike, said he were taking somebody for a ride in the countryside.' She grinned knowingly. 'Talk about ships what pass in the night! He never said nothing about who were getting this 'ere ride, but I reckon he's piked off up your way looking for you.'

Magsy's joy could not be contained. It spilled out of her mind and spread itself in the form of a huge smile all over her face. 'Thank you.'

Bertha waddled over, dropped her voice. 'He's not been right, love. She were a pest, but she were his mam, and he's took it bad ways, wouldn't talk to nobody, wouldn't open yon door. He come round, like, just the once, to give me Lois's bits and pieces – string of nice imitation pearls, lovely shopping bag and a couple of ornaments. I tried talking to him, but he were a shut shop. Ooh, I hope this van's a good sign, Magsy – I were getting feared for him.'

'Thanks for telling me, Bertha. And thanks for caring about him, he's a decent man.'

'And he loves the bones of you, so fingers crossed. Happen he's coming to his senses.'

There was no more she could do here, so Magsy retraced her steps and walked up to Derby Street. As she waited on Moor Lane bus station for the vehicle that would carry her back to greener pastures, Magsy saw the funny side of the day. The mountain had come to Muhammad, but Muhammad was out in a borrowed van. It was plain that great minds did, indeed, think alike.

While Magsy was knocking on his door, Paul Horrocks was sitting in her upstairs living room, jacket off, shirt sleeves rolled to the elbows, mind jumping everywhere.

The old dear was downstairs with Beth, both heads bowed over a chessboard, nothing to be heard but some heavy sighs as the game progressed. He had been offered salad, had refused, because his stomach was tied in a granny knot, while his head was all over the place, would she be pleased to see him, would she understand about his mother, would she ... would she marry him?

Games finished, Beth dashed upstairs. She entered the room with Tinker and threw herself into a chair. 'She'll be visiting the new baby,' she said by way of comfort, 'and Miss Hulme. Then she'll have gone to your house.'

Paul extracted himself from beneath a fast-growing Tinker and grinned ruefully. 'That's a very affectionate dog, Beth.'

'Yes.' She studied the man for a few seconds. 'Sorry about your mother.' She paused, assessed his mood. 'If you go back in the van, you might catch her, because that's faster than a bus.'

He thanked her for her condolences, but stated his intention to remain.

'You love my mother, don't you?'

He stared hard at this troublesome, lovable child. 'That's a grown-up thing, Beth, not something you need to know about.'

The lovable child tut-tutted in an adult fashion. Why weren't adults plainer and simpler? They had to run three times round the houses just to find out where they were. As far as Beth could work out, life became more complicated once maturity set in. Children played, liked some people, didn't like others, got on with it, didn't question themselves. Whereas the older and wiser folk spent so much time thinking about stuff – well – they needed to get on with things.

'She'll be back,' he said.

'I know, she's my mother.'

He stared at his shoes, at the rug, at the recumbent Tinker. 'Beth?'

'Yes?'

He raised his head. 'When your mother does come back, make yourself scarce, will you?'

Beth stood up, indignance in her expression. 'I wasn't born yesterday,' she said haughtily. Then she stalked off to her bedroom, leaving him to indulge his nervousness. Sometimes, grown-ups were just too stupid for words.

Magsy was hot, tired and rather cross as she climbed the hill from the bus stop. The dress hung sadly, any semblance of crispness destroyed by this afternoon's murderous heat; the shoes rubbed, her hair hung damply around a face that screamed for cold water, she was thirsty and well on her way to exhaustion.

She saw the van, dust all over it, remembered the night when he had stayed with her outside the hospital. Her heart rose unbidden, and she swallowed, the movement almost painful in a mouth as dry as blotting paper. She had half expected him, had half dismissed such expectation, as he must have been here for a couple of hours. And she was a mess and—

'Mam?' Beth was leaning out of one of the upper windows. 'Paul's here.'

'I know.'

'He's been waiting ages.'

Magsy sighed, remembering how proud she had always been of Beth for knowing exactly how to behave, yet now, at this crucial time, the child was yelling all over the road while Paul Horrocks listened, no doubt.

She entered Katherine's kitchen, dabbed cold water on her forehead, pulled the dress into some semblance of order. When she had consumed a large glass of lemonade, she began the climb towards a moment that might well shape her future, each stair a mountain in the relentless heat. It was after seven o'clock, yet the earth continued to burn.

Paul stood up as she entered the room.

'Thank you for waiting,' she said. 'We must have passed each other. Shall I make some tea?'

'No.' He walked past her and closed the door. 'Little ears,' he said.

They stared at one another for a few moments. 'Where have you been?' she asked.

'Getting through the guilt,' he replied.

'Ah. Your mother. I am sorry.'

He pushed a damp curl from his slick forehead. 'This may sound ridiculous, but it is too hot for a proposal. I thought I should make an appointment for some other time, though.'

Magsy grinned. 'So you are proposing to set a time for a proposal?'

'That's it,' he replied.

'I accept your proposed idea for a proposed proposal. Of course, I have no idea what my answer will be. We must make an appointment that is mutually suitable.'

'Saturday,' he suggested, 'Town Hall steps, two o'clock, don't be late.' He picked up his wrinkled jacket and walked to the door, pausing as he touched the handle. He turned and looked at her for several seconds. 'By the way, you have a black mark on your nose. And you are still beautiful.' He left, a huge smile on his face as he descended the stairs. She would marry him, so all was well in the civilized world.

Beth dashed in. 'What did he say?'

'That I have a dirty mark on my nose.'

'You have.' Beth stood, feet planted apart, arms akimbo. 'So he sat here all that time, waited for you and never asked if you would marry him? That was all he said? About your nose? He only stayed about two minutes after you got back.'

'Yes.'

'Mam?'

'What?'

'He wouldn't come all that way for nothing.' Adults really were stupid, absolutely mad. 'Tinker's got more sense than you two,' offered the young genius before stalking out, head in the air, scruffy puppy at her heels.

Alone, Magsy looked in the mirror, spat on a thumb and rubbed the smear from her nose. She picked up William's photograph and kissed it. She would meet him again one day, when the world was a little older and real time had been left behind by her earthly self.

But for now, while her life remained fastened to this globe, Magsy O'Gara had discovered her new love, so she whispered a goodbye, then went to wash her face properly.

Peter Smythe watched the van as it drove away, wished with all his heart that he could have begged a lift. But a lift was out of the question, because he had to remain invisible, safe and totally undetected.

He had done his stint at the shop, had come home to his little summer house, was about to embark on one of the more adventurous of his journeys through a well-travelled life. He brushed his shoes, washed his face, found a pair of bicycle clips. The bike was a borrowed one, though he had failed to inform the owner about the loan. Well, that should present no problem, because the man whose bike this was had gone away for the week. 'No harm done,' he told his reflection in the small mirror.

The time had come. He stuffed a small package into

his pocket, took a deep breath, left the summer house. Dusk was still not happening, but he had no time to waste. The route would take him through fields and narrow country lanes, as he needed to be anonymous to the point of non-existence.

He slipped through a gap in the hedge, skirted a field, found the bike where he had left it, began the journey of several miles. Once at the outskirts of Bolton, he would wait for the light to fail before continuing along the populated section. He was afraid, yet he knew that he was doing the right thing; he was doing it for Dorothy.

At the age of sixty-two, Peter had arrived at love very late in life, but Dorothy was his life, his hope, his future, however brief that might be. The main thing was to make sure that his life was not ended by the hangman.

Because Peter Smythe was on his way to free Dorothy; he was going to rid the world of Ernest Barnes.

Nineteen

Paul and Magsy Horrocks were among the early arrivals at Chedderton Grange.

This was the first night of *Olivia Tangle*, a play written by one of the seniors. It was a comic and all-female version of *Oliver Twist* and Beth, proud as a strutting peacock, had the meatiest role. As Ferocia McFadden, she was to play the Fagin role, her face covered in warts, body bent in the shape of an old woman, several teeth blacked out.

'You look lovely,' said Paul as he drew the final wrinkle across his stepdaughter's face. 'A picture of glowing youth and innocence if ever I saw one. In fact, if I were single, I'd ask you out for a date Saturday night.'

Beth grinned at him, showed him the 'bad' teeth. 'I do not associate with commoners, Mr Horrocks,' she informed him. 'I only pickpocket the high and mighty. Am I ugly enough?'

'Yes,' chorused her adult companions. She looked like nothing on God's good earth, thought Magsy, face a greenish-white, dark circles around the eyes, stringy wig dangling down to her shoulders, black clothing that looked as if it had come straight from one of Charlie Entwistle's rubbish wagons.

Chedderton Grange school had outgrown itself. As its reputation had spread to encompass the whole of England, another location was earmarked, a huge, rambling mansion about a mile away, a place large enough to take a dozen boarders. So this would be the final dramatic effort from the Grange.

Magsy was sad. The very size of the school had been its strength, yet she must continue to believe, because the headmistress had reassured all parents that standards would not slip, that each girl would have her own needs covered.

Magsy squeezed Paul's hand. Her happiness was so precious that she had to make sure of it, was having to damp down her fears that this man, too, would disappear. William had been lost in a war, and there was no war now. But she feared for Paul each time he set off for work on that motorbike, was happier when he borrowed Murphy's van.

He knew her fears, squeezed her hand in return. He was a happy man at last. Living at Knowehead was all right. He actually liked the old dragon downstairs, but he wished that they could get their own place, a proper house with two floors all to themselves. Nevertheless, he was grateful to be out of the slums, happy to be married to the most wonderful woman on God's earth.

It had been a quiet wedding, just close friends, little Beth and Paul's neighbour from Bolton. Magsy had forbidden him to take instruction, so he remained a Protestant, though he had agreed that any children would be raised in his wife's faith.

Magsy's opinion was that all men were equal, that Catholics and Protestants were basically the same, human flesh, human blood, divided only by the likes of Ernest Barnes, whose remains had been lowered into the earth just a few months ago. A stroke, the certificate said. And how lonely had that man's last journey been? Just a few old Lodgers and the undertaker's men, no wife, neither of his sons, no friend to see him on his way. Even his paltry legacy had been given away by Dot to a charity for children. She had muttered a few dark words about how Ernest had abused his own boys, had declared that he would now pay for a couple of orphans to be fed, had never since mentioned his name.

Beth looked in a mirror. 'Jesus wept,' she exclaimed.

Magsy put a hand to her mouth, held on to her laughter. Beth was not a child who took the good Lord's name in vain, yet these words had tripped so easily from that sweet mouth.

'Mam, I look terrible. Isn't it brilliant?' She pulled faces at herself in the glass. 'Perhaps I'll be an actress.'

Paul looked at Magsy, Magsy looked at Paul. In the past few months, Beth had been a doctor, a scientist, a mathematician and now she was an actress. They waited for each change of mind, smiling at each other as the world unfolded before this wonderful, mercurial mind. Whatever she chose, Beth would do it well.

Other parents and children arrived, fussy voices and bodies filling the classroom until Paul and Magsy decided to leave in order to escape the nervousness. They said ta-ta to Beth, noticing how she did not fuss. Other girls recited lines, stared in mirrors, pulled at hair that would not obey its owners. But Beth simply sat and read a book. 'Keats,' said Magsy quietly.

'I'll bet you ten bob she'll be a poet tomorrow,' replied Paul.

Magsy shook her head. 'No,' she answered, 'I'm not playing that game. She was talking about being an astronaut last week, said there'd be people on the moon in twenty years. No, I'm betting no money, love.'

Arm in arm, they walked into the small hall where a stage and curtains had been installed. It was time for Beth to make yet another of her débuts.

*

A much thinner Nellie Hulme and a much plumper Lily Hardcastle travelled on the bus up to Hesford. Closer than sisters, these two were welded together by lacework so strong that only God would ever undo that stitching. They also shared the rearing of Roy and the control of Aaron, whose marketing skills were amazing. In fact, he had done so well that several dozen homeworkers were now knitting day and night to fill the orders he had taken without informing his employers. 'But Mam,' he had answered when reproached, 'I can sell it, I can sell it all.' Which was true, because the lad might have sold coal to folk from Newcastle.

'Nice up here,' said Nellie, whose speech was coming on in leaps and bounds.

'Lovely,' agreed Lily, her mind fixed on Aaron and Roy. 'They'll be all right, won't they?'

'Yes, they will.'

Each woman carried a shopping bag containing night-dress, clean underclothing and toiletries. After the play, they were to take supper with Magsy, Paul and Beth. Tonight, they would sleep under the roof of Miss Katherine Moore of Knowehead, once owner of the house to which they now travelled, Chedderton Grange. Lily swallowed a lump of nervousness. 'I can't remember the last time I slept away from home.'

'You'll be all right,' said Nellie, 'you're with me.'

'I know. But she's reckoned to be fierce.'

Nellie laughed. 'Yes, well, so are we. And there's two of us, so she had better watch out.'

'They'll remember to feed Skinny and Spot, won't they?'

Nellie sighed. 'Yes, they will. Now stop worrying, here's where we get off.'

They walked up the road to the Grange, each looking forward to the play. It was good to be out, good to be together even in the chill darkness of October. The house hove into view, its gardens lit by lamps, the driveway long and winding.

Yes, this would be a good night.

Katherine had not picked up Peter Smythe's book in weeks, but she had asked Beth to fetch it for her this very afternoon. Weary and made cross because of her inability to watch the play, Katherine decided to indulge herself.

She opened it at her mark, chewed absently on a rare treat, Belgian chocolate with strawberry filling. Yes, the man had enjoyed an interesting life, but the new pain-killers were extremely effective. After just a couple of paragraphs, her eyelids closed and she was asleep.

The author of the slim volume walked smartly along by the side of his wife.

They moved at exactly the same pace, even strides, she swinging her left arm, he his right. The other two arms were linked, while Peter bore in the free arm that famous cane which had become his trademark.

They had married within weeks of Ernest's death. Peter, who had come late in life to love, insisted on keeping his little wooden house. It was snug, tiny, and just about adequate for the couple. They had a bedroom, a sitting room, kitchen, bathroom and an enclosed wrap-around porch. They talked endlessly, listened to certain programmes on the wireless, had obviously been created with this partnership in mind.

Dot had not expected a second chance. She kept her independence, was still employed by her son, but the centre of her life was now this small, lovable man who was well read, kind and very affectionate. 'Peter?' she said.

'Yes?'

'We were lucky, weren't we?'

'We were indeed, my dear.'

She tutted quietly. 'Fancy him dying just like that. As if God had planned it so that we could be together, you and me.'

She seldom mentioned her dead husband, and she plainly expected no reply, so Peter kept his counsel. He had led Dorothy into his ways, had encouraged her to wander country lanes with him, to learn about plants and wild flowers, about cuttings, cultivation, about growing from seed. But his knowledge of poisons sat deep within him and he would never tell her that particular truth.

Peter Smythe owned no God and was owned by none. He saw humanity as an extension of the animal kingdom, a layer not above, yet slightly apart from the rest. Humans had developed beyond plucking berries from trees, beyond digging for roots and scratching for grubs. Humans killed. They killed not just for food, but also for territory. And he had made Dorothy a widow.

'I hated him,' she said now.

'I know. So did everyone else, or so it would seem.'

He looked back on that night, shivering as he wondered anew that he still owned his freedom, though he regretted not at all the action he had taken. Peter had helped rid the world of a rodent, a creature who would not have been allowed to remain alive as a member of any other animal group.

'Are you all right?' she asked. 'That were a big shiver, love. Do you want to borrow me scarf?'

'No, thank you. It is rather cold, but we shall soon be inside.'

Monkshood, sometimes called Monkshead, had done the trick. Peter pulled his coat tightly to his chest, relived that fateful evening. Dot paced along beside him, quiet, adoring and adorable, a loving woman who had required just a small amount of respect and affection to bring her back to life . . .

Aconite in his pocket, Peter let himself in through Ernest Barnes's back door. He listened, just as he had listened many times before, to the moaning of this abandoned 'widower'. Dot was a bad bitch, Dot had never fed him properly, she was a parasite, a thief, a nightmare. She had spoilt his sons, had turned them into nancy boys, had driven the whole household into madness.

Peter boiled the kettle, made tea, dropped the aconite into Ernest's cup, poured a measure of scotch into the drink so that the taste would be disguised. This poison, brought into England in the Middle Ages, had been used by ancient cultures to finish off old men who had become burdensome and useless. How apt.

'What are you thinking about?' asked Dot. 'I can tell you're thinking.'

He returned to the present. 'Vermin control,' he replied.

The first symptoms were negligible, just a slight numbing of the tongue, a tingling sensation around the mouth. Ernest sat back, empty cup placed on the table, tongue flicking around lips that were suddenly pale.

'Ooh, very nice, I'm sure,' laughed Dot. 'Here we are on our way to see Beth in a play, and you're thinking about rats.'

Yes, very nice. The sensation of small insects crawling over the skin, cold sweats, irregular breathing. Peter knelt beside the perspiring man and whispered, 'Your pulse is slowing and breathing is difficult. You are so cold. In a moment, you will vomit. I do this for Dorothy, the woman I love. I do this for all those Catholics who live across the street, decent people whose faith I do not share, but whose rights I defend.'

He stood back then and watched Ernest's final agony. Without digitalis, there was no cure. But Peter had saved Dorothy, had brought her a gift whose value was beyond price, beyond measure. He had given her the freedom to move about Hesford without jumping every time a vehicle approached.

They reached the gates of Chedderton Grange. 'He deserved that stroke,' said Dot, 'Ernest, I mean. God knows he stroked my lads' backs with a cane often enough.'

'Stop thinking about him.' He released her arm and put his hand on her shoulder. 'Fear is dead,' he told her. 'And nothing will ever hurt you again.'

He removed the cup, placed it in his pocket, abandoned the corpse where it was, half on and half off its usual chair. With his own heart beating like a bass drum, Peter Smythe left the scene of his crime and steered the bike into Prudence Street's back alley. Like a shadow, he had come and gone for weeks, had gained the confidence of a hateful man.

Well, it was done. As the priest had said at the end of a Mass Peter had attended just once out of interest, *ite missa est*. It was over. And Dorothy was free at last.

'Come on,' she urged, 'you've gone all of a dream. Peter?'

'I am sorry, my love. Yes, we must hurry, or we shall miss the first scene.' He led his wife towards the next episode in their joint lives, and guilt was not in the equation.

She woke with a start, the book still held in her hand. Oh, she was always falling asleep these days. It was probably a side effect of these new painkillers, great big white things that required breaking into four pieces before she could swallow them.

Once her focus settled, she fixed her eyes again on the work of Peter Smythe. The man who lodged with his wife in Katherine's summer house was courteous, well-spoken, almost willing at times, but there was something, a sort of challenge in his eyes when he addressed her. Was he wondering whether she had found herself in this book?

She read on, learned a little about his background, his mother, his home. Peter's only parent had been cursed by drink, had been a weekend imbiber. During weekdays, she was sober, reasonable, a good educator of her only child. But at weekends, she raged about the man who had cast her out after impregnating her. Good God, Peter Smythe had no shame, was screaming his illegitimacy all over the page.

I am a bastard, but a privileged soul for all that. Mother taught me to enjoy nature, to nurture all things that grow, to respect creatures of the earth. She had a brain that encompassed more than I shall ever know, yet her bitterness twisted that sweet mind, driving her further each year, then each month, then each day into the madness that would finally engulf her.

Katherine sniffed and rested her vision for a moment. At least he had owned a mother. As she thought about what she had just read, she realized that she and Peter Smythe had much in common, since her parent, too, had been married to a bottle. Like her, Peter had been lonely; like her, he had remained alone. Until now, until he had suddenly married Dot Barnes.

Lifting her hands again, she continued to read.

Nellie stopped in her tracks.

Lily carried on, realized that she was suddenly alone, turned on her heel. What was Nellie playing at now? 'Nellie?'

There was no reply.

'Nellie? Come on, we'll be late.'

An owl cried mournfully into near-darkness. Nellie, scarcely breathing, heard the bird's wings as he raised his body into the night sky. Water. Water splashing onto a cotton dress, a woman's laughter. Mother. The same fountain, silent now, no water because of the frost of autumn, but that cherub would be there, the little angel with a chip taken out of his nose. Hard ball, tiny hard ball, Father with a stick. Golf club.

'Nellie!' Had the poor woman gone deaf again?

Powerful eyesight adjusting quickly to darkness, Nellie took in the lie of the land, tall Edwardian windows, a lion couchant at each side of those double front doors. She recalled two knockers, again with lions' heads, brass, a word printed somewhere, the name of the house. 'I cannot read yet,' she whispered.

She would see the injured cherub soon, once she got close enough. The hall floor would be marble, black and white. There was a red room ... Oh, dear God, no, please, no, have mercy upon me, your child. Balustrade. Tiny infant, female, peering through the gaps, watching that lady, teacups on the lawn, dark laughter from him. Him. He was Father, strange smells, tobacco, amber fluid from a tantalus, crystal. Mother – 'Don't drink any more, Bertie.' Here it came, now, full circle, dream spilled into reality, sanity a lifetime away.

Lily, poleaxed to the spot, could only watch and wait. Ah, here came Dot with her new husband.

At the rear of the house, there would be cobbles, a horse trough, stables forming three sides of a square, the house itself providing the fourth, except for gaps, gates, latches high, she would have to climb the gate to lift the mechanism. The wail of dry hinges, Father's dogs barking. Red. He wore a red coat, many horses, many dogs, the wail of a horn. Run, foxy, run. So much scarlet, such anger, very little love from the man.

Lily rushed to greet Dot and Peter. 'I can't do nothing with her,' she jabbered, 'she's come over all peculiar, like.'

Peter left Lily to the care of Dorothy, ran to the side of the woman whose neighbour he had terminated. 'Miss Hulme?' he asked.

She turned slowly, like one in a dream, a person forced to obey the farcical rules of unreality. 'I am Helena,' she said.

A shiver ran the length of Peter Smythe's spine, but he held himself together. 'Take my arm, Helena,' he suggested, the tone gentle and persuasive.

'I know you,' she replied. For one terrible moment, Peter thought that she had recognized him from his expeditions to Prudence Street, but no, she spoke in the voice of a child.

'Come along,' he urged.

Nellie held her father's hand as she walked the rest of the way. Father pretended to be kind, but he wasn't. Bloodied birds hanging in a shed, eyes turned to glass, flesh decaying into tenderness for cooking. Large table, white from scrubbing, beefy arms on the woman who made the meals. 'Where's Mother?' she asked.

'We shall find her,' was the answer from Peter Smythe.

They walked up the steps and she knew that there would be seven, dips in their centres worn down by many years of feet, touched a pillar that supported the outer porch. Twin lions, twin doors, black and white marble on the hall floor.

Pulling herself away from her guardian, not noticing groups of people chattering and laughing, she walked to the staircase. Yes, handrail in reddish-brown wood, stairs that curved away and round towards ... the red room.

Peter remained at the foot of the stairs. He turned to

his wife. 'Go and find Miss Earnshaw, she is the head teacher – a very approachable woman – I do the gardens sometimes. Go, Dorothy. Something very strange is afoot here.'

The knob was in reach – she had grown. When the door swung inward, Nellie Hulme failed to see the head-mistress's office with its desk, filing cabinets and book-cases. Instead, Helena saw a four-poster, its side curtains half drawn, its foot facing the door.

Father roared at her, 'Go away, Helena.'

But she could not move. Nailed as firmly as Christ to His cross, she watched a small body, saw it lifted high into the air, a woman holding its feet as if it were an item in a butcher's shop. The noise came then, a horrible sound that cut through her head as if threatening to slice it in two. Mother screamed and screamed and . . . And the red, the red . . .

White sheets, father shouting, that woman holding the newborn. White sheets stained, red flowing, pumping as if some mechanism stronger than a human heart drove it onward, outward until it filled the room, flooded the house, poured and poured and the scream would not stop.

She raised her hands, covered her ears, she was Helena, was Nellie, was two people. Lace at the windows, lace on the sheets, white lace edging pillow cases, lace in an upstairs room at home, Prudence Street. Lily. Where was Lily? That thin scream, baby crying, cover those ears tightly, do not hear. Deaf. The colour of deafness was solid red, darkening, closing in, no more birdsong.

Father slammed the door in Helena's face; Nellie left the headmistress's study. A clock chimed. 'I can hear,' she said aloud, just to make sure.

They came for her then, Dot Barnes-as-was, Peter

Smythe, the head of the school, Lily Hardcastle, her forehead lined deep with worry. There was a fuss, a cup of sweet tea, the faces around her were kind. But it was over.

'Miss Hulme,' Martha Earnshaw touched the stricken woman's arm, 'would you like to go home? I can arrange transport.'

'No. Thank you, but no. I have come to see my friend's daughter in the play. Yes, my voice is strange, but I was profoundly deaf until some months ago.'

Dot, Peter and Lily glanced at each other. 'Are you sure you want to stay?' asked Lily eventually.

Nellie nodded. Oh, yes, she was determined to stay. She handed cup and saucer to the headmistress, smoothed her hair, picked up her bag. Then, in a voice that was unusually clear, she dropped her bombshell. 'My name is Helena and this was my house.'

Mother was cast out without a penny to her name. But she did not go quietly. Just before she died, she gave me the silver-headed cane which has become a part of my uniform. The spherical handle is worn now, but the crest remains partly visible, while the initials of my father, BM, intaglio and partially erased by time, seem as clear to me as they did then, just days before her death.

Katherine shifted uneasily, the slight movement causing her to wince. Peter Smythe had stated earlier in the work that he had deliberately returned to the scene of his male parent's misdeeds, that his original intention had been to register his claim against any estate. But, as he had also said, how could he prove paternity? And why was her skin crawling so?

With that cane, Mother smote the man who had so mistreated her, then she kept it as a souvenir, a memento of her life with the man who had introduced her to the fruits of Bacchus. Then she moved to Northampton where, rejected and neglected by friends and family, she gave birth to me.

Our life was not unhappy. Mother taught sons and daughters of the rich, dragging me in her wake wherever she went. Thus I gained my knowledge and my love for the English language, for the classics, for paintings and music. I learned languages modern and ancient, mathematics, geography and history, all at differing levels dependent on the age of her pupils on any given day.

I was lucky. My education was wide and varied, while my mother encouraged me to read anything and everything within reach.

Her drinking worsened until we reached a point where she could no longer work. Even then, she would imbibe infrequently on weekdays, saving the more glorious moments for weekends.

Glorious moments became spectacularly bad. Her skin yellowed and became an outward advertisement for the state of her liver. As she lay in her bed during those final weeks, I became her nurse, her companion, her comforter. Realizing only too well that she was the architect of her own doom, she apologized repeatedly, sobbed in my arms, told me that she loved me and that I had been the light of her life.

She had but two days to live when, her mind as clear as a bell, she summoned me to her bedside. In a steady voice, she told me who I was, identified the man who was my father. It transpired that she had taken a job in the north of England, a governess's position that was residential. Her charge was a young girl whose mother had died in childbirth, an only child who needed a sensible woman in her life. Judged as sensible, Mother moved into the house and took responsibility for the child's educational and emotional welfare.

Mother's employer plied her with gifts, with hints of marriage, courted her so determinedly that she succumbed to him. The drinking began then, while the man attempted to persuade Mother to abort me. But she refused to listen to him, refused to go into the exclusive clinic where certain secret procedures were executed.

Finally, he turned on her. She packed her belongings that night, fought him off, beat him across the head with the very cane I carry on a daily basis.

History speaks for itself. The man who fathered me, who abandoned my mother, raged his way to death by the very same means which abbreviated the life of my adored and wonderful mother. He drank away all his possessions and was laid to rest many years ago.

Thus I find myself…

The story continued, his life on the road, rejection by the army because of a spinal curvature, his eventual arrival at the place where he was conceived.

Katherine Moore closed the book. There remained no vestige of doubt in her mind – Peter Smythe was her half-brother.

Twenty

The play was a roaring success.

Beth, hilarious as the villain, stalked about the stage, trained her young pickpockets, even sent some of them into the audience, where the screams of parents and siblings made the occasion all the funnier.

It was a clever piece of work, one that underlined the high standards of Chedderton Grange academy. In the interval, a string quartet played, delivering pieces whose excellence was certainly upheld by girls almost too small to control their instruments. This was clearly the place for Beth to be, thought Magsy as she enjoyed the talent on display.

Paul dug her gently in the ribs. 'Nellie looks a bit fussed,' he whispered.

Magsy glanced across to where Lily and Nellie sat together. Nellie's face was flushed and she seemed not to be concentrating on the events that surrounded her. Perhaps her hearing was not quite right yet. Nellie Hulme had been forced to learn everything all over again and had possibly experienced difficulty while interpreting noises delivered by the lightweight voices of young girls. But Magsy noticed that Lily, too, seemed slightly out of order, eyes sliding sideways towards her companion, hands picking nervously at the scarf in her lap.

As this was the interval, several people were milling

about and talking quietly, voices muted so that the playing of the excellent string quartet would not be drowned. Magsy rose from her seat, caught Lily's eye and beckoned her to the rear of the hall.

Lily told Nellie that she intended to get some refreshment, then she joined Magsy at the back of the room. 'Dear God,' she muttered, 'I don't know whether I'm coming or going.'

Magsy pulled her old neighbour out into the foyer. 'What's wrong?'

Lily's eyebrows shot northward as if they intended to disappear into her hairline. 'What's wrong? What's right would make a shorter list. I'd want a bloody crystal ball to work out what's gone on here tonight. I don't know where to start.'

'Just tell me. Come on, Lily, it'll be the second act in a minute and my Beth will get her comeuppance – I can't wait to see it. And you'll want a cup of tea to take back to Nellie.'

Lily swallowed hard. 'Well, it's this way. You know how Nellie goes on about red and screams and birds singing?'

'Yes.'

'All them years when she couldn't hear nowt except when she were asleep?'

'Yes, yes.'

'It were here, Magsy. It were here. This is where she comes from. It's this house what were in her dreams. She knew where the bedroom was – well, it's not a bedroom now, it's like an office. Her mam died here, I think. Ooh, I don't know. I mean, I think I know, but I'm not sure.'

Magsy's thoughts were all over the place, bouncing about like a ball in a game of O'Leary. 'But she might have dreamt about a house similar to this.'

Lily nodded quickly. 'Then why has she got a newspaper cutting, a photo of this house left in Prudence

Street by her mother? By Mrs Hulme, I mean. I recognized it right off tonight when we got here, knew them lions near the front door and that there fancy fountain.'

Magsy chewed on her lip. 'The dreams could have come from the photograph. We may have this all the wrong way about altogether. She saw the picture and it sat deep in her mind, coming out only when she was asleep.'

Lily disagreed. 'That photo were years in yon cupboard, Mags. You know the state that place were in till she kicked off sorting it out. I were there when she started on her mam's sewing cupboard. I can tell you now that nowt had been disturbed on them shelves for many a year. Then there's that other photo, the one she says is her real mam and dad. I know it's very old and brown, like, but why was that there? I can tell you now, there's a look of Nellie round that woman's face, and I can tell you why that photo's there and all. It's there because Mrs Hulme knew who Nellie really were.'

Magsy's left hand found its way to her throat. Surely not? Surely—

'She's from money,' continued Lily. 'She still gets money. Not a lot, but enough to keep body and soul together. The rest, the lace money, she saves. Aye, it's very fishy, is this.' She dropped her voice even further. 'I'll tell you this and I'll tell you no more. There's summat about Nellie Hulme, summat as was there even when she were filthy. It's called class. Her's a lady, Mags. And she's as rich as bloody royalty, thousands in the bank.'

'Nellie has worked hard and she has saved,' replied Magsy.

Lily fished around in her mind, could not lay her tongue across the words she needed. It wasn't the money, wasn't this house, wasn't anything tangible. The fact remained that Nellie Hulme was set apart, was different

314

from the normal run of folk. Lily wished that she had time to read more, to learn the words she needed to express herself, but lacemaking, collecting items for the stall, placing orders among homeworkers – all these tasks required time and concentration.

They collected cups of tea and hurried back to their seats. The curtain rose, Beth O'Gara sobbed her way through Ferocia's downfall, Olivia Tangle was saved and all was well with the story.

When the applause died down, Paul and Magsy rose to leave. 'What was all that about in the interval?' he asked.

Magsy sighed. 'I have no idea. But I suspect we have some interesting days ahead of us.'

They went to collect Beth, found her in the changing room with her nose buried in Keats. They congratulated her, kissed her, shook their heads when she returned to 'Ode to a Nightingale'. 'Come on,' tutted Magsy, 'we've to take Lily and Nellie back with us, it's getting very late.'

Beth turned a page and sighed, the wig slipping as she raised her head. 'Miss Hulme's with the head upstairs, says she'll be ten minutes. Mrs Hardcastle went up with her, so we've got to wait.'

'Ah.' Magsy lingered, expected further information, got none. She took her husband on one side. 'Wait here with madam, would you? I'll just see if I can find out what's what.'

Lily was seated on a chair in the corridor, her hands twisting in her lap. Magsy joined her, sat beside her on a second chair. 'It feels as if we are waiting to be punished by the head teacher, two naughty girls about to get the cane,' she whispered.

'Eh? Oh, hello, Magsy.' Lily shook her head resignedly. She didn't understand what was going on, but she was ready for her cocoa and her bed. 'I don't think we'll be coming back with you. Miss Earnshaw said summat about one of the teachers taking us home in a car. Nellie's a bit shaky.'

'Ah.'

'So she wants to go straight home.'

'I see.'

The older woman reached across and touched Magsy's hand. 'Tell your Beth she were magic. If there hadn't been all this carry-on,' she waved a hand in the direction of Miss Earnshaw's firmly closed door, 'I reckon I would have been laughing me head off.'

Nellie emerged from the office, stood still for a moment, her eyes flicking from Magsy to Lily. Her skin, always pale, was now whiter than ever, while a nervous twitch had developed in her left eyelid. It was plain that she was distressed, though she said not a word as Miss Earnshaw followed her into the corridor.

Magsy jumped to her feet. 'Nellie?'

Nellie raised her hand. It was plain that she had nothing to say, so the other three women followed her down the stairs. Whatever had happened in that office, the two women who had met in there were remarkably subdued.

As the teacher's car pulled away, Beth expressed everyone's disappointment. 'I was looking forward to them staying.'

Magsy said nothing, but her bones spoke loud and clear. There was something afoot and her unease was deep.

Dot and Peter made their way homeward, each enjoying the crisp night air and that companionable silence that was so much a part of their life together. Dot, who had endured enough noise to last a lifetime, was glad of the peace. Peter, a loner, a man who had travelled several decades in his own company, could not have endured the company of a mindless chatterer. He had found the ideal soulmate and was glad to have her.

'It were good,' she said when they were halfway home. 'You don't expect kiddies to be as clever as that, do you?'

'My mother would have,' he replied after a few moments' thought. 'My mother expected excellence and accepted nothing less. The school may be unusual in its approach, but it works.'

Dot had known from the start that this second husband was a clever man. He knew the proper Latin name of every weed, every plant, every bush and tree. He could grow just about anything from seed or cutting, read books on remote subjects like psychology, fine art and philosophy, was always learning something new. Peter was of the opinion that everyone should learn as much as possible, that each man had a duty to expand his brain.

Not another word was spoken for the rest of the journey. They turned into the driveway of Knowehead, walked down the side of the house and through the garden until they reached their own comfortable little home, 'our wooden hut', as Dot called it.

Like a team that rehearsed regularly, they stepped into a mode that was almost automatic, he damping the fire, she warming milk for their bedtime cocoa. The chime in a nearby church tower announced nine o'clock. Dot and Peter sat by their fire, each staring into dancing flame, each content in the presence of the other.

They dozed, sipped cocoa, dozed again. When half past was announced, they rose, Dot removing the cups, he going to fetch nightwear from the bedroom in order to warm it in front of the dying embers.

Someone knocked at the door. Dot, on her way to the kitchen, opened it. 'Hello, Magsy. Come in.'

Magsy stepped inside, bewilderment printed all over

her features. She decided to hit the nail on the head straight away, as she had no intention of trying to explain the inexplicable. 'Dot, Katherine wants to see Peter.'

'Now?' Dot's eyebrows came together in a frown. 'It's half past nine, Magsy. We get up at six o'clock – Peter thinks that's the best time of day. Is it important?'

'I'm not sure,' replied Magsy, 'but she said to come now.'

'So it's not an emergency? She hasn't had a fall or anything like that?'

'No.'

Dot went to inform her husband that his presence was not requested, it was demanded.

Magsy sat on the edge of a chair and waited. She had never seen Katherine Moore in such a state of agitation. Had Rachel Barnes not been pregnant, Magsy would have gone to the shop to collect her, because Rachel's calming effect was extremely useful where Katherine was concerned.

Peter came into the sitting room, paused, noted the expressions on the two women's faces. So, the time had come. He walked to a small chest of drawers, removed a small package, pocketed it, kissed his wife, grabbed a coat, then followed Magsy to the door.

'Peter,' called his wife, 'it's going on half past nine.'

'My dear,' he replied calmly, 'it is almost 1952. Time is short. It is also irrelevant.' Then he followed Magsy towards a moment that had been for ever preordained. And his pulse did not quicken at all.

Katherine Moore sat upright on her chaise, frail bones supported by feather cushions.

Beth, sensing an atmosphere, had taken herself off to bed, sensible girl. Where was Margaret? How long could it possibly take to fetch someone a few strides through a garden? The clock on the mantel ticked, louder and louder with every beat, marking the passing of her life, the fruitlessness of it.

It had been the longest of evenings, the loneliest of hours, because she had faced the situation alone, just as she had faced most of her seventy-plus years. Alone, isolated, neglected and bitter. Was that a footfall?

No, it was Tinker, the cross-breed with yellow eyes and a temperament so gentle as to be almost self-denying. Look how he was sitting, head in her lap, golden irises concentrating intently on her face. 'You know, don't you?'

He 'talked' back to her, a throaty 'grrr' that was almost as soft as the purr of a contented feline. Yes, Tinker knew about life, had been born knowing. While this was Beth's pet, his loyalty to Katherine was undeniable. He adored her, supervised each painful movement, each creak of her bones. 'Good dog,' she said absently.

Tinker waited, sat through a dimension created by humans, his own sense of time non-existent. He was here, so he sat; he was here and he offered comfort, warmth, steadiness. Her tension reached him, so he reached her, head in her lap, not too heavy, merely present, just there for her to know, for her to trust.

The back door swung inwards. Katherine stiffened, watched the door. It swung open. And, for a few seconds, time was frozen.

They were silent all the way home in Mr Allwood's car. Mr Allwood, taciturn scientist, would probably not have noticed even if they had spoken, so engrossed was he in the intricacies of his brand new internal combustion machine. He drove with his head cocked to one side, ears concentrating on every squeak, every groan, every whirr.

319

In the back of the Austin, Nellie and Lily sat, each peering out of her window as if riveted to the view. There was nothing to be seen until they reached the bottom of the moor, because country lanes were unlit and as black as chimney backs, but they pretended to be interested.

For the first time in months, there existed between them a tension, an awkwardness created by whatever had happened tonight. Nellie, who knew perfectly well what had happened, did not wish to discuss the events; Lily, acutely aware of her companion's confusion, was reluctant to encroach upon territory that clearly caused pain to a person she valued so highly.

In Prudence Street, they alighted from the vehicle, thanked the driver and stood for a moment in embarrassed silence while he drove away.

'I'll ... er ... I think I'll go straight to bed. Night, Nellie.'

'Good night.' Nellie fished the key from her pocket and let herself into her dark house. There was no fire and no Spot – the dog was next door in the care of Lily's sons, as the two women had expected to be out for the whole night.

Nellie lit a mantle and, with her outdoor clothes still fastened tightly about her, sat in a chair next to the cheerless grate. On the mantelpiece, the photograph of her parents leaned, a silver frame surrounding the two sepia-coloured figures. These were her real parents, not the Hulmes. And yet the Hulmes had been real parents, gentle, decent people who had truly loved their adopted child. But these other subjects, depicted in palest brown, were her instigators, her inventors. It was too much to take in; it was too awful.

She closed her eyes and leaned back. Devoid of hearing for much of her life, Nellie had accepted her lot, and understood nothing beyond her immediate environment. There had been holidays in Fleetwood, hot days on sands, visits to zoos, to fairs, to the circus whenever it visited the town. The Hulmes had done their best. No-one could improve on his absolute best. How could they have explained the truth to a hearing child, let alone to a deaf one? No, no, the Hulmes could not have acted differently.

And now, after such a settled childhood, after years of hard work as an adult, after finding such wonderful friends, it had come to this. She bit down on her lower lip, stopping only when she tasted blood. Oh God, what now? Did she need to do anything? Did she need to follow the trail to a conclusion which, though providing little surprise to herself, would shock so many other decent people?

She realized that she had started to weep, great, fat drops of salt water squeezing their way down her cheeks. Almost halfway through her eighth decade, Nellie Hulme was too old for this. In six years, she would be an octogenarian if God spared her. Oh, for some peace, for some blessed freedom.

'Nellie?'

Spot bounded in and threw himself at his mistress. Lily brought up the rear, flustered and hot from trying to contain the young dog. 'He knew you were back, wouldn't stop, wouldn't behave, kept yap-yap-yapping–' The visitor stopped in her tracks. 'Nay, love, don't cry.'

Nellie dried her eyes. 'I'll be all right.'

'Oh aye?' Lily marched in and stood in front of this dear friend, the woman who had taught her to make lace, the one who had provided a job for Aaron, who had given the lad a chance to sell things made by deaf people and housewives, poor folk who earned by sewing or knitting while supervising children. Nellie Hulme was the best person Lily knew. 'Nellie, you don't need to tell me nothing till you're ready, but I'm here, you know.'

'Yes.'

'So knock on that wall when you want me.' She turned to leave.

'Lily?'

'Yes?'

Nellie took a deep breath. 'We have to go back up there tomorrow.'

'Right.'

Determined to ask no questions, Lily left her friend and went back home. There was nothing she could do at the moment, but she would be there for Nellie tomorrow, would always be there for Nellie.

He leaned his stick against the wall. 'You wanted to see me?'

Katherine noted his arrogance, had been aware of it in the past. 'Sit down, please.'

He obeyed, placing his hat on a small table. The book rested beside her on the chaise, but he would not mention it; no, it was up to her, because he had known all along.

'So. We are related,' she said.

He inclined his head slightly.

'And you wrote that book just as a means to let me know?'

Oh, she did flatter herself. She actually imagined that he had spent the best part of a year scribbling just in order to inform her of their relationship. 'I wrote because I felt the urge. The decision to tell some of the truth came late.'

'Miss Farquar-Smith,' she said quietly.

'Was my mother, yes. I changed my name to Smythe, as there are rather too many Smiths, you see. And a tramp with a double-barrelled surname seemed . . . well, too odd even for me.'

Katherine closed her eyes and pictured that pretty young woman, belly swollen, hair tousled, face made pink by tears. She remembered the night when the governess had made her escape, recalled the screams, the woman's fury, her father's rage. 'She was good to me and would have been an excellent governess except for ... well ... the drinking. And that was my father's fault, I should imagine.' Her eyelids opened. 'I am very sorry,' she said.

'It is not your fault,' came the quick reply.

The silence that followed was awkward. She had read his book, so she had read his mind; on her side, she owned few confidences to offer in return. She knew this man, yet did not know him, had employed him, had read him, yet he remained new, because he had acquired a different identity. The man was her brother; her brother was a stranger.

Peter understood the woman's discomfort. He leaned forward, hands clasped together between his knees. 'I came here a very long time ago, after my mother's death, an angry young man, Miss Moore. I don't know what I sought – revenge – compensation – but you were already frail. The man I wanted to see was recently dead and it was he who had worn you out. There was no point in hurting you. You sold the Grange, then I went away.'

'Then why did you return?'

'For many years, I came and went. I made my way back because I like the people, the hills, the life. And I thank you for the summer house. I am sheltered, yet not con-tained. There is a little of the gypsy in me, Miss Moore.'

Her face relaxed slightly. 'My name is Katherine.'

'I know.'

As they studied one another, the atmosphere suddenly changed. Each felt a wetness in the eyes, a tightening of the throat. They were half-brother and sister, one father between two, neither with a full-blood sibling.

Katherine swallowed. 'I was nervous tonight.'

'That is understandable,' he replied, 'but I am not here to make any claims, Katherine. I have no child, no need of money. My home is dry and warm, my wife is a decent, honest soul who cares for me. All I ask is that I might spend some time with you, because we share blood. I was afraid that you might be ashamed of me – my lifestyle has been rather bohemian.'

She considered that last statement. 'At one time, I might have been reluctant to admit our connection. But I, too, have learned a great deal from the people of Lancashire. There is a place where we all meet in the end, and I do not make reference to an afterlife. The fact remains that we are of the same species and, if we are to survive, we must connect.'

He found himself smiling. Rising, he took one of her transparent hands, bent over and kissed it gently. 'Hello, sister,' he whispered.

Katherine blinked rapidly. 'Hello, brother.'

Then he announced his intention to make cocoa, turned on his heel and left the room.

When he returned, he took a package from a pocket of his waistcoat. He studied it, turned it over, seemed to weigh it both literally and figuratively before speaking again. 'She died a horrible death. I have never witnessed such pain before or since, nor would I wish to. Drink your cocoa while it is hot.'

She obeyed, her eyes never leaving the item in his hands.

'I think she must have written to you quite early on, possibly before I was born. It is addressed to you, Miss Katherine Moore, Chedderton Grange, Hesford, Lancashire. The inner envelope remains sealed, though I have replaced the outer wrapping several times.'

Katherine nodded just once. 'Why did she not post it to me?'

He had wondered about that many times. 'You were probably too young early on and your father might have intercepted it. Who knows? Only my mother has the answer, and that lies with her in a Northampton grave-yard. As she grew older, she may have forgotten that this letter existed. Then, as you know, drink affects behaviour and ... well ... here it is.'

A cold hand gripped her heart and she looked at the packet as if it were a snake, a reptile ready to pounce. Her fingers trembled and she found herself incapable of reaching out for the message. She looked up, met his gaze. This was an honourable man who had kept this letter for many years, who had guarded the privacy of his mother and of his half-sister. 'Open it, please,' she begged. 'Read it to me.'

'Are you sure?'

'I am absolutely positive. There have been enough shocks. If you read it, you may cushion whichever blow may be contained in that envelope.'

He sat, placed his cocoa on the little table, tore at paper so frail as to be almost decayed. But his mother's hand-writing, bold and clear in Indian black, was as legible as it had ever been. His quick eye scanned the contents and he glanced at his companion. 'This is another shock,' he advised her.

'Then so be it. Fire away – at least on this occasion I am not alone.'

Peter cleared his throat. This woman was unwell and he dreaded her reaction. But it had to be done; truth was truth, it was there for the telling.

My dear Katherine,

Firstly, I must apologize for having abandoned you

without warning and in such a hurried fashion, but circum-stances dictated that I must leave Chedderton Grange very suddenly, as I needed to address certain issues within my own family. I take this opportunity, however tardy, to tell you that you were a delight to teach, that I grew fond of you and that I wish you success and happiness in your life.

There remains, however, a matter deserving of your attention, a subject about which I believe you have no knowledge, but which will be of great import as you grow older. I believe that your father has no intention of convey-ing the information to you; I therefore presume to take upon myself the burden of relating to you this subject of vital importance.

'As you are already aware, your mother did not survive your birth. However, you were not the only child of that marriage; you have a sister who is two or three years your senior. I have no information regarding her exact where-abouts, though she resides in the town of Bolton and is in the care of a decent married couple.'

He paused, looked at Katherine's inscrutable face. 'Shall I continue? Would you like me to fetch your housekeeper?'

Katherine shook her head. 'No, thank you. I may as well hear the rest of it. Please go on.'

The little girl developed normally, but was unfortunate enough to be a witness to your birth and to the death of your mother, which event occurred when you were just minutes old. Afterwards, she became withdrawn and diffi-cult to the point where your father could no longer bear to have her within his sight. It transpired that she was very deaf, though her hearing was, apparently, perfect before her mother's passing.

'Sweet child, when you are older, take care to find this sister, for you are born of the same mother and may have

326

need of each other. I beg you to forgive me for any distress caused by this letter and I remain your sincere friend and governess,

'*M. Farquar-Smith.*'

Katherine looked at him, her lower lip quivering so badly that speech proved difficult. 'What sort of man was our father?' she asked.

'I don't know,' he replied, 'because I was fortunate, since I never had the dubious pleasure of meeting him.'

She inhaled a long, shuddering breath. 'How might I find her, Peter? She could well be dead.'

But Peter's mind was working very fast, too quickly for him to be able to organize its contents. He stood, paced about, hand rubbing his chin. Dot's former neighbour, who had been deaf for years . . .

'Peter?'

He held up his hand. 'A moment,' he begged, 'please allow me to think.'

Then it came to him and he stopped dead in his tracks. 'There was a fuss at the school tonight, just before the play started. Dot's neighbour ran upstairs, recognized the house . . . Oh. Oh, my goodness. Nellie, I believe her name is.'

'She was meant to stay here tonight,' said Katherine, 'with another woman. Where is she?'

'Someone drove them home,' said Peter slowly. 'A science master got out his car – very proud he was, too, of his car – he said that he was taking them home. After the final curtain, Nellie went upstairs, which was why Dot and I walked back separately from Margaret and Paul – they waited because those two women went to see the headmistress.'

Katherine could scarcely contain her excitement. She made him go through it all again, watched him closely as he gathered together the jigsaw pieces of memory. Then she leaned forward. 'Can you see a light in the shop across the road? Upstairs, I mean.'

'Yes,' he replied, 'but why—'

'Because today you have found two sisters, Peter. Now, I want you to go across to that shop. Do not worry, they will understand. Ask Frank Barnes to collect us here at eight o'clock tomorrow morning. You and I shall go to Bolton.'

Peter's jaw dropped. 'But you never leave the house, you will be in pain, this is not possible—'

'None of this is possible,' she answered, 'yet it is happening. We shall pack me in with cushions and we shall travel at the pace of a snail. It will be done, Peter.'

The determination in her tone was very evident. Peter picked up his coat and went to do his new-found sister's bidding. Once outside, he realized that he was shaking, that the shock had affected him, too. He remembered a quote about a tangled web called deceit, forgot it immediately. There was a job to be done and he was the only man who could do it.

Nellie Hulme woke with a start, her body as cold as ice, her mind alert within seconds.

Spot was barking like a demented hound, was hurling himself at her repeatedly. She had not been to bed, had dozed from time to time, was still sitting in a chilled room in yesterday's clothes, outdoor garments included. What on earth was happening now?

'Hello?' A man's voice, one she did not recognize. At least she was beginning to categorize voices – until just a few weeks ago, she had experienced difficulty separating the tone of a male voice from that of a female. The door must have been unlocked all night. Her body shook.

He entered the room, a little man who was strangely familiar, someone she had seen recently. Last night? That school, the play, a bedroom that was no longer a bedroom . . .

'Miss Hulme?' he asked.

'Yes?' Still drunk from sleep, she attempted to stand.

'Stay as you are,' he said, 'I can see that you have slept badly.' Peter Smythe took a step towards her. 'I know you are in shock,' he said softly, 'but there is more to come. We have brought your sister.'

Her hand flew to her throat, icy digits causing her to jump as they contacted flesh that was slightly warmer.

'Please, please do not be afraid,' he urged. 'Had I known that we were disturbing you, I would have made sure that we stayed away.' Would he? Could any force on earth have kept Katherine Moore away from here this morning? In unbelievable pain, the younger of these two women had not uttered a single groan throughout the journey from Hesford to Bolton. 'Mr Barnes is about to carry in Miss Moore.'

Nellie nodded.

'You know that Katherine Moore is your blood sister?'

She nodded again.

The door swung wide and Frank Barnes entered the room, a bundle in his arms. Here was Nellie's baby sister, no substance to her, small enough to be a child, but with old eyes glowing as brightly as two stars in a winter sky.

It was too much for poor Nellie. She began to cry, great heaving sobs that shook her all the way to her chilled feet. Here came the child who had been dragged from a mother's defeated body more than three score years and ten before this day.

Frank placed Katherine on the sofa, his own chest racked by feelings he could never have explained in a whole lifetime. He looked from Katherine to Nellie, back again to the woman whose weightless yet pain-filled body he had just borne in his arms. Frank guided Peter out of the room and closed the door on a scene whose poignancy verged on the unbearable.

Katherine, too, began to weep. She was tired, confused, yet filled with a strange joy that proved uncontainable. 'I am Katherine,' she managed, a handkerchief blurring the words.

'I am Helena,' sobbed Nellie.

Outside in the hallway, two men whose emotional brotherhood-by-proxy had been created overnight, upheld each other silently, each leaning on the other in the search for more than one kind of support. 'We must make a fire,' mumbled Peter, 'and a hot drink. They are too old to be left in a room as chilled as that.' So they busied themselves in the time-honoured way employed by humanity in times of great stress, by beginning to deal with practicalities.

The sisters calmed themselves, each eager to unearth the missing years, each needing to know the other, greedy for news, for evidence, for reassurance. Nellie was introduced to the unpalatable memory of their father, Katherine 'met' the Hulmes, that sweet couple whose lives had been dedicated to the care of Miss Helena Moore. For some minutes, they stared in silence at the silver-framed photograph of their parents on the mantelpiece.

After a decent interval, the men tapped at the door, entered bearing hot tea, sandwiches, coal and kindling. Silently, Peter made a fire while Frank fed the two old ladies. The room crackled with emotion and burning wood as Peter and Frank withdrew from it.

'You must come and live with me,' suggested Katherine, 'away from all this grime. There is so much to say—'

'No,' answered Nellie, 'let's do this properly. You must come to live with me.'

The surprising truth was that Katherine knew that she would do just that, that she would leave Hesford and come here, to this mean little house set among thousands of such dwellings. This was her sister, and the bonds had been recreated instantly.

Nellie's trembling hand guided an uncertain cup towards its resting place, a saucer balanced on the fire-guard. She managed a weak smile. 'Not here,' she said, the newborn voice steadier, clearer. 'Oh no, we can't stay here, Katherine.' As if trying the new word for size, she repeated it slowly, 'Katherine.'

Helena heaved a deep sigh, though a sad smile encompassed her next words. 'I must wash,' she said, 'because I need to go out. Today, sister, I am going to buy a house, lock, stock and head teacher's office. We are going home. To Chedderton Grange.'

1952

Peter Smythe was as happy as Larry. He had his own little workshop in one of the stables at the back of the big house, with shelves, benches, hundreds of terracotta pots. There were pipettes, Bunsen burners, bottles, test tubes, copious notes and heaps of books. He also had an assistant, a sweet-natured child with a down-to-earth attitude and a mind that was never satisfied. She was far from satisfied at this moment.

'It's the deposits,' she reminded him, 'and they could come from anything. So what do we do? Stop her eating altogether?'

'No, but—'

'But what? If you are right and food is giving her the inflammation, where should we start? We all need food. She's too old to start doing without what she's used to.'

Peter shook his head. 'Beth, she can walk more easily, thanks to us. I shall do another brew of boneset and motherwort, then—'

'Well I think she did better on the slippery elm and prickly ash.'

'With or without devil's claw?' he asked.

Beth picked up a jar. 'With. And we put wild lettuce and skullcap in that – with valerian, of course.'

He scratched his head. 'She will always need valerian.

I say we take her off all raw foods, make sure everything is cooked.'

They looked at each other and burst out laughing. The thought of actually forcing Katherine Moore to do without anything was ludicrous. If she wanted an apple, she would demand an apple; she certainly would not sit there while said apple was cooked, mashed and cooled.

It was a hot day in June. The pair of amateur scientists wandered to the door of their workshop and breathed in some fresh air. The trouble with herbs was that they could get rather pungent at times. 'Are you happy?' Beth asked him.

He was becoming inured to Beth's odd questions; her mind flitted from subject to subject like a worker bee seeking the best pollens. 'Yes, I am. I have my wife, my summer house, this workshop, a victim to practise on – oh, and a very inquisitive assistant.'

'Then you are happy. Peter?'

'Yes?'

Beth wanted to be happy. She was in love with her family, with Knowehead, the house that now belonged to Mam and Paul, but she didn't know what she was going to become. At almost eleven years of age – well, ten and a half – surely a person should know? 'When will I know what to be?'

He considered that question. Peter had never known what to be – he had allowed life to arrive, had accepted it as it had come. 'Well,' he said, 'I suppose I just found plants, because plants are everywhere. Living with gypsies taught me the remedies, the natural painkillers, the poisons.'

'You know poisons?'

'Yes.'

'Have you ever used them?'

He could not lie, would never be able to tell the truth. A stroke, the official papers said. 'Just once. I had to get rid of a very large rodent. He was making life impossible for everyone else, so I put him down.'

Beth thought about that. She would never be able to kill, wanted to save lives, to make lives better. 'Whatever I do, I keep coming back to medicine,' she said, almost to herself. 'Women can become consultants now. Come on, let's go in for lunch.'

So the man who was of pensionable age and the girl of ten and a half walked through the yard and in at the back door of Chedderton Grange. Helena was at the table peeling vegetables. At her feet sat Spot and Tinker, offspring of that famous failed racing dog, Skinny-Bones of Prudence Street.

Helena looked up. 'Katherine's in the conservatory. She has decided to learn lace-making and her hands are stiff, so stay away unless you want Beth to learn some interesting language.' Proud of her speech, Helena Moore was stringing longer sentences together with every passing day. Her sister was wont to remark that Helena never shut up, that the day would arrive when the full works of Shakespeare would be delivered on the lawn of Chedderton Grange.

Beth, who was on this earth to learn, shot off towards the next lesson, which promised to be swearing. She found Katherine Moore with a small lace-making pillow, a few hundred brass pins, four pairs of bobbins and a face like thunder. 'Hello, Katherine,' the child said sweetly.

Katherine looked up. 'If they can do it, I can.'

Beth looked at the twisted fingers and wished that she could wave a magic wand and destroy arthritis for ever. 'Would you like me to help?'

Katherine tutted impatiently. 'No, thank you. Lily is on her way from town – she will tidy this up.' She threw down the work and smiled at this terrible, adorable girl. 'Is my sister cooking?'

'Yes.'

'And Dorothy?'

'She is at the shop minding Pinta.'

Katherine tut-tutted. Rachel Barnes's baby, born prematurely, had been compared to a pint pot because of her size, and the nickname had stuck. 'She is Katherine Helena,' she insisted.

Beth placed herself on a stool at Katherine's side. 'Tell me again.'

'Dreadful girl,' complained Katherine for the hundredth time. But she went through it all again, the reading of Peter's book, discovering that she was his half-sister, finding out on the very same day that she had a full sister.

'Then Helena bought this place and you all lived happily ever after. And you gave us Knowehead, which was very kind of you.'

'Yes, it was very kind of me. Now, go and fetch me a drink of lemon tea, you impossible child.'

The impossible child scampered off, leaving Katherine with her own thoughts. It occurred to the old woman that she was, indeed, happy. For the first time in her seventy-three years, she was content. With the aid of a stick, she could walk; with the aid of a wonderful sister, she was back where she belonged, in Chedderton Grange, in a house that had belonged for several generations to the Moores of Hesford.

She dozed, travelled back in time, met her father once more, cursed him all over again. Nellie, sweet little Helena, had been given away because she had not worked properly. Father had treated his elder daughter like a domestic appliance, something that must be sent back to the factory as sub-standard.

Miss Farquar-Smith, another of his victims, banished from the Grange because she would not allow some practitioner to attempt an abortion … Thank God, because Peter was immensely valuable, sensible, kind …

Alone at Knowehead, endless days staring through that same window, Rachel across the road, the shop, a new blouse, smiles so broad, so grateful. Lily and Dorothy, Frank, dear Frank …

She woke. 'I am blessed,' she told Beth. 'Thank you for the tea.'

Beth reached out and took a hand as fragile as a sycamore leaf in the autumn. 'We all love you,' she said quietly.

'That's a miracle,' replied the old woman. 'Look at us, the old and the young, best of friends.'

Beth sat again, told Katherine about the herbal experiments, about Aaron and his stall, about Lily using both the Prudence Street houses, about the lace Helena and Lily were making for the new queen. 'If the new queen sends for Helena, she will go this time. She loved the king. Ever since she sent him that first gift when he was Duke of York, she has loved him.'

They sat together and remembered Nellie's grief, how she had travelled to London with Lily, how she had stood in the chill of February to watch that fine man on his last journey.

'It must be true,' announced Katherine.

'What must?'

'The old poem. Saturday's child works hard for a living. You, your mother and my sister, all born on Saturdays. You will be a doctor and that is a very difficult road. Your mother looks after me – which job is harder than that?'

Beth laughed.

'I am fortunate,' the old lady concluded, 'that my sister is another Saturday child. Her labour bought us back our home. But best of all, I got to choose my family. You, your mother, your wonderful stepfather. Rachel, Frank,

Dorothy, our new baby. My sister and my brother whom I found late in life. Do I deserve you all?'

Beth giggled once more. 'What was the day of your birth?'

A gleam entered Katherine's eye. 'Friday,' she replied eventually.

They stared at each other for several moments.

'Friday's child is loving and giving.' Beth's voice was solemn.

'That can't be right,' said Katherine.

Beth agreed with her. 'Wednesday would have been better. Full of woe. Miserable.'

They screamed with laughter, an old lady who had seldom laughed, a young girl who brought joy wherever she went.

In the garden, a man with secrets tended his herbs. The laughter of his older sister and his young friend travelled through sun-baked air and kissed his ears.

From Bluebell Woods, a cuckoo called.

Everyone was home and the world was well.

THE END

Tales of
love, loss and life
in Liverpool
from bestselling author

RUTH HAMILTON

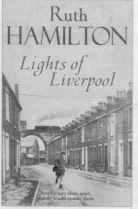

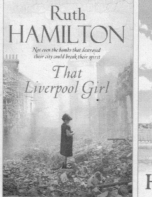

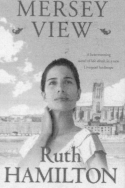

Lights of Liverpool
978-0-330-52225-0

That Liverpool Girl
978-0-330-52224-3

Mersey View
978-0-330-50753-0

For more information visit www.panmacmillan.co.uk